THE SALTWATER HEIR

CASSIDY CLARKE

Website : cassidyclarkewriting.com
Cover Designed by : COVERDUNGEONRABBIT
ISBN: 9780578838748
First Edition: June 2021

10 9 8 7 6 5 4 3 2 1

Content Warnings

THE SALTWATER HEIR includes content that may be triggering to some readers, including:

Graphic violence

Amnesia/memory loss

Abduction

Death

Religious terminology/rituals

Possession

Food Descriptions

Anxiety/panic attacks

Mild language

Body horror

Please read safely.

CHAPTER 1

SOREN

"**M**ove."

Soren didn't give the half-asleep lump in her bed the chance to listen. She shut her door with a sharp backward kick, toed off her boots, and stomped over. Irritation prickled up her legs at the unsatisfying thumps her feet made against the floorboards. She should have kept her boots on until she was done fuming.

She rolled onto the bed and shoved Elias with her foot, ignoring his groans est until he finally shifted to give her room.

"Give me some blanket," she said, wriggling her toes against his leg.

His only response was a grunt.

She grabbed a fistful of the heavy down quilt and tugged, revealing broad, thickly tattooed shoulders and a rumpled mess of tar-black hair. Wrapping the quilt around her head and shoulders like a cloak, she nestled back against the headboard, scowling at the far wall.

Childish? Maybe. Did it help her mood any? No. But at least she was warm. It wasn't like he needed it, anyway. He slept hot.

A longsuffering sigh from beside her. Elias turned over groggily, not quite opening his eyes. His hand wandered, searching for his stolen cover. "Thought I told you to use your own blanket."

She scooted away, smacking his hand. "It's *my* bed, jackass."

"It's *my* blanket, smartass."

Soren snorted softly, wrapping the quilt tighter around her shoulders. "Wake up and take it then."

A pause. Then Elias sighed again, loud and heavy, dragging himself up into a sitting position beside her. Even in the dim light from the flickering candle on her nightstand, he was halfway handsome—not in the way of princes, not fine-boned and sharp-jawed, but in the way of warriors: square and sturdy and rough-hewn, as though he'd been carved from the russet stone of the mountain ranges to the west. A string of black beads dangled around his neck, a matching skull charm resting over his heart.

"What's got you all pouty?" he asked, blinking drowsily at her.

"I'm not pouting. I'm stewing."

He rolled his eyes, twisting one of her curls around his finger and tugging. "Fine. What's got you *stewing?*"

Her mouth went dry, the words clinging to her tongue.

It wasn't fair. None of it was. She didn't want to admit what she'd tried . . . or that she'd failed. But he deserved to know, and he'd find out eventually, anyway. "I finally tried to talk with my mother. About finding a cure."

Some of the drowsiness cleared from his eyes, and he rubbed his prayer beads, his expression softening as he connected her confession with her glower. "She said no, huh?"

A lump tried to make itself known in her throat, so she ignored the question, rubbing the cold out of the tip of her nose with her palm. She smelled ice and wind . . . and something warmer. More fragrant. "Did you open my window earlier?"

He gave a weary nod toward her nightstand and the incense burner beside her candle, an ebony ceramic skull with blood-red crystal roses blooming from its eye sockets. The thinnest curl of smoke still danced from the tip of one of the sticks. "I know it gives you headaches."

Superstitious man. *He* was the one giving her headaches. "I thought we agreed you'd do your praying in the royal chapel. Or that it could wait for morning. Mortem won't miss your mumbling for a night."

His mouth crooked upward, a wordless apology. He scratched at the back of his neck, avoiding her eyes. "It wasn't for prayers. I was . . . warding something off."

She reached out to fuss with the sweat-damp ends of his hair. "More nightmares?"

His silence was answer enough.

Soren grumbled curses toward religious boys and their sad, manipulative eyes, but slid the ragged red quilt from her shoulders, arranging it so it would cover both of them. "You're lucky I love you."

Elias reached down to the foot of the bed, tucking the blankets under his heels and pulling them up over her ankles, just the way they liked to sleep. "You're lucky I mostly tolerate you."

And this was the man she'd chosen to be her best friend. Soren punched his arm. "I *will* make you walk home in the dark."

"To the forge or the barracks?"

"Oh, definitely the forge."

He twisted to peer dubiously at the window behind her darkwood headboard, frosted with so much snow they couldn't see through it. His family's forge was a good five miles away from the castle, if not more. "With or without my shirt?"

"Take a guess."

Elias's laugh was soft, disbelieving. He buried his head back against his pillow, gazing up at her, sleep already glazing his eyes again. "Is everyone ready for tomorrow?"

Any amusement shriveled up and died, adrenaline tightening her chest. She shifted, resisting the urge to check for the knife she kept under her pillow. "As ready as they can be. Word is Atlas forces were spotted moving toward one of the border cities—Ursa, I think. We'll have to leave at dawn if we want to cut them off." Elias's brow furrowed, and he spat a quiet curse. Soren's hand flew to her chest. "Such language from a holy man!"

"Oh, stop. Should I even bother sleeping?"

"If you keep me up all night with your muttering, I'll end you."

"I didn't say I'd spend the time praying."

Heat bloomed in her core, but she smothered it quickly. She knew better than to hope he'd finally figured out how to flirt. *That* would truly be a miracle. "How else would you spend it, exactly?"

The look he gave her held all the solemnity of a funeral. "I've been thinking about taking up crochet."

She pressed her lips against a smile, ignoring the thin thread of disappointment that tried to tie itself around her heart. "In that case, I could really use a new pair of socks."

Elias snorted softly, and for a time there was silence, only the roaring of the winter storm outside and the muffled laughter of castlefolk in the hall to break it. "I know you tried your best," he finally said. "It's okay."

Fresh anger bit at Soren's hands, and she curled them into fists. "It's really not."

"We knew she wouldn't let you go."

Soren settled against her own pillow, the warmth of his breath brushing against her cheek as she stared up at the glass ceiling. Even though she couldn't see them through the snow, she knew stars glittered far beyond, cold and distant and unhelpful. Her mother had always told her to give her dearest wishes to the stars, and they would carry them straight to the moon to see them granted.

Whatever stars Soren had been wishing on lately, they must have been pathetically slow.

"I still have months left, if not longer," Elias added. "One victim lived two whole years before the poison kicked in."

She refused to look at him, or at the bandage still wrapped around his right arm, hiding a wound festering with a death sentence. The sight of it was like a kick to the ribs every time. "You're absolutely right. You'll make it to twenty-two, at least. Practically ancient."

His teeth clicked. "I'm just saying I have time."

Soren kept her eyes on the ceiling. Her words barely reached past the wind howling outside. "Not enough."

It wasn't like she'd expected her mother to *eagerly* accept her proposal. The idea of sending Soren through the kingdom of the very people who dealt Elias his damning wound . . . no, she hadn't expected it to be an easy victory. But she'd practiced her argument for weeks, reciting it with her sisters until they were confident they'd explored every counter-argument Queen Ravenna could offer.

But in the end, it hadn't mattered. Enna had barely bothered to listen before telling her in no uncertain terms there would be no excursions through Atlas. Not even to save her battlemate's life.

"Who knows if Arborius would even help," Elias mumbled, his voice muffled by sleep and a silken pillowcase. He adjusted to lie flat on his stomach again, the muscles in his back relaxing, smoothing the runic tattoos he'd received during his time in the temple of the Death Goddess. "The Arborian queen is Atlas-born, you know. Queen Adriata's sister."

"That doesn't matter. Their healers swear an oath to treat anyone who comes to them for help, no matter the kingdom, no matter the station. If I have to make it through Atlas to get the antidote from Arborius, I'm more than happy to do it."

"You wouldn't even make it past the border. Your Atlas accent is horrible."

She snatched up an extra pillow at the edge of her bed, popping him over the head. "Not as bad as yours."

Her battlemate barely flinched, his mouth stretching open in a yawn. His hand fumbled out again until he found hers and squeezed. "Don't worry about me. It's not worth risking your life, anyway. I have time, and when it runs out . . . I know where I'm going. I'm not afraid."

Soren swallowed hard, her eyes drifting to that skull charm hanging over his heart. A tangle of frenetic emotions knotted up her throat, each one stinging worse than the last.

Elias's faith had always been a puzzle to her. She'd heard the rumors floating around the barracks when he first joined up: a priest-in-training who abandoned his calling, trading prayer and peace for bloodletting and vengeance in the name of his father, who'd died on an Atlas blade.

So gods-damned unfair that the same fate that cost Elias his father would now cost him his own life.

I'm not afraid, he'd said, and she knew he wasn't. That was Elias—fearless and fire-touched.

"But I am," she said, louder than she meant to.

His only answer was a snore.

"Rude," she mumbled, just to be sure he was asleep. Then she sat back up and pulled her hand away from him, twisting to dig under her pillow. Her fingers brushed past her knife, closing over the small book she'd stashed there instead— the only one she'd managed to find on poisonwork in the public library. Most potentially dangerous books were in the Queen's private library on the fourth floor of the castle, and she knew better than to get caught snooping around in there. The last time had landed her and Elias both in hot water, and as fun as it had been to see who could shovel horse manure the fastest, she wasn't eager to be thrown on stable duty for a month again.

The cover was worn and soft against her calloused fingers, the pages dog-eared from hours of frantic research whenever Elias wasn't around—which wasn't often these days. They'd always shared her room in the castle the night before being dispatched, but since he'd been poisoned, it was hard for him to sleep in the barracks at all. He claimed the pity from the other soldiers was making him nauseous.

Distracted by the book in her lap, she stroked Elias's hair while she read, his snores deepening as the candle began to burn itself out, its flame fading from limpid gold to dying red. Her eyes snagged on bits and pieces of text, scanning for portions she'd underlined:

Slow-acting poisons are rare, but no less deadly . . .

Victims can live anywhere from a few weeks to a few years without symptoms . . .

Once severe symptoms present themselves, victims often don't survive past a week.

Fresh terror tore through her, and she had to move her hand to Elias's back to make sure it was still warm, still moving with every breath, still guarding a beating heart somewhere beneath.

It was her fault. She'd lost focus for half a second, and an Atlas Viper had cut through her guard, burying a knife to the hilt in Elias's arm. Her mistake had marked him as the newest victim of that elite sect, warriors with a particularly cruel poison on their knives. Atlas's aim wasn't only Nyx's defeat, but Nyx's suffering. A Viper could poison upwards of twenty soldiers in one battle simply by grazing their knife against them. Some didn't even realize they'd been hit until months later, when they began showing symptoms from a wound that had long since healed.

She closed the book with a sharp snap. Elias jumped and snuffled, but didn't wake.

There was no use lingering on this tonight. There was war to wage tomorrow, and she needed her rest. She could ask Enna again when they came back . . . she *would* ask, and if that didn't work, she would demand. She was going to make it to Arborius, no matter what it took.

But when she blew out the candle, smothering them in darkness, she couldn't help wondering what she would do if she had to spend her nights before deployment alone.

CHAPTER 2

ELIAS

The armory was in chaos.

A cacophonous chorus of "Toss me my boots!" and "That's *my* sword, dumbass," and "Who took my bracers? Una, I know it was you! Give them back!" rang through the room as Elias squeezed around adrenaline-high soldiers in various states of combat dress. The walls of their company's armory had wooden compartments like linen closets built into them, stuffed full of everyone's possessions and armor. Anxious silences peppered the laughter and verbal sparring, each tick of the clock above the door bringing them closer to their departure.

For some of them, it would be their last time in this room.

Elias brushed his fingers against his beads, casting out a prayer to Mortem that one of them wouldn't be him.

The armory was stuffy and dank despite the chill outside, the crisp scent of fresh snowfall drowned out by nervous sweat and flasks of fine Nyxian whiskey passed between friends. Things were always tense before a battle, but something was different this time—as if everyone had a muscle that was too tense to loosen, a pain that was too sharp to shake. Some pulled out religious tokens and figurines, laughing at the jabs thrown around while clutching their symbols in white-knuckled fists.

For once "Elias the Pious" wasn't the only one flaunting his superstitions, but that didn't comfort him. He could taste the sour tang of fear in the air.

"Elias!"

Soren's voice cut through the din, her red hair flashing in the early morning sun as she waved him down. She was less armored up than he'd expected, dressed in warm pants the color of blood and a sleeveless white top that showed off her muscular, freckled arms. Her left shoulder sported an old, deep scar from a knife that had barely missed her neck; the other was a complete mess, the skin warped from the fire that had burned down her childhood home. Her hair was pinned up in a messy bun, strands falling loose over her shoulders, and her eyes gleamed like she'd already been in a fight this morning and was spoiling for another one.

Elias's chest tightened and warmed all at once, something relaxing in him at the sight of her. He didn't often rely on people for peace, but somehow everything made a little more sense with Soren there. Like she brought everything into focus.

"You're late," she scolded as he sat on the opposite bench, facing her. "Did you get lost?"

"Some of us don't wake up the morning of a battle as excited as a child during Winter Fair." He paused, eyes snagging on her feet. "You're wearing my socks again."

"Oops," she deadpanned. "It was so dark this morning . . ."

He reached down and tugged at the toe of the sock, pulling it halfway off her foot. "Get your own, will you? My mother's running out of wool."

"Mine aren't nearly this warm, and you know your mother doesn't mind—let go!" She kicked halfheartedly at his fingers, her attention wandering down to the end of the room. She dropped her voice to a whisper. "Don't look now, but you've got eyes on you."

Elias obediently lowered his gaze to his boots as he tugged them on, lacing them up. "Lily?"

"No, she's moved on to Kriss."

"What sort of eyes, then?"

"Well, it's more like *eye*, if you don't count the glass one."

Elias groaned softly. "Not this again."

"I'm just saying, you could do worse than Raquel. She's clever, funny, and beautiful besides—"

"Is she? I hadn't noticed." He'd noticed. It was fairly impossible to *not* notice Raquel Angelov. "Is she still looking?"

"I'm not sure she's even blinking." Soren craned her neck, and he kicked at her boot, heat flushing up the back of his neck.

"You're being obvious."

"No, *she's* being obvious. Quick, take off your shirt."

He did not. "I'm not having this conversation with you again. *You* can court her if you think she's so amazing."

Soren sighed heavily, bending back down to lace up her boots. "Unfortunately, I promised Jira years ago I wouldn't court any of her siblings, and now that she's dead I actually have to hold to that. If you break a promise to a friend, you're just mean. If you break a promise to a dead friend, you're an asshole."

"Soren."

"*Elias.* You're not going to be young and slightly less than ugly forever. She's smart, she's pretty. What else are you looking for?"

Elias looked up, studying Soren while she was distracted: the cluster of freckles at the hollow of her throat, the crooked bend of her nose from being broken more than once, the absent way she fiddled with the hem of her pant leg before tucking it into her boot.

"I'm not looking for *anything* right now," he said. "Everyone knows I'm not long for it, anyway. No one wants a dying man sharing their bed."

"Some people might. They do that, you know. Marry old or sickly so they can inherit the estate. Keeps things exciting, anyway. Every night together could be your last."

Elias scowled. "Oh, thanks. I feel so much better."

She scuffed his boot with hers, abruptly serious. "I'm just playing. Besides, you don't need to worry about that, because you're not dying. I told you I'd get you help."

"Right. And remind me how that went over with Enna?"

"Someone called?"

The dry, amused voice of his queen jerked Elias to his feet, a quick flush heating his cheeks. How she always showed up right when someone was talking about her, he didn't know. He gave a quick bow. "Majesty."

"Oh, don't do that. You're embarrassing us both." Queen Ravenna waved him off impatiently, lowering herself to sit at Soren's other side. She'd been a warrior princess before she was a peaceful queen, and it was still visible in her bearing: the way her shoulders cocked back at the sound of swords being sharpened, the way her hand wandered toward her hip like she was looking for a weapon of her own. She was more than capable of leading a diplomatic summit or an army alike in her lavender silk gown and opalescent slippers. Her ebony skin sparkled, shimmering silver dust streaked across her cheekbones like the trails left behind by shooting stars, and her coiling black hair swayed as she leaned close to Soren, licking her thumb and rubbing a spot on Soren's cheek. "Hold still, love, you've got some syrup."

Soren groaned in protest, pushing her hand aside as snickers and hoots of *Mama's girl* rolled through the armory. "Mama, *please*. I'm not a child."

"Debatable," said Elias, earning himself another kick to the shin.

"And yet you eat like one." Enna scowled playfully, but the set of her jaw said she was worried. "I don't think you should go."

"You never think I should go."

"Well, I *especially* don't think you should go this time."

Soren held her mother's shoulders, giving her a look. "I'm never going to make general if you keep trying to take the sword off my belt. Besides, you want me to leave Elias without his battlemate? He'd be dead in seconds."

"She's right," Elias agreed, leaning back against his compartment and gesturing at himself. "Look at me. I'm utterly helpless."

Soren frowned at him. "Stop flexing when you say that. It ruins everything."

"You ruin everything."

"Your *face* ruins everything—"

"Enough," Enna interrupted, rapping Soren's head with her knuckles. "Just be careful. You have your mask?"

"Check."

"Sword?"

"Obviously."

"Socks and underwear?"

"Mama!" Soren scolded as Elias's face went hot. "You're embarrassing Elias."

Enna frowned. "It's nothing he hasn't seen before."

"Battlefield triage is hardly intimate." Soren shot him a grin, wicked as an adder's bite. "Besides, I wasn't even wearing my good stuff."

Pain pierced his tongue as Soren hauled up her bag, still arguing with Enna as she walked out. He tasted something metallic—blood. He'd bitten his tongue.

Mortem save him. He needed to get himself in check.

The whole company was looking at him now, fighting grins and fluttering eyelashes. Lily went so far as to make kissing noises at him, and he threw his discarded shoe at her. "What's with all of you?"

"Poor fool," sighed Jakob, the blond, bulky captain of their company, barely two years Elias's senior. "You still haven't told her?"

"I have no idea what you're implying."

A chorus of groans went up around the room, and Jakob turned his back to Elias, flipping his palms out. "You heard him. Who had money on him confessing by the end of the week?"

"Tomorrow is the end of the week," protested Frigga, a middle-aged soldier with hair shorn to her scalp and a gnarled scar across her mouth. "We still have a day!"

"It's not gonna happen by tonight, Frig. Pay up."

"Are you—" Elias spluttered, heat pulsing from his injured tongue to his cheeks and neck as coins flashed between palms, at least half the soldiers in his company handing over money. "You're taking *bets*? On *what*?"

Jakob pocketed the money, flashing him a grin brighter than any coin. "Don't worry about it, Pious. Just consider how much torture you're really willing to endure here. The princess somehow manages to be sharp as a tack *and* dumb as a brick."

It was true. Soren handled many things with a deftness of intellect that rivaled most others, but when it came to common-sense matters, she tended toward idiocy. However, that didn't answer his question. "I still have no idea what you mean."

"Then you're even dumber than a brick." Jakob clapped his shoulder and called, "All right, fun's over! We have a sun to outmarch and some Atlas heads to remove. Gather your things and get out. Anything left behind stays behind."

"In that case, why don't you hang out here for a bit?" asked Varran, Jakob's battlemate. Jakob flashed him an rude gesture in response, catching him in a headlock as they filed out, knuckles digging into Varran's scalp as he struggled and laughingly cursed Jakob. He shoved Jakob's hands off, immediately reaching to check that the twin braids knotted at the back of his head hadn't come undone.

Elias instinctively followed suit, finding his own mourning braid in his hair. Those strands hung twice as long as the rest, the rough cloth tucked within chafing at his fingertips.

Nyxian custom—when a battlemate died, the survivor of the pair cut a section of their dead battlemate's uniform and twined it into their hair. Some saw it as a mark of shame, a broken vow. Others cherished them as memoriam to their fallen.

He wore his like dishonor. Soren wore hers like a dare; a dare to try and blame her for what happened, a dare to even *try* and forget her wild and wicked battlemate Jira, who'd died in the same battle as Kaia, Elias's first. He sometimes wondered if that was part of why he and Soren fit so well—their griefs matched, in a way.

He caught up to her outside the door. Enna and the other soldiers were already gone, but in Enna's place stood three other girls—Soren's adoptive sisters.

Yvonne, the oldest, was fussing with Soren's curls, her own pencil-straight white-gold hair braided in a crown atop her head. The Crown Princess groaned, spitting out a curse from between her pert, pink lips. "Gods, I swear your hair has a mind of its own. Em, you have any pins?"

Emberlyn, second eldest, was the opposite of fair-skinned, fair-haired Yvonne. Her bronze skin was striped with scars from her forgework—Ember was a master weaponsmith, having somewhat recently returned from serving an apprenticeship in her birth kingdom, Artem. She plucked a pin from her own pitch-dark hair, opened it with her teeth, and handed it to Yvonne, who wrinkled her nose.

"With your mouth, Em, really?"

"If you wanted manners, you should've asked Auralee."

Soren laughed, pushing Yvonne's hands from her head. "Will you *stop*? You three are going to run us late."

Auralee, the youngest of the four sisters at fifteen, crossed her arms with a pout, button nose turned up, her dark chestnut hair shifting as she moved. "Elias isn't even out here yet."

"Sorry to disappoint," said Elias, and the eyes of all four girls flickered to him.

"Elias!" Auralee ran straight into him, her head thumping the air out of his chest, her thin arms wrapping around his middle. "You weren't at dinner last night!"

Elias forced a smile, aware of Soren's eyes boring into his skull. "Sorry, Aura. Didn't have much of an appetite. I went to bed early."

Auralee's beaming smile faded some, and he silently cursed himself, catching the older sisters exchanging looks behind Auralee's head. Auralee reached for his sleeve. "Is it the Viper bite? Maybe you shouldn't go with the others."

"Already tried it," said Soren lightly, but he heard the strain hiding in her voice. "He goes where I go."

"Then maybe *both* of you should stay." Auralee worried her bottom lip with her teeth. "I have a bad feeling."

"What have I said about your bad feelings?" Soren freed herself from Yvonne's grip and gently pulled Auralee from Elias's embrace, wrapping her muscled arms around her younger sister instead. She planted a kiss on the top of her head. "The only way to prove them wrong is to ignore them. Besides, we can't just stay home. Our company needs us. Elias is the one of the few praying sorts we have, and who knows what'll happen to us without Mortem's blessing, right?"

Auralee pouted once more. "You don't even believe in Mortem."

"Shh. Don't say that around him, I'll get lectured all the way to Ursa."

While Soren pulled Auralee further down the hall, Ember stopped Elias from following with a hand on his chest. "I have something for you."

"Me?"

"That favor you asked of me? I finally finished it." Ember set a small parcel in the palm of his hand, a slight smile tugging at her normally stoic lips. "Good as new."

Heat flushed up Elias's neck, and he hastily pocketed the parcel. "Thank you. How much do I owe you?"

"Elias. You know better than to ask. It wasn't any trouble." She tipped her head to one side, dagger-sharp eyes seeking out any chink in his armor. "What's wrong? You don't look pleased."

Before he could come up with an answer—or, better, a plausible lie—Soren called him from the end of the hall. "C'mon, jackass, we're getting left behind!"

Elias offered Ember a sheepish smile and a quick bow. "Duty calls."

"Elias," Ember said, stopping him again as he started to pass her. She looked him in the eye, her jaw flexing, her brows furrowed. "Don't leave her side out there, you hear me?"

Uneasiness flickered in his gut like a poorly fed fire, but he nodded. "Never."

She smacked the back of his good shoulder before pulling away. "Maybe one day I'll be back out there with you."

"I'm sure every Atlas is praying against that day ever coming," he said, earning him a rare laugh from the weaponsmith.

By the time he caught up with Soren, Auralee was walking hurriedly away, wiping at her face as she went. Soren's eyes weren't entirely dry either—goodbyes weren't her strong suit, no matter how many times she said them.

He looped his arm around her shoulders. "Never gets easier, does it?"

Soren sighed, circling her arm around his waist, and they started to walk in lockstep. "It is easier. When you're with me, it's easier."

CHAPTER 3

SOREN

The city of Ursa glittered like a cluster of stars in the pre-dawn light beyond the mountain plain, its distant beauty a discordant backdrop for the screams of battle below.

Soren wiped at her running nose and tucked her spyglass away before dragging her scarf back up over her face, a smattering of rocks tumbling down from the ledge as she shifted a bit, trying to relieve the tension in her body. An hour had already passed, cramps beginning to crawl up and down her bent legs as she watched for the signal that their company was to join the fray.

"Restless?" asked a voice from further up the path, and Soren twisted to find Raquel approaching, her scarf pulled down to reveal her startlingly beautiful face. Her gait was steady and strong, her deep brown skin showing only the faintest hint of wind-beaten blush. Her ebony hair was split into twin braids, revealing the deep scars that stretched from her left eye all the way past her temple. Her left ear was half-mangled as well, and no hair grew from the stripes along the side of her scalp. Rumors abounded over how she came by the scars, ranging from a farming accident to a battle with some great mountain beast, but she'd never confirmed any of them.

She looked at Soren, one sharp black brow raised. "Jakob's taking his sweet time letting us loose, hm?"

"As usual," Soren mumbled, avoiding her gaze. Raquel's voice sounded too much like her dead sister's to ever be easy on Soren's ears. Every discussion with her felt like talking to Jira's sterner, more boring ghost. "Atlas brought Anima-blessed soldiers with them. Biomancers."

Cursing, Raquel took out her own spyglass and dropped down beside Soren, holding it up to her good eye. Soren reached up and guided the spyglass in the direction of the bramble thickets she'd spotted earlier—definitely non-native. Nothing like that grew in these mountains. "I don't suppose you're feeling a bit more inclined toward magic yourself?" she asked Raquel.

Raquel's shoulders stiffened. "Not particularly."

Raquel's magic was a secret very few were privy to. Jakob knew, because he was their barracks captain; Soren knew, because Jira had told her; and Elias knew, because Soren didn't see the use in keeping secrets from him. Despite of being one of the rare people in Nyx blessed by Tempest, God of Nature, Raquel refused to use her magic. Soren hadn't been told why.

She didn't push the issue, though it would've been nice to have a touch of magic in their ranks for once. It didn't seem fair that Atlas got to keep that advantage. Instead, she said, "You don't have to babysit me, you know."

"I know. That's Loch's job." There was a question in Raquel's voice that Soren didn't much care for. "Seems you two are joined at the hip since he got bitten. Well, more than you were already."

"Why don't you just ask me if he's available, Raquel?"

Raquel's eye rolled as she lowered her spyglass. "That's not why I'm here. Though I should warn you that Jakob is starting up the next round of betting soon."

"I'll save you some money. Elias and I aren't like that." Not that she hadn't tried to drop a hint here and there when she felt particularly brave.

Raquel sighed again. "If you two were buried any deeper in denial, it would take the whole company to dig you out. But really, that's not why I'm here. Do you know what's different about today?"

Soren decided it was best to ignore that first remark and focus instead on the last. She fussed with a buckle on her boot. "Soleil. Their dead princess. It's her birthday today."

The corners of Raquel's eyes feathered. "You know what that means."

Hatred heated the back of Soren's neck. "*He's* here somewhere."

Most soldiers lost in this pointless war didn't get any true retribution for their deaths. The battlefield rendered everyone faceless, cutting them down to the crest on their armor and the flags they fought under. She was just as likely to kill a fresh face as she was the one that had killed a friend. Targeted revenge was a pointless venture; better to go for numbers than for specificity.

But not this one. She'd been gods-damned *lucky* enough that Jira's killer was perhaps the only identifiable man in the Atlas army.

Raquel stared sightlessly ahead, not a hint of emotion furrowing her brow. "My sister is two years dead. Two years he's been allowed to outlive her . . . I feel them, you know? I feel every breath he takes that she'll never get to."

Soren's throat tightened. That pain wasn't a stranger to her; there were hollow parts of her left behind by loss that would never quite feel right again, like a broken bone poorly mended.

Jira, slain in battle. Her birth family, her brothers and sister and parents, killed when their village of innocents was burned down in retaliation against the Nyxian king's attack on Atlas. Countless other friends whose pyres she'd helped build.

Tonight, each and every one felt closer. They clung to her shoulders like condensation, weighing her down, whispering notions of revenge into her ear.

Elias had told her a story once in hushed murmurs masked by the moan of the wind, sitting shoulder-to-shoulder by a campfire, so close that her breath would have mingled with his if she hadn't been holding it. He'd whispered to her of souls without rest. How they wandered the world beyond with backs bent by the burdens they carried, clothes torn by winds like claws as they begged Mortem for sanctuary.

But they would find none. No peace, no rest; not until their deaths were avenged.

Atlas's First Prince wasn't responsible for every death. She couldn't free every soul she loved from the suffering Elias had described. But avenging even one would be a good start.

She offered her hand to Raquel. "First one to see him takes the kill?"

Raquel snorted, tapping at the corner of her glass eye. "First to see him? Doesn't sound very fair to me."

"Don't even try to pretend you're not twice as deadly as any Atlas, with or without two eyes."

A smirk tugged at Raquel's full lips. "Fair enough." She clasped Soren's hand. "First sight gets the kill."

Just then, the sound of boots scraping rock reached her, and she looked over her shoulder to see Elias come around the bend of the path, his mouth set in a grim line. The slow-blooming dawn lit his dark hair with a halo of fire, his eyes gleaming with battle nerves.

"It's time," he said.

Oh, gods, this was taking *forever.*

Soren flexed her grip against the hilt of her sword, glancing over her shoulder to the body her battlemate prayed over. "Elias, the dead can't hear you. You do know that, right?"

He sighed, his palm pressed to the dead soldier's brow, his knee digging into the blood-soaked battleground dirt. His black armor was spattered with mud and blood from his own kills, his prayer beads wrapped tightly around his knuckles. "The more you rush me, the longer I'm going to take."

A groan rumbled from her chest as she bounced on her heels, rotating her shoulders to loosen them. They'd been fighting since sunup, and she should have been exhausted. Instead, bloodlust thrummed new energy into every part of her that had begun to tire. "The battle's winding down. We're going to be accused of deserting if you don't hurry *up.*"

"We are not going to be accused of deserting. Relax. There's plenty of blood left for you to spill."

"I'm more concerned with Jakob telling my mother I spent half the battle watching my battlemate on his knees. Which I wouldn't mind under other circumstances, but . . ."

She could have sworn his face flushed under the layer of dirt and gore. "Smartass."

She stuck her tongue out. "Jackass."

"If you want me to rush, you need to stop talking. Mortem can't hear me over all your whining."

"You are *so* mean to me."

A small smirk tugged at the side of his mouth, but he wrenched it back into a solemn line. "Just let me finish, will you?"

She could have kept growling at him, but it wouldn't do any good; he was stubborn about these things. When he'd first joined the army, chants of "Elias the Pious" had echoed through any barracks he walked into. Soldiers could be so cruel to new blood—especially a particular young soldier who had spotted a handsome new recruit wearing *prayer beads*, of all things, and hadn't been able to help herself.

It had taken him a while to forgive her for that nickname.

She kept watch while he said his piece, taking in the snowy battlefield sprawling before them. The storm had halted just before they arrived, thankfully, so visibility was good. They'd climbed a hill where only the dead were left, the enemy forces withdrawn, Nyx's forces chasing them.

Atlas was retreating.

It should have been a good thing, but suspicion twinged deep in her gut. Atlas never retreated. It was more likely a regrouping, maybe even a trap. And she hadn't yet caught sight of the man she was looking for.

Elias's voice reached through her worries, a reverence in his tone she never heard outside of his prayers. "You fought with honor and courage. May Mortem guide you home, friend—and may no living being disturb your slumber."

The last part was familiar, the final words to a prayer recited at funerals just before the coffin was locked and the key melted down. A superstition from a much darker time; old, but hard to shake.

She dragged her feet behind Elias as he climbed further up the hill, moving from body to body, murmuring the same prayer over and over. She was inches away from ripping her hair out, and he wasn't even speaking to her. Mortem must have either been deaf or in possession of a divine amount of patience.

"If you try to say that prayer over me one day, I'll come back to life just to punch out your teeth," she said over her shoulder.

"I wouldn't waste my time. Mortem is going to need more than a prayer to be persuaded to let *you* into Arcaea."

Oh, he was going to get kicked for that. Snooty bastard.

But as she was about to follow him to the next body, her gaze caught on an Atlas soldier fighting his way out near the foot of the hill. Something about him . . . the way he fought was familiar.

A shiver ran down her back. "Elias."

He didn't answer, didn't look. She inched away from him, her heels sliding on the blood-slick slope as she peered past the blinding gleam of dying sunlight.

The soldier's armor was of considerably finer make than the others, padded with extra reinforcement in the vulnerable spots, made specifically to fit his body and limned with gold detailing. Beyond that, he fought with just an inch more finesse, just a hint more caution. He pulled back where others might have pushed in. He ducked where others would have met the blow.

The hairs on the back of her neck stood on end, and it had nothing to do with the deeper chill falling over the battlefield as the sun hid itself beyond the horizon, the orange-gold light bathing the field in a bloody glare.

Even at this distance, Soren knew the soldier with the gilded armor.

Not a soldier at all, but a *prince*.

Atlas had only two of them, and according to their spies, the younger never deigned to step foot on anything as dirty and dangerous as a battlefield. Which made this soldier First Prince Kallias Atlas, second-born of Queen Adriata.

Two years of searching, two years of that hollow place aching inside her chest whenever she thought of Jira . . . and there he was.

"Elias." A request. A warning. She had first sight—she had the right of the kill. But if she didn't hurry, she would lose him.

Elias didn't answer, and when she turned, she found he'd made his way to a body several paces behind, out of earshot. He knelt to the ground, bracing himself first with his injured arm—then wincing as it buckled, catching himself with his other hand.

The inkling of an idea pierced her mind.

Enna would not allow her to travel through Atlas to reach Arborius, and Atlas wouldn't offer the antidote for their deviously slow-acting poisons for all the gold or jewels in the world, not even for peace.

But for their prince?

He could be the breaking point, the chink in Atlas's armor. They doted on their royals—loved them. It was strange that the Queen allowed one of them on the field at all. She had started this war to avenge the death of her youngest daughter, after all. What lengths would she go to in order to avoid digging another premature grave?

Determination singing in Soren's veins, she fastened her simple metal mask over the lower half of her face, set her sights on the Atlas prince, and *ran*.

Her feet pounded against the ground, every step sliding in the bloody snow, but she'd trained for such conditions. This was her world. This was her day.

Her vision tunneled in on the prince, still retreating but doing his best to take down as many who chased them as possible, handling his sword with surprising deftness. He fled backward, heels constantly catching on patches of ice, likely afraid of turning his back to the enemy army.

So Soren got to see the moment he realized retribution had come, his eyes blowing wide as she lunged, a battle cry ripping free from her throat as her sword arced toward his leg.

Their blades met with a sharp *clang*, echoing across the rapidly emptying battlefield.

"You," she spat. "It's been too long."

His eyes narrowed. "I'm sorry, have we met?" His voice was too pretty and polished for a soldier, Atlas accent sharp as the ridiculously beautiful blade in his hands.

Soren didn't bother with a reply. She stepped forward to sweep his leg, but he locked himself in place, slamming the hilt of his blade against her jaw and knocking the mask loose, sending her reeling. She hit the ground headfirst, her mask knocked clean off, and her braid fell free from its pinning. It swung like a tongue of fire as she jolted back to her feet, shoving his blade aside with hers and driving her elbow upward. As she connected, the knob of bone cracking under his chin, a vicious bolt of glee thrilled through her veins.

This was going to work. She could feel it in her bones.

The prince straightened with a growl, his gloved hand reaching up instinctively to feel at his jaw. Even with her mind wrapped in a battle-hot haze, she noticed little things—the vivid blue-green of his eyes, the freckles thick as the stars in Nyx's skies across his skin, the well-trimmed red beard and matching streaks of long hair that had fallen free from the knot at the nape of his neck.

Meeting the challenge in her eyes with one of his own, baring his teeth, the prince readied himself to lunge, muscles bunching like a wildcat about to pounce.

And then he looked at her face. Really looked at it.

He stopped dead. His blade sagged until the point nearly brushed the ground, his expression slackening as if he'd forgotten entirely what he was there to do. His trembling hand—honest to gods *trembling*—lifted to his mouth like he might be sick.

"*Soleil?*" A curse, a gasp, a prayer.

His voice. That name.

Bedtime stories, hide and seek, candy floss, fire and smoke.

Soren couldn't think. Couldn't move. For several heartbeats too many, she was frozen, every moving part of her locked up by the way this prince was looking at her.

"Soleil?" He came a step closer, barely an inch from the outstretched hand of one of her fallen people. His gaze was only for her, devastated, aflame, *awed.*

That sound, that sight, shook Soren back to herself. A roar of fury tore out of her, and she lunged, driving her sword toward his thigh. Getting him off his feet was the only way the plan would work. She could solve the rest later.

His eyes flicked behind her as he twisted instinctively to avoid the blow, horror brimming in those startling eyes. "Wait, no! Stop—!"

His feint threw her off balance, but her blade still made contact: not a stab into his thigh, but a deep gash along his calf. The terror and lingering wonder on his face snapped into pain, and he stumbled backward, shouting at someone to *stop, please stop, I'm ordering you—*

Not shouting at her.

Snow crunched behind her, and she whirled. A shadow loomed over her, a flash of steel, and then pain ripped up her torso like she was being torn in half, burned alive from navel to chest. The ground met her body with a thump that drove what breath she had left from her chest, the kiss of snow against her middle briefly shocking the burning into numb. She desperately tried to scramble up, but her hands plunged into what felt less like snow and more like a puddle.

Slowly, she looked down.

The slush beneath her fingers was stained dark crimson.

Huh. That's a lot of blood, was her first thought.

Oh, Mortem's pits. That's my *blood,* was her second, slightly more concerned thought.

She rolled herself over, years of battlefield training kicking in quickly—*use gravity to your advantage, don't let the wound face downward*—and propped herself up against one of the boulders scattered across the valley. And after that, she didn't do much of anything, because it turned out blood loss made that kind of thing difficult.

Past the ringing in her ears, she heard the Atlas prince screaming, "Go back! Go back, go back for her, *damn it* go back for her! *Soleil!*"

Screaming like he would never stop.

CHAPTER 4

SOREN

When she opened her eyes again, there was only blood.

The taste of it coated her tongue, the smell stronger than the incense-spiced smoke of the funeral pyres burning around her. The warmth masked the dwindling temperature as night finally fell on the battlefield, casting long shadows over blades and bodies. It was the reason for the scarlet snowmelt beneath her, her wandering hands leaving streaks wherever they touched.

And the pool in her lap told her she was minutes away from being dead.

The smoke . . . if they were still burning the enemy dead, she hadn't lost that much time.

She braced herself against the boulder and forced a shaking hand to the gaping wound in her gut, fingertips running over jagged edges of broken armor and frayed pieces of her tunic beneath. They came away dripping.

That damned blade had cut straight through her favorite armor.

Well, she thought fuzzily, *that's just lovely. Elias is going to pitch a fit.*

Fumbling a dagger from her belt, she clamped the wooden handle in her teeth until the bitter taste of polished wood mixed with the tang of iron and salt on her tongue. Then she shoved her palm back against the wound.

It took every ounce of her strength to choke down a scream. The agony left her dizzy, barely clinging to consciousness, but she couldn't stay here and wait to be found. She couldn't die *this* unimpressively. Gods, it was hardly even a story.

Princess Soren of Nyx bled out on a hill with a knife between her teeth. We found her a day later and no one heard her last words. They probably weren't that great anyway.

Not a chance. She was going out spectacularly, or she wasn't going out at all.

If you can walk, you'll live, so get up and walk.

She spat out the knife, her half-delirious mind focusing on the grooves her teeth had left and the blood that now stained the hilt. Pushing her dirty hair out of her face, strands catching on her sticky palm, she forced herself to her feet in one quick movement.

Lightning lanced across her abdomen, the pain blinding her, and she barely noticed her knees buckling, her limbs failing, darkness crowding in until all she could hear was her own heartbeat.

Thump.

Thump.

Nothing.

Thump.

Nothing.

The pauses between each beat grew as she lay still, waiting in breathless, dull terror for that next thump . . . or for silence to fall. There was no telling how many beats her slowing heart had left in it, no telling whether—

"Soren!"

She tried to raise her head at that shout, but found it to be disobedient. Blurs of sunset and snow spun in lazy circles as she tried to get her bearings. Her cheek was pressed into the melting snow, sharp stems of dead grass poking her skin. Her left hand was still draped loosely over her middle, doing nothing to slow the bleeding anymore, her right arm pinned underneath her.

Dead weight. She couldn't move.

So much for walking, O Glorious Warrior. This is an embarrassing way to die.

The voice shouted again, louder, more worried. "Has anyone seen Soren? Does anyone know where—" Then, worry melting into exasperation: "Soren, where *are* you? This isn't funny, I tell you every time, it's not funny to scare me like this—will you come out already so I can skip straight to kicking your ass for leaving me behind? *Again?*"

Elias.

She spat out the blood pooling in her mouth, trying to shout to him. Instead, her voice caught in her throat, and a clotted cough was her only rallying cry against Mortem's gentle hands.

Oh, pits take me.

Apparently Elias could track her down well enough on his own, because moments or hours later, his voice came again, louder, sickened, horrified: *"Oh gods."*

Oh, that's not a good sign.

Soren blinked emptily, a blur of black armor consuming what little vision she had left. As he lifted her by her armor and propped her back against the rock, she tried to find his face, tried to remember how to say his name, but death was too close now. The shadow of it hung low over her body, stealing away thought and memory and will.

"You *stay awake*, Soren," ordered Elias, every word choked with a terror so deep it nearly broke her heart. "Stay with me. You—hey! Didn't you hear me? Keep those eyes open! For once in your damned life, just do as you're told!"

His warm hands, sticky with blood—*her blood*—clasped her face. She blinked to find death-dark eyes gazing into hers, black glowing gold in the light of the pyres.

"Do as you're told," he repeated, battle-dry lips pressing against her forehead.

Her swollen tongue moved, and she barely managed to rasp, "Don't . . . boss me around, jackass."

A broken laugh against her forehead. "I hate you, smartass."

"Do not," she mumbled back, her eyes sinking shut. Even this far gone, she knew that.

"Soren. Hey. Soren!" His hands clapped against her face, trying to rouse her. "Where do you think you're going?"

"Mortem's pit, probably."

"It's called Infera, smartass. Don't be crude."

A blood-laden laugh burbled from her throat, sending a rivulet down her chin. "Jack . . . jackass."

He cursed under his breath, pulling away for a moment to yank the string of black beads from around his neck and wrap them around his fingers, the polish catching the fading light. "Keep breathing, all right? You're not allowed to stop breathing."

That distracted her momentarily from the pain; his prayer beads were for dying or dead people, not *well, she looks a bit rough, but she'll live* people.

The next laugh caught painfully in her chest. "Damn. There go my . . . my plans for . . ."

The cracked, rasping noise he made could have been a chuckle or a sob. "There go your plans for the evening? Are you seriously trying to joke with me right now? Because this isn't funny. I don't know how you think this—"

"I'm sorry." She wasn't sure why she said it, wasn't sure whether the pain in her chest was because she was dying or because he sounded like he was going to cry.

"For what? Running off to get yourself killed? I certainly hope so—"

"No." She blinked slowly, tears welling in her eyes. "My armor."

He frowned, brows knitting together, gaze flickering downward. "What about it?"

"You worked so hard on it." Her throat tightened. "They ruined it."

His eyes flashed back up to hers, widening first, then gentling in a way she'd rarely seen. "Gods, Soren, don't worry about that. I'll make you a new set, okay? I promise. Winter Fair is coming up anyway."

"He . . . the prince." A flash of gold armor sparked to life in her memory. "Saw him first . . . thought we could . . . trade. For the antidote."

His hands pushed against her torso, but she didn't feel it anymore—another bad sign. His next curse was helpless, shaky, and his grip tightened around his beads. "You went after *Kallias?* Soren, you can't just . . . you should have waited for me!"

"No time." She reached out one hand, and he caught it, twining his blood-soaked fingers with hers, leaning close to brush sweat-clumped hair from her forehead with his other hand before pressing it back against her wound.

"Did you kill him, at least?"

"No." Shame bloomed in her aching chest at the shred of memory. "Got away."

"That's fine. That's fine. I'm sure the son of a—hey. Soren. *Soren.*" He smacked her again, his voice getting louder and louder, but her head was beginning to feel heavy, like one of the grainsacks they beat apart in the barracks training rooms, and her hands . . . she couldn't feel her hands at all. "I'm going to get you home, okay, smartass?" He paused, as if waiting for a response, then repeated himself: "Hey, *smartass*, I'm talking to you. *I'm going to get you home.* Tell me you hear me!"

You hear me, smartass?

I hear you, jackass.

It was their version of affectionate nicknames that doubled as code for *I'm okay, are you?* Call and response, question and answer. But she didn't have the strength to speak.

He shifted, as if about to stand, and panic pierced the warm haze slowly drowning her thoughts. Was he leaving? He couldn't leave. She had to tell him, had to make him stay . . .

Gods, she didn't want to take her last breaths alone.

Not again. The nonsensical thought broke through the fog. *Don't let me die alone again.*

Then he reappeared, a shadow hovering over her. His hand cupped her cheek, his voice gentle despite the frustration creasing his blurred face. "I can't move you with my arm like this. I'm going to get a physician and bring them back, okay? I need you to hold on until I get back. You remember how to do that?"

She moved her lips, but no sound came out.

His grip on her tightened. "You anchor yourself. Find your anchor and hold on. Tell me when you have it."

She couldn't. Her head started to loll—

"Soren!" He caught her and forced her to look at him, his voice cracking as he stroked his thumbs over her cheeks. "Come on, tell me when you have it."

She nodded—the barest dip of her chin.

He brushed a stray tear away from her cheek, his lips quivering as he tried and failed to smirk. "That was too fast. Tell me what it is or I won't believe you."

Keep them talking. They'd all been taught what to do to keep the wounded fighting. She hadn't realized it was so irritating. So *hard.*

A flash of red hair that wasn't her own. Boyish voices yelling her name, hands gripping her and hoisting her over a shoulder while she shrieked in delight.

"Summer Fair." Gods, was that her voice? She sounded halfway to being a ghost already. "I'm . . . I'm six. My brothers are playing hide and seek with me."

He blew out a breath and nodded, leaning down to press one last fierce kiss to her forehead. "Hold on to it. I'll be right back."

He wouldn't come back in time. She knew it. He probably did too. "Don't."

His expression was torn, agonized in the firelight, his face streaked with soot, his stubble caked with blood from an open wound on his cheek. An old god, a lost boy, a mourner who'd arrived too late to the pyre.

Beautiful.

He clasped her hands, then let them fall. "I'll be *right back*."

She couldn't do it. She couldn't let him leave, couldn't die cold and lost and *alone*— "*Elias*. Don't go."

But he was already gone, his shadow replaced by stars—thousands upon thousands of glittering swathes strung across the sky like drapes over a bedframe, like waves thrown up against a shore of broken shells.

Waves. Shells. Things she'd only read about in storybooks, but here, in this pocket between life and death, she could imagine them: the gleaming bits of color dotting the shoreline, water with a life of its own heaving itself at the land, devouring anything in its path before retreating back to the depths.

Was Atlas's ocean as vast as Nyx's sky? There had to be a reason they practically worshipped it, why they spent so much of their lives in the water.

Exhaustion, cold and dark and final, crept over her body. Settled in her muscles. Weighed down her eyelids.

So this was her great end, her final goodbye. The winking of faraway, irreverent stars. A sudden, strange, visceral longing for a sea she'd never seen.

For a heartbeat, just one, she could have sworn she smelled salt and damp and brine. The snow balled in her fist could possibly feel like sand, if she believed it hard enough, if she pretended . . .

The ocean never leaves us, you know, said a voice she only remembered in dreams. *It gets in your blood. People get addicted to saltwater.*

But what if they go somewhere else, Papa? What if there's no ocean?

It follows them. Once you taste the ocean, you can never forget it. You will miss it forever.

And then darkness swept her away.

CHAPTER 5

ELIAS

Elias Loch had prayed uncountable prayers in the past ten years.

From the moment he stepped over the threshold of the church where Priestess Kendra had founded her school, taking his first breath of dusty, incensed air, he knew one thing: he was meant to serve his goddess whatever way he could. Even as his eyes had stung and watered, half-blinded by the kaleidoscope of colors from the stained-glass windows vaulted high above him, he'd known with a shiver of *rightness* that he was exactly where he belonged.

His first true prayer that was wholly his own and not a recitation from his little holy book had been simple, whispered under his breath as his knees knocked and his stomach churned.

Please don't let me throw up on the Priestess.

He guessed it wasn't a request the Goddess of Death received often.

His mother's hand on his back and his father's on his shoulder were all that kept him steady that first day. And that first prayer led to thousands more—none of them quite as desperate as this one, chanted in his mind as he sprinted across the frozen valley. None of them as fervent as the one that slipped out in sobs between gasping breaths: *Not her. Not her. Please, please, please not her.*

Gods, how had he let this happen?

I'll give you something else. Anything else. You will have whatever you ask of me. But not her.

His feet barely kissed the ground as he tore through the mountain-encased valley, and it still wasn't fast enough for him. For her. The sky was fading rapidly from orange to gray to black, night cloaking the evidence of the bloodshed they'd wrought today, and it should have been a comfort. Nyx was the kingdom of night, after all. It was their home.

But this time it only spurred him faster, panic pumping alongside his pulse, his arm throbbing with agony. It was weak again, numb and tingling like the day after he'd first been wounded. That probably wasn't good, but he didn't have time to worry about it. Night was falling, and if he got lost in the dark, he'd never find the tents. Soren would slip away from exsanguination or shock or hypothermia—whichever stole her first.

Breathe. Breathe. Breathe. As much a command to himself as a plea whispered to the battlemate he left behind, soaked in her own blood, her laughing mouth still and pale with cold.

The next breath he took shattered into a ragged sob, the noise muffled by the blood-beat in his head and the crunching of snow beneath him.

"You are going to live," he prayed between gasps. Prayed to her, his Soren, and not his goddess—perhaps the first heretical act he'd ever committed. The first of many he might be willing to commit if it kept her *here*.

"You are going to live." Not a question, not a plea. An *order*. "You listen to *me* for once: you are going to live, or so help me, I will kill you myself."

Gods, he wasn't running *fast enough*. His lungs burned, every breath scraping as he pushed, and pushed, and pushed—

There. Lanternlight flickered in the distance, cutting through the pitch-black Nyxian night. He hurtled into the tents, screaming for help, and everyone stopped what they were doing and stared at him like he was some kind of specter. Only when he looked down did he realize he was covered in enough blood to look like he was dying himself.

"Someone help," he choked out, doubling over with his hands on his knees, trying to drag in enough breath to explain. "It—the princess—Soren is—"

Two of the physicians were on their feet in an instant. The elder one, grim-faced and pale, said, "Take us to her."

If the run there was a century, the run back was an eternity. The physicians passed him as his strength flagged, but that was all right. As long as they reached her, as long as they *saved* her—

They stopped running.

Elias skidded to a halt between them, desperately trying to pull breath into his searing lungs. "What are you doing? We're almost . . ."

What little breath he'd managed to muster slipped away as he took in the scene.

Blood-stained grass and snowmelt. A blood-streaked boulder lit up eerily with lantern light. Empty, discarded armor.

She was gone. Not dead—*gone*.

The world fell away from Elias's feet, horror dragging sharpened claws down every one of his bones. *No. No. No no no no no*—

"Maybe someone else found her," he heard himself say. "Maybe someone found her and took her to the tents . . ."

Or she died, murmured his thoughts. *She died and they dragged her off with the rest of the bodies. Maybe she's already burning.*

The world tipped on its side, further, further . . .

Elias crashed to his knees.

CHAPTER 6

SOREN

Sometimes, on the loneliest and darkest nights, Soren dreamed of her father. Almost everything about her first family was lost to smoke and time, her memory clouded after the injuries she'd suffered the night of the fire. But she remembered how his beard scratched against her face when he gave her kisses, how tall she felt when he carried her on his shoulders, and how, if she begged just the right way, with just the right pout of her lip, she could steal permission to stay up past her bedtime.

Those nights were her favorite. Her father would hold her head against him and stroke her hair as her eyelids grew heavy, his voice rumbling deep in his chest as he murmured tales of other kingdoms and beautiful princesses, singing lullabies about the stars and the sea and questions left unanswered.

All memories she'd found hiding deep in her mind, returning through dreams and half-formed thoughts. And here, in this shadowy place between life and death, she found him again.

"Papa. Papa. Papa Papa Papa Papa *are you* listening *to me?"*

"I always listen to you, Sunbeam. Give me a moment, then I'm all yours."

Soren gripped the edge of her father's desk and leaned across it, her braids brushing through fresh ink scrawled on parchment, staining the edges of her hair black. Hope fluttered between her ribs like nervous butterflies as she took in the mess. "Are these for my party?"

She couldn't remember what the room looked like, or what her father's profession was, but she would never forget how the work wearied him. That day, he was bent over a pile of envelopes, some hastily torn open, others tossed aside with their wax seal intact. His thick copper hair was tied in a small knot at the nape of his neck, held in place by a gold-and-emerald clip Soren desperately wanted to pilfer for her own jewelry box, and his spectacles slid down to the very tip of his nose, threatening to fall right off his face and into the letters he'd been reading for hours now.

He offered her a warm smile over his work, but his brown eyes were narrowed, glassy. He always squinted when he got tired. "A couple. But most of them have to do with other matters."

She took in a quick breath, doing her best to hide her disappointment. But a frown tugged at the less-obedient side of her mouth, the side that had been looking forward to her birthday for just about a year now and very much wanted the presents that would come with it. "Oh. What, then?"

He pushed his chair back, opening his arms, an invitation she never ignored. Soren scrambled up onto the chair with him, perching on his lap, stretching her arms over the armrests like his as he scooted the chair back up to the desk. She couldn't see his face, but she heard his smile when he said, "Tell me what you see, Sunbeam."

Well, that didn't sound like a very good answer to her question. But she bit her tongue and obeyed, studying the letter before her carefully. "Incentives," she read aloud. "What's that mean?"

"Incentives are like rewards. They're offered to encourage people to do or not do something."

Soren studied the paper more closely, her tongue poking into her cheek as she read, her own eyes squinting in concentration. "Mm . . . incentives for . . . an alliance. Alliance with who?"

"Tallis. We think they would make good allies for us in the event of . . . if anything were to happen."

Nervous energy thrummed down Soren's legs, and she kicked her feet gently to get it out. She leaned her elbows forward on the table, inky braids brushing streaks down her father's newly written letter, ignoring his quiet groan of protest. "I thought we were already friends with Tallis."

The smile was gone from her father's voice when he answered, gently sliding his hands under her elbows and coaxing her away from the desk. "We were. But we recently got word that they've been putting out feelers to other kingdoms."

Soren wrinkled her nose. "Feelers?"

Her father wrapped his arms around her, resting his chin on her head, his beard tugging strands out of her carefully done plaits. "They're trying to find a kingdom that can give them more than we can. So we're going to be the ones to offer more first."

"Why? If they don't want us—"

"Nobody wants an alliance, Sunbeam. If kingdoms only wanted for alliances, they would never bother to make them. We need Tallis—and we have to show them that they need us, too."

Soren craned her head back to look at him. "Do they need us, Papa?"

Her father's gaze drifted back to the letter, and his chest rose and fell in a sigh. "I hope so. I really do."

Death smelled like mint and a cool breeze.

That was a surprise. Being around Elias always gave her the impression that it would be a fiery sort of place—or, at least, he'd told her that if she made one more comment about his ass being somewhat nicely shaped, she was going to taste soot and sulfur when she died.

"Worth it to see you blush," she'd replied cheerfully, and he groaned something about her being unbelievable.

But there was no fire here, though she dreamed of it, somewhere past birthday letters and her father's voice and the sharp smell of fresh ink. Fire that roared and bit at her heels and hissed to *run, little princess, run* before the tar-thick darkness choked it out.

At least that was over. But remnants of that darkness still clung to her mind, dragging at her consciousness like it wasn't ready to let her out yet.

No pain—that was the first thing she noticed when her mind fumbled back to wakefulness. Where she'd once felt like a fish with its belly slit, there was only a gentle, tingling warmth. But she was bone-achingly, unbearably tired, and her mouth tasted awful, like old meat and morning breath had taken a tumble over her tongue. Death might have smelled pretty, but the taste was horrendous.

Somewhere far away, she heard a cracked, breathless moan. It might have been hers.

Something settled over her forehead; a hand, soothing and cautious, smoothing over her hair like a mother fussing over a feverish child.

She found her tongue and managed to rasp, "Hey, jackass."

The hand on her brow stilled. "Pardon me?"

That was . . . definitely not Elias.

She'd never woken after a battle without Elias beside her since they'd taken their battlemate vows, injured or not. Not even *once*.

Her eyes flew open to the face of a murderer.

Prince Kallias.

Sunfire hair hung in a long braid over his shoulder, resting against his long-sleeved turquoise tunic—fine silk, filigreed with gold, very easy to stab through. His eyes were the palest shade of blue-green she'd ever seen, like shaken stardust, like mold. His face was oddly open, vulnerable, wearing nothing but hope.

She could change that.

Soren flung herself up, snarling, her hands going for his throat, ready to crush the life out of his pretty neck. "You!"

He sharpened from friend to warrior in the span of a heartbeat, catching her wrists and pinning her with no trouble at all.

Damn it. *Damn* it.

Her body couldn't handle a fight in this condition. She was shaking just from the effort of that one lunge, wave after wave of dizzying pain deadening her limbs.

So the lack of pain was contingent on her not moving. That was unfortunate, mostly because she'd just thrown herself straight into the arms of Jira's killer, his heart *inches* away, and she had no weapon to drive hilt-deep into it. No strength to force the breath from his lungs. Nothing.

Raquel had trusted her with his death-right, and she'd *failed*.

She hated his face—handsome in the way Elias was not, all sharp angles and graceful features—more than she'd ever hated anything. And that was saying something, because she hated quite a few things, and hated them very well.

"That's a fine way to treat someone who saved your life," he scolded her.

"Go to the pits," Soren spat in his face, jerking her knee into his groin.

The prince released her immediately, barking in pain, anything gentle in his eyes hardening from stardust to limestone. He limped backward, but stood as straight as he could, clinging to his composure. "Try to kill me again, and you'll find our dungeons are much less welcoming than this room."

This room—rounded like a castle turret, the walls colored a gentle shade of cream, with creeping vines and strange flowers painted from floor to ceiling in cheerful swathes. Jars of poultices and bunches of dried herbs were spread out on the nightstand beside her bed—some medicines to ward off infection, and others she couldn't guess at. A broad window sat across from her would-be deathbed, framed in raw wood, and outside it . . .

That explained the roaring that hadn't faded even when she wandered out of her flaming nightmares into quieter dreams. Not fire at all, but water that went on and on with no end in sight.

Ocean.

Mortem's rusty *scythe*. She was in Atlas.

They stayed where they were for several heavy heartbeats—Soren with her palms braced against the mattress, poised to attack, and the Atlas prince staring at her like she was breaking his gods-damned heart. She closed her eyes, taking in a slow breath, trying to steady herself. There was something she was missing here, and she was going to die in very short order if she didn't figure it out.

"I didn't think Atlas took prisoners," she said finally, trying again to stand. But her head twirled like a spinning top, and she stumbled.

Prince Kallias, either truly foolish or suffering from an overabundance of pity, caught her again, holding her by her wrists. "I didn't think Nyx trained their soldiers to be suicidal."

She tipped her head back, grinning her most feral grin, letting her hatred spread over her face like a growing weed. "You have no idea what we're trained to do, you bastard. Now let me go."

Something in his eyes shuttered at her grin, but he didn't answer her hatred with a spurt of his own, didn't match her mocking look.

He seemed . . . sad. If she didn't know better, she'd call it grief.

Whatever it was, he obeyed, guiding her down to the edge of the bed and taking three long steps back. He wasn't much taller than Elias, but his legs made up a good portion of his body, more awkward than she would've guessed when he was armored. His posture was too perfect, his shoulders held back like the statue of some long-dead king. Not a warrior's build, but a politician's.

"You don't know who I am, do you?" he said softly.

"Kallias, First Prince of Atlas, second-born to Queen Adriata herself." She sketched a mocking half-bow from her seat, trying not to be conscious of how stiff the movement was and hoping she didn't look too pathetic in this patchy infirmary gown. "I'd say it's a pleasure, but I promised my battlemate I'd make a real effort to be more honest."

Kallias's expression didn't change. "I don't mean my names and titles. You don't know who I *am*."

Soren's grin faltered. "What else is there to know, Your Royal Gangliness?"

That got a reaction, a brief flicker of shock before he schooled himself into indifference. "Get some rest. Our healers took care of your wound, but your body still needs to recover. You lost a lot of blood."

Soren's heart dropped into her gut, and her hand moved instinctively to cover it. Beneath the gown, she felt it—a thick rope of scar tissue, the healing accelerated by unnatural means.

Magic.

Not entirely unknown in Nyx, but certainly not common, especially for healing. That was in Anima's repertoire, and Nyx had mostly rejected the other gods, devoting their temples to Mortem alone with the odd altar built to Tempest.

But never Anima, Goddess of Life. Never Occassio, Goddess of . . . something about mirrors and snakes and reading the stars that gave Elias a special kind of heebie-jeebies. And never, *never* the fifth god, What's-His-Name—a god in charge of something else unpleasant she couldn't remember.

Maybe she should have listened to Elias a little better.

"No thank you," she finally said. "I would like to be allowed to go home, please."

Kallias's eyebrow cocked. "That was polite."

"Is it working?"

"No."

"Then forget it. Go to the pits, Atlas bastard." Wait . . . she'd already said that. Gods, her tongue felt heavy, every word running into the next with a drunken slur.

His eyes darkened again, pain of his own cracking that icy gaze. But instead of a retort or a threat, he simply said, "Rest. We'll talk more later."

Before she could dredge up the energy to demand to be told why she'd been brought here, why they'd bothered using their magic to heal her, why they hadn't killed her like the others . . . the prince turned on his heel and walked out.

The lock clicked in place as the door shut behind him.

CHAPTER 7

KALLIAS

The howling in Kallias's head refused to quiet. Like a storm whipping apart the palm trees, like the crash of waves thrown against the shore. He knew nothing, saw *nothing* but that Nyxian girl's hair, her face . . . a face he knew. A face he'd thought long-buried.

A stranger, but not a stranger at all. Unfamiliar in adulthood, but as familiar as his own heartbeat.

He leaned against the door to the infirmary, the grooves digging uncomfortably into his spine. He didn't care about the discomfort; barely felt it, really. Past the noise in his head, everything else was muted, numb, dream-like.

This couldn't be real.

Alive. Alive. Alive.

"So?"

Kallias rasped his hands down his beard and looked up to find Jericho propped against the opposite wall, arms crossed, back straight like she still sat on her throne. Like it followed her everywhere she went.

His older sister couldn't look any more poised in that pink, flowy chiffon gown with sleeves that cuffed at her wrists. Her scarlet hair pulled back in a neat bun, and her porcelain skin practically glowed with shimmering gold cosmetics and subtle gloss on her lips. But the look on her face was built for war. He'd never seen her so furious, the blazing green fire in her eyes threatening to sear right through the door holding him up.

"She doesn't know me." The words bit the tip of his tongue like acid. "I mean, she knows my name, but she . . ."

Spat at me. Insulted me. Told me to go to the depths. Tried to kill me.

"She doesn't know me," he repeated lamely. "Whatever Nyx did to her . . ."

"Are we sure it's her? Not just some unlucky redhead you happened to run into?"

Resentment twinged in his gut. He tamped it down. "I'm not a fool, Jericho. You saw her face. She looks exactly like you, like Mama. And gods, the way she talks . . ."

"Like Finn?"

"Disturbingly so."

Jericho's expression softened, and she pushed herself up from the wall, coming to squeeze his shoulder. "I know you did your due diligence, Kal. I just want to be careful." She frowned, licking her thumb and rubbing his neck. "Hold still. You've got something there."

"Probably blood," he sighed. "I've bathed five times already and I'm still finding spots."

Her freckled nose wrinkled, and she jerked her hand back, grimacing at the red-brown stain on her thumb. She unceremoniously wiped it on his jacket. "Well, ew."

That would've coaxed a laugh from him if fury and grief weren't taking turns squeezing his heart to the point of pain. "Can you send for Vaughn to witness the blood match? I don't want to tell Mama and Papa until I'm sure."

Jericho's smile wavered. "Kal, I don't know . . . he's had a bad couple days, and you know how hard it is for him when—"

"I know, I know." His brother-in-law had always been a sickly man, but the past couple years had seen a sharp decline in his strength. On bad days, he could hardly pull himself out of bed. "And you know I wouldn't ask if it wasn't important, but we have to know, Jer. And we're going to need someone to back us up. If it's her . . ."

Jericho swallowed, grief showing in the tears that lined her eyes, in the press of her arms against her stomach like she was going to be sick. "If it's her, she's been a prisoner of Nyx for gods-know how long."

"Whatever they did to her, if it is her, she doesn't know us like she should." Kallias forced himself to be the First Prince, composed and analytical, stating the facts and gathering what he could from them. Emotion had no place in this discussion until he knew for sure. "Nine was old enough to remember. If she doesn't, it's because they *made* her forget."

That should have been impossible. Nyx had very little magic, and it didn't include magics of the mind as far as he knew—which, admittedly, wasn't much. He was a man of politics, not miracles. Not dead baby sisters all grown up and trying to murder him, found on the wrong side of a war *her death* started.

A slow pain began to pulse in his temples. "Get Vaughn. I'll start finding the others."

"Mama and Papa are at the country house," said Jericho. "Mama needed to get away over Soleil's birthday. And Finn . . ."

Oh, perfect. He knew that lilt in her voice, that little wince, a look on her face that said she'd gone down a path she hadn't meant to.

"All right," he muttered, pinching the bridge of his nose. "Break it to me fast. What's the prick up to now?"

CHAPTER 8

FINN

"Now, hang on. I think we can all agree this was an honest mistake."

Prince Finnick Atlas backed away slowly from the rough-hewn table, the soles of his sandals sticking to dried puddles of beer and discarded bits of candied coconut, an innocent smile decorating his face. Not that they could see it with his scarf wrapped carefully around the lower half of his face and his hat jammed over his telltale hair. He was a lot of things, not many of them good, but he wasn't a complete fool.

Just half of one. Maybe a third, if he was being generous with himself.

He had three minutes to wrap this up before the barkeep kicked one of them out.

He caught said barkeep's eye and tugged twice at his earlobe. She narrowed her eyes at him, a silent groan of *Must you?* written all over her face.

He gave her a pleading look. She sighed, but gave in with a weary nod, plucking all breakable glasses from the bar itself. Not exactly the best show of faith, but he'd take it.

The hulking mass of a man he'd just beaten in a game of cards—not all that high-stakes, definitely not worth all this fuss—drew himself to his feet, his club-like hands slamming into the table with such force the driftwood chandeliers on the ceiling rattled. "Oh, it was a mistake, all right. But far from an honest one."

Finn resisted the urge to sigh. It was so cliché he couldn't even be bothered to find it funny. "Tomas, let's call it beginner's luck and leave it at that, shall we?"

"Let's call it *being a cheat*."

Finn gasped, putting a hand over his heart. "You wound me."

Tomas grinned, showing surprisingly perfect teeth. "Oh, I haven't even begun to wound you, pretty boy."

Stammer. Pat your pockets. You're a nobleman's son out of his depth, so act like it.

Finn put his hands up, forcing his knees to quake just enough to be noticeable. "Look, it's not a big deal. You want the money back? Here, have it back. I've no use for it."

He tossed the bag onto the table. Tomas didn't even look at it.

"You're a cheat and a thief. I want double."

A cheat and a thief? He was one to talk. It had actually taken *work* for Finn to keep his hand high enough to win with all the face cards this man kept shoved up his sleeves.

Finn coughed out an anxious-edged laugh. "Oh, come on, I don't have double on me. Only a fool carries that much coin."

Tomas flicked out a wicked-looking dagger. "Double."

"O-Okay, okay, no need to get . . . pokey. Look, I'll have to make a trip home and bring it back. Where are you staying?"

Tomas gave a quick glance about, and as he gave Finn an address, it was an effort to keep the earnest terror in his eyes. The tremor in his hands. Every little costume he wore.

Gods, it was so easy, it almost wasn't fun anymore.

He hit his heel on the doorjamb in just the right spot to make his stumble look real, tripping out onto the street, stammering out promises to leave the money on the man's doorstep by evening and looking appropriately frightened by the promises to shove that knife in unpleasant places if he failed to deliver. The moment the door swung back into place, he loosened his posture, finally letting himself chuckle, and pocketed the bag he'd snatched from the table as he tripped and stumbled about, the tipsy noble they were all used to seeing . . . and swindling.

So they thought, anyhow.

"*You're a cheat and a thief,*" he mimicked under his breath, rolling his eyes. "You're the dumbass that stiffed a seer, but sure, *I'm* the thief."

He tugged off his jaunty hat and scarf and stuffed them into his satchel, then pulled out a cloak in their place and fastened it around his shoulders, throwing the hood up over his head. Hurrying down the cobblestone street before the tavern door could swing open again, he slipped into a glassware shop, peering out from behind colorful suncatchers while two men swaggered out and made their way past the store without a second look—a tail sent by the man he'd swindled, no doubt.

"Finnick Atlas," called the clerk at the counter—thankfully the only other person in the store, or else he'd be in trouble for using Finn's real name—"You'd best not be bringing trouble into my shop."

"Of course not, Mr. Pollock. Just looking today."

The old man grumbled under his breath, but didn't protest further—after all, Finn was still a prince before he was a scoundrel.

Once enough time had passed, Finn left the shop, taking a leisurely walk down several side streets before finally ducking into an empty alley, taking in a deep breath of salt-heavy air. Even this deep in the city, he could always find traces of the sea: stray shells, sand, the telltale scent. Port Atlas wound itself around the shoreline like a sunning serpent, its people never too far from the beach to hear the waves roaring just beyond the sand-lined streets and whitewashed walls. There was no escaping the ocean here.

There was a gentle bite to the breeze that stirred his hood, chilling the sweat gathered on his brow under the edge of the cloth. The humidity was lighter than usual, the sun just a touch cooler. Winter was on its way, robbing the tropical heat of its usual potency, but Finn didn't mind it. He wasn't a fan of humidity; it did awful things to his hair.

Speaking of, his scalp was already itchy as a sand-coated seal. He tugged off his hood, raking his fingers through the dark auburn waves, grimacing as strands stood up with a mind of their own.

Near the back of the alley, a second cloaked figure rounded the corner, propping herself against the wall. She lifted a hand, knuckles knocking three quick beats against the whitewashed stone wall. In response, Finn gave a low, three-note whistle. The all-clear.

"That took you long enough," sighed the shadow, knocking back her own hood as she stepped forward. "I thought Neesi would've kicked you out sooner."

"I bargained for more time." Finn held out the bag of coins. "This should be about half the payment he owes you, but I'm guessing he lost the rest to another game before I got to him. He's at the old green building on Riptide with the weird windows, if you want to drop a hint to a guard. And good to see you too, Luisa. Thanks for saying so."

Luisa snorted, taking the bag from him, weighing it with a practiced hand. She was dark as a Nyxian night, her skin matching her onyx hair. Her curls seemed to stand up on their own—it always looked a bit like she'd been caught in a windstorm or struck by lightning, and Finn liked that about her. "You're sure it's my guy?"

"He still smelled like those awful candles in your shop."

Her smile widened. "Observant as always. You're sure I can't pay you? I feel bad imposing . . ."

Finn snorted softly. "I'm good, thanks. I'd do it just to keep my mind busy. Feels like there's not enough to think about lately."

Luisa chuckled quietly. "Truly the kind of problem only a prince would have."

"Business been busy, then?"

"Busier every day."

Finn dared to ask, "The day business or the night business?"

Luisa's mouth quirked. "Both. People are coming to the shop all day looking for poultices and potions to ease their aches from the cold, and as for the night . . . with the war so close to ending, people want a peek into the future more than ever. You should know. Your visits alone could keep my shop afloat for months."

A stab of discomfort squirmed deep in Finn's stomach, and he instinctively glanced over his shoulder. "I prefer we don't talk about that. Confidentiality, remember? You promised."

"Afraid someone will find out their prince is visiting a seer in the wee hours of the morning?"

"More afraid that you're swindling me and everyone's going to find out I got duped. Can't be risking my title as the cleverest man in Atlas on the hope that you're honest."

Luisa snorted. "I am not *swindling* you. My readings come from actual magic. That's more than half the other seers in the city can say."

"They can say it all they like, and so can you. That doesn't make it true."

"Have I ever been wrong?"

Finn threw his hands up in helpless plea to the silent gods. "Are you done? Or are you going to keep bickering until someone spots us? I'd rather not risk my reputation by getting caught outside the palace."

"Your reputation for being a lazy arse, you mean?"

"Yes, that. Exactly that."

Luisa chuckled softly, pocketing her bag of coins. "All right, Finn. Tell your pretty brother I said hello."

"I'll pass. Kal's got enough admirers without adding you to the mix. It's getting to his head."

"It'll *cost* him his head if he's not careful."

Finn smirked in spite of himself as she walked away, tossing her hood back over her riotous hair. He leaned one shoulder against the brick wall, watching her go. "Is that an observation or a prophecy?"

"You'll have to guess!" she called over her shoulder, mischief playing tag between her words. "Or pay me for it tonight!"

Greedy, cunning woman. He wasn't sure he had a better friend.

Tugging his hood back up, Finn slipped out from the alley, plotting out a path through his mental map of the city. There weren't many shops left that he could pass by safely in this particular costume. Lord Jaskier would have to retire soon.

A shame, really. He'd put a lot into that particular role. He was almost fond of the poor fool.

Rubbing an itch behind his ear, he turned down a quiet street, absentmindedly counting how many doors, how many houses, which colors they were. All white stone houses. Six red doors, four green, seven blue, two purple. The last door caught his eye, a whirlpool of paint and glued-on crystals. It was buttermilk yellow the last time he came by; likely under new ownership, likely an artist.

Damn. That was a shame. An artist meant a shop wasn't far behind, and a shop meant customers, and customers meant he'd have to adjust his map. This street was going to end up too crowded to be safe for his exploits.

He may have been dead last in line for the throne, but he did more to keep his city in order than either of his siblings ever did. And as nice as it would've been to get some credit for that, his effectiveness relied heavily on working outside the influence of the palace.

A sigh slid through his teeth, and he paused for a moment, bracing the back of his neck with both hands as he took in the sounds of the city beyond this bubble of quiet. The screams of gulls. The laughter of children. The crashing of waves.

Losing this street would be inconvenient, but it couldn't be helped. With the war supposedly on the edge of ending in their favor—or so his brother and mother claimed—people were chock-full of optimism, starting new businesses, building new homes. And they were heading for *something*, Finn knew that; he could taste the change in the air, sense the silent shift in the tide. His contacts were on edge. His marks were on edge. Even the path beneath his boots seemed less forgiving than usual, like the city itself had braced every muscle, anticipating a blow that hadn't yet struck.

But he wasn't so sure triumph was the thing that was coming. It felt . . . darker than that. More like a warning knell than a victory chime.

A vague shiver of dread played hopscotch down his back, and with every step he took toward the palace, that dread grew and spread until it took root in his stomach. Until it was difficult to force one foot past the other.

"Ah, stop it," he muttered, knocking himself in the head with the heel of his hand. "Paranoia's a killer, Finn. All this skulking around is getting to you."

Still, dread held on, clinging to his heels like a second shadow. So when two guards stepped into his path out of absolutely *nowhere*, being incredibly intentional about blocking his way, he wasn't as surprised as he should have been.

He tugged down his hood, offering a smile even as he recited a litany of curses in the back of his mind and considered turning on heel and running. "Hi, there. Fine time for a stroll."

"Prince Finnick," said one, saluting with a fist over his chest. "The princess has summoned you home."

He'd been afraid of that. Jericho didn't care much for his insistence on the occasional trek through the city with only himself for company. Thank the gods she hadn't sent for him an hour earlier. It took every ounce of his very fragile self-control to hold in a groan.

"I hate to break it to you, Seamus, but my sister doesn't summon me anywhere." He gave the guard a cheery pat on the shoulder as he tried to shimmy around him, leaning up on his toes to seem a little taller. It was a trick he'd learned from someone a long time ago . . . someone he didn't like to think about anymore, someone he only visited in accidental dreams or on the anniversary of her death.

Seamus took a step back to block him, effectively cutting off his shimmy. His older siblings' favored guard gave him a tired look, golden brows raised in silent apology. "She said it was an emergency."

Damn it. He wasn't getting out of this one.

"Fine," he sighed. "I suppose if she was kind enough to send an escort, I can't really refuse. Can we stop and get some cookies first? I'm starving."

Seamus and the other guard Pyrra—a young woman who was new to their staff, had two younger sisters, and loved jasmine tea—exchanged looks. Seamus already looked resigned. "Whatever you wish, Prince."

Indeed. As it had been, as it was, as it forever would be: Finnick Atlas always got what he wanted. The spoiled brat of the royal family. The lazy prince who couldn't be bothered to polish a sword, let alone wield one. The scholar who filled himself up with knowledge to the point that he had no room left for more amicable traits like compassion, work ethic, or manners in general, really.

But those things were masks, and good ones too. He was practiced at wearing them, not like an actor, but a chameleon. The same form cast in slightly different colors, just enough to be convincing.

It had to be that way. No one was threatened by a lazy man. No one gave him a second thought.

He enjoyed playing the layabout, the jester, the fool. It made it that much easier to be what he truly was.

But as they approached the palace, that strange foreboding growing heavier and darker with each passing moment, he suddenly wasn't sure the fool would be adequate to handle what was coming.

CHAPTER 9

KALLIAS

Honestly, some days it seemed like his younger brother made a sport of trying to drive him mad.

The rhythmic thumps of Kallias's pacing steps weren't helping, the repetitive slap of sandal against tile grating on his already-sore nerves, but he couldn't hold still. Every inch of him buzzed with anxious energy, adrenaline surging like high tide in his veins every time he remembered what was coming.

Finn and Soleil had been born barely a year apart, practically twins, so similar in personality there had been a betting pool around the palace over which one would get in the most trouble each day. Soleil came out on top nearly every time, for one reason only: Finn had learned how to lie well and early. Soleil never managed it, not even as she grew up. Finn felt so bad about Soleil being the only one punished for their antics that he actually started taking responsibility himself.

The two were inseparable. And when Soleil died, no one took it harder than Finn. The boy who followed Kallias on his tiptoes to try and seem taller, who echoed everything he said with a haughty tone and an upturned nose, who skinned his knees and cried for Kallias over their parents . . . he died, too.

And while the rest of them eventually learned to live with their grief, Finn chose instead to lie—to himself, this time. To convince himself he felt nothing, that Soleil never mattered, that she was nothing but a ghost left behind in his childhood. He didn't even visit her grave anymore.

Kallias tried not to be angry with him for that. The last time he'd given that righteous anger its head, Finn hadn't spoken to him for nearly a month. And in the end, he'd rather let his brother keep his lie than lose him to the truth.

But there would be no forgetting now, no drowning of memories in wine or avoiding the door in the royal wing that still sported colorful scribbles drawn by a child's hand. Finn's decision to erase Soleil entirely would be hard to cling to when he came face-to-face with her.

There was no telling how his brother would react to having that lie snatched away from him. And Kallias didn't really feel like trying to guess.

Thunder rumbled outside, goosebumps shivering to life across his arms as lightning flashed, blanching the world of color for a single moment. This particular hallway was covered in paintings on the right side, with a glass wall on the left, an endless window showing off what was normally a spectacular view of the sea beyond. But today the sea was pitch-dark and angry, clouds the color of soot roiling across the sky, stripes of lightning shrieking between them like arrows shot into hearts.

It was not a good day to be out in the city.

Typical that the one day he actually *wanted* his younger brother to be lazing about at home, Finn had chosen to wander, and without an escort no less. Kallias was going to strangle him when he got back.

That is, if he hasn't already been murdered in some back alley by mercenaries or Nyxian spies or someone who found him particularly annoying.

No sooner had that thought actually started to worry him than a hand clapped down on his shoulder from behind, his brother's pretentious drawl following it: "While I'm glad to see you made it back alive, I feel obligated to tell you that you're going to wear a path in the floor dragging your heels like that."

Kallias brushed Finn's hand off, arranging a properly displeased scowl on his face before turning around. "I'm gone for a couple days and everything comes apart. You know better than to leave the palace alone. If Mama caught you—"

"Oh, gods, you're right!" Finn made an exaggerated show of looking around, shading his eyes and craning his neck to search the hallway. His hair was wet, his clothes damp, and he smelled of rain, pipe smoke, and Kallias's favorite cologne . . . the one he'd *thought* he'd misplaced over a month ago. "Hmm . . . strange. Mama doesn't seem to be here. Has she turned invisible? Hiding under one of those frames, perhaps?"

"Don't be an ass. If something happened to you—"

"You'd be devastated. I know, and I'm touched, truly." Finn pressed a hand over his heart, imitating a look of appreciation—which was so out of practice on him that it looked more like an ugly wince.

"I'd be the one getting *blamed,* actually."

"Guilt and grief aren't all that far off from each other. You remember when Jericho was painting her office and kept asking us if she should choose mint green or seafoam green? It's like that."

Kallias blinked at him. "You know, half the time I'm not even sure *you* know what you're talking about."

A grin cracked across Finn's face. "You're just now figuring this out?"

Kallias jerked him close, catching him in a headlock, digging his knuckles into Finn's damp hair. Even as Finn protested and wriggled and good-naturedly shoved at him, even as they laughed and tussled, Kallias's skin prickled with the wrongness of it. But he forced himself to take it in anyway, to enjoy it, because he felt it already; the walls of this moment were fragile, coming apart at the seams before it even passed by.

After this, there would be no turning back. Whatever normalcy they'd managed to achieve in the past ten years, whatever off-kilter way they'd managed to stitch their family back into some semblance of a whole . . . it was all about to collapse. And Kallias was the one to deal the final blow to its foundations.

"All right, enough!" yelped Finn, finally shoving Kallias off, fixing his hair with a quick ruffle and scowling as he straightened his maroon jacquard coat. "What's eating you? You only torture me when you're stressed."

"I'm always stressed."

"Exactly."

Kallias feigned a lunge, and Finn fell back, putting his hands up. For a moment, they stayed like that, each trying to gauge if the other was about to attack. Finally, Kallias sighed, letting his arms fall to his sides. "Walk with me. We need to talk."

Finn gazed at him cautiously, but fell into step with him as they made their way to the infirmary wing of the palace. "Is this about my leaving today? Because last I checked, you and Jericho far outweigh me in the sneaking out category."

"No."

"Is someone dead?"

Kallias's gut tensed. "No."

"Then spit it out! You know I don't have the patience. Is this about my snoring? Have people been complaining again? Because I'm seeing a specialist, you know, once a—"

"Once a week, I know. Funny how I still wake up to the roof shaking every night."

"Oh, ha-ha, hilarious. You're not any better, Mister I-Give-Rousing-Speeches-In-My-Sleep. Everyone can hear you, you know, your walls aren't that—"

"*Finnick.* Will you stop talking for a second so I can tell you what happened?"

Finn winced in earnest then, mimicking a gag. "There is *no* need to pull out the full name card, thanks. You're not my nursemaid."

"Could've fooled me," Kallias grumbled.

Finn simply shrugged, and Kallias tried not to envy how easy it looked. Tried not to think about how unfair it was that because of dumb luck, because of birth order and nothing else, he had the weight of a kingdom on his shoulders, while Finn had nothing heavier than that gaudy coat. "Are you going to tell me why we're walking to the infirmary if no one's dead?"

Kallias stopped before the main infirmary doors, painted stark white and decorated with two wreathes of greens and yellow-tinted hibiscus—a tiny tribute to Anima, the Goddess of Life, and therefore the goddess most healers prayed to.

He wasn't much for religion; he believed the gods existed, and prayed to Anima out of duty, but as for devoting his life to her service . . . he had enough on his plate as Atlas's First Prince, ensuring the Heir's safety. He'd already failed once. He didn't have time to play disciple on the side.

Besides, there was only one place where he felt anything close to worshipful. And that particular area wasn't under Anima's jurisdiction.

Slowly, Kallias turned to face his brother. Finn leaned one shoulder against the wall, fussing with the hem of his coat, his expression abruptly serious. The dimple in his left cheek deepened with his frown. "Kal. Come on, you're scaring me."

There was no way to make this blow land gently, so he came right out and said it: "Soleil's alive."

Finn stared at him without blinking for five seconds. Ten seconds. Thirty. Kallias counted every one, never breaking his gaze, waiting for him to take a breath. To ask questions. To shout. Anything.

Instead, Finn laughed. A dark, humorless laugh that raised the hairs on the back of Kallias's neck. "That's not funny."

"Finn." But he shook his head, another dull-edged laugh breaking Kallias's composure, dragging anger out of him as he stepped forward, trying to grip his brother's shoulder. "Finn, this isn't a joke—"

"You're right, it's not a joke!" Finn snapped, shoving Kallias's arms away and pressing his fist into Kallias's chest, pushing him back a pace. "What is wrong with you? Are you drinking again, huh? Because you'd have to be *stark raving drunk* to even *sort of* think this would be funny!"

Shame chilled Kallias's hands, his knees already aching to hit the ground and beg for forgiveness, but he gritted his teeth against it. He'd apologized enough for that; Finn was only bringing it up to spite him, to try and hurt him back. "Finn. Look at me. I am not joking, I am not trying to pull some kind of prank, I am not trying to hurt you. Come and see her."

"See, I'd love to do that, Kal, except she burned to death. Do you remember that? There was a fire. Nyx burned half the palace down. Did you miss it? I could've sworn I saw you there."

Frustrated, Kallias tried to catch his shoulders again. "If you'll just *look* at her—"

Finn stumbled back so quickly that he nearly tripped, his back hitting the wall with such a hard *thud* that the windows shook in their frames. "Stop trying to grab me! Gods, Kallias, did you hit your head out on the battlefield? Someone dent your skull with a sword . . . handle . . . thing?"

"It's called a pommel—"

"I don't give a damn what it's called!" Finn's voice pitched an octave higher, his eyes shining with anger—but there was fear there, too, just barely peeking out. "Just tell me you're being a bastard or playing some ridiculous game, or you made a bet with Jer, and I won't even be mad. Just come clean, right now."

Kallias spread his hands helplessly. "I'm as clean as I can be. Look, if you walk into that room and I'm lying to you, I'll be at your beck and call for an entire week—a *month*. A whole month where you can ask me to do anything, and I'll do it. But I need you to go in there and *look at her*, because I can't . . . gods, Finn, I have no idea what to do and I need your *help*. Our sister is alive. Nyx had her all this time. And I need you and Jer both with me when I tell Mama and Papa. I can't do that alone."

Finn stared at him, jaw twitching, eyes brewing with something unfamiliar. Something he'd never seen in him before.

"Please, Finn," he whispered. "Us before all, remember? You, me, Jer, Vaughn . . . we're a team. Always will be. I'm not going to break your trust now." *Not ever again.*

Finn lowered his eyes to his gold-fletched boots. And just when Kallias had given up: "Two months."

Relief tumbled through him like a landslide. "Deal. I'll come with you."

Finn took in a deep breath, pushing up from the wall, walking to the infirmary doors. He stopped with his hands on the gilded doorknobs, glancing at Kallias from the corner of his eye. Then, with a quick twist of his wrists, he opened the doors and stepped inside.

CHAPTER 10

FINN

Finn had always known Kallias wasn't the brightest candle in the candelabrum, but he'd never known him to be cruel before.

Soleil's alive.

Rage or worry, he couldn't tell which he should be feeling. Kallias was normally an easy read, but this time he couldn't tell if his brother was pulling some kind of revolting joke, or if he'd gotten seriously hurt in a way no one could see. Confusion, memory loss, those were symptoms of head injuries, and with all that ridiculous hair in the way, maybe the triage healers had missed something—

Then he saw her. And then he didn't feel *anything*.

For the first time in a very long time, Finnick Atlas couldn't think.

Atlas-red hair, closer to Kallias's gold-tinted fire than the rich, bloody crimson of his mother and older sister. Paler, too, like the sun had turned its face away and left her to darkness. Her head was angled to the side, her hair pulled up off her neck, and he thought he could see a Nyxian mourning braid hidden inside it. She was bandaged and bloodied, sleeping too deeply to be fully natural.

No. Gods, no. This wasn't happening. Kallias couldn't be this much of a fool. Couldn't possibly think this girl was . . . that she could be . . .

"Oh yes, well done, Kallias." Sarcasm dripped from every word, so saccharine he could taste it. "Congratulations! You found a redhead! Truly your greatest accomplishment."

He waited for Kallias to laugh, to deliver his grand *gotcha*, because this could not be the person Kallias claimed it was, whom Finn almost thought he recognized until he remembered that impossible things were called so for a reason. Miracles weren't real, no god or goddess was listening, no one was around who could possibly possess the power to do . . . this. And even if they were, none of them loved him enough to have finally answered the prayers he'd wept through at his bedside at ten years old.

It couldn't be Soleil on that bed. Not *their* Soleil.

Kallias was rambling somewhere behind him, something about a battlefield and an injury and a mask, and then he went silent, the weight of his gaze boring into Finn's back. Finn took a step away from the bed, toward the door. A slow shaking started in his fingers and staggered up his limbs, spreading until he quivered like a frightened child. He turned desperately to Kallias, who couldn't be trusted to stick to a lie if it would save his life.

"Tell me the truth," he begged. *Admit that you're lying. Admit it.*

But the expression on Kallias's face told Finn all he needed to know.

"Jericho performed a blood match, the girl's blood against mine. It's her," Kallias said, too carefully. The way someone broke bad news, not good news.

He knew what that meant. Even if this was real, when the girl woke, she would be *only* that—a girl who was no more his sister than any person he picked out on the street. Her body might've been alive, but Nyx had had their way with her mind—her clever, quick-witted mind that was the nearest match to his he'd ever found. The mind of his very best friend.

Without that, what good was this stranger, this *nobody* wearing the face of a memory?

He was feeling too much, remembering too much, too many variables had just been introduced and he couldn't see a way forward—

"Finn!" Soleil tugged on his sleeve, all gap-toothed grin and freckled cheeks. "Come on, I think I figured out how to get the cookies down without anyone seeing!"

"Finn!" Soleil sobbed after a nightmare, knocking on the wall between their rooms, knowing he would always come running.

"Finn!" Soleil screamed in his nightmares, muffled by fallen debris and crackling flames, his imagination convinced she'd called for him as she died, and he hadn't been there to answer.

He backed away, images crowding his mind, his mouth dry as cotton and his heart in a vise. His hands didn't feel like they belonged to him. He couldn't feel his face. So when his back hit the door and his hand found the knob, he turned and ran as fast as he could, ignoring Kallias's shout—ran until he was out of the hall, out of the palace, out onto the wide stretch of shore that belonged to the royal family alone. Ran while his razor-sharp memories sang a funeral dirge, the ghost of his sister screaming his name—a plea, an accusation, a death sentence.

He didn't stop running until he hit the beach, empty thanks to the recent storm, the sand damp and cold, the waves swollen and overfed. He dropped to his knees, not caring if his pants got sandy, not caring who might be watching, not caring about anything at all.

And with nothing to cling to, nothing to stop him, he vomited his breakfast all over that perfect, pristine sand.

CHAPTER 11

Soren

Never had she been more grateful that Emberlyn and Yvonne taught her how to climb out of windows.

She'd woken from that medicinal-herb-prompted sleep yesterday, clearer than before, stronger—her stomach still wasn't perfect, and she was weak from being bedridden for gods-knew-how-long, but she was still strong enough to shimmy down this rope.

She couldn't afford to wait. Who knew what else Atlas had planned for her.

Humid breezes stroked Soren's cheeks like sweaty hands, and she felt like cringing out of her skin, hating that damp caress. Wind shouldn't be wet. Wetness was for *water*.

"I hate water." She inched down another knot on her rope. "Hate, hate, hate hate hate *water*."

Her stomach spasmed, but the magic of those Anima-blessed healers was no joke—she felt like she'd gone through a particularly rigorous workout rather than a near-death experience.

Not even near death. One step into it. One whole foot and four toes from the other.

She'd be sure to thank Kallias for being foolish enough to save her life later. From a distance. Preferably from the comfort of her own bed, middle finger raised to the west in salute.

She was a mere thirty-foot stretch away from the ground when her rope went taut. She had to swallow down a groan as she slowly tipped her head back.

"Princess," sighed an exasperated voice that was already becoming familiar. "This is getting tiresome."

"You're tiresome."

"And childish—"

"You're childish."

A head popped out of the window above her, belonging to Seamus, her special guard friend. And by special, she meant especially annoying. "Please don't make me drag you back in, Princess Soleil."

"Stop calling me that."

She still hadn't seen any of the royals except Kallias, and him only briefly since his first visit. Only long enough for him to break it to her, oh-so gently, that she was actually the youngest daughter of Adriata Atlas. That she was his sister.

His very, very dead sister.

She had to give him credit—she hadn't laughed that long and hard since Elias got his ass kicked by a trainee boy half his size whose father happened to be a high-ranking military officer. The prince had promised he could prove it, but he had yet to do so—probably because he couldn't, because it was a bald-faced lie, and Soren wasn't sticking around until he could find a way to make something up. The only Atlas blood she possessed was what had dried in the unreachable parts of her nails.

"How did you even get the rope?" Seamus the Especially Annoying Guard detached the rope from where she'd lashed it and began pulling her up, and as much as she would have loved to jump off, a thirty-foot fall would probably kill her a little better than that slice to the stomach. And there was no hope of him tiring before he got her to the top; he was built like a mountain. A dimwitted blonde mountain.

"Found it." Made it, really. She'd spent hours tearing her sheets into strips to make it happen. "How did you get to be so intolerable?"

Seamus only sighed again, loud enough for her to hear even past the sticky breeze. Somewhere inside her prison, a door opened and shut.

"She giving you trouble?" chirped a too-cheerful voice Soren hadn't heard yet. It sounded . . . obnoxiously arrogant.

"Your Highness!"

Soren squeaked in brief mortal terror as the rope started to slide before skidding to a halt again, like Seamus had let go to salute before remembering he was the only thing between her and a very messy incident.

His voice came again, harried, embarrassed: "It—I came to check on her and she was halfway to the ground."

"Two-thirds!" she yelled up toward the window. She wasn't about to let him downplay it to save his own ass.

A new face peered out from the window, resembling Kallias but younger, not as freckled or angled. No, this face was softer, still handsome, but his eyes . . .

Oh, all the sharp things about this boy lived inside his head. She could tell from that one look. His hair was darker than Kallias's, closer to dark auburn than true red, and his suntanned skin didn't have a single blemish or scar.

The boy studied her for a moment, then ducked back inside. "I'll handle it, Seamus. Go stand out there and look guard-ish, will you?" A pause, then the boy poked his head back out. "Are you done being a dumbass," he asked, still cheerful, his grin cutting like a razor, "or would you like to hang there for a bit longer?"

She glowered at him, clinging more tightly to her makeshift lash, wondering how likely it was that she would break a leg if she decided to slide down rather than climb. "Go to Infera and rot."

Elias would've been proud of her for remembering the right name this time.

The man above her only leaned his elbows on the windowsill, casually poking the rope. "Already been. Don't care to live there, but it makes a nice vacation spot."

Soren blinked. Most people didn't have the wherewithal to come back at her that quickly. "Who exactly are you?"

That mockingbird grin faded at the corners for a moment. "You can't guess?"

"I *can*. But it seems like a lot of effort to put into something I don't care about."

His lip pouted out, and he pressed his hand over his chest. "That's hurtful."

"Bite me."

"No thanks." He studied her with narrowed eyes. "You're a lot meaner than my little sister used to be."

Soren's hands stilled on the rope.

"Thought you were going to make me guess, Prince Finnick," she said lightly.

He groaned, waving his hand. "Please don't call me that. It's just Finn. *Prince* implies I have some kind of authority." A delicate shudder. "Or *responsibility*, gods forbid."

"Someone sounds bitter."

"On the contrary. I'm perfectly happy to be third-best. If you're looking for bitter, it's Kallias you want." He held out a hand. "It's sunny now, but a storm's blowing in any minute, you know. You don't want to be out there when it starts."

Soren contemplated refusing, but then he'd just call more guards, and they'd drag her inside regardless. At least this way she could keep her dignity.

What remained of it, anyway.

She hauled herself back up the rope, smacking his hand aside when he tried to offer it again. "Back away or I won't come inside."

"Don't trust me?"

"Not one damn bit."

"Then you're already smarter than most of the people in this palace," he chuckled, but to her surprise, he obeyed.

She caught herself on the sill and pulled herself up, reluctantly marveling at the way her body allowed it, at the weakness that had already begun to recede. She tumbled inside, definitely less than dignified, but quickly straightened, dusting off her leggings and plain linen tunic. "You're shorter than I expected."

"Jericho says I traded height for wit. You look scarily like her, you know." His tone was just as lighthearted as before, but he looked stricken as he took her in—the first sincere emotion from the Second Prince of Atlas.

She didn't like it. An outright bastard was one thing, but that hint of genuine feeling . . . that made him unpredictable. The hair on the back of her neck stood on end, and she leaned her shoulder against the wall, protecting her back. "I suppose you're here to help your brother play his little game."

Finn crossed his arms, his fine cream shirt billowing with the movement. The thin, soft material clung to his body, but the long sleeves were puffy, airy, like marshmallows. He wore black pants stitched with gold and a golden belt buckled around his waist. Matching earrings clung to his ears, and a necklace of hammered gold rested against the hollow of his throat. With every movement, she caught the scent of cologne, the kind people only wore to brag about how expensive and rare it was.

Showy. Bordering on ridiculous. Bragging with every breath, every move, every pose. But that was exactly what it was—posing. She could see the cogs moving behind those eyes, the split seconds of thought before each action.

She'd heard all the gossip about Finnick Aurelias Atlas from their spies. He was lazy, an insufferable brat who couldn't be bothered to look at a sword, let alone lift one.

It was strange that no one had ever noticed he was dangerous. Or maybe, if someone had, they were one of the ones who never made it home.

"Stop looking at me," she said.

"It's rude not to look at people when you're talking to them."

"It's rude to kidnap people and lie to them about being your dead sister."

"You've got the hair."

"Maybe I dye it."

"It's strange," he said. "I came in here planning to despise you, and you're actually making it hard."

"Funny. I'm finding it rather easy."

Finn's next laugh was a thing of wicked delight. He leaned back against the door, gazing at her up and down, and she had the sudden sense she'd just passed or failed a test. She wasn't sure which. "So. You really don't remember us at all."

"I remember very little before I was nine years old," Soren hedged.

That smile faded at the edges. "Nine. And you're how old now?"

"Five hundred and three, but I moisturize."

He didn't laugh, which was annoying, because that was the one thing she'd meant to be a joke. He pushed up from the door, approaching her with crossed arms and eyes that weren't hiding their menace any longer.

"You should hope," he said finally, "that my brother is mistaken, and you're nothing but a Nyxian with very unique hair. You should get down on your knees and pray to whatever gods you know, because if he's right, then your kingdom did worse than kill my sister. And you might have noticed, but Atlas isn't the forgiving sort."

Chills skittered down every chink of Soren's spine, but she kept her head up, refusing to cower before this trickster prince and his deceivingly bright eyes. "He's wrong. I could never share blood with that monster you call a queen."

"Watch how you talk about my mother."

Soren looked down toward her mouth. "I could never share blood with—"

He snorted out loud, interrupting her. "You're quite the smartass."

Her heart clenched at that, flashes of tar-black hair and affectionate laughter echoing in her mind. "Don't call me that."

There was a knock on the door. "I'm coming in," said Kallias's muffled voice. "Is that okay?"

Finn rolled his eyes, tugging the door open, Kallias nearly tumbling inside as he did. "You're a *terrible* captor. Is that how you think people speak to prisoners?"

A flush crept up Kallias's neck, and he straightened quickly, smoothing back his hair and clearing his throat to regain some composure. "I didn't want to startle her."

"Lest she think you're one of those *mean* kidnappers who enters a room without knocking?"

Kallias's teeth ground audibly, but he looked to her instead of his strange brother, his mouth slanting sideways. "Are you ready to see our proof?"

Soren sat primly on the edge of her bed, crossing her arms. "Sure. But I know a trick when I see it. Whatever it is, you're not going to convince me."

"Good thing we're not tricking you, then." Kallias grabbed Finn by the nape and pushed him out, ignoring his protests. "Please come with me."

His tone was calm, kind, but there was an edge to it that told her he wasn't really giving her a choice. She could go on her own, or she could be tugged along by Seamus, who was now safely stationed outside her door. And as entertaining as it would be to brawl with two Atlas princes and a guard, she couldn't help hearing Elias's voice in her head pleading with her not to be a *complete* fool.

She owed it to him to get out of this place alive. Besides, her body was already quivering just from the effort of climbing back up into the palace.

Let them play their games. She could pretend to fall for their tricks—she was good at that. Years of listening to Emberlyn wax poetic about her latest weapon design or Elias lecturing her on proper religious terminology had prepared her well. If she could fake interest for them, she could certainly fool two strangers who didn't know what it looked like when she lied.

So she stood back up, making a show of stretching, wincing at the sharp popping of her joints. Finn actually jumped a little at the sound, then covered it up with a scowl, brushing imaginary dust off his sleeve. "You're sure this is her? She's got the bones of a crone."

"Just walk," Kallias sighed.

And that was how Soren found herself walking with Prince Kallias before her and Prince Finnick behind her . . . two enemies who had been faceless till now, the politician and the layabout.

She never thought she'd rather have the politician at her back. But Finnick didn't try anything; he simply stuck his hands in his pockets and sauntered along behind her, looking for all the world like he couldn't care less whether this test was successful. In fact, she was half-convinced that she could have reached out and broken Kallias's neck, and Finn would have merely stopped to complain about the mess before stepping over his corpse.

The corridor was empty besides her and the princes and Seamus, who walked directly alongside her, pinning her close to the wall so she couldn't run. The floor was odd, smooth and glazed on top but filled with crushed shells forming swirling patterns beneath, mimicking waves. It was an effort to force herself to walk with her bare feet, even knowing the broken shells weren't actually going to stab into her heels.

Shells.

A ripple of unease tumbled down her ribcage. She'd never seen such things in Nyx. She shouldn't have known their name.

She shook it off. She'd read about shells before, she knew that. Maybe there'd been an illustration included.

The corridor fed into a larger common area with a domed glass ceiling arched over a round-cornered space, pale marble floors peppered with chaises and seats and plush rugs in all colors. The four large corridors branched to the north, south, east, and west. They'd just come from the south, judging by the angle of the morning sun coming through the glass, fracturing into beams that cast everything in a white-gold glow. She'd never seen the sun so bright. So *warm.*

But that wasn't what made her muscles go stiff, her toes digging into the cool marble, half-poised to turn and run. It was the people. Palacefolk lounged on those chaises and seats, laughing and warbling with gossip muffled by mouthfuls of their breakfasts.

That all stopped the moment Soren crossed into the space.

Maybe she should have been more intimidated. But in the moment, all she could think of were those plates of food, piled high with strange fresh fruits and pastries and steaming piles of eggs. Gods, when was the last time she'd eaten? The morning before the battle?

Her stomach chose that moment to growl embarrassingly loudly, and she did her best to ignore the hushed laughter behind her.

Kallias offered a polite nod to his people, and they bowed their heads in return, but their eyes were locked on her dirty hair and bare feet and borrowed tunic that was hardly fit for a supposed princess, let alone an *actual* princess from a different kingdom.

Not all those gazes were merely curious. Some were outright hostile, especially when they caught sight of her mourning braid, black cloth twined with a strip of hair shorter than the rest, cut at her shoulder rather than her chest.

"Nyxian filth," murmured one as she was paraded past. Another spat at her feet.

She flashed the spitter her biggest, brightest, most infuriating grin, the sort she only pulled out of her repertoire if she desperately needed a fight and Elias was unwilling to give her one. "Your aim's a little off, love."

"As if you can do better," he jeered. "Nyxians can't hit the broad side of a boat."

Soren smiled serenely, taking a moment to gather herself—and her saliva. Then, neatly, she spit directly into the Atlas man's eye.

Finn snorted out loud.

The man surged out of his seat, but before he could even make it a step, Finn held up a hand. His smile was easy, kind, a thing of patience. But his eyes pierced the other man like needles. "Relax, Hagen," he said, the amused lilt to his voice framing the whole thing as a lovely joke. "We're taking her to Jericho."

Apparently that meant something, because the man immediately moved back and sat down. She guessed it wasn't a pleasant something, either, because he seemed satisfied with it, as if it was a punishment being meted out.

Kallias didn't seem inclined to correct their behavior, though his shoulders were tense; whether he was offended on her behalf or worried his ruse would suffer from his people's obvious disgust, she couldn't be sure. He led them to the west corridor, saying, "Keep moving. It's not far."

This corridor was decorated differently, the ceiling made of hammered gold, lush green rugs spread like grass over polished wooden floors. The left wall was decorated with five paintings: one for each god or goddess except Anima, who had two. Their gilded frames shone in the near-blinding sunlight.

Soren had never seen illustrations of the entire pantheon outside of rough sketches in the oldest of Elias's books, but she knew Anima when she saw her: freckled brown skin, sleek hair the color of freshly tilled soil, flowers budding in great swathes around her . . . and *through* her. Marigolds blooming in her pupils, creeping vines twining around her wrists and throat, cascades of forget-me-nots in her hair, baby's breath cradled between her lips.

But not roses. Never roses. She couldn't remember the reason, but Anima hated roses.

Kallias tugged her past the paintings—Soren swore they followed her with their creepy, flowery eyes—to a simple green door at the end of the corridor. He knocked, and an impatient voice called, "What do you want, Kal?"

"How did you know it was me?" he called back.

"You're the only one who knocks in this roguish family."

"Told you," Finn said.

Kallias mumbled something in mocking tones under his breath, but pushed the door open. "Are you ready for us, Jer?"

Over his shoulder, Soren caught glimpses of what appeared to be a small workshop. Vases hung from the ceiling and perched on the white shelves covering the back wall from left to right, entirely dedicated to storage. Alongside the vases full of living flowers, bunches of dried ones were strewn about, along with herbs and cinnamon sticks and leaves that looked entirely too tempting, the sort Soren loved to crunch under her boots during harvest. Nyx only got three seasons to Atlas's four: winter, the warm season, and harvest season. And as winter made up half the year, she normally only saw this many flowers in the castle greenhouse.

A woman moved into sight, her impatience shifting to vulnerability when she caught sight of Soren. Older than the others, likely closer to thirty than twenty, she was easily the most beautiful of anyone Soren had met thus far. Her face was soft and perpetually blushing, her eyes a pale shade of green with no blue to be seen, and she was covered in more freckles than all the others combined— someone who spent her days in the sun. Her hair reminded Soren of poisonous berries, a deep scarlet that stood stark against the spring-green walls of the workshop. Her mouth was a rosebud, pressed thin like petals between book pages. She looked at Soren like she was the most tragic creature she'd ever beheld.

"Hello," she said, her voice too soft to be true. "I'm Jericho."

Princess Jericho, firstborn of the Atlas royal children. Heir, but not because of birth order—the Atlas throne fell to the youngest daughter. Something about women living longer, and younger women living longest of all, allowing for careful transitions to the next queen, not often sudden or traumatic. Queens of Atlas did not put themselves in harm's way, and neither did their Heirs. The former Heir's death was the first premature one in a very, very long time.

"Princess," said Soren. "I'd say it's a pleasure, but—"

"We told her we'd get her proof today," Kallias interrupted, flashing her a warning look.

"Has she consented to this?" Jericho crossed her arms. "You know I can't do anything if she doesn't consent."

Soren's toes curled against the floor. "Consent to what?"

Jericho pinned her with a surprisingly sharp look. "Kallias wants me to break the spell Nyx put on you."

Soren blinked at her. "That won't happen," she said slowly, "because no one put a spell on me."

"Then you won't mind if I try to break it."

"I sure as the *pits* mind if you shove your magic into my brain."

The princess's nose wrinkled at her profanity. "If there's no damage to be found, my magic will touch nothing. It only heals, it doesn't harm."

"Pretty words," Soren said, her hands curled into white-knuckled fists, "but the answer is no."

"If Jericho finds nothing," said Kallias, every inch of him corded with tension but his eyes still unbearably gentle, "we will let you go. You have my word."

Her tongue curled, tasting the words before she spat them out: "And what good is the word of a prince in Atlas?"

Kallias's eyes shuttered. Jericho stepped in, her gaze flickering sympathetically toward her brother. "You have my word too. Our parents are away on business, which means I currently hold the authority in this palace. If we find nothing, you go home."

Home.

Her mind hummed for a moment, weighing their faces, their words, their promises that were undoubtedly false.

Elias was going to kill her for this. But if she played it right, at least he'd be alive to do the killing.

"I want your oath," she said, "that when you discover I am not who you think I am, you will release me and allow me to return to my kingdom unharmed. And I will require one more thing from you."

"Name it," said Jericho.

"I need the antidote to the poison your Vipers carry."

Kallias was already shaking his head, mouth open to speak, but Finn voiced his objection before the others. "Not a chance. You think we'll give up the antidote to our favorite weapon so you can duplicate it?"

"No," Soren snapped, even as guilt brushed up against her heart. That should have been her plan at the start. It was considerably less selfish than what she was about to counter with. "Give me enough for one person . . . just enough that if I even spill a drop, it won't work. You'll know then that I can only use it to heal my . . . my friend."

"How do we know this friend even exists?" Finn scoffed. "If you take it home, you could just turn it over to your physicians and let them have their way with it."

"How long would it take for them to do that?"

"A month, if they're good," Jericho guessed. "Perhaps longer."

Soren narrowed her eyes at Finn, drawing herself up to her full height—pleased to find she was just as tall as him if she stopped slouching. She put on her best diplomatic face, the one Enna told her to practice in the mirror after a particularly embarrassing outburst at a summit with Artem, when the kingdom of glass and metalwork agreed to grant Emberlyn her late father's diplomatic status to clear the way for her to apprentice with them as a weaponsmith. Soren, fourteen years old and often described as *that little royal gremlin*, had done her best to sabotage the meeting and keep her sister home.

"My friend is already beginning to show symptoms," she said. "Not the dangerous kind, but I can see it. He gets tired faster. He eats less. I wouldn't risk waiting another month."

Finn's eyes glittered as he took her in, his hair shifting when he tipped his head to one side. "I don't believe you."

It was the first truly smart thing he'd said to her. She hated that it happened to be when she was telling the truth.

Jericho studied her closely. She was more difficult to read than her brothers, made of pretty things and strange energy that crackled in the air like static when she moved. Jericho, she remembered, was a rare dual-wielder—Anima-blessed twice over. She could perform both healing and biomancy.

Soren had been around magic before, but it had never felt this wild and exciting and *alive*. She could taste it on her tongue, syrupy and sharp like a shot of flavored liquor, promising fun and thrill and *power*.

Intoxicating. Terrifying. Soren wanted out of this room *now*.

But for Elias . . .

"Agreed," Jericho said finally. Finn widened his eyes at her, but she met his gaze with a warning glare. "Please, sit down."

The Heir of Atlas moved back into her workshop, Kallias a step behind her. Soren briefly, shamefully considered taking the opportunity to run, but Finn nudged her from behind with an impatient noise, and Soren growled halfheartedly before stepping inside.

It was a small but surprisingly pleasant space with a worn-out wooden worktable in the center, similar to what Soren had seen in more intense infirmary spaces where they used knives to heal instead of kill. Jericho gestured to it. "Really, sit. It'll be more comfortable."

"For me or for you?"

For the first time, she caught a hint of wickedness in the delicate princess's smile. "Both."

There wasn't much point in resisting. Soren climbed onto the table, feeling very much like a small child trying to reach a confiscated toy from a high shelf.

"Make it quick," she said, crossing her arms.

Jericho exchanged a look with Kallias, and he nodded, resting his hand oh-so-subtly on the pommel of the sword strapped to his hip. Discomfort streaked across Soren's shoulders, curling them inward. She was weaponless and armorless, deep in the heart of Atlas, allowing an Atlas princess to dig magical claws into her most vulnerable spot.

Elias was *definitely* going to kill her for this.

Jericho placed her fingers on Soren's temples, shutting her eyes.

Awkward silence stretched on for several seconds. Soren glanced between the three siblings, kicking her feet slightly, clearing her throat. Finally, she sighed and said, "Should I be feeling any—?"

Lightning lanced through her skull, searing from front to back, tines of shuddering pain stabbing outward into her brain. Her head jerked back, her back arched, and then—

"Hey! Get back here, minnow."

Soleil giggled as she ran away from the teasing voice floating between booths and stands decorated for the holiday. Colorful lanterns hung from braided cords far above her head, her sandals catching on cobblestones and nearly snagging her sparkling golden skirt as she wove between booths until she was absolutely, utterly certain she'd lost her brother.

She ducked behind a kite salesman's cart, peeking around the side. The salesman, a kindly older man with a handlebar mustache and colorful suspenders, smiled down at her, eyes twinkling. "Need a hiding spot, Soleil?"

"Just for a minute, Mr. Hargreeves," she whispered, muffling her giggles behind her hand.

"You're not the only one," he said, stepping back to reveal her other *brother, his own hand clapped over his mouth. When he saw her, his eyes went wide.*

"Get your own spot!" Finn hissed, though he still laughed when he shoved at her shoulder.

"No, you!"

"I was here first!"

"I was here last. *"*

Her brother opened his mouth to argue, but a hand gripped his collar and another snagged the back of Soleil's dress. A familiar voice, teenaged and amused, came from behind them. "Harboring fugitives, Mr. Hargreeves?"

"The boy threatened to rip a hole in every one of my kites," said Mr. Hargreeves very solemnly. *"I had no choice."*

"Kallias!" whined Soleil, even as she laughed and kicked, trying to escape her brother's hold. *"Let us go! Finn, kick your feet!"*

Finn obeyed, both of them wriggling and protesting and trying to shove down their giggles until Kallias finally set them down, keeping his hands on their shoulders as he knelt down. His hair was twisted back in a bun, an embroidered headband tied in it, and he was wearing far more casual clothes than usual—a yellow cotton shirt and dark trousers. If not for the color of his hair, he could have been any ordinary person on the street. Definitely not a prince.

It was a stark contrast to Soleil and Finn, who had been forced out of their favored play clothes into much stiffer, fancier stuff. As much as she loved the way her dress sparkled in the sun, it was the kind of thing she'd get punished for tripping in, and Finn didn't seem much more at ease in his silk pants and colorful shirt.

"Why did you get to wear normal stuff?" Finn complained, his mind in the same place as hers, like always.

"Because I'm older."

Finn and Soleil glanced at each other, then leveled twin glares at Kallias.

His lips quirked up sheepishly. "Fine. I changed when Mama wasn't looking. You two ready to start shopping yet?"

Soleil frowned, scuffing her sandals against the cobblestones. There was a thin line of blood on her big toe where she'd scraped it against the ground one of the times she tripped. "I thought we were waiting for Jericho."

Kallias smirked, licking his thumb and wiping at something on her cheek. She gagged and groaned, trying to crane her neck away. "We could. Or we could get our shopping done now *and split the treats between three people instead of four. How does that sound?"*

Soleil glanced at Finn, and as one, they smiled.

"Stop!"

Soren's scream shattered through whatever sick, twisted illusion Jericho had woven into her head, and she lolled forward so swiftly Kallias had to lunge and catch her. She tried to push him off, but her arms were limp and numb, unworkable. Something warm dripped from her nose, trickling down her lips.

Blood. Her nose was bleeding.

"What did you do?" she choked, reeling, flashes of that memory—clearer than she'd ever seen it, *far* sharper than when she used it to anchor her on the battlefield—threatening to drag her back into her own head. *"How did you change it?"*

"I didn't," Jericho said. Her cheeks were slick with tears, her eyes bloodshot and wet. She was crying. Legitimately crying.

"What did you find?" Kallias demanded, sitting Soren back up. Even Finn looked shaken, one hand slightly extended toward her, his eyes flicking between his older brother and sister.

Jericho's eyes were only for Soren. "Saltwater Festival. Playing hide-and-seek with you two. She hid behind a kitemaker's stand."

Kallias let out a slow breath, and Finn made a choked noise, but Soren couldn't look at either of them. Her eyes were caught on her bare feet, on the tiny scar beneath her big toe, exactly where she'd cut herself in that memory.

Her chest began to heave. "How did you change it?" she asked again, weaker, because gods, that memory was real. It was hers. It was all she had of her brothers from before the fire, before they all died, but until now she'd thought it was the Summer Fair, the celebration Nyx threw in the warm months. It was very similar, the colors, the vendors . . . but not the clothes. Even in the warm season, Nyxians would never wear sandals. And she'd never remembered the names of her brothers before, only that they'd existed . . . that she'd loved them.

And in that memory, her name was Soleil.

She slowly raised her head, looking first to Kallias, then to Finn. "I'm going to throw up."

They both moved, Kallias to grab a discarded bowl, Finn to stand at her side. Kallias shoved the bowl into her lap, Finn's hands tugged her hair back, and by the time she spewed bile and water and whatever tonics they'd forced into her while she slept, they were surrounding her just like in the memory: Kallias's hand on her shoulders, Finn's steady presence beside her.

No. *No.* Why was she thinking their names that way, like she knew them, like she . . .

"Get off me." To her surprise, they obeyed, leaving her hunched over the bowl, clutching it as tightly as her deadened, trembling fingers could manage.

"Soleil," whispered Jericho. "Oh, Soleil."

Her cool, gentle fingers touched Soren's cheek.

In that moment, she had a decision to make.

She could get out. Finn was unarmed, Jericho was close enough for her to knock out, and Kallias was . . . well. If she could get ahold of one of the paring knives on the counter nearby, maybe she could plunge it into his heart. She could even take out Jericho before she had to flee, leaving Finnick as the only possible Atlas Heir. And from what she'd seen of him, though he was cunning, she doubted he possessed the motivation to use it properly.

Or . . .

These three royals were staring at her like she might be their salvation. This war had only been so long and brutal because of their undying love for the sister they'd lost. To them, Soren was that sister—not that she believed it. She couldn't believe it, despite the whisper that said she *knew* that memory, that it was deeply, truly hers.

She could face that later. For now, she had two choices: she could try and fight her way out now, escaping empty-handed, and she and Elias would have those few months or years before the poison took him.

Or she could play pretend, just a little longer, and see what came of it. See what she could do, what she could save . . . what she could bring to an end.

Nyx had never been able to establish a spy in the palace, only on the outskirts. Atlas was too careful about who they allowed inside their glittering gold walls.

Maybe it was suicidal. Maybe it was mad. Maybe this would be the last mistake she ever made. But she raised her head and met Jericho's gaze and the hope there with awe, with tears she dredged up from the pain of her vomiting session.

"It's true," she whispered. "All of it. You were telling the truth."

Jericho's grin was a thing of joy, brilliant and perfect and terrible. "Welcome home," she whispered, her arms enveloping Soren like a vise. "Soleil, welcome *home.*"

CHAPTER 12

KALLIAS

"I just don't understand," Vaughn said yet again, sitting across from Kallias's desk, his elbows propped on his knees and his head buried in his hands. "How could they have possibly stolen Soleil?"

Repeating the story for the second . . . fourth . . . gods, maybe even fifth time seemed beyond Kallias's abilities. Even telling it once had been an effort, especially because it didn't even have an ending. Just a chaotic, impossible beginning and a very thin slip of a middle. But as Vaughn was Jericho's husband, Prince Consort and future king of Atlas, he couldn't exactly tell him he didn't feel like talking about it.

A thorny ache was beginning to burrow itself right in the center of his skull. Whether it was from the absolute disaster his life had become or because he was on his third glass of wine within the hour had yet to be seen. He wasn't normally a day drinker—not since the incident—but after the events of the past few days, he'd *earned* this wine, damn it. Every biting, horrendously dry gulp of it.

"Ten years ago, when Nyx's warmongering king got the brilliant idea to extend his reach west, he figured assassinating all of us was easier than an outright attack," Kallias mumbled, staring into his wine, "so he sent those agents to burn the palace down—"

"I know, Kallias." Vaughn gave him a reproachful look. "I was there. He killed twenty-six people that night."

"Twenty-five, it looks like." He sipped at the wine slowly. "We thought Soleil didn't escape . . . the fire turned her to ash like the rest of them."

Vaughn tapped his fingers against his hollow cheeks, his gray eyes unfocused and troubled. His black waves were tamed back in a messy knot, like he'd barely had the energy to tug it back that far, and his cheekbones were looking sharp enough to slit a throat, but at least there was color in his face. That was better than yesterday. "You're saying they took her instead."

Again, that rage that rose and fell like a dying wave. "Yes."

"Which one is she? What name was she going by?"

"Princess Soren, the third eldest. The soldier."

Vaughn nodded. "And they took her memory? Some kind of magic? That doesn't make any sense. Mortem and Tempest don't possess magics of the mind."

"That's the thing. Jericho couldn't find any trace of magic. So either the memory loss was a side effect, some injury she suffered, or Nyx has something synthetic we can't trace."

Vaughn sat straight at that, horror creeping over his face. "A poison that can erase memory? *And* hide from magic?"

Kallias's throat tightened. "Gods willing, no. But we have to consider the possibility."

Nyx had never been able to produce poisons the way Atlas could. Strange how worshippers of Death could be so poorly practiced in dealing it out delicately. But what they lacked in elegance and precision, they made up for with their skill in weaponry. If they'd somehow mastered poison studies too . . .

Vaughn leaned forward again, studying Kallias with narrowed eyes. "So. She doesn't know us."

"No. Not even Finn." It was an effort to keep his voice steady. "Jericho unearthed a single memory, but Soleil won't let us back into her head. No matter what we offer."

"And without her consent, Jericho won't try it herself."

"Exactly."

Vaughn rubbed his temples, shaking his head in disbelief. "And how do you feel about that?"

It took him a moment to process the question—no one had asked him that yet. "Well, we got one memory free for her. So at least she's not threatening to kill us anymore." The weak, jagged laugh he tried to dredge up caught in his throat, sounding more like a cough. It wasn't funny, anyway.

Reconciling this snow-and-stone girl who bared her teeth like a wolf when she saw his face with the sister he'd carried on his shoulders and taught how to swim was proving to be damn near impossible. That little girl had blown bubbles in her milk and shared her dessert with him when she worried he hadn't eaten enough. *This* one had tried to rip his throat out with her bare hands, and when he'd told her who she truly was, she'd laughed and spat at him for even suggesting she had a drop of saltwater in her blood.

"This changes everything," Vaughn said absently, tapping his fingers against his knees. "An assassination is one thing. That's basic warfare. Kidnapping and brainwashing an Heir . . . that's another."

Kallias's head pulsed. "I know."

Vaughn's gaze softened. He stood up before the desk, placing his palms flat on it as he leaned down, level with Kallias. "You're doing it again, brother."

"Doing what?"

"Putting the entire kingdom on your shoulders. Set it down. It doesn't belong there. Jericho's the Heir, and she knows what she's doing. We're in this together, remember? You don't have to carry this alone."

The words settled over Kallias in a strange way, sitting uncomfortably in his gut. But he forced a smile anyway. "I know. Thanks, Vaughn."

"I'll see you at dinner?"

"Of course."

He kept himself poised as Vaughn left, his pen to his paper, giving the illusion of busyness. Then, when the door closed, he finally slumped, settling that weight back on his shoulders. Because even though it wasn't his, no one carried it better than him. His shoulders had bent and sloped to make room for it, growing used to its weight, and when it was finally lifted away . . . he thought he might actually miss it.

He closed his eyes, taking a moment to breathe in the heavy sea air blowing in from his open window, listening to the roar of the ocean. Every window in the royal quarters faced the sea. The palace backed right up to the beach, its walls delineating a section of shore that was for them alone. Citizens weren't allowed there except with special permission from Adriata herself.

His siblings would be expect him at dinner tonight. There would be talk of Soleil, and her future, and Atlas's future with her in it. There would be debate on how best to reacclimate her and how to bring her lost memories back. How best to tell their parents that Nyx had done something worse than they'd ever imagined.

Kallias stepped into the hall. Looked one way, then the other. No one was around, no one he had to smile for or accept orders from or solve problems for.

At the very edge of the silence, the sea purred to him. Beckoned him.

As if they had a mind of their own, his feet turned towards that chaotic, masterless thing beyond palace and land and wars. Beyond dead sisters and living sisters and all the things he was doomed to lose.

And then he was running.

The ocean was bitingly cold, shocking the feeling from Kallias's toes long before he reached the good waves, but he didn't mind. The cold invigorated him, woke him up, shaking off that daze of palace politeness and that feeling that always haunted him for a few days after a battle—phantom blood on his hands and his fingers constantly feeling *wrong*, too light, like they should still be wrapped around the hilt of a sword.

He was trained for the battlefield, but he was raised for throne rooms, and most days he wasn't sure which one he was better suited for. If either of them.

He sat up on his waveboard, letting his legs dangle, licking salt from his lips, the hot-pink rays of the setting sun dancing off the turquoise sea around him. A long, wobbling sigh unwound from his throat.

He'd been away too long.

He reached his hand out, letting the undulating water kiss his palms, waves arching like purring cats against his fingers. Peace flooded his senses, and he closed his eyes, afraid to even breathe too deeply—as if this contentment was truly a skittish animal, liable to bolt away at any sudden movement.

"She's alive," he said out loud—not sure why he felt the need. "All this time, she was alive." Nothing but the call of sea birds and the lapping of water against his board answered him. The raw, aching hollowness in his chest yawned open. "She doesn't know us. Any of us. Maybe I should feel worse about that, but right now I'm just . . ." A cracked, rasping laugh. "I'm just so gods-damned grateful she's alive. And if you had a hand in this, we're grateful."

What was he doing? Praying to a god his kingdom feared wasn't something a prince should be risking, but . . . well. He'd never felt much in the way of worship toward Anima. Life hadn't been easy on him, and he didn't feel much like thanking her for it.

But the sea had given him gifts he could never hope to repay. So instead, sometimes, when there was a wind to blow his words out to the horizon and there was no one around to hear him whisper, he prayed to Tempest.

He didn't know if the supposedly malevolent sea god listened. Or cared. Or even existed. But it made him feel better anyway. Besides, Tempest may have been the god of storms and shipwrecks, but he was also the god of lost things. And who better to thank for Soleil's return?

He reached up to run his fingers through his hair, but they jammed halfway through, locked in a mass of brine-roughened knots. A low groan rumbled in his chest. It was going to take an hour of stealing Jericho's fine conditioners and yanking a brush through to get it smooth again, but that was a problem for later. For now, he simply twisted it into a bun, tying it with the leather band he always kept on his wrist.

A flicker of movement on the shore caught his attention—a flash of coral and persimmon. Crossed arms and a tapping foot. A hand beckoning him back.

That fragile peace he'd managed to find fizzled away like mist, and he blew out a frustrated breath. He hadn't expected to get caught quite this fast.

For a single, uninhibited second, he thought about going out further, until he could no longer see Jericho waiting for him, until he lost sight of the palace and the city and all his problems. But the sun was rapidly fading, and surfing in the dark was practically an invitation for the sharks to devour him.

So instead, he waved back to her, then flipped off his board.

He crashed beneath the water, icy thrill shooting up his veins as he plunged, nothing beneath him and nothing above him but open ocean. He drifted there for a moment, only moving enough to keep himself from sinking too deeply, until his lungs began to ache for air. His soul might find the water welcoming, but his body liked it less.

When he finally dragged himself and his board from the sea, dripping and knocking the side of his head to clear his waterlogged ears, Jericho was waiting with a towel outstretched. "Better?" she asked, one eyebrow cocked.

"Much." He took the towel gratefully, goosebumps pricking up and down his arms as he dried himself off. "Am I late?"

"You would have been. Vaughn faked an awful migraine, just unbearable. He bought you time."

"He's a godsend."

"Believe me, I know." She tugged playfully on his knotted hair. "You forgot to braid it again?"

"Maybe I like looking a little rugged."

"You look like a rat made its nest on your head."

Kallias elbowed her in the ribs and she squeaked, shoving him away, flinging pitiful kicks toward his legs. "Stop! You're dripping wet!"

"If you don't fix that attitude in about two seconds, you're going to match."

They ribbed each other and picked their way through the sand, Jericho laughing when Kallias somehow managed to step on every sharp shell in his path, until the shadow of the great Atlas Pier rose up before them. Kallias hopped up and gripped one of the support beams, hoisting himself up onto the sandblown wooden structure. Jericho opted to walk up the ramp instead.

He sat on the edge of the pier, legs dangling, and rested his elbows on his wetsuit-sheathed knees. After a moment, Jericho's wispy skirts settled beside him, her bare feet stopping several inches above his. She gave him a look—*that* look. The *I'm your big sister, spill your guts to me, I swear I am the most loyal and true of all your friends* look that he'd never trusted but always fallen for. "Tell me what's bothering you, Gills."

A soft huff of a laugh. "Gods, Jericho, what isn't bothering me?"

"You're worrying about the engagement again?"

Always. "No."

"Because if you're having second thoughts—"

"It's not that. It's . . ." He gestured weakly at the sea, as if that could encompass all the wretched, tangled feelings he couldn't seem to get a grip on.

Jericho reached over and undid his hair, running her fingers through it bit by bit, tugging through the snarls with businesslike efficiency. "You don't want to leave."

Kallias averted his eyes, focusing instead on the ocean beneath them. He could just barely see tiny fish wriggling beneath the surface, shards of silver flashing in the dying sun.

This had been a long time coming. It wasn't like his parents had ambushed him—in fact, they'd waited a considerable while after the more traditional mark of his twenty-first birthday. If he'd been like most eligible royals, he would have been married before that year was out. But his parents had put it off. First, because Nyx had held the upper hand at the time, and no kingdom had been willing to risk even the *suggestion* of an alliance with Atlas, marriage or otherwise. And after they'd started winning . . . he liked to think his skill with warfare had something to do with it, that by turning the tide with his insight and occasional personal involvement, he'd proven himself invaluable.

It seemed with the war close to an end, his usefulness had run out. And while he'd never relished the idea of leaving his kingdom, he'd never dreaded it, either. Not like he did now. Until this past month, it hadn't felt *real.* All those premonitions of wedding a mysterious royal and being swept off to a new and exciting kingdom had seemed like an exciting promise, an adventure he would embark on when he was older—when he was ready.

But now he was twenty-five, and he'd run out of time to become the kind of man who was able to leave everything behind him without a backward glance. Now he'd have to settle for being a man who wanted to serve his kingdom however it required, but ached at the thought of stepping foot outside its borders.

Jericho clucked her tongue when he held his silence too long. "Kal, no one will begrudge you that. Atlas is home. The ocean, it's a soulmark. It gets in people's blood. Of course you're going to miss it."

He closed his eyes as she worked through his snarls. "Not just the ocean."

Her hand stilled for a moment, then resumed. "You'll always have us, you know. Mama will definitely require more than the usual standard for visits. And Finn and I, we'll come see you all the time. I'll expect a present every visit, naturally."

Something warmed in Kallias's chest, a single thread in the tangle loosening. "*Every* visit?"

Jericho chuckled. "Well, the first five or so, anyway. Mama will probably ask for you home more than that in the first year."

Kallias's lip tried to curl into a wince, and he took a slow breath to stop it, forcing a laugh instead. "Somehow I doubt it. She's more excited than anyone for this marriage." And that shouldn't hurt him as much as it did.

They stayed quiet for a moment, listening to the gulls, watching the waves.

"This news doesn't leave us four and Seamus," Kallias finally said. "Mama and Papa have to be next to know."

"Then how do we explain her presence in the meantime? We can't keep her locked up, Kal, that's hardly going to convince her she belongs here."

"I know, I know. I'll come up with something."

Lines carved across Jericho's brow, deeper than usual—she hardly ever had something this weighty to worry over, thanks to him. But she merely nodded. "I know you will. Let's start with dinner. I'll have Finn bring her tomorrow. She can meet Vaughn, she can ask questions . . . we'll get her comfortable. Maybe she'll let us back into her head after that."

Kallias frowned. "Is it really safe to let Finn be in charge of her? We can't trust her yet, and Finn's not exactly the fighting type. If she attacks—"

"You remember what they were like as children. They stuck to each other like tar to a shoe. That kind of thing doesn't just go away."

"You're making me feel like I'm being paranoid."

"No—well. Maybe you are. A little. But after the week you've had, I think it's earned." She pulled back from him, her gaze falling to his hand. Sadness clouded her eyes. "I'm going to miss you when you're gone."

Kallias folded his left hand under his right, hiding the simple golden band on his first finger.

That damn ring. He wanted to bury it in one of the sea-caves along the cliffs and never lay eyes on it again. "They only just started searching out an arrangement, Jer. We've got time."

"It could be a decade and it still wouldn't be enough time. What are Finn and I going to do without you to keep us out of trouble?"

"I shudder to think. Gives me nightmares," Kallias deadpanned, and she punched him in the ribs.

"Rude."

"I give it a week before the kingdom's completely collapsed."

"I am the *older* sister, you remember that, yes? The future queen? I'm technically more qualified than you to handle these things."

She was right. The matter of their sister wasn't even his to solve. As First Prince, it was his job to take what the Heir handed down and see that it was done. It was his job to make it palatable to the people. Never the decision-maker, only the decision-enforcer.

He shook that thought off, trying desperately to curb the sharp edge of jealousy. He couldn't keep indulging in those thoughts, couldn't let the bitterness take hold. He smiled ruefully instead. "You know I'm teasing, Jer. You're going to be a brilliant queen."

Jericho laughed too, a sound that reminded him of chirping birds. She ruffled his hair, planting a kiss there before pulling herself to her feet, offering him her hand. "You're going to be fine, Gills. No matter where you land. I promise."

He gazed at that hand, then at her face. "And if I'm not?"

Her smile was uncompromising. "I'll do whatever I have to for that to change."

CHAPTER 13

ELIAS

All Elias could see was blood.

The water inside the basin was already murky and rust-colored, and still his hands weren't clean. No matter how hard he scrubbed, no matter how fiercely he dug under his nails, traces of Soren's blood still remained.

And he couldn't stop shaking. His legs, his arms, his gods-damned *hands* were trembling so badly he could barely hold the bar of soap.

He didn't realize he was crying until a ragged sob tore from his throat, and he had to clasp the edge of the basin to steady himself.

Not her, not her, not her. His prayers had devolved since he'd run to each of the healing tents like a madman, demanding to know who'd found his battlemate and whether or not she was still alive. Since he'd been told no one had brought the princess in, dead or otherwise. Since he'd realized what had happened might be worse than even that. *Not her, not her, not her.*

Every breath grated painfully against his chest. His lungs still hadn't quite recovered from his rush to the tents and back to where he'd left Soren and then back *again,* not even after he borrowed a horse rather than walking all the way back to the capital city, Andromeda, riding at breakneck speed to bring news of Soren's capture to the Queen.

It wasn't a good sign that he was still struggling, but he couldn't worry about it now. It was probably just his panic making it difficult for him to breathe.

It had to be.

"She's not Kaia," he whispered to himself. "She's not dead, you bastard, so stop acting like it."

Kaia. His last battlemate—his best friend. There had been no goodbyes for them, either.

It was hard to say goodbye when your head was cut free from your neck.

The memory invaded with such force that Elias barely had time to twist himself over the nearby wastebasket before his sparse breakfast made a hasty reappearance. Bile burning in his mouth, he turned back to the basin, spitting into the bloodied water.

A sharp rap on the bathing room door made him start, his hands tightening on the edges of the basin. "Just a minute!" he called, gritting his teeth against the tremor in his throat. There was no chance he was going to embarrass himself or Soren by looking like a hysterical mess in front of the royal family and their court.

They were meeting now to discuss how to go about a rescue. Elias had only been allowed in for a few minutes before being sent away to clean himself up, and honestly, he was glad for it. He couldn't recall the rules of decorum right now if his life depended on it.

Soren was always the strong one of the two of them. She faced tragedy with an irreverent quip and a dare-you-to-try-it grin, and the weeping came days or weeks or months later. She held it together until everyone else was okay again. She was the pillar that held the rest of them up.

But she couldn't be his pillar now. It was his turn to stand. His turn to hold.

She needed him. He would not fail her.

So he straightened, pulled his hands from the wood, and took as many deep breaths as he had to for his chest to stop heaving. Then he dried his face, slung the towel over his neck, and pushed the door open, locking himself into a stance that said he was ready to receive an order. "Yes?"

A grim-looking page stood at the door. "You've been summoned back, Officer Loch."

Hope, dizzying and hot, nearly put him on his knees. "They've decided?"

The page nodded, but seeing the expression on his face, Elias's hope fled as fast as it came. He took a single step back as if he could escape what was coming, as if it would change so long as he didn't hear it.

But refusing to hear it would be cowardice, and he was not a coward. So he rasped, "Tell me."

"What do you mean, *no?*"

Shaking hands balled into fists, disbelief swelling painfully in his chest, Elias stood at the end of a long table, staring straight ahead at his queen, certain he'd heard her wrong.

"Officer Loch," Enna said too gently, in a way that promised bad news. "We cannot afford to send more soldiers into Atlas—"

"Like the *pits* we can't!"

"*Officer Loch.*"

"Enna—Your Majesty," he amended quickly, catching the way her eyes flashed in warning. This wasn't the armory or the dinner table. Here he was a Nyxian soldier, not Soren's battlemate, and calling the Queen by her first name would earn him nothing but a trip to the dungeon for a night or two. "They stole my battlemate. Our *princess*. We cannot let this stand!"

"Elias," said Enna, her voice tight, "can I speak with you outside, please? Yvonne, Emberlyn—you stay here."

Soren's older sisters didn't look much better than Elias felt. Yvonne's face was stony and pale, jaw clenched, her fingers tapping against the dagger ever-strapped at her hip, even in her fine silk gown. Emberlyn seemed moments away from outright raging, her dark eyes mimicking the flame tattoos climbing up her arms as she settled herself back in her chair, fingers curled so tightly into her red silk sleeves that he thought she might rip them apart.

The Queen led Elias out and came to a halt in the hall, her back to him, only the stiffness in her shoulders giving away her true fear. She buried her head in her hands. "I can't send our people on a suicide mission," she finally said, though her voice wobbled like she might fall into sobbing at any slight push. She turned to face him, frustration teeming in her eyes. "I can't. Not for her, not for anyone. Gods, we don't even know if she's still . . ."

Alive. The word pulsed bright and terrible in the silence between them.

"Then don't send our people," he said. "Send me."

Her eyes went to his arm. That damned arm. "Elias," she began, in the voice he had come to recognize as the voice people used when they spoke to dying men.

He cut her off before she could finish, gesturing wildly to his own shoulder, wishing he could lop the damned thing off and be done with it. "This only means I'm *definitely* the right choice. I have months left, if not weeks. And I don't want them without her."

Enna's eyes flickered with secrets, her lips pressed thin against things she wanted to say. "I cannot approve a rescue mission. I'm sorry."

Anger flared, dark and dangerous. "How can you do this? She is your *daughter.*"

Any softness that lingered in Enna's eyes hardened to stone. "Do *not* suggest I do this lightly, Elias. Don't you *dare* suggest—"

"I suggest nothing, Majesty," he said, coating every word with venom twice as potent as what swam in his veins. "I am *telling* you that you are abandoning her to die. And if they kill her, or Mortem forbid they find a way to *break* her, her blood is on *your* hands!"

He turned his back on his queen and left the hall, his palms burning with anger, the soles of his feet aching to run with every step. But even as the fire of his rage heated his throat like a forge, guilt lurked, waiting to rise up when anger was spent. Because no matter what he said to Enna . . .

Her hands. Her hands.

Not hers. Mine.

He was the one who abandoned Soren. And though her blood may have been on Enna's hands, it was also buried under his nails, dried on his uniform, crusted on his boots.

He'd been *right gods-damned there.*

"Elias!"

He didn't turn, not even when Auralee came up behind him. "What did they decide?" she asked breathlessly, her shoulder bumping his elbow—Auralee barely brushed five feet, even to a generous eye. "When do they leave?"

"They don't."

Auralee's steps faltered, then she picked up her pace again, chestnut curls falling from her bun to coil gently at her brow. "What are you saying?"

"I'm saying Enna refused to approve a mission. No one's going. They're leaving her there." Leaving her in Atlas hands to be tortured, to be flayed with nine-tailed whips and then bathed in saltwater, drowned and revived and drowned and revived again, told over and over that she'd been abandoned, and what worth was there in being loyal to a kingdom that didn't care enough to rescue her?

And that was only if they'd taken her alive.

Nausea surged, and Elias barely had time to stagger to the side and snag the closest thing resembling a wastebasket—a priceless Artem-made blown glass vase on display beside the window—before he surrendered what little he had left inside his stomach to it.

Vaguely, past his heaves and the strangled half-sobs that accompanied them, he felt Auralee's small hand rubbing soothing circles in the center of his back, her palm rasping uncomfortably against an old scar there. Soren always did that when he was sick, too, but she knew to rub between his shoulder blades instead.

Gods, it was ridiculous, that such small things could make him *ache* so badly.

"Sorry," he rasped when the retching finally calmed.

"I'll hide the vase," Auralee offered kindly, and he would have hugged her for it if his breath wasn't absolutely horrendous. He hadn't brushed his teeth in two days, and the bile scalding the back of his throat wasn't helping matters.

"Don't bother," said Emberlyn, suddenly appearing at his other side. The weaponsmith plucked the vase from his hands, her nose wrinkling as she carefully arranged her fire-scarred fingers to avoid any mess. "I'll throw it out."

"I should be better than this," he said instead of thanking her. "Stronger for her."

Emberlyn eyed him for a long moment, her lips pursed, and he couldn't read the look on her face. "When my battlemate died," she said finally, "I spent a week drinking myself sick, puking my guts up, then drinking again to make myself forget I was sick. If Vonnie hadn't dragged me out of my room and dunked me in a bucket of ice water until I sobered up enough to grieve, I'd still be there. Or I'd be dead too. Strength has nothing to do with it, not when it's grief. Or guilt. You fought for her. You did the best you could."

Panic shivered down his arms, threatening to bring on a new round of retching. She sounded too much like his mother did when his father died, like his first captain after he found Kaia's head. Like Soren was already buried beneath the frozen dirt. Like she was already lost to them. "It's different. Soren's not dead."

"We know," said yet another voice, Yvonne sweeping up to them in a blur of velvet skirts and set jaw. Her angular features were still shocky, her fists clenched, but there was a look in her eyes that he recognized: a look that said she'd made up her mind about something, and wouldn't be budged. All the Nyxian princesses carried more than their share of stubbornness, and the Crown Princess was no different. "And Mama knows it too. But she's right—sending any number of rescuers over the border is just sending Atlas more prisoners to play with."

Elias leaned against the wall, breathing through the aftershocks of vomiting, his body not quite sure if it was done. All three remaining princesses stood before him, silent exchanges passing between them, occasional glances pointed his way.

"So," said Emberlyn finally, "who's going to say it first?"

Auralee's tearful eyes narrowed in confusion. "Say what?"

Yvonne looked to Elias. "You saw her before it happened," she said. "How bad was she?"

A blurry flash of blood and dimming eyes and a death-kissed grin.

"Bad," he rasped, and even stoic Emberlyn winced, her scarred fingers drifting to her mouth. "But I . . . I believe she's alive." Gods, he had to believe she was alive.

Emberlyn's eyes, golden-brown and ever-thoughtful, skimmed up and down his body in a frank assessment. "And you?"

He met her gaze unflinchingly. "I'm not dead. That's enough for me."

Yvonne covered Auralee's ears, ignoring the youngest princess's groan of protest. "You know, it's always better to ask forgiveness than permission," she said. "And it seems to me you've already tried asking permission. But if I recall correctly . . . Ember?"

"The guard shift at the stables changes at seven," Emberlyn supplied immediately. "The gate guard changes an hour after that. With a fresh horse, you could be over the Atlas border in a few days."

Shock bristled inside his chest. "You're telling me to go get her."

"I'm not telling you anything." Yvonne shrugged. "I'm just discussing the guard rotation with my sister, and you happen to be overhearing."

"I can still hear you through your hands," Auralee grumbled. "This is silly."

"Hush," Yvonne scolded. "I prefer not to corrupt you just yet with schemes of this nature."

"And we don't trust you not to tell," Ember added dryly. "Mama takes one look at you and you fold like a bad hand of cards."

Mortem save him. What they were suggesting was worse than disobedience; Enna had given him a direct order to stay here. Defying her would be treason.

Being stripped of his title and dishonorably dismissed from the army was the absolute *minimum* punishment, and at maximum . . . execution.

His gaze fell to his bandaged, bruised arm. What was he thinking? He was dying anyway. Weeks from now, months, years—what did it matter? His fate was already sealed, but Soren's didn't have to be. Not if he pulled this off.

"Damn it, smartass," he muttered, running one hand over his face. "The things I do for you."

The echoing ache that bounced back to him from the absence of a quick and snarky "jackass" was the last straw. The princesses had given him everything he needed—if he hurried, he could still beat the armory shift change. He could get out of the castle before night fell, and by the time anyone realized he was missing, it would be too dark to bother chasing after him. And by morning, they'd never catch up.

"I'll bring her home," he rasped.

Yvonne's eyes glimmered with unshed tears. "You'd better."

"And when you find her," Emberlyn added, covering Auralee's ears again, ignoring the way the girl flailed, "make sure you kick her ass for scaring us."

He steeled his shoulders, gave them a quick bow, then quickened his pace. He tried to look as dejected as possible as he rushed back to Soren's room and gathered up his remaining things, whatever he needed that wasn't already jammed into his pack.

As he jerked open the drawer of her nightstand and tugged out his holy book, the flash of a metal box at the bottom of his bag caught his attention. The parcel Ember had given him just before his departure to Ursa.

He scooped up the box and flipped it open, revealing the treasure inside: a a simple band, a ring crowned with a raw black diamond, a row of raw white diamonds arching over the center stone. He used to wear it at the end of a chain, using it as a good-luck charm, dousing it in blessed water before every battle. He stopped wearing it when he and Soren became battlemates. But recently, a new purpose for it had come to his attention, a purpose that had required resizing and restoring, something Ember was thankfully skilled at.

At least, he'd been *considering* a new purpose for it, before the Viper bite that had rendered any dreams of that nature useless. Before the gentle simmer of poison in his veins had tugged him back to sense.

He should definitely leave it behind. But where he was going, he might just need an extra dose of luck.

So he slipped the ring back inside his pack. He looked both ways as he crept out of Soren's room, quietly shutting the door behind him.

And then Elias Loch marched off to commit treason.

CHAPTER 14

SOREN

Up until Soren's knee gave out on her in the middle of her workout and dropped her to the floor like a bag of spoiled apples, she was actually having a fairly pleasant day.

Seamus had brought her breakfast, and she'd gotten *much* closer to impaling him with a thrown fork this time than the morning before. Or the one before that. In fact, it was the first of six forks that hadn't ended up tines-deep in the doorframe or the wall, so it counted as a win in her book.

Practice made perfect, and she certainly needed something to keep herself busy, because being trapped in this room with nothing but her thoughts for company was making the inside of her skull itch. Turning to the revelation that had been forced on her only brought a bubbling vat of disgust to her stomach, a haunting feeling of un-belonging, of utter and complete discomfort. Like she was living in a skin that no longer fit, that had told her lie after lie about where it came from and what it was made of, and now that she knew the truth . . .

Atlas blood. Bile welled in her throat.

It was just a manipulation, her unearthed memory a trick of magic. The faint familiarity of Finn was his own careful manipulation. None of it was real, and she couldn't afford to lose sight of that.

She rolled from her side onto her back, relishing the healthy burn in her muscles, forcing her aching lungs to take in a steadying breath. She draped one wrist over her forehead, squeezing her eyes shut.

In for five, hold for five, out for five. That was what Enna taught her that first day in Nyx, when she woke burned and terrified in an infirmary bed and couldn't remember what put her there. *Breathe in, hold it, breathe out. Control what you can.*

The breathing helped. The bruises drowsily beginning to raise color on her legs and the throbbing in her shoulder, decidedly less so.

"You're all right," she murmured. "You're all right."

As all right as someone could be after finding out they were the daughter of a revenge-addled woman whose hands were soaked with the blood of some very precious people.

Jira, dead and buried, never to scale the barracks wall after a glass of wine too many or dye Soren's hair purple while she slept ever again. Kaia, Elias's sister in heart, her body burned in a private pyre because she was too mangled to bother carrying home. Elias himself, dying piece by piece every day, soon to be another name scrawled on a gravestone she'd have to kneel and cry and pretend to pray over.

Steel straightened her spine, and she clenched her hands into fists, her nails pricking bits of sense back into her. She had to pull herself together. Everything else could be solved later—she had to pull this ruse off *now*.

A knock on her door. "It's time, Princess," said Seamus the Especially Annoying through the door.

Soren's eyes drifted to the hanger near her borrowed bed, to the decadent outfit and jewelry that waited there. She contemplated showing up with just her plain tunic and unwashed hair, but . . .

Well. It couldn't hurt.

Okay, fine. So the wrapped blouse, made of crushed velvet in the most vivid shade of purple she'd ever seen, was damn near the best thing she'd ever touched in her entire life, including that time she'd managed to persuade Rian from the barracks class above hers to pin her to the armory wall and teach her exactly how a princess with her sort of mouth ought to be kissed.

Her neck flushed hot, her fingers balling up her black chiffon pants in her sweaty palms. Elias had been pissed for days after he'd walked in on them . . . not because she'd been kissing *someone*, but because she'd been kissing *Rian Loch*, of all people. But it wasn't her fault Elias's cousin was so good at what he did when he managed to stop *talking* for thirty seconds, and it wasn't her fault Elias didn't seem to feel the need to explore whether the skill ran in the family . . . at least, not since that game of truth-or-dare their company had played a couple years back.

Gods, she had to stop thinking about that. It was completely the wrong time to indulge those sorts of thoughts.

"There you are!" A far, far too friendly arm slid around her shoulders from her left, and she found herself once again in the sparkling company of Finn, who'd opted not for finery but for simple dark pants and a brownish sweater with a hole near the collar. He wore gold-framed spectacles, which might've helped give a scholarly air if they weren't about to slide right off the end of his nose.

Off-kilter. Messy. Lazy, almost.

Soren blinked, casting a glance down at the accessories that had been provided for her, sapphires dripping from her fingers and her throat. Already over-the-top, and that wasn't even taking into account the golden cuffs that crept up each of her ears and wrists. "Are we going to the same place?"

"Yepperoo. I'm just horrendously underdressed. Bilberry?" He held a handful out to her, and when she leveled a glare at him, he flashed her a grin that showed off his mottled purple tongue.

Maybe she'd been wrong about him hiding a cunning mind behind the shield of the fool. He certainly seemed perfectly legitimate now.

"No, really. Am I going to walk in there and find I'm the only one dressed like I'm trying to get mugged?"

Finn sighed in a tight, painful way, throwing the rest of the berries in his mouth and chewing glumly. "And here I thought we were learning to trust one another."

Soren snorted, shrugging off his arm and fluffing up the curls he squished, cursing quietly at the static his sleeve stirred up. "I'm not sure anyone should trust you, least of all me."

Something in his smile faltered. "Soren, I'm not trying to trick you."

Interesting. He called her by the name she'd given them, not the name of his sister. "Aren't you?"

"Not at all. Well, not right now, anyway."

"Do let me know if that changes."

"I definitely will not." He jerked his chin at Seamus, who was following behind at a close distance—too close for comfort with that beltful of blades he wore. "You're dismissed. I'll take her from here."

"But she—"

"Seamus. If she tries to kill me, I pinky-promise I will scream like someone lit the backside of my pants on fire. I haven't had the privilege of walking my little sister anywhere in a very long time, so if you wouldn't mind . . ." Finn made a shooing motion with his hand.

Tension wrapped a tight hand around the back of Soren's neck, and she reached to rub it away. She knew what it sounded like when this prince lied; he'd been doing it almost every moment since she met him. But he sounded different just then, and she didn't like the way it made her feel.

Left alone—albeit reluctantly, Seamus slinking off with several backwards glances just to be *sure* she wasn't trying anything—they made their way to the common area at the center of the palace. No jeerers or bug-eyed palacefolk this time; it was eerily empty, her footfalls echoing, each slap of her sandals a new note in an off-putting symphony.

"Remind me again how this works," she said.

"Now that you're home, you're invited to your first sibling dinner. We use it to talk kingdom matters behind our parents' backs. Not that you're ready to be involved in any sort of official business." His eyes slid over her, narrowing slightly. "This is more of a . . . I guess you could call it a peace offering. Kal doesn't want you to feel like a prisoner. But we're not about to trust you with the goings-on just yet."

"I thought we were learning to trust one another," Soren mimicked, and he flicked his last berry at her.

"Learning doesn't mean we're going to hand you the keys to our kingdom. As far as I'm concerned, you're ninety-percent Nyxian."

"And the other ten?"

"Five percent Atlas, five percent closet gremlin."

She snorted in spite of herself. "Closet gremlin?"

He nodded seriously. "Little terrors. They steal your socks and buttons and gnaw holes in the crotch of your pants."

"I can sincerely promise you I have never gnawed at any kind of clothing."

He held up his finger like he'd caught her in a lie. "Ah! But nothing against sock-stealing."

The reluctant swell of laughter died in her chest, leaving behind an ache that throbbed like a hunger pang, like a heartbreak. "Guilty. My battlemate's socks are better than mine. His mother knits them."

Elias. What could he be doing now? Enna would never approve a rescue mission, and that was assuming they even realized she'd been taken and not killed. He was going to hate that. He was angry, she was sure. Blaming himself like an idiot, she'd bet her life on that.

Maybe he'd already started a new braid in his hair.

Finn's hand, more hesitant this time, settled back on her shoulder as they turned down the correct corridor. "Battlemates. That's a Nyxian custom, yeah?"

She resisted the urge to break his wrist. "Mmhm. We're paired up when we graduate from training."

"They choose pairs for you?"

"No." Her lips quirked. "Well, not usually. My battlemate didn't choose me. And I only chose him because I had to."

That one.

Soren, he just lost his battlemate too, he may not be ready—

I fight with him, or I fight alone.

"You love him," Finn observed. His brows were raised, eyes slightly wide. Too innocent.

"He's . . ." The words shriveled and died, leaving behind an aftertaste of fear. What was she doing, giving these things away to him? She knew his type. They fed on secrets, on knowledge, and she wouldn't add hers to his stash. That quiet hunger glimmering behind his spectacles was the same as mountain wolves on the hunt.

She would not give him a weakness to exploit. Especially not when that weakness was Elias.

It was only then that she realized just *how* alone they were. She hadn't seen anyone since they crossed into the common area.

"He's good at what he does," she said stiffly, shrugging off his arm again, putting some distance between them and angling herself toward the nearest weapon she could see: the pull cord to the curtains. She could tear it off and use it to strangle him if she had to. It might even make a better story than the time she impaled a grabby trainee's hand to a table with a butterknife. "Love's got nothing to do with it. Admiration, maybe."

"I know what admiration looks like. If you admire this boy, you must get completely useless when you love someone."

She bared her teeth. "Watch it."

He frowned at her, his nose crinkling. "What is that?"

"What is what?"

He clicked his teeth mockingly her way. "The teeth-gnashing. The *grrr* sound you make. Do Nyxians throw their kidnapped children in a wolf's den?"

"Yes. In fact, I can run on all fours better than on two legs."

To her annoyance, he took her humor in stride. "Understood. Should I tell the chef to prepare your meat rare?"

"The bloodier the better."

He heaved a sigh as they made another turn, entering a new corridor. Similar to much of the rest of the palace, this hall was utterly ornate, every surface made of either polished gold or glimmering gemstones. The entryway at the end was huge: double doors, hammered gold, inset with a sunburst design. The seal of Atlas.

"I wish I didn't like you so much," Finn muttered under his breath, slipping his fingers through the handle-rings. "It would make all this much easier."

A chill fluttered across her body, and gods *above* did she wish she had her sword. "Make what easier?"

He gave her a wry, wretched smile over his shoulder, but didn't answer. Instead, he flung the doors open and led the way inside. And as Soren followed, all eyes in the room landing on her, she thought: *No,* this *is what a den of wolves looks like.*

She raised her chin and followed the Second Prince inside.

CHAPTER 15

FINN

The way Soleil—*Soren*—was acting, one would've thought they'd dragged her to the dungeon and strapped her to a stool covered in spikes, not a cushy chair in the Queen's private dining room. She was stiff as a dried-out sea sponge, sitting at the very edge of her seat, her fist wrapped so tightly around her fork he could've sworn the metal bent beneath her white-knuckled grasp. Her arms were mottled with purple and green below the elbows—from the battle, he guessed—and when she shifted, her draped sleeve slipping a bit, the light caught wrong on her bare shoulder.

He wasn't often startled, but when his eyes snagged on her shoulder, his breath caught in his throat, a jagged cough that brought every eye to him.

He wasn't sure how he'd missed the ridges of ruined skin sloughed from the right side of her collarbone down to the bend of her elbow, discolored and poorly healed. An old wound. Maybe even a decade old.

He suddenly felt like bending a fork or two himself.

Soren's eyes silently dared him to speak. "Weak stomach?"

"It's not that." Normally he would have gone further, made a joke, asked a ridiculous question, anything. But that scar . . .

Smoke tarred the walls of his lungs, heat searing his eyes, his mind whirring at a speed impossible for most. Map after map flickered through his mind—routes he could take from here to a door, a window, anyplace *that would free him from this fire. But every possibility fell short. Every option was too far, too dangerous, or already destroyed.*

He needed help.

"Kallias!" His brother's name ripped down his throat, and he staggered to a stop, coughing so harshly his lungs refused to take in new breath. At ten years old, small for his age and completely alone, he didn't know what to do. And that ignorance would have killed him if his father hadn't found him moments later, bundling him against his chest and rushing him out through one of the routes he'd been too scared to try, pushing him into his mother's arms.

"Is that everyone?" Adriata's shriek pitched above the sickening symphony echoing down the beach, screams instead of strings, wails instead of brass. Finn buried his face in her nightdress, only to find that it smelled of the same smoke that had stolen his breath. He gagged, which began a new round of coughing, and his mother's hands held him closer, rubbing his back. "Ramses, is that everyone? Where's Kal?"

"I'm here!" Finn barely heard Kallias's shout past his own wheezing. "I'm here. Jericho got out with me, she's down the beach with—"

He felt his mother's chest stop rising and falling. "What about Soleil? Wasn't she with you, I thought she was with you!"

"What?" Kallias's voice cracked with panic. "No, she left us to go find you just before we got told to—"

"Ramses!" Adriata screamed, and Finn only realized then what this meant, because his mother never screamed. Not in fear, not in anger, never. "Ramses, Soleil's still in there, Soleil is still in there*—"*

She pushed him into Kal's soot-stained arms, and he was too numb to fight it, shaking too badly to move as he realized that . . . that Soleil . . .

"No," he whimpered. "No, no. She got out, didn't she? She must've gotten out! Soleil!" His gaze devoured the beach, taking in every burn and scream and sob, every face that wasn't the one he needed, every voice that wasn't his sister's. His panic grew until he felt like he might burst out of his skin. "Soleil!" His voice caught, doubling him over in a hacking, wheezing fit.

Kallias's face was paler than the sand they stood on, every one of his freckles ink-dark. He rubbed Finn's back, murmuring hushed reassurances, but his eyes were fixed on their parents, arguing before the burning palace over who would go back in, both fighting to keep the other safe.

Finn realized it at the same time Kallias did. Felt his stomach drop at the same time Kallias's jaw tightened, his hands falling away from Finn's back.

Soleil would be dead by the time a decision was made. There wasn't time to wait.

"Kal," Finn choked, tugging on his sleeve. "Kal, you have to get her out. We have to get her out please Kal we can't leave her in there—"

Kallias's hands tightened around his shoulders, holding him in place. "You stay here," he said slowly, absently, like a boy already one foot past the line between life and what lay beyond. He moved that way too, inch by inch, drifting so gradually their parents didn't realize what was happening until he was too far for them to stop.

Then Kallias bolted.

"Kallias!" Adriata and Ramses both lunged at the same time, shouting with one voice, their panics twining together and echoing Finn's. But before they could even make it a step, Kallias was through the half-scorched door, his hair flickering like another flame, swallowed by blaze and ash and smoke.

"Finn?"

He blinked his way back to this room, this time, this table full of his family. And this girl, this stranger wearing his sister's face, watching him with her thumb flicking at the tines of her fork. She leaned casually against the arm of her chair, tipping her head to one side, narrowing her eyes. "Are you going to sit? Or do my scars repulse you that much?"

"It's not that," he said blankly, before realizing he'd repeated himself. Dimwit.

More than the others, Finn was haunted by that fire. Jericho and Kallias and Vaughn had moved on, pushed past it, but Finn was the one cursed with flawless, vivid memory, his entire life arranged in a neat series of pictures in his head. He would give anything for time to soften the edges like it did for the others, blurring them until he could no longer relive every terror-soaked second of that awful night with sickening accuracy.

His perfect memory was an asset most times. But not when it came to this.

He sank into his chair, ignoring Kallias's eyes burning a hole into his temple, ignoring Soren's smirk at his obvious discomfort.

He couldn't let this girl get into his head. He couldn't let himself *care*. She might have the same body as his little sister, but that mind, that woman peeking out at him from shrewd, indifferent green eyes . . . he didn't know her. Nyx had created her, and believing anything else was base sentimentality at best, idiocy at worst.

Of course, he had to play idiot if he wanted to keep ahead of whatever game she was running. But he couldn't lose himself to memory like that. He would move forward as if nothing had changed. As if his best friend was still a pile of ash buried beneath the rebuilt palace floor. As if Jericho had never found the remnants of a festival and a game of hide-and-seek hiding in this Nyxian decoy's mind. He knew the truth: Soren was a shell, a chunk of fool's gold dressed like a diamond, and he wasn't falling for it.

But still, that scar spread uncomfortable chills across the pit of his gut, echoes of a grief he'd burned and buried far too long ago.

"So, Jer!" He plucked up his glass of wine and scooted his chair back, kicking his heels up, lounging back and pretending to take a leisurely sip. He didn't drink; loosening his tongue, however slightly, could be disastrous for a good many people. "Where's Vaughn?"

Jericho reached over and pushed his sandals off the table. "On his way, you rogue. Keep your feet on the floor. Who raised you?"

"A swamp witch named Nora. Lovely lady, very greedy. Mama and Papa paid a hefty price for me, you know. They struck out with you two and needed at least *one* child with half a brain." A quiet snort and mutter from Soren. Finn flashed her his best grin. "What was that?"

"It's a shame, is all."

"What is?"

Soren gestured at him like that was enough of an answer. "That she so obviously cheated them. Think they can still get their money back?"

Kallias choked on his wine. Jericho outright laughed. And something very small broke in Finn's chest. Something that wasn't as convinced as it should have been that Soren was no one . . . something that heard the echo of a younger girl in those taunting, playful words.

He forced a poor imitation of a laugh, all breath and rasp, no voice or charm to it. "Funny."

"I know." Soren took a long drink of her wine, her eyes flicking over him. But when she set the glass down, it was just as full as before. Finn narrowed his eyes at her. Her smile merely widened, a challenge shining in the gleam of her teeth.

Touché, kid.

"So," he said, "tell us about Nyx."

"Finn," Kallias hissed.

Soren's smile vanished. "I don't feel like discussing it."

He shuffled through the cards in his mental hand. Playing dumb was a queen, a safe bet but possibly not enough to beat her. This girl was one of the few people who might manage to find a king up her sleeve. Claiming hurt feelings wasn't even a face card, he could count that out. And while he always had a perfectly fine ace ready to throw down, he never wasted those on people who hadn't earned them.

So he chose his own king: acquiescence. Changing the subject. "Fair enough. Then what would you like to talk about? Open forum, kid."

She studied him with pursed lips, weighing out the silent challenge in his voice. "Kallias mentioned you performed another test while I was sleeping," she said, her glare flicking to Kallias, who averted his eyes with a sheepish crook to his mouth, pushing his food awkwardly with his fork. "What was it?"

"A blood match," said Vaughn, appearing in the seat beside Jericho without any of them noticing, one pale arm draped around her shoulders like he'd been there for hours. His black hair was messy, barely brushed, and deeper circles framed his dove-gray eyes than usual.

A bad day, then. No wonder they hadn't seen him at breakfast.

Out of the corner of his eye, he watched Soren flip the fork in her hand, holding it at an angle more suitable for stabbing. Kallias jolted in his seat and swore. "How do you *do* that?"

A tired smile, but no answer from their brother-in-law. "Princess Soleil. I'm Prince Consort Vaughn. It's a pleasure to meet you—again, anyway."

Finn liked plenty of people, but he counted very few as friends. Vaughn was one of them, if only because he was the most frustratingly genuine person Finn had ever met. Even if he wanted secrets to hold over Vaughn's head, he'd never find any. The worst thing he'd ever seen him do was steal Jericho's last strawberry tart and blame it on *him*, and he'd been so impressed that Vaughn bothered to lie, he'd simply admitted to the crime.

The Prince Consort was a gentle man, a talented physician who loved Jericho with a ferocity that rivaled what Finn believed possible when it came to love. The only time he'd seen anything comparable was with his parents . . . before the fire, anyway.

Afterward . . . well. It wasn't that things had faded between them, but they'd changed. No longer did Ramses pull Adriata from stuffy bureaucratic meetings just to dance her down the hallway, trying to sing a sea shanty through his laughter. No longer did Adriata light up like the sun when Ramses walked into the room.

In fact, Finn couldn't think of the last time he'd seen his parents having *fun* together.

"The feeling is mutual," said Soren, in a tone that assured them it was *not*. "What's a blood match?"

"Something I can do with my magic. Vaughn came up with the theory, and I proved it worked." Jericho offered her husband an adoring smile as she nestled her head against his shoulder. "A way of testing parentage or other such relations. Healers can test bloods against each other and see if they share anything in common, but it only works on immediate family. Brothers and sisters, parents and children . . . useful when there's a complication with claims to a throne."

Finn kicked at Vaughn's foot beneath the table, hoping to get his attention, but he was too busy losing himself in Jericho's eyes or smile or whatever people who liked to look at other people cared to stare at. He kicked again, and Vaughn finally looked up, one eyebrow raised. "Is there a reason you're playing footsie with me? You're going to make my wife jealous."

"Let it happen. She can't hope to compete with our love."

Vaughn looked to Jericho. "Your brother is flirting with me again."

She fluttered her eyelashes at him. "Are you flirting back?"

"Not at the moment."

"Then I suppose it's all right."

A smile tugged at the corner of Finn's mouth despite himself. Despite how dissonant this whole thing was. Despite the fact that Soren hadn't yet lowered her fork.

"How accurate is a blood match?" she asked, teeth gritted so hard a muscle in her jaw began to tick.

Vaughn gave her a measured look. "It hasn't failed yet. Would you like to see?"

Soren simply offered her palm. But Kallias blanched, a nervous laugh cutting off whatever challenge Soren's lips were poised to give. "Let's not deal with blood at the dinner table."

Soren cocked her head at him. "Oh, now you're squeamish too? I thought Atlas would be made of stiffer stuff."

To Finn's surprise—and slight disappointment—Kallias didn't rise to that bait. Instead, he calmly sawed off a piece of his fish and popped it in his mouth, chewing and swallowing before saying, "Only when it involves a meal."

"Oh, gull*shit*," said Finn. "Who's the one who took three years to stop getting seasick on his own boat?"

"Who fainted the first time he saw Papa gut a fish?" Jericho chipped in.

"Who got the spins after he gave himself a paper cut and had to lie down for an entire day?" Vaughn added.

Finn snorted. "I forgot about that one. And who—"

"Enough!" Kallias moaned, throwing down his silverware and putting his hands up in surrender. But even with annoyance twitching between his brows, it seemed he was an inch away from grinning. "Soleil, don't buy a word out of these liars."

Jericho and Vaughn made twin noises of protest. Finn shook his head, clucking his tongue. "He's in denial, see. It's so sad."

There was a noise—the softest snort, the slightest chuckle pitched just below a breath. Slowly, all of them turned to look at Soren.

"Did you just laugh?" asked Kallias.

Her mouth wrenched into a scowl, and she stabbed her fork into her fish like she wasn't convinced it was fully dead. "It was a sneeze."

"Sure, killer." Finn picked up a napkin between his first two fingertips and flicked it across the table at her. "It's nothing to be ashamed of, you know. I'm hilarious."

Soren caught the napkin, raising one eyebrow. "So you've mentioned."

Quick, this girl. Quicker than he'd thought a Nyxian could be. Even the sharpest of the spies her kingdom sent to try and infiltrate the palace were barely worth his attention; most were caught by guards well before they even got through the main foyer, and only one or two had gotten far enough to bother involving himself with. One had fallen on her own blade rather than face the famed Atlas dungeons. The other had been braver, or duller; he'd made it three days before he broke, begging Finn to put an end to him.

All without him ever laying a hand on the man.

"So," Kallias said, and Finn flinched internally. He knew that tone; his brother was about to say something he really shouldn't. "Soleil. Do you . . . do you remember how you ended up in Nyx? Do you remember being taken?"

It took real, concentrated effort not to roll his eyes. Oh, so *he* wasn't allowed to ask about Nyx, but First Prince Kallias could do whatever he wanted. Typical.

Predictably, Soren stiffened up again. "I wasn't *taken*."

Kallias's jaw clenched. "Well, we certainly didn't ship you off there ourselves, and I somehow doubt you wandered all the way there at nine years old."

"Hard to say. I do like walking."

Vaughn coughed out a chuckle, a rare grin flashing across his face. And right then, the doorknob twisted with a creak that cut through the room like a schooner through a wave.

Adrenaline flooded Finn with shocking speed, lighting his ribs up from the inside, bringing him to his feet at the same time as Kallias, who'd gone utterly pale. They met each other's gazes, both wide-eyed, both already resigned to what was about to happen.

Seamus guarded the door. And he was under very strict, very painful orders not to allow anyone in . . . except the two people no one in this room could outrank.

They turned as one to the door, Kallias straightening his shoulders and adjusting his jacket, raising his head like he was balancing a crown as King Ramses and Queen Adriata swept into the room, smiling and open-armed, not realizing yet that there was an extra head at this table.

This time, when Finn took a long swig of his wine, it wasn't fake.

This wasn't going to go well at all.

CHAPTER 16

SOREN

Damn every single one of these people straight to Infera. They'd told her King Ramses and Queen Adriata wouldn't be back for another two days at *least*. She could have been long gone by then; she'd planned to search for and steal the antidote after this weird display of sibling banter, slipping out while they were all tipsy and tired. She could've been halfway home before the King and Queen even showed up.

But now they were here. And they hadn't seen her yet.

She gripped her fork as she stood, the handle cold and comforting in her palm. It wasn't much, but at least it was something.

"I thought we'd find you all here." Queen Adriata was recognizable by her legendary hair, blood-red and hanging well past her waist. The heavy gold necklace around her neck was just as telltale: an amulet in the shape of a flaming sun, the crest of Atlas. She seemed younger than a queen of forty-six years should look. But then again, Soren thought she could remember Elias mentioning something about how the Atlas royal line had been blessed long ago by Anima herself, granted long life and beauty in exchange for some favor they'd done for her. It certainly seemed to be the case with this woman sweeping up to the table. "Why are you all so somber? Was Finn telling ghost stories again?"

As the Queen wrapped her arms around Finn and motioned for Kallias to lean across the table so she could give him a kiss on his head, hatred roiled in Soren, so hot and deep she thought she might catch fire. Finn's eyes flickered to her, and his arm came up in front of his mother—a protective stance.

This would've been a lot easier if he was dull like the others.

Her eyes found brown ones across the room, and they didn't belong to Finn. King Ramses had seen her sitting at the other end of the table.

Oh, gods.

Copper hair. An emerald clip. Tired, loving smiles.

He saw her, and she saw *him*. Not just now, but before; in an office, writing letters, treating for an alliance Nyx needed but didn't want.

He was older. Sadder. He had new creases under his eyes. Frown lines around his mouth.

And he hadn't been working for the sake of Nyx after all.

Horror curdled her blood, and suddenly she couldn't breathe. Her knees went weak, threatening to drop her back into her seat.

"Papa."

A whisper against the roaring disbelief in her head. The faintest wisp of memory that curled from her tongue like smoke, like a prayer whispered over a loved one's grave.

She'd refused to believe their lies, even her own memory, but she couldn't deny this. Not her father. Not the one person she truly remembered from her first life.

He stared at her, mouth half-open as if he'd been about to speak and the words had been stolen off his tongue. His eyes were wide behind his glasses—*those glasses, she knew those glasses*—and she'd seen less pain on the faces of dying men, in the eyes of soldiers relieved of their guts and counting their breaths until Mortem decided to grant them mercy. He looked at her like she'd looked at an Atlas blade that had found its way into her leg one unlucky day.

He made a noise like something broke deep inside him. His knees hit the floor.

"Papa!" Finn and Kallias cried out in tandem, rushing to his side, but he didn't move. Didn't blink. And neither did Soren.

They gazed at each other, frozen, fearful. Two bodies thought lost to fire, found alive.

Everything was falling apart. The plan, the deception, her own self-preserving denial . . . all of it.

Atlas blood. Atlas blood. Atlas blood.

"Ramses?" Adriata knelt by her husband, swiftly gripping his cheek and turning his face toward her, her voice frantic. "Ramses, what——?"

Then Adriata followed her husband's fixed, glassy eyes straight to Soren.

Not to her face, not to her hair, not to any of the places where all these people had looked first to prove her lineage. No, this woman looked to the mourning braid that brushed against her shoulder. The crescent moons tattooed on the middle finger of each hand. The fork she held like a dagger.

And though it s*houldn't* have surprised her when the Sun Queen lunged from the king's side and shoved her back against the wall, bashing the breath from her lungs, drawing an *actual* dagger from gods-knew-where and holding it tight against her throat . . . after the considerably less-violent welcomes from the rest of the Atlas royal family, it actually took her somewhat off guard.

"Who are you?" The question was sharper than the razor edge she slowly pushed further into Soren's neck. Blood welled, dribbling down her neck, staining that perfect blouse. "What are you doing in this palace?"

While her lungs tried desperately to pull in a breath, she tried to think of a lie, a truth, *anything* that wouldn't get her killed. She came up empty.

No. The word echoed, hollow and terrified, in her very core. *Not like this.* Not here, not this close to a victory, not this far from home.

It wasn't supposed to be like this, gods damn it. She should have died back in the valley—she should have let Elias's hands on her face and his voice in her ear be enough of a goodbye. This would be a far more impressive death, but gods, it wasn't the one she wanted. With the roar of the ocean in her ears and a king who looked too much like her father and an Atlas dagger poised to bite too deeply for her to come back from . . .

She didn't want to be a legend anymore, didn't want stories or songs. She wanted Elias.

Instead, she got Kallias, who shoved his way around the table and caught his mother's wrist. "Mama, stop! It's not what you think——"

"What I *think* is that Nyx did a brilliant job of crafting a decoy." Adriata lifted the dagger from Soren's throat only to shove the tip under her chin, tilting her head back, studying her with glittering green eyes, her face carved into a regal sneer. "And *you* fell for it. Is this why everyone in the halls is whispering about how my son retreated from a battle he was inches away from winning?"

Soren *felt* the disappointment in her voice, and it wasn't even directed at her. Kallias flinched like he'd been struck.

"Addie." The king's hand joined Kallias's, and the metal tip lowered from Soren's chin. A new bead of blood welled, but she didn't dare wipe it away. She only watched them, breath baited, hands splayed flat against the wall, one still pinning down the fork.

Jericho, Finn, and Vaughn were on their feet but hanging back, watching cautiously to see how this would end. Jericho's hands were stretched out just slightly, as if she was ready to try and stay that knife's path as well.

Ramses hadn't stopped looking at her yet, eyes wet behind his glasses. He reached out with his other hand, and Soren flinched back instinctively, hand tightening on her fork.

Fine. If this was her death, fine. She'd go to it fighting. The moment he laid a hand on her, the moment he decided to strike her death blow, she would—

Fingertips, calloused and ink-stained, brushed against her cheek. Soren stopped breathing as the King of Atlas touched her face, his lips parting in a shaky gasp, another shattered sound grating from his chest.

"Sunbeam," he whispered, "is that you?"

That name broke the spell that had settled over her, broke her composure, all of it. *That* name, she remembered.

She had no time to take that in. She could survive this . . . whatever this was. She just had to *think*.

The Queen was too enraged to listen, and none of Soren's claims would convince her, anyway. So what did a little sister do when she needed help?

She turned to her older siblings.

She looked at Kallias, letting the tears she'd been fighting well in her eyes, letting him see all the fear and none of the cunning. The stern angle of his jaw softened, and he moved to stand between her and his parents, arms spread out in supplication. The cutlery in her hand practically sang for his blood. His back was so close she could feel it rising and falling with every breath he took. "Mama, Papa, I can explain everything, but I need you to listen. Just . . . just come with me. Finn, Jer?"

The other siblings moved, Jericho immediately, Finn only briefly hesitating. They took up on either side of Soren, and to her surprise, Vaughn moved to flank his wife, throwing in his lot with them.

Adriata's face slackened in shock and fury, but Ramses squeezed her shoulders, murmuring something in her ear, finally tearing his gaze away from Soren's face. Something in her chest loosened without his scrutiny, and she started to feel the wobbling in her knees, the tightness in her chest, the burning in her eyes.

Atlas blood. Atlas blood. Atlas blood.

Enna had *lied* to her.

Only when Kallias ushered his parents from the room did she peel herself off the wall, her back tacky with sweat, her neck and chest sticky with blood. And, annoyingly, she was trembling from head to toe.

"I'm so sorry, Soleil," said Jericho, squeezing her shoulder, her horrified gaze locked on the door. "I never expected her to react like that."

"I did," said Finn as Vaughn begrudgingly deposited a couple coins into his palm. "I thought it would be worse than that, actually."

Soren glowered at him, resisting the urge to shield her neck as Jericho came close, a bud of green light held between her fingertips. "Hold still," she said, and it wasn't like Soren could protest. So she obeyed, and tried to stop shaking, hearing Elias's groan of *What am I going to do with you, smartass?* as she let Jericho run her fingers over the cut on her neck. A gentle static buzzed over the surface of her skin, the magic fizzing against the cut, pulling it shut unnaturally fast. The smell of flowers tickled the edges of Soren's senses for a moment before the sensations faded.

"There," said Jericho. "Perfect."

No. Not perfect. Nothing about this was *all right*, let alone *perfect*.

"What now?" Soren croaked.

It was Finn who answered, and she didn't like that smirk he was wearing when he drawled, "Well, I'm going to go eavesdrop while Kallias gets reamed out. Anyone want to join me?"

CHAPTER 17

KALLIAS

Thirty-five minutes. That was the record for how long Adriata Atlas could rant without pausing.

Finn was the one who'd set it, the day he'd lost his temper and told a particularly disrespectful emissary from Tallis exactly where he could shove his eagle-feather pen. Of course, Adriata had been holding back laughter the entire time she yelled, and Finn's only punishment had been banishment from any further meetings involving the Stone Kingdom, so perhaps that didn't entirely count.

Adriata wasn't laughing now. And they were coming up on minute thirty-three with no signs of her anger dissipating.

"Of all the foolish, impulsive things you could have done," Adriata fumed, pacing from one end of his office to the other. He was hiding—*sitting*—behind his polished desk, made of Arborian-imported wood. It was rumored that anything made of it was indestructible, and he'd never hoped more for that than now, because his mother looked ready to break something. Possibly his nose. Or his spirit. "We aren't the only family in the gods-damned world with red hair, Kallias! And even if we *were*, Nyx produces the finest cosmetic dyes on the continent, it would be so *easy*—"

"Why does everyone keep talking about the hair?" Kallias threw his hands up. For gods' sake, he was a soldier and a prince. He wasn't a fool, no matter how much they all liked to pretend. "You think a hair color is enough to make me see the dead? You *saw* her, Mama, you—Papa. Papa, I know you see it. Don't you?"

A thin thread of desperation wove through his words, a crack in the ice he'd forced over his voice to shield against his mother's flaming anger. She might question him, but his father had fallen to his knees at the sight of Soleil's face. Where Adriata saw only her Nyxian parts, Ramses saw what Kallias had: the dimple in her cheek, the sea-green shade of her eyes, the razor-sharp grin that was the honest side to Finn's lying, smirking coin. The tattoos, the braid, the faded freckles . . . none of that could turn her into a stranger. Not to Kallias.

Ramses worried his lip with his teeth, looking to his queen with furrowed brows. His feet were angled toward the door, as if he was about to run back to the dining room where his lost daughter had been left behind. "Addie. Listen to him, love—"

"No! No, no, no. I don't want to hear it." Adriata's voice wobbled for a moment before she steeled it, grinding away the weak spots like a blade on a whetstone. "Our daughter is dead, Ramses. *She's dead* and I cannot . . . I *will not* indulge him in this. Wishful thinking has no place in war."

Gods, didn't he know it. "I did my due diligence. I had Jericho test her blood and search her mind. She *is Soleil.* I can prove it to you, I will prove it ten times over if I have to!"

Adriata met his gaze, her trembling mouth pulled taut. "Then prove it."

He was afraid she would say that. "Fine. We'll perform a blood match again, if my word's not good enough. She's not going to be happy to give up more of her blood to us, though."

Ramses's eyes sharpened. "What do you mean, more?"

Kallias hesitated, scratching the back of his neck with one hand, tapping his pen on the lacquered surface of his desk with the other. "I . . . well, the way I found her . . . we were about to fall back and regroup, to give the final push, and she . . ."

You. It's been too long.

"She might have . . . attacked me?" Kallias ventured.

Adriata threw her hands up in plea to the gods, turning on her heel as if she couldn't even bear to look at him anymore. Even his father looked a little pained. "She *attacked you.*"

"Only a little."

"Kallias."

"Really, Papa. Jericho fixed me up in seconds."

"And what did you do?" asked his mother, still turned away, the bridge of her nose pinched between thumb and forefinger. "When she attacked you, what did you do?"

It was a bit of blur between the awful thrust of her blade sinking into his calf muscle and his own screaming. His shoulders went taut, and he sat straighter. "One of our soldiers came to my aid. I ordered them to stop, to capture her alive, but they didn't hear, they . . . they wounded her. Badly."

The noise she'd made, the way she'd fought to get up even as she bled . . . gods, he'd seen much worse in this war, but that was a sight he'd never forget.

Not as bad as the fire, though. Nothing would ever haunt him half as much as that night; nothing could be worse than remembering searching through burning rubble for his baby sister, screaming for her from a throat nearly closed up from breathing smoke, dodging flames and falling debris while the palace staff fled in the opposite direction from him.

And worst of all, he still remembered the look in his mother's eyes when he woke up outside with a concussion from a falling beam. The guards that had gone in after him had found him, had gotten him out, but not Soleil.

"I went back," he said, shaking off the memory. "I had the battlefield healers work on her just enough to live, so that I could question her to be sure. And I *am* sure."

Adriata stood still for a long moment, a gentle breeze the only moving thing among them as it uncoiled from the open window and tumbled around the room, fluttering papers and stirring wispy strands of her hair. He and his father exchanged glances, then looked back to her, waiting with drawn breath.

"Get Jericho," she said, much quieter than before, her fists clenched at her sides. With her head bowed, she looked less like a queen and more like a mother, and some of the strain eased from his shoulders. "We'll meet wherever you've been keeping her. I . . . I need to see this for myself."

Kallias bowed his head, even though she wasn't looking. "Yes, Majesty."

That finally softened her, and she turned to look at him, eyes losing some of their fire. "Kallias. Formality isn't necessary here."

His ears went hot. "Sorry, Mama. Habit, I guess."

Forty minutes. A new record. He made a mental note to update Jericho and Finn when he had a moment.

His mother came to him and leaned on his desk, her eyes searching his with their usual penetrating power, probing out any secrets he would have rather kept hidden. "It's not that I don't trust you. You know that. But this . . . this is . . ."

"Impossible," said his father. His eyes were fixed on the window, and Kallias was worried by the blank look in them. He'd been prone to bouts of absentmindedness since the fire, and they only got worse around Soleil's birthday. Now was potentially the worst time for the King to be lost in his own head.

"Papa," said Kallias, and Ramses slowly looked to him. "You're the first one she knew without our interference. She remembered you out of all of us. Maybe you can reach her where we can't."

A shaky breath, and Ramses ran his hand over his beard. "I can . . . I can certainly try. I would like to try. Do we know why her memories are damaged?"

"All we know is that it isn't magical in origin. Whether it was an injury from the fire or something Nyx did . . ." Kallias shrugged helplessly. "Jericho can only see so much."

"We'll cross that bridge when we get to it," Adriata said with the same stiff tone Kallias wore when he was trying not to let himself feel. "For now, let's make sure Nyx didn't just manage to get their first spy into our palace."

His throat went dry. "I'll get Jericho."

CHAPTER 18

SOREN

As it turned out, a blood match was considerably less magical and mysterious than Vaughn and Jericho made it sound. First, they took a drop of her blood and Vaughn's and mixed it together. Jericho hovered her hand over it, gentle green light budding at the tip of her finger and falling to mingle with the blood. The mixed droplets turned slate-gray.

"No blood in common," Vaughn explained.

"Thankfully," Jericho added, with a wink at her husband. Vaughn went pink in the cheeks before taking Soren's blood and Adriata's. That time, the drop of magic set the bloods flashing with bright white light.

A match.

Ramses started to weep. Adriata simply left the room. Soren didn't see her afterward and didn't know what to make of that, if the Queen was convinced or not. But that didn't matter—not when the rest of them believed it.

Barely a couple days passed before Ramses insisted on announcing her return to the kingdom. A celebration, he said, to welcome her home. Kallias disagreed, Finn and Jericho outvoted him, and now . . . now she was *sweating*.

Not just because of the gods-damned humidity, either. Honestly, where did they get off on calling this sticky, lukewarm-bathwater-weather *winter*? If the wind didn't gnaw on their faces with icicle-tipped fangs and chap their lips to flaking, they had no right calling anything winter.

She said as much to Jericho, who merely rolled her eyes with another sharp tug on Soren's hair. They'd been at this for *hours*, Jericho attempting to wrestle Soren's uncontrollable mane of snapdragon curls into some semblance of deliberate placement, and Soren was beginning to think Jericho took a sadistic pleasure in wrenching squeaks of pain from her. She'd had an easier time controlling herself when she was nearly ripped in half.

Enna never cared if her hair was wild. But then, Enna never cared to inform her she was from Atlas, either. So.

"You haven't changed a bit," Jericho said suddenly, her next tug a little gentler, meeting Soren's eyes in the gold-framed mirror. Atlas was widely known to have the most prosperous gold mines on the continent, and they weren't shy about showing it off in everything from walls and décor to clothes and cosmetics. "From when you were little, I mean. We practically had to tie you to the chair to get your hair fixed."

Soren forced herself not to squirm. "In my experience, all little girls are like that." Even prim, proper Yvonne had been a nightmare child when getting her hair done for some royal occasion, and Ember had once nearly shattered a maid's eardrum while getting a particularly terrible snarl combed out.

"I wasn't. I used to beg Mama to sit and do my hair for me. I loved it." Jericho absently twisted one of Soren's curls around her finger, her eyes drifting off to some distant place Soren couldn't follow. "I stopped asking after you . . . after the fire."

I don't care, Soren thought. But that wasn't the part she was playing, so she said, "What changed?"

"You were gone," Jericho said. "It was harder to get her to sit with us after that. She didn't have the energy to focus on anything but the war. Or . . . I don't know. Sometimes I think the grief was too much for her, so she shut herself away. And then Finn copied her, like he does with everything, and Kallias . . ."

The comb rustled gently against Soren's hair as Jericho's hand dipped, one corner of her mouth tugging downward, her eyes glimmering with the thin sheen of tears.

"It wasn't just you we lost," said Jericho. "We lost ourselves, too. And it took a very long time to find our way back to each other."

"I'm sorry," Soren whispered, even though she wasn't. "That you all suffered that way." *I hope your tears will keep the flames at bay when you're all rotting in Infera.*

A quiet scoff, and Jericho lifted the comb again, coming back to herself in one quick motion. "It wasn't your fault you were *kidnapped,* Soso."

Soren wrinkled her nose. "Soso?"

Jericho lifted one shoulder in a shrug, smiling at her in the mirror. Soren felt an uncomfortable yank on her gut when she got her first glimpse of their faces next to each other.

Finn was right. Jericho's cheekbones were more pronounced, her jaw less square, and her eyes were a much paler green, but they had the same nose. The same slight divots in their chins. The same fake smile.

"I like nicknames," said Jericho. "Soleil became Soso, or Leia if you were being grumpy. Kallias has always been Gills, we haven't been able to keep him out of the ocean since he learned to swim."

"And Finn?"

Jericho grinned in earnest then. "Nicky. But only when he's being a brat. He *hates* it."

"Hey, Elias the Pious! Going to read us a story from your little book before bed?"

"Sure. Maybe the one about what happens to heretics when they die?"

"Does it have something to do with chains? Cause I could be into that."

"You're insufferable."

"You're boring."

"Those are the best kind," Soren said, meaning for it to come out much more teasing than it did. Missing robbed her voice of its strength, an ache throbbing in her throat.

If someone had told her back then that Elias would become the person she leaned on more than any other, she would have laughed in their face. He'd been so . . . *proper,* so stiff and quiet and polite. He folded his napkin in his lap before every meal. He said a blessing over his food. He pressed the wrinkles out of his uniform every morning.

And gods, had he despised her.

The faintest smirk tugged at her mouth. She'd earned that disdain, no doubt about that. Their spats had annoyed the others so much that one night, during one of many sparring matches thrown in the barracks by older recruits to work the nervous energy out of the newcomers, the two of them had been pushed into the circle and forced to settle their feud with fists and feet.

Jericho rapped her head lightly with the comb, distracting her from the memory of sweat-soaked clothes and broken noses and the way her heart stuttered the first time she saw Elias grin at her with blood on his teeth, the first glimpse of the wolf beneath the worshipper. "You sound like you know from experience."

Soren shrugged, grimacing at the odd feeling of pale orange tulle brushing against her shoulders. She wasn't used to wearing such light fabrics. A garment like this would have left her frostbitten back home. "I'm a soldier. Doling out embarrassing nicknames is a competition in the barracks."

"Is it a competition you won?"

"Once or twice."

Jericho made a soft humming noise in the back of her throat, then held her silence for a time, the swish of comb against hair the only thing to break it. Then, at last: "I'm sorry."

Soren tensed, hands bracing against her chair. "For what?"

Jericho wouldn't meet her eyes, gaze fixed steadily on Soren's hair. "That we didn't find you sooner. You were right there, all this time, and we didn't . . . I'm . . . I'm just sorry."

Soren found she didn't have an answer for that.

"Anyway," Jericho continued, suddenly brusque, setting aside the comb, "We have some things to discuss, you and I."

"Like what?"

"Well, you've been away for a long while, and with your memory out of sorts . . . now that you're being introduced to the people, I don't think it's fair to throw you to the sharks with no lifeboat. It might not help much, but I can give you a refresher on Atlas customs. I assume you don't know much?"

"You assume correctly." That wasn't entirely true, but what she knew was mostly useful for fighting Atlas, not winning them over. She hadn't exactly cared to make any Atlas *like* her before she drove her blade through their chest. "What's your plan, then? What lies do you want me to tell them to make them love me?"

To her surprise, Jericho grinned ruefully. "Quite frankly, I like you just like this, even if they wouldn't. Some . . . *tweaking* . . . is necessary. But take it from an Heir, lies won't fly with the general populace. Royals don't lie, we just . . . selectively tell the truth."

"You ever heard of lying by omission?" Because she'd mastered it long ago.

"We'll tell them what happened," said Jericho, as if she hadn't said a word. "That Nyx stole you and kept you as theirs for ten years. But maybe don't mention the, ah . . . bloody bits."

"Like the part where I stabbed the prince."

"Yeah, it seems best to leave that part out."

All right, then. If earning the trust of this family and these people was the way to get the antidote, and if she could potentially gain war-ending information on the way, she wasn't about to refuse free assistance.

For her sisters, for her friends, for Elias, she could bide her time. She could smile and simper and pretend to be grateful, pretend to be rescued. She could play the game of lost princess. Especially if that game included dresses with strategically sheer fabric that would've made Elias choke. And when it was over, she'd hear the truth about her lost memories and what Atlas was to her from Enna's mouth instead.

"All right, Princess," she said, meeting Jericho's gaze in the mirror and banishing every thought of how they looked alike. "What do I have to do?"

CHAPTER 19

SOREN

The celebration of Soleil's return was opulent and crowded and terrible, and Soren's delight over her dress quickly wore thinner than the tulle encasing her body. Not to mention the crown was making her head itch.

The Atlas dining hall was huge, the back wall made entirely of glass so the ocean could always be in view. The rich light of sunset bathed the room in shades of orange, pink, and gold, complementing the finery of the gold plates and utensils and decorations. Chandeliers dripped diamond tears, fragmented light spinning in dazzling circles across the dozens of tables set around the room. There was a space left open in the center for dancing or speeches or for larger groups to gather and gossip.

And gossip they did. Hundreds of eyes watched her on all sides, distrustful and worshipful all at once, belonging to palacefolk and friends of the royal family and high-ranking members of their council. Some were claiming she must be divinely blessed to have survived the *cruelty* of Nyx for so long. Others, smarter, said nothing. They merely watched her—waiting, maybe, for her to attack.

She smiled pleasantly at everyone who dared meet her eyes, and carefully marked which ones she'd need to kill first if it came to that.

Jericho and Vaughn hadn't bothered taking their seats at the royal table; Vaughn had already stolen a place with the palace workers, and Jericho sashayed straight after him. Though Vaughn's ashen pallor was the complete opposite of the gold-and-scarlet Heir, when she perched on his lap, delicately picking cherries off his plate, he beamed so brightly Soren was surprised it didn't blind her. He wrapped his arm around his wife, not bothering to look away from his conversation with the man across their table while Jericho kissed his temple and stole more of his food. The actions of two people entirely attuned to one another.

That new, painful divot in Soren's chest deepened, and she tried not to think of a different man while she turned her attention to her own plate.

Finn sighed heavily from his place at Soren's right, sprawled across his chair, arm slung over the back, the picture of irreverence and boredom. "I hate parties," he announced to no one in particular, though he glowered toward Soren as if it was all her fault he was being subjected to this pomp. Which it sort of was.

"Sit up, Finn," Kallias said tiredly from his seat across from Soren, his nose buried in a stack of what appeared to be military reports. "You'll twist your spine like that."

"It's already bent wrong from all that reading he does," Ramses pointed out from the foot of the table, flashing his wife a hopeful smile at the head. She didn't so much as look up from her plate.

Finn pointed at his father, his eyes going to Kallias. "See? He knows. I'm already beyond hope. Let me live my crooked life."

Kallias buried himself deeper in the reports, one eye twitching. "Your choice if you want to be hunched over before you're thirty."

Finn tossed a grape at his brother—what was it with him and throwing fruit?—ignoring the snarl Kallias threw his way. "What's wrong with you? You're grumpier than a stingray with its tail stuck."

"He's just on edge because Seamus is waiting on him to sort out the scouting reports," Adriata said placatingly.

"He should be! Seamus is going to kick your ass," Finn said to Kallias, finally sitting up straight and picking at a fuzz on that ragged brown sweater he seemed overly fond of, the gold wrist-cuffs and sash Kallias had forced on him shimmering in the light. "You were supposed to have those done last night."

Kallias gave an aggressive gesture at the papers in his hand, still scowling. "Why do you think I'm doing them now? You think I *like* bringing work to dinner?"

Their bickering faded to a low buzz as Soren's blood ran cold.

Scouting. That meant they were searching out new weak spots, new battlegrounds to claim from Nyx. They were getting ready to attack again.

The thought made her stomach twinge and twist, the memory of being ripped open seizing her mind and body with clawed hands, digging in *hard*. She tasted death-tack on her tongue. Cold sweat broke out on her forehead. Her lungs seized up.

Finn's hand closed tightly around her wrist before she could stand. He glanced at her, reading her face, her heaving chest, her white-knuckled grip on her chair. He stood up, making a show of stretching, his spine indeed popping with the movement. "Soleil, care to accompany me for a quick walk?"

Soren's immediate instinct was to say *go rot, Atlas bastard* or *I'd rather throw myself into the boiling lakes of Infera*, but another wave of dizziness crashed over her whole body, and she found herself nodding. She left with Finn out a back door, both of them ignoring Kallias's hisses of protest.

This hallway was windowless, dark, and blessedly cool; no one had bothered to light more than a couple lamps. Shadows flickered and whimpered across the wall, ghosts of darkness writhing against the rich purple paint.

"You looked like you were about to vomit all over our pretty floor. Again," Finn said as they walked; walked, not ran, because running gave the impression there was something to run from, and she'd never calm down if she gave her adrenaline that kind of encouragement.

"I'd like to see how strong your stomach is while listening to someone talk about fighting the kingdom you were raised in, Prince," Soren retorted, gathering the excess tulle of her skirt in her hands to prevent tripping. It was hardly the first time she'd worn a fine dress, but Nyxian fashions weren't so damned *long*.

Some of the eternal amusement in Finn's eyes dimmed at that, but before he could speak, one of the shadows in the hallway moved.

Soren was already in a fighting stance when the shadow flicked a small, wickedly sharp piece of steel against Finn's neck.

"Is she dead?" demanded a masculine voice, deep and coarse, ragged with rage, Nyxian accent heavy.

And even in the clothes of an Atlas servant, Soren knew him.

She knew his voice, knew the angle at which he held his knife, knew he held it with the wrong fingers because he was missing one on his dominant hand. She knew his fury, knew his gleaming black eyes, knew the gravel-rough rasp that rubbed his voice raw.

"Is she dead?" Elias snarled again, the blade just barely drawing blood from Finn's neck. "Is she *dead*, you Mortem-cursed bastard?"

Soren's heart cracked at what only she could hear in his voice, the fear and the grief.

Elias—her Elias had come for her.

Finn clearly didn't understand the peril he was in, because when he spoke, it was only with indignance, no fear at all. "I don't think I appreciate your tone."

She should have let Elias rip his throat open. But instead . . . maybe it was the kindness he'd shown in saving her from that room, maybe it was a rare glimmer of mercy, but Soren quickly said, "You just can't help being a dramatic bastard, can you?"

Elias's eyes flicked up as fast as his knife had, and she waited for the shock, the anger, the betrayal as he took in her Atlas finery.

None of it came. Instead, his face crumpled.

"*Soren.*" Her name was somehow both a laugh and a sob on his lips, and he shoved Finn away with a sharp blow to the temple, tugging her into his arms, clutching her against him in a bone-cracking grip. Or maybe that was just Finn's head connecting with the floor.

Trading one Atlas for another.

Something very, very cold dropped into Soren's stomach, splashing her insides with unease. She hadn't stopped to consider what Elias would think, what he would say when he learned of her Atlas blood.

Gods, no. What was she thinking? This was *Elias*. He wouldn't turn his back on her for something as petty as ancestry.

"Are you hurt?" He felt her arms, her sides, the place where the new scar stretched her skin thin. He scanned her with disbelieving eyes that knew she had one foot in Infera the last time he saw her. "What happened? Have they done anything to you? Soren, I swear to Mortem, if they've—"

"No one's hurt me," Soren lied, emotion threatening to choke out her voice at the sound of her name on his lips. She hadn't realized how much she'd missed it—missed *him*. "I'm fine, but what in the pits are you doing here? Did Enna send you? *Alone?*"

The gleam in his eyes darkened, his hands tightening on her shoulders. "No. She wouldn't approve a mission. She said it was too dangerous."

"And she was *right*, you absolute dumbass—"

"But I had to know." The catch in his voice tugged at her heart. "Gods, Soren, I . . . when I got back and you were just *gone* . . ."

It was then that the absolute insanity of the whole thing struck her. Elias was *here*, in Atlas's *palace*, where not a single spy had managed to get a foothold in the entire decade they'd been at war. "How did you get in here?"

Elias grimaced. "That is a story I don't have time to tell."

She'd never met anyone so good at making her want to hug and slap him at the same time. "Elias, I cannot stress enough how much you *cannot* be here right now."

Confusion and worry tugged his brows together. "I mean . . . I am, though. See?" He poked her shoulder, as if to prove he was corporeal. "You're not imagining me. Did they drug you? I didn't think Atlas had access to hallucinogens but—"

She smacked away his hand. "No, you jackass, and stop being such a fussbudget. I'm *fine*. I don't mean you *can't* be here, I mean *you* can't be here!"

"Not really clearing anything up for me, smartass." But even as he said it like she was driving him crazy, a grin was creeping across his face, joy that bordered on delirium.

"What are you smiling about?"

"I missed you."

The words wrung her heart out like a damp towel. "Elias, there's something you need to know."

"I know. I have things to tell you, too. We can talk on the way, but we need to get out of here. I'll take care of this one—"

"No, see, that's kind of part of the problem—"

"I knocked out the guards at the front of the hall—posed as a servant, served them some drugged tea, they were none the wiser," he said, tugging at his Atlas-blue tunic in demonstration. "They'll just think they dozed off. We can get out of here before they find the body—"

"I'm Soleil!"

Oh, that was a mistake. She knew it the moment the words left her mouth.

That foolish grin on his face wiped away in an instant, and for once, she couldn't read him. Couldn't tell exactly what he was thinking from a flicker of his jaw or a twitch of his nose. She'd seen him furious, seen him grieving, seen him happy and sick and drunk and affectionate and sad and silly. She'd thought she'd seen everything Elias Loch could be.

She'd never seen *this* look on his face before.

Carefully, like she might bolt at any sudden movement, he shifted forward, his boots making no sound on the marble floor. Slowly, so slowly, his hands slid over her cheeks.

"They *think* I'm Soleil," she amended, but he was already shaking his head.

"Soren," he said, *so gods-damned slowly,* "did you let them use magic on you?"

Her cheeks burned. "No."

"*Soren Andromeda Nyx, did you let them use magic on you.*"

"Oh, are we really going to play that game, *Elias Tiberius Loch*—"

"Soren!" he snapped, giving her a quick shake. "This isn't a joke, okay? Answer the question!"

It took all her strength not to sigh. Maybe her fish breath would shake him back to sense. "Maybe! Yes. Only a little."

He swore, a filthy curse that would've impressed her if he hadn't looked so angry—so terrified. "Did you let them into your *head?*"

"Only once! Just for a second, and it wasn't . . . it didn't . . ."

How could she explain that she'd *clung* to that same desperate notion, hoping that Jericho somehow altered her memory to fit their narrative? How could she explain that she'd lain awake these past couple nights chasing theory after theory, failing to see a motive, failing to see where claiming a Nyxian as Atlas made any gods-damned sense? All they could possibly hope to gain from her was intimate knowledge about Nyx, but Kallias wouldn't have known she was one of Enna's adopted daughters on the battlefield. She hadn't worn anything with the royal seal, and no one used her title out there either. And even if they *had* known, why take the risk of bringing an enemy into the palace when Nyx was already losing?

And besides, it wasn't *that* memory that had truly made her wonder. Made her doubt.

"It wasn't like that," she said simply. "Elias, gods, stop looking at me like I'm broken. It's *me*. You think I'd fall for some silly magic trick? I know better than that. *You* taught me better than that. It had nothing to do with what they showed me. It's King Ramses. I recognize him. He . . . gods, Elias, he has my father's face."

Elias took in a harsh breath, his eyes widening. He knew the implications of that, knew she sometimes woke up crying for a father she'd lost long ago. But he shook his head again. "Soren, their princess is *dead*."

"Well, apparently, Mortem doesn't feel like keeping me," she joked weakly, gesturing to her stomach. "Maybe if you'd bothered to say those prayers . . ."

He didn't laugh. He merely held her, studied her, searching for any crack, any flicker of *wrong* that would reveal her to be magicked. She *hated* it.

"Come on, jackass," she croaked. "If they'd done something to make me theirs, I wouldn't be standing here talking to you. I'd be screaming for help, or . . . or attacking you or something. Right?" Mind magics weren't exactly something she was familiar with, but she'd heard some truly terrifying stories over war campfires and Jakob's half-edible stew. Enough that she understood why Elias was staring at her like *she* was the one who might not be real.

Finally, he blew out a slow breath and let her go. "I know you would be. I just . . . gods. Don't scare me like that."

She wrinkled her nose. "Not like I forced you to overreact."

"Oh, you haven't gotten anywhere close to seeing me *overreact*." He ran his hands down his face; he hadn't shaved lately, she noted, not exactly *displeased* by the development. His gaze drifted to where Finn was slumped, drooling onto the floor. "And that's . . .?"

"The Second Prince. Finnick."

Elias took a deep breath, the kind that said she was fraying his last nerve. "Right. Great. So what exactly are you suggesting we do?"

She hesitated. "Don't shout at me."

His face dropped. "I hate when you lead with that."

"It's just . . . look, I spoke to them, and I was thinking, even if it's not true, as long as they think I'm their sister or daughter or whatever the case may be—"

"Spit it out, smartass."

Her eyes flickered to his injured arm.

He blinked. Once. Twice. "No," he said. Then, considerably *shoutier*: "Absolutely not! Soren, this is how we ended up in this Mortem-cursed palace in the first place! Forget it!"

She groaned. "See, yelling! And after I specifically asked you not to!"

"Yelling is perfectly appropriate in this situation!"

A pout tugged on her bottom lip. "Yeah, well, it's not very *nice*."

Elias paced away from her, raking his fingers through his hair, his broad shoulders tenser than a tightrope as he leaned his forehead against the wall, hiding his face from her. The eerie half-light from the sparse torches fluttered over him, rendering him into another shadow, another phantom that could fade with a quick blow of breath.

For all her bravado, that distance was too much. Every step he took away from her sent a new wave of terror crashing through her body, like this might be a dream she was moments away from waking up from.

So she crossed that space between them. Settled her hand between his shoulder blades. "We won't ever get this chance again. The antidote is in this palace somewhere."

"I cannot let you take that risk for me." His voice rasped like a blade being drawn from its sheath, but she shushed him with a flick to the back of his head.

"Oh, I'm sorry, who's currently standing in the middle of an enemy kingdom on a solo rescue mission with only a sewing needle and a stolen uniform to his name, hm? How is it fair that you can be an idiot for me, and I can't be an idiot back?"

"You started it," he mumbled, but even in the darkness, she saw the corner of his mouth lift. The faintest smile.

Their fights never lasted long anymore, and this was exactly why. Elias Loch, at his core, was not a fighter. He was composed of all things soft and gentle and good, and though there was a wolf living under his skin, it wasn't a wolf she found difficult to tame.

Which was a very fancy way of saying her best friend was a complete pushover.

So she pushed, leaning her forehead against his injured shoulder, hating that the skin felt feverish beneath. She could've sworn she smelled rot and ruin buried in his blood. "You came all this way alone. Why?"

"You know why," he said. "Together or not at all."

The last words of the battlemate vow echoed in this quiet hall, words that she guessed had never been spoken on Atlas soil.

Where you walk, I will follow. When Mortem takes us, she takes us. Together or not at all.

"You kept your vows," she said into his borrowed shirt. "Now let me keep mine."

His shoulders rose and fell in a long, unsteady breath. He was quiet for a heartbeat. Two. Three. Then, turning to face her, he said, "Tell me you have a plan."

"Better. I have two. I convince them that I believe I'm Soleil, whether that's true or not . . . stop that, you're going to get wrinkles," she added, reaching up and pulling his furrowed brows apart with her fingertips. "Once they get used to me, I'll get them to tell me where exactly the antidote is. Or, if that fails, I go back to the first plan."

"And what was the first plan?"

She hesitated. "Kidnap one of them, drag them back to Nyx, and ransom the antidote with their life."

Elias gave her a *look*. "So are you going with the suicidal plan or the one that's going to get you killed?"

She sighed. "Elias."

"Don't *Elias* me. Those aren't plans, those are barely ideas! There's no way you can pull that off alone!"

She gave a dramatic gesture his way. "But I'm not alone, am I?"

He snorted. "Right. And what do you expect me to do?"

A door creaked down the hall. A loud burst of music and laughter and chatter flooded out before it shut again; then, footsteps. Coming closer to where two disguised Nyxians were standing suspiciously close to an unconscious Atlas prince.

Soren met Elias's wide-eyed gaze—and grinned. "Follow my lead."

In a flash, she gripped Elias's wrists and tugged his arms around her waist, forcing him to hold her arms tight against her chest, like he'd pinned her. And at the top of her lungs, she shrieked, "Get *off me*! Let me *go!*"

Elias swore under his breath, but he shifted to hold her tight, his heart hammering against her back like a battering ram. His breath stirred her hair as he hissed, "What in Mortem's name are you doing?"

"You might want to get used to using Anima's name instead."

"Why?"

"Just play along. You're an Atlas servant who's always dreamed of being a guard."

"I'm *really* not—"

"*Let go of me, you Atlas bastard!*" She jerked her elbow into his gut, and past his wheeze of pain, she heard Kallias shout and start running.

"What in the *depths* happened here?" Cold hands tugged her out of Elias's arms, Kallias pinning her down much less comfortably as she struggled and spat. He tightened his grip, looking to Elias, his breath huffing in her ear. "You! What happened?"

Elias blinked, a rabbit staring down a wildcat. "Uh. Um."

"I was almost out!" Soren snarled at him, hate scalding every word; but where Kallias couldn't see, she shot Elias a look, mouthing, *Play along, jackass!*

Elias pinched his lips together, an expression she recognized as him silently calling her names in his head. Then he cleared his throat and snapped to attention, head bowed. "She was trying to escape, sir. I saw her attack the Second Prince."

Hmm. His Atlas accent wasn't half-bad; he'd been practicing.

First Prince Kallias, she mouthed to him, rolling her eyes back to where she thought Kallias's head was. Elias blinked twice to signal he understood.

Kallias's fingers tightened like a vise around her arms. "And who are you?"

"Elia—er, Eli," he said like an idiot, his eyes flickering back and forth, like he was searching the hallway for something. "Eli . . . Door . . ."

He did *not* just say his last name was *Door*. She made another snarl-y noise, a warning buried in it this time, and he quickly amended, "Dorian. Eli Dorian."

"Dorian." Something pulled taut in Kallias's voice, a string out of tune, pinching Soren's airway shut. If she'd played this wrong, if he shouted for help . . . "I don't believe we've had the pleasure."

Please, please, she prayed to any gods that might be listening, hoping desperately that at least one of them loved Elias as much as he loved them. *Let this work.*

Elias's head rose, and his stance shifted; not so frightened, but still respectful. "I'm new, Highness. I was seeking a place in the guard, but I was hired on as a page instead."

She couldn't breathe. There was no air left for her in this darkness-doused hall, caught between her second battlemate and the man who murdered her first. How fast could she move if Kallias tried to shout for help? He was armed, she could feel the hidden hilt tucked beneath his long military jacket, and what did she have? Nails she'd pared down to the quick with her teeth and a particularly solid grasp on how to kick someone in the groin? If she hadn't let him grab her, maybe she could have disarmed him, but it was too late to be thinking of new ideas.

Either he'd buy it, or he wouldn't. Either she and Elias would live, or they wouldn't.

Kallias was quiet for so long that her pulse began to roar in her ears, beating louder than anything had a right to.

"Well," he said, his voice easing into something almost impressed, "it seems to me I need to have a word with whoever made that decision, because they obviously made a mistake. Eli, you said?"

Elias saluted with a fist over his chest—an Atlas salute, not a Nyxian one. "Yes, Highness."

"Find a place in the garrison to sleep, Eli. I'll handle this from here. And expect a summons from me in a day or two to discuss your placement."

Elias bowed with another mumbled "Yes, Highness." But when he straightened, his eyes lingered on Soren, jaw clenched so tightly it spasmed.

She gave him a quick, careful wink. *Trust me, jackass.*

He shook his head, infinitesimally, so slightly it might have been a twitch. *Only you, smartass.*

When he left, air flooded back into the hallway, into Soren's lungs. She tried not to let her chest heave as she dragged in a breath, dizziness and relief whirling in her head like snow borne on an indecisive wind.

Elias was here. Elias was *here.* And as awful as that was, as awful as *she* was for being happy, it felt like a weight lifted from her shoulders.

She wasn't alone anymore.

A cleared throat behind her dimmed her euphoria. "What exactly possessed you to pull this stunt?" Kallias snapped, releasing her after making sure she held no weapons. He blocked her way to the door Elias had left through; she could only stay put, or run back to the dining hall. Either way, she was caught.

She gazed at the prince, taking in his frown, his eyes darker than storm clouds. For the first time since the battlefield, she caught a glimpse of the warrior wrapped in the politician's skin.

Which weakness did she pick at? Which one would buy her safety?

She sniffled. Hard. Stopped blinking until the air burned her eyes, until tears welled, a dam threatening to burst.

It had worked before. Hopefully it would work again.

His face dropped. "Soleil?"

"It was too much," she choked—not a lie, really, and maybe that was why it came out with a crack that nearly sounded real. She let her chin quiver, let the shrieking cataclysm of emotions that had been building up explode with a force that sent tears streaming down her cheeks. "All of that, in there . . . I don't know those people, any of them, and they're all *looking* at me, and you were talking about attacking Nyx, and it . . . I just wanted to run. I'm sorry. I'm so sorry. Oh gods, did I hurt Finn?"

Mortem *must* have been smiling on her—maybe Elias was chanting his own prayers from the other side of the door—because her acting was atrocious, but somehow, it worked. Kallias softened faster than a snowbank in the sun, storm clouds breaking to reveal tears lining his own eyes. "Gods, Soleil, I'm sorry. I told them not to do this yet. I told them it was too soon. Let's just get you back to your room, and—"

"Oh, sure, don't worry about Finn," came a groggy moan from the sweater-clad lump a few feet away. "He just got his *skull* dented. No big deal, I'm sure."

Damn it. She had to screw her lips up to hold her curses in. She'd hoped Elias had dealt him a more damaging blow than that.

Kallias rushed to Finn's side, cradling his brother's head between his hands, angling it to try and illuminate the wound. "Damn, she got you good."

Despite Finn's dazed expression, his eyes narrowed. "She?"

Oh, pits. She hadn't thought of that.

"I knocked you out," she supplied quickly. "I . . . panicked. Sorry."

Soren had been looked at like she was a fool before; had *earned* that look plenty of times. But this one topped them all, Finn's disparaging scowl screaming *gullshit* louder than his voice ever could.

She bit her tongue, stirring more tears to her eyes. "Really, I am," she said, pretending his doubt was for her apology. Maybe if she really stuck to it, he'd give it up.

His scowl relaxed, but she didn't like his tone when he said, "If you say so."

Oh, she was really in trouble now.

CHAPTER 20

FINN

Well.

Now things were getting interesting.

Everything from yesterday was just a bit fuzzy around the edges, but alas, his perfect mind hadn't failed him yet. And he knew very well that Soren was not the one to knock him unconscious in that hall. The snarling voice in his ear had definitely been male, and Nyxian, and *mean*.

So. That left them here: him with a headache from the deepest pits of Infera even after Jericho healed him, Soren playing like she was trying to remember the girl she used to be, and an extra head in the garrison.

He could have stopped it all right now—*should* have. A prince would have. A lazy man would have. And those two so rarely agreed on anything that when they did, it was usually a no-brainer. But a third man, the cunning man, the *bored* man, was in charge today. And that man wanted to see how far this fool's gold girl could go before she forced his hand.

But first, he needed a break. He couldn't stand the brokenhearted joy on his father's face every time he beheld Soren, the eagerness with which Jericho welcomed her in, the hope that Kallias wore on his sleeves and his eyes and just about everywhere else. Not today.

So as dusk fell, he slipped through the kitchens, flipping a coin to the chef on duty before leaving out the back door.

He loved Port Atlas, inasmuch as one had to love the place they called home. But he loved it most for its nights—for its chirping crickets and salt-heavy damp, for the empty echo of his sandals against the cobblestone paths, for the lanterns glowing cheerily from strings wound between buildings like beacons welcoming him home. For the fireflies and the laughter that floated from taverns that never closed. For the moonlight dancing on the ocean and the giggling adolescents out past their curfews. For the clink of coins changing hands in alleyway card games and the tipsy laughter of friends stumbling home together, arms linked so they wouldn't lose each other.

He watched a group of three staggering past, taking no notice of his hooded visage, smelling of wine and lost money and counted cards. Music floated after them, a lively fiddle-and-voice duet that tickled the soles of his feet with a wild, absurd urge to dance.

Kallias would like it out here; that kind of wishing-well thinking had always appealed to him. They could rule these nights together, if he ever stopped being so gods-damned obsessed with his image and their mother's approval. If he ever came to terms with the fact that she hadn't bothered to care about any of them for a very long time in any way that mattered, and if he wanted a crown so badly, he was better off building one from the bones of the city they reigned over.

Finn had already learned that lesson long ago, the first night he'd finally broken, unable to bear the silence from the room beside his another moment. The first night he'd wandered into the city, twelve years old and entirely trusting of the home he'd never roamed without an escort.

That first night had bruised him, scarred him . . . and transformed him. When he finally made it safely back to his bed, he'd closed his eyes and dreamed about a different kind of king, one who ruled cloaked in silhouettes and masks, who could achieve his own ends without the scrutiny of councils and advisors and allies.

From then on, Finnick Atlas ruled his kingdom from abandoned alleys and seedy tavern tables. He forged himself a crown of shadows and secrets, and gods, did he look good wearing it.

But the boy who'd started down that path would've given it all up to have his little sister back. To have his parents, his *family*, whole and laughing and alive.

But here they were. His father was still broken-hearted. His little sister was still as good as dead. And all that was left of his mischievous, vibrant mother was a war-wager, a conqueress . . . a woman who forbade her children to wander anywhere without an escort for fear of losing them, but didn't even bother to talk to them unless necessary.

A child's loneliness tugged at a corner of his heart. The man shoved it away.

He wasn't out here to miss his mother. He was out here to gamble away an exorbitant amount of money in exchange for the secrets falling from drink-loosened tongues. He was here to learn where his kingdom stood on the news of their lost princess returned.

Sure, it was Kallias's job, technically. But Kal would never get the answers he needed. People told a prince what he wanted to hear; they told the bottom of their mead tankard what they were really thinking. And as little as Finn cared for the stranger posing as his sister, he didn't want her fate in anyone's hands but his.

The sound of his sandals was too loud, too obvious; he couldn't move the way he needed to with them on. So he kicked them off, the cobblestones beneath his toes still warm from the sun. Winter, it seemed, was having second thoughts about closing its grip around Atlas just yet. Even with the sun gone, his favorite sweater was almost too thick, sweat gathering in the small of his back and along the bridge of his nose, beneath the nosepiece of his spectacles. Plucking them off, he leaned against the wall of a barred-up antiques shop, cleaning them against his pants and putting them back on, heaving a sigh.

"Where am I even going?" he mumbled, scratching a phantom itch behind his ear.

The scent of pipesmoke and alcohol hit him with the force of a battering ram, the viscous, gritty smells jamming pain through his still-sensitive skull. He wrinkled his nose, digging the heels of his hands into his temples, trying to rub the pain out of his head.

Black curls and lavender soap and lightning-strike looks. "Working late, Prince?"

The images flickered through his mind like shuffled cards, barely there before they vanished. And when he opened his eyes, Luisa stood before him, the smells of a tavern trailing on her heels, her lips pursed in amusement. "Working late, Prince?"

A shiver pinched the base of his spine, and déjà vu spread discomfort through his gut. But he simply smirked back, shrugging off those sensations like he normally shrugged off the weight of his title. "It's hardly *late*. The sun's barely set."

"I suppose." She settled against the wall beside him. "You missed your appointment last week."

"I've been busy. You may have heard the news."

She stiffened. "Ah, yes. The princess. She's still here? I saw her trying to run."

Of course she had. She was the best seer in the city, the most accurate, the most consistent. It was why she was the only one he would hire.

"Seems she hasn't found what she's looking for yet." Apparently she was telling the truth about needing an antidote to their Viper venom for her *friend*, if she was desperate enough to stay even after someone came to get her out. Thank the gods all their Vipers were strewn across the border cities to help hold the line; if any of them had been in the palace, this game would have been over already, long before Finn had what he needed.

Luisa pursed her lips. "Are you going to tell her?"

He played dumb, chewing the corner of his thumbnail. "Tell her what?"

"That there is no cure." Her eyes narrowed. "Here, or anywhere else."

He cocked one knee up, resting the sole of his bare foot against the wall, projecting his best casual air. "You can see the future. You tell me."

She gave him a look that could've fried shrimp. "Finn."

"*Fine.* We talked about it, but Kal and Jer are buying her little act. They don't think she'll even want one now that she knows Nyx kidnapped her."

"And what do you think?"

"I think she's not going to give up that easily. Not if she's still here. And . . ." Honesty, a rare and strange taste on his tongue, welled up just enough for him to admit, "I don't know what kind of havoc she'll wreak if we *do* tell her. They as good as killed her, Lu. She's Nyxian at her heart. I don't think anything's left of . . . of who she was."

Luisa's eyes darkened. "A shame."

He glanced at her, sliding his gaze up and down, looking for a hint of an answer before he even asked. "Did you know?"

She blew out a wine-soaked breath, regarding him with a tipsy tilt of her head. "You'll have to be more specific, love."

"Did you know she was alive?"

Her silence tickled an old, rarely seen monster in Finn's stomach: a simmering, black-edged anger that he did his best to bury. Anger didn't lend itself well to cunning; it was too impatient to play a long game.

"Why didn't you tell me?" he rasped.

She shrugged delicately. "You never asked."

He hated that it was an answer he couldn't fault her for, because it was exactly what he would have said. "A hint wouldn't have been out of place!"

She knocked her head back against the wall, tipping her face toward the stars, pulling her silken sleeves up to her elbows and tucking her arms over her chest. "You have to ask yourself one question, Finn." Her eyes speared into him without warning—a fizz of pink light playing in her irises before it faded, so quickly he might have imagined it. "Would you have believed me if I *had* told you?"

Well, damn. She had him there.

"I might have," he protested, but she was already rolling her eyes.

"If I'd tried to tell you Soleil was alive, you would've ruined my reputation faster than a seal swims from a shark. You wouldn't believe someone if they told you your shoes were untied."

"Well, obviously not. Sandals don't have laces. Why would I believe someone if they—"

She cocked one eyebrow, and his lips quirked sideways.

"Fine," he said. "I guess that's fair."

"Will you forgive me if I give you something interesting? Free of charge," she added, when he opened his mouth to tell her his pockets were a little light at the moment to be paying her steep fees—and that was coming from the prince of a kingdom rich in gold.

"I hate when you finish my sentences," he grumbled.

"Then you shouldn't have made friends with a seer, hm?" But Luisa's lighthearted voice was heavy now, a wrinkle hovering between her brows he'd never seen before. She looked genuinely troubled, an expression she never wore; at least, not in his company.

Unease woke in place of anger. "What have you got?"

She shook her head. "Not here. The walls listen in the lower city."

He cursed himself silently; he really was dangerously off-kilter tonight. "Of course. Your shop?"

"No." She kicked off the wall and started walking—not inviting him, because she already knew he'd follow.

"Seers," he muttered under his breath, but who was he to argue with the future? He followed her, padding through sun-bleached streets that glowed spookily in the light of the moon.

Before long, he found himself gazing *down* at those streets, the shingles of the roof they perched on digging uncomfortably into his backside. Luisa, on the other hand, seemed perfectly comfortable, one knee cocked up, her loose linen pants stirring gently in the breeze blowing in from the sea, revealing delicate rings of tattoos around her ankles.

"All right," he said. "No ears left but mine."

Still, it was another full minute before she murmured, in a voice that lifted the hairs on his arms, "Has anyone at the palace mentioned the string of grave robberies that took place a couple months back?"

"Yeah, a little." A sick crime, but not necessarily an unusual one. It was Atlas custom to be buried with valuables. People had been known to dig up coffins for the sellable goods within.

"Well, it seems there's a copycat running about." Luisa tightened her arms around herself. "Only . . . they're stealing something besides gold now."

Finn frowned. "Jewels?"

Luisa shook her head. "Bodies."

Revulsion curled his tongue. "*What?*"

"*Bodies.* The dead are disappearing, and nobody knows why." But her gaze was slanted sideways. Her frown dug a divot into her cheek. Her fingers clenched the loose fabric of her pants.

"You have a theory," he prompted.

Luisa worried her lip with her teeth, nervously scratching behind her ear. "It's not one you want to hear."

"Try me."

She stared at the sky, the stars lighting her gaze with eerie light, and ghostly fingers of foreboding clenched around his heart. "Whoever is responsible, they aren't targeting rich graves," she said finally. "They're not targeting specific graves at all. There's no pattern in anything beyond where the graves were located . . . near the edges, far from others. Graves that clearly haven't been tended to in some time."

They were taking the dead that had no one left to mourn them, no possible witnesses to catch the robbers in the act. "So?"

"I think," she said reluctantly, as if voicing it may make it true, "that we might be seeing the work of a fledgling necromancer."

Finn blinked. Once. Twice.

"Tempest's rotted *teeth*."

Luisa's pursed mouth looked ready to spew a curse of its own. "I consulted with my former mentor already. He hasn't seen necromancy at work in a very long time, but he agreed the signs are similar. The isolated graves . . ."

"Anima's leafy pits."

"The random timing of the thefts, like they only take when the craving hits them . . ."

"Occassio's grimy—"

"Stop it," Luisa groaned, rubbing her ears. "You're a prince, for gods' sakes. You've had the best scholars in the world at your disposal since before you could speak. You can do better than cursing me out."

He merely shrugged, heart pounding, mind racing furiously to get ahead of the problem.

Necromancers. The only kind of magic that was entirely outlawed in Atlas, the reason worship of Mortem was banned as well. A magic that hadn't reared its ugly head in *decades*.

Gods, he hated surprises.

"Any idea what could have triggered it?" he asked finally.

"Unfortunately, Occassio's the goddess of foresight, not hindsight. I can't tell you for certain, but smart money's on Nyxian death-worshipping spies."

"Necromancy's outlawed in all the kingdoms. Including Nyx."

"Officially, sure. But if you were about to lose a war, wouldn't you start thinking outside the box?"

Maybe, but something about that didn't taste true. Nyx was a kingdom of superstition. Dabbling in the occult didn't necessarily seem like their style, worshippers of the Goddess of Death or not.

Still . . . Luisa's logic was sound. And Nyx had been the *last* kingdom to outlaw necromancy, if he remembered his schooling correctly.

"So you think they're raising the dead to bolster their armies?" he asked, just to be sure.

"Something like that. But I can't tell you for sure, Finn. Like I said, my vision's . . . clouded." Again, that troubled tilt to her mouth. "Occassio must not be ready to reveal those secrets to me."

His nose wrinkled. "Well, your goddess is going to be having a word with *me* if she doesn't loosen her tongue."

Luisa laughed, but it was rough-edged, ringing false against the rooftop. She wrapped her fingers around her ankles, tapping at the tattoos erratically. "You shouldn't talk like that. Occassio's one of the only gods that listens to us anymore, and not even the great Finnick Atlas could handle having a goddess as an enemy."

He savored the taste of heresy on his mouth before he gave it voice: "I don't want her as a friend, either. She can only tell the future, not change it. Between your magic and my impressive brain, we can do both. So tell me which of us should really be getting bowed to."

Luisa tensed in earnest then, and he smelled something besides wine on her breath this time . . . something dizzying and spicy-sweet, like a dream spun to life by hemp smoke and incense. "You can believe whatever you like, Finn, but if you're going to invite my goddess's wrath, I'd prefer if you left me out of it."

She seemed to count that as a proper goodbye, because she sidled down the drainpipe in a sweep of curls and cloth, and within seconds she'd vanished into the Port Atlas alleys they both loved to haunt.

Leaning back against the chimney, the bricks snagging at his sweater, Finn let his head fall back, his eyes taking in the night sky above. The moon gazed back at him impassively.

He probably should've felt guilty for disrespecting the goddess his only friend . . . ally . . . colleague? . . . adored so much. But he didn't have the time or the energy to waste paying homage to something that either never existed or died off long ago.

"Sorry, Cassi," he said, pulling off his knit cap and giving a mocking, sweeping bow to the moon. He pocketed the knowledge Luisa had handed him where he could reach it easily—later, when he had the energy to study it more closely. "Don't mean to be rude, but you can get the credit when you and your deadbeat family decide to do something worth worshipping."

He'd stopped believing in the gods shortly after digging a grave that was too small to be fair. But even so, he caught himself looking over his shoulder the entire way to the nearest tavern, the weight of eyes pressing heavily between his shoulder blades.

But there was nothing behind him besides empty cobblestone streets and the distant, dead-eyed moon.

CHAPTER 21

ELIAS

This was definitely not how he'd envisioned this night going.

He couldn't close his eyes even as darkness fell in the Atlas garrison, his body flinching wider awake at every snore and snuffle from the cots above and below him. Every inch of his skin sang with adrenaline, with exhilaration, with sheer, unabashed terror.

He was in Atlas. In their *palace*.

Atlas's garrison was set up differently from Nyxian barracks, where they were all piled into a huge communal space, shoving cots wherever they would fit, sometimes combining them to make more room and provide more warmth. Like a giant sleep-over. Atlas's garrison was split into several different rooms, six beds to a room, three stacked on each side wall. There were two closets, two washrooms, and no windows.

He hated it.

It was so gods-damned hot, hotter than he imagined the lakes of Infera might be. Even the thin blanket stretched over his cot was too much. He couldn't sleep with his feet untucked, but he couldn't sleep with that blanket on him, either. Everything was sweat and swelter, the stuffiness heating his body to the point that he found himself desperately wishing for a snowdrift to dive headfirst into.

He could have gone into the washroom and soaked himself in a cold shower—at least Atlas had plumbing, something he and Soren sometimes joked was beyond them—but he didn't want to risk waking his new roommates. More than that, he didn't want to abandon his pack, which he'd managed to recover from the decorative plant he stashed it in on the way to find Soren. Leaving it open to these Atlas guards' curiosity wasn't a smart move.

He knew how things went for new recruits to any cause. Thanks to his fellow soldiers in Nyx—mainly Soren—he'd been hazed enough for this lifetime and the next.

Soren. Mortem damn her, she somehow always managed to take whatever absurdity she was handed and raise it to a new level of utter insanity. He was beginning to think the chaos that clung to her heels was *contagious.*

I'm Soleil, she'd said to him, her voice cracking under the weight of the lies they spun in her head, her eyes heartbreakingly earnest.

He'd taken too long to get here. Even when she walked it back, blustering her way to the mischievous, irreverent battlemate he knew, that doubt still swirled in her eyes.

Gods, he didn't know what to do, how to save her from that. He hadn't even had time to see how deep that illusion went.

What had they promised her, to get her to let their magic into her head? Anima was the main goddess of Atlas, which meant all kinds of magics that toed the edge of morality. Mortem had her share of magics that were mishandled in the past, sure, but nothing like Anima. The most innocuous of Life's magics was healing, but there were other things in her repertoire that were far more dangerous, and Elias didn't know what sort he was dealing with here. And even those were better than if Soren had been handled by someone Occassio-blessed. Those gifted by the Goddess of Time could do things that Elias sometimes had nightmares about.

He slipped his hand beneath his pillow, finding his pack and rifling around until his fingers brushed his beads. He squeezed his eyes shut. *Mortem, please, whatever they've done to her . . . keep her strong. Bring her back to me one more time. Just one more.*

Letting Soren talk him into this half-assed plan was a mistake. There was a reason Nyxian spies never made it into this palace. There was a reason he'd had to connect with several of their agents in the city just to figure out how to make it through the gates. Each of them had sent him off with the same warning: *Someone in that palace knows how to spot a Nyxian, no matter how well they play Atlas. Watch your back—and Mortem bless your soul.*

He'd likely used up every bit of favor he'd stacked up with his goddess just to make it to Soren's side alive. At this point, he was pushing his luck much further than he'd ever intended to.

They were going to get caught. It was only a matter of when.

He tried to roll onto his side, but a sharp ache pulsed in his shoulder, and he had to bite his tongue on a curse. He rolled his sleeve up to check the wound for the first time in days, his fingertips brushing over skin hot and tight—not just from the Atlas heat.

The smell of fester shoved up his nose so violently he had to clap a hand over his mouth to muffle his gag. The wound was closed over, technically, but the scar remained, a sickening red-and-purple splotch with angry red veins beginning to carve their own paths under his skin. In the center of that scar, the skin had begun to fade to gray—dead.

His stomach fell to his toes, and he quickly rolled the sleeve back down.

His time without symptoms couldn't be up *already*. It had only been weeks since he was bitten. Only old men died that fast from this poison.

Or at least, they had up until now.

Maybe he really had used up his favor with Mortem. Maybe she'd given him that one mercy—seeing Soren alive—and that was all she was willing to offer.

"Not yet," he said out loud, the words so quiet they came out with no voice, only breath. "Please, if you ever loved me, if I ever served you well . . . please just give me a little longer. Just let me get her home."

There was no answer he could hear; there never was. But he thought maybe, just maybe, the pain receded slightly. And when he checked the wound again, the flesh in the center seemed pinker—like death had drawn out of it, if only a little, if only for now.

Gratitude tightened around his throat like a noose. *Thank you.*

If saving Soren from the jaws of Atlas was the last thing he ever did, it would be enough of an epitaph. That was something his mother and siblings could be proud of, something that might get his name carved on the castle gates with the rest of Nyx's honored dead.

He could let her try one last time to save him . . . she'd earned that trust. And she'd been right in the hallway. It wasn't fair for him to be the only one allowed to fight to keep his vows.

So he'd let her try. But the moment she realized it was hopeless, the moment he saw an opening, he was taking his best friend home, where they could laugh and spar and argue until it was finally his time to say goodbye.

Soren might hate him for leaving her. But at least she'd be alive to do the hating.

CHAPTER 22

SOREN

On the edge of Soren's mind, between memory she could recall and memory she could only dream about, fire burned.

It purred and popped, crisping the edges of her thoughts like paper held to a candle, rendering them muddled and dull and tasting of soot. She was nearly convinced that if she scraped her tongue with her nail, it would come away blackened and burnt.

But there was no fire here in this new corridor, one she hadn't been let into before; and not by this pretty pink door, colored halfway up with clumsy doodles painted by a child's unpracticed hands. This door that made her want to run through it and run away from it all at once.

She trailed her fingers over those paintings, absently worrying her bottom lip with her teeth. One, two, three, four, five, six . . . seven. Six redheaded drawings, one dark-haired.

"You said you wanted all of us close by. In case you started to miss us."

Every muscle in her body jumped, her teeth jamming down into her lip. She tasted blood.

Breathe in, hold it, breathe out. Control what you can.

But she couldn't breathe at all when she turned to find King Ramses standing behind her, his hands in his pockets, his gaze fixed on her over the edges of his spectacles. He'd kept his distance in the day and a half since the party. After her "escape attempt," they'd all been a little more leery of her, except for Seamus the Especially Annoying, who mostly seemed smug that he'd been right about her eventual intentions. But Ramses was here now: wearing dark pants, a long-sleeved cream shirt, and an orange-brown vest held together with brass buttons, along with a strange gold band around his wrist.

"Is that a clock?" Soren blurted, her eyes caught on that strange, tiny thing around his wrist. Better, safer, to focus on that instead of his face, which sent shivery pangs of homesickness through her that she didn't want to understand. She didn't feel like interrogating any part of this too closely until she could get back to Enna and hear the answers from her.

Ramses glanced down to his wrist, a fond smile smoothing away the tired lines around his eyes. "More or less. Finn made it when he was a boy . . . he noticed I had a bad habit of being late everywhere I went. He thought carrying the time with me might be of service."

"Was he right?"

Another smile, a little more amused, and suddenly she could see his pair of sons in him, the clever side of Finn and the soft side of Kallias. "Unfortunately not. All this really does is *tell* me that I'm running late."

She managed a huffed laugh, forced out of her jammed-up throat, past nerves and discomfort and phantom pain. "I was just . . ."

Just what? Following a trail of smoke to a room she almost recognized? Tracing old paintings with her fingers to see if they remembered making the shapes? Being a complete and utter disaster of a spy?

"Would you like to go inside?" he offered, saving her from having to find an end to that sentence.

Like to was a bit strong. But she nodded. "If that's all right."

"Of course it's all right. It's yours." But still he hesitated, gazing at the knob as if he couldn't quite remember how to turn it. Then he caught her gaze, his mouth twisting from a hesitant grimace to a sheepish smile. His brown eyes softened as he admitted, "None of us have been inside this room for quite some time."

"Lost the key?" she asked lightly, but the joke tasted wrong. Her smartass remarks didn't fit here. Not with him.

His throat bobbed, and something in his gaze dimmed. He didn't answer, merely twisted the knob and let the door drift open.

Something very cold slid through Soren's blood as she took one step forward—like a ghost had stepped the other way, past her, *through* her, trailing the damp chill of the grave through her bones.

This was not a room, she thought, stepping over the threshold.

This was a tomb.

Cobwebs hung from every corner: from the ridiculously large four-poster bed shoved against the left wall, from the blush-pink curtains sheathing the huge window and plush patterned windowseat on the center wall, and the gold-and-ivory vanity on the right. There were dolls and playclothes scattered on the floor, like the little girl who'd spent her days here had vanished in the middle of a trip into her imagination, part of the daydream herself. There were two doors on the right and left of the room—a washroom and a closet, she guessed.

She bent and scooped up one of the porcelain dolls, its sable-brown hair chopped unevenly, its painted face half wiped clean, stains on its dress that looked like chocolate.

A squeal burst from her chest as she snatched her doll out of her brother's hands, cradling her close, gripping her ruined hair in one fist. "Finn, you made her ugly! I love it!"

Her fingertips brushed the bristly ends of the doll's hair, hot pinpricks stabbing into the back of her eyes. Gods, her head was *pounding*.

Ramses stood guard just beyond the door, like he really couldn't bear to follow her in. He had one shoulder braced against the doorframe, his eyes following her every step, every breath. "Do you remember it at all?"

She shook her head, clinging tighter to the doll. "No." *Yes. Maybe. I don't know.*

His next question was even softer, even more hesitant: "What *do* you remember?"

So much. Not enough. Nothing helpful. "My father's office," she said, running her thumb over the doll's chalky face, her calloused skin finding it somehow rough and soft all at once. "It was before my birthday, I think. Lots of letters. I got ink in my braids. And I . . . I remember . . . a fair. Or festival. Playing hide and seek with my brothers."

He made a quiet noise, something between a sigh and a hum. "You aren't ready to believe it yet, are you?"

So he hadn't missed the way she'd carefully hedged. "No offense, but up until last week, you all were nothing but faceless enemies trying to put an end to my home for the sake of a princess who was killed by a long-dead king. I'm not sure what lengths you would go to in order to finally win."

"Of course not. And you shouldn't be."

"Listen, you're not going to convince—wait, what?"

Ramses approached her, gingerly crossing the wooden floor like it might burn him. He came to her side, holding his hand out in silent request. Slowly, she handed him the doll.

Gods, the longer she looked at him, the harder it was to pretend she didn't know him. She knew that look on his face, the divot between his brows that only appeared when he was stressed or sad, that one spot on his beard that didn't grow in as long as the rest.

This wasn't fair. Whatever cruel joke the gods were playing on her, she wanted it over. *Now.*

"Soren . . . that's your name, isn't it? The one they gave you."

She nodded, a single bob of her head, unwilling to go further than that, unsure what he was going to say.

Ramses studied the doll, brushing his fingers over its hair with heart-wrenching gentleness. "This was your favorite. You called her Princess Flowerpetals."

"Clearly I've always been a creative genius."

A laugh ground out of him, sounding out of practice. "You were, actually. Between you and Finn . . . you two were a challenge. But we loved it, you know. Every second." He finally met her gaze, brown eyes serious, earnest, and she saw no trace of deception in them. No lie. No cunning. So different from his younger son, from his queen. "I'll call you Soren, if it makes you more comfortable. Until you are ready to believe it—if you ever are. You're safe here, as long as it takes, as long as you need. We don't expect this to be quick—me, or your . . . or Adriata."

Her fist clenched at the sound of the Queen's name. She wasn't sure she could stand to be in a room with her again. "I'm not sure *Adriata* would agree."

Ramses grimaced. "You have no idea how your loss broke her. How much it changed her."

"I have some idea. She took it out tenfold on my people."

"The blame doesn't rest solely on her. Your queen is not innocent either."

Soren gritted her teeth. "She offered peace talks when her father died. Eight years ago. You denied them."

Ramses's eyes sharpened, and he set the doll aside, crossing his arms. "We did not deny them. We sent Jericho to barter. The escort your people sent turned on her and her chaperones. She was the only one who escaped."

Any smug, self-righteous argument dried up on Soren's tongue. "That not true. That's not what happened."

"Ask Jericho. She barely made it out with her *life*." Finally, a bit of that Atlas anger burned in the king's eyes, but it was different with him, calmer. A simmer rather than a flame. "We were willing to forgive a queen who was only a princess when her father started his war with us. We are *not* willing to treat with a queen who tried to divest us of another daughter, no matter how desperate she is now. She gave up that chance."

She'd thought the emotions in Jericho's eyes were merely the result of a softhearted princess fearing the kingdom they fought against. But either Atlas was very practiced at churning out lie after lie, or some of these had to be true.

If not all of them.

"You only have one side, then," Soren finally said. "You don't know what happened. All you have is Jericho's word."

"Jericho is our daughter—our Heir. We trust her with our kingdom and our lives." He shook his head, looking away from her, toward his feet instead. "But I can't expect you to."

Soren's throat closed up, and she barely managed to rasp, "No. You really can't."

Ramses cleared his own throat, taking a few steps back from her, heading for the door. "I'll leave you to it," he said, gesturing limply at the room, at the mess. "But if you need anything . . . answers, company . . . I'm just down the hall."

The barest dip of her head was all she could manage, and blessedly, he took that as his cue to leave. Only when the door swung shut did she finally slump, lowering herself to the floor, staring around at the curtains, the cobwebs, this crypt.

It didn't feel like home. It felt like a broken music box containing a stranger's childhood, playing a disjointed song she almost knew but not well enough to hum along to.

She missed her sisters. She missed her home.

She missed her mother.

She swallowed hard, balling her fists against the floor. She would search this room for anything that could help her in this game. Elias could glean gossip from the guards, maybe even valuable information about battle strategies and scouting missions. And when the time was right, she would get him the antidote, and they would run.

And she would never have to think about these almost-memories ever again.

CHAPTER 23

KALLIAS

"You're going to get sunburned."

Kallias peeked one eye open to find Jericho standing over him, hands planted on her hips, twin braids hanging limp and dripping onto his feet and Finn's, who lifted his brimmed hat to squint through the sun at their sister.

"I've made my peace with that," said Finn. "Go glower at your husband if you need someone to nag."

"Her husband is wearing plenty of sunblock," said Vaughn from Kallias's other side. "Don't drag me into this."

Jericho threw her hands in the air in exasperation. "The last warm day we're probably going to get this year, and you three want to spend it dozing on the sand instead of swimming?"

On the contrary. Kallias fully planned on getting in that water. But for once he was perfectly content on land, the warmth of the sand beneath his towel soothing away the ache in his back from being bent over reports all night . . . some more disturbing than others.

A sharp pain pulsed in his temple. He rubbed it away. Those worries were for his office, not here.

"Don't worry about us, love," said Vaughn, lifting his hat to flash his wife a tired smile. He tapped his head. "I'm not feeling up to fighting the waves today."

That put an end to Jericho's complaints. With a soft huff and a kick of hot sand over Finn's feet, eliciting a yelp from him that sent both Kallias and Vaughn laughing, she jogged back out to the waves, Vaughn watching her appreciatively the entire way.

"Quit drooling," Finn complained. "You're making me nauseous."

Kallias socked Vaughn's arm. "You can't play the headache card every time, you know."

He shrugged, placing his hat back over his face and settling against his towel. "I'm not playing anything. You think I'd rather be napping on the sand then out there with her?"

"Yes?" said Finn. "If you have the option to nap and you don't take it, you're not the kind of person I want to associate with."

Vaughn pointed back toward the palace. "Feel free to un-associate from me, then."

"And deal with Little Miss Concussion-Giver? I think not. I need a break." Finn rubbed his temple with a grimace, his mouth screwed up in a bitter knot. "She still hasn't apologized."

"She did, actually. A lot."

"Well, you could tell she didn't *mean* it."

Tension edged Vaughn's laugh. "Speaking of Soleil, I heard Jericho had a meeting with your parents about her this morning."

Kallias's attention piqued. No one had mentioned any meeting to him. "What about her, exactly?"

Vaughn heaved himself up again, propping one leg up and wrapping his arm around it, squinting out at his wife past the blinding sun. "About what happens now that the Heir is back from the dead."

Oh. *Oh.*

Finn sat up, some of the heat-flushed color draining from his face. "They can't seriously be thinking about reinstating Sor—Soleil?"

A rock clunked from Kallias's chest into his gut, dragging it down to his toes.

He hadn't even *thought* of that. Of course, now that Soleil was here, she was the youngest daughter. Jericho was no longer the Heir—not traditionally, anyway. But the title didn't shift until the Queen approved it.

"I don't know." There was a hint of frustration in Vaughn's tone, something he didn't hear often. "She wouldn't talk to me about it. She just said they're handling it, whatever that means."

Kallias struggled to wrestle down the jealousy, the *anger* that tried to rile itself up in his gut. Of course they'd had that meeting with Jericho alone; it affected her first and foremost, not him. They would bring him into things when it was time for that. Maybe they'd talk tonight.

At least, they'd better. He couldn't do his job if he didn't know what that job *was*.

Besides, Finn was right. It wasn't likely they'd reinstate Soleil this soon. And they definitely wouldn't do it without consulting him first.

"I don't know about you two, but personally, I'm not too keen on this," said Finn. "She's barely out of Nyx! She tried to kill me!"

Vaughn sighed. "Your head's fine."

Finn tossed his hat aside, gesturing agitatedly at his skull. "There's a *dent!*"

"There's really not, though," said Kallias.

Finn leaned over, offering his head for examination with a dramatic point at the correct spot. "Here. Feel. You'll see."

Kallias popped him on the back of the head instead. "You're being dramatic."

Finn pouted, gingerly rubbing the spot. "I'm being expressive. It's different."

Mischief, rare and dangerous, bubbled up in Kallias's chest. Stretching, he said, "I'll give you something to be *expressive* about."

Finn didn't have time to react past a very shrill yelp before Kallias had him thrown over one shoulder, Finn's weight dragging him sideways as he laughed and staggered out into the water, Finn shouting impressively varied curses and kicking at Kallias's hip until he heaved them both into the salt-laced waves, Finn's shouts cutting off with a splutter and a splash.

"That," said Finn crossly as he dragged himself back to shore, dripping from his hair and wringing out his sleeveless cotton shirt, "was not *nice*."

Kallias grinned at him, the weight on his back easing some. "But it was *funny*."

How long had it been since things had felt this normal? Days—weeks? However long it had been since he'd dragged Soleil home. He couldn't remember the last time he and Finn had laughed and sparred together. Both of them had been absorbed with other things—other people.

Finn rolled his eyes, but a smile fought his annoyance for dominance on his face. "You're an ass."

Kallias made a sweeping bow, his soaking wet hair flying in an arc with his movement. "Guilty as charged."

Vaughn and Finn both protested this time, Finn throwing his discarded sandal at Kallias's head, Vaughn wrinkling his nose as he shook droplets of seawater from his book. "Thank you for that. I was just thinking I needed to wash this."

Kallias had to bite down on a laugh, that wild ecstasy born of salt and sand pushing against the walls of his chest, desperate to find its way out, to be embraced fully. But he couldn't give in to it all the way, not with them.

Soon he'd find time to escape out here on his own. Maybe during the Saltwater Festival, when everyone else would be occupied on the public beach instead of their private stretch.

"Sorry," he said to his brother-in-law as he straightened up, slicking his hair back. "Didn't mean to catch you in the crossfire."

"Sure," Vaughn sighed, staring forlornly at his damp book. "Now the pages are going to get crinkled."

Kallias's laugh stuck in his throat as he glanced back out toward the sea, watching Jericho bob on her board, face tilted back to the sun, shoulders relaxed in the sheath of her wetsuit. He'd fought for years to keep her protected, determined not to fail another sister. He'd spent so much effort and time preparing Atlas for her eventual rule, gently coaxing public opinion her way after the loss of Soleil, carefully polishing her image until it shone: the firstborn of Atlas, the mirror image of her mother with the gentle soul of her father. Adriata was a queen of war, a conqueress. Jericho would be a queen of peace, and he was careful to paint her as such.

It wasn't too hard these days; she'd rarely involved herself in the messy side of the war since Vaughn's illness worsened and Atlas started winning.

"Kal." Vaughn's cold hand clapped down on his shoulder, shaking him gently. "Don't worry over it before there's something to worry about. Jericho's got it under control, just like always."

"Right. I know she does." *Just like always.*

Finn stood up abruptly, brushing the sand from his body, his brow carved with lines. "I'm going to head in. I need a snack."

"Bring some back, will you? I'm starving," said Vaughn, and looking at the Prince Consort's bony wrist, Kallias believed him.

"Good to see your appetite's back," he said quietly as Finn picked his way across the hot sand, his disgruntled swearing floating back to them on the warm breeze.

Vaughn shrugged, the light in his eyes dimming. "Good days and bad days, yeah?"

"Jericho still hasn't found anything that can help? Or what might be causing this?"

Vaughn shook his head, crossing his arms over his chest, his eyes seeking out his wife again. Sadness weighed down his features. "Turns out 'wasting sickness' encompasses a lot of conditions documented over the centuries. She hasn't found anything that helps for more than a few days."

"I'll send word to Arborius again. They have to have something."

"Jericho did already. Your cousins have been experimenting, sending us things to try, but . . ." A miserable, tired smile. "Seems Anima may have decided to hand me over to her sister's care."

A lump formed in Kallias's throat. He cleared it, rasping, "Don't say that."

"No use fighting the inevitable, Kal."

"There's every use. Your death is not an inevitability."

Vaughn's eyes twinkled, which seemed completely out of place in this conversation. "I love the optimism, but I think you'll find that death is an inevitability for everyone."

Kallias checked Vaughn's shoulder with his. "You know what I mean. We made a promise, remember? Us before all. You're part of that. We're going to find something to help you."

The mask that he so often saw Vaughn put on wavered, showing just a glimmer of the fear that lurked beneath, the shadow beneath the stars. The Prince Consort's throat bobbed, a slight sheen welling in his eyes. "Jer's barely sleeping lately. I keep finding her in the library facedown in a book. She's making *herself* sick over this."

Something softened in Kallias's chest. "I don't blame her."

"I don't either. If it was her instead . . ." Vaughn shrugged, hugging his book to his chest. "But I wish she would take better care of herself."

Gods, he was a horrible brother. Here he was sitting around and complaining to himself about how little Jericho had to worry over, all while she was facing down the possibility of losing the center of her world. "I'll see what I can do. Maybe I can take over some of it for her. Find some new places to look."

Vaughn gave him a look. "Yes, because you don't have enough on your plate between Soleil and the war and your upcoming engagement."

Kallias wrinkled his nose, his gut rushing back up from his feet and shoving up against his chest instead, tightening every breath. "It could be years before they even find someone willing to make an arrangement."

"I doubt it. Have you seen yourself? There's a reason everyone in Atlas is at least a little bit in love with you—eight reasons," Vaughn added, gesturing at Kallias's abdomen. "Honestly, what are they feeding you? Because Finn and I could use some of it."

Kallias's cheeks went hot, and he covered his middle with his arms. "It's not my fault you two spend all your time reading. And not *everyone* is in love with me."

Vaughn nodded solemnly. "I've spoken with each citizen personally. The result was unanimous."

If he hadn't been afraid of breaking one of Vaughn's ribs, Kallias would've dug his elbow into them. "Stop."

"There has to be someone asking after you. Maybe one of the Tallisian twins?"

"*Please* don't bring that up." He wasn't allowed in meetings with Tallis either, but not because of poor conduct like Finn—the Tallisian prince and princess were so gods-damned *pretty* he hadn't been able to get a coherent word out. He'd stammered and blushed like an idiot until his mother granted him mercy and invented an emergency calling him away. "Besides, I think Everin might have an arrangement set already, and Raini . . ."

"Scares you?" Vaughn smirked.

"She could step on my neck and I'd thank her."

Vaughn laughed in earnest then, clapping Kallias on the back. "I thought that was exactly your taste when it comes to women?"

"You and Finn teaming up on me now?"

"Jericho, actually. She's been weighing in on the whole thing, trying to get your parents to pick a kingdom we share borders with."

That softened the last bitter edge on Kallias's heart. "She's too good to us."

Vaughn's grin softened to something so utterly lovestruck Kallias almost made a face. "Isn't she?"

Jericho was lucky to have escaped the fate that now hung over Kallias's head. When she was First Princess instead of Heir, sixteen and rebellious, she'd met Vaughn during her training with the best healers Atlas had to offer—she a prodigious magic wielder, he a gifted young physician—and they'd quickly grown close. But Jericho hadn't been allowed to have any kind of romantic trysts, not when her hand was already promised to another kingdom.

She hadn't cared. And for two long years, she and Vaughn had hidden their relationship, claiming Vaughn was training her privately in the craft of healing without magic. Which was partially true, but Kallias alone had known the truth: his sister was in love, and when she turned eighteen, she planned to revoke her title and elope with Vaughn, fleeing Atlas and never looking back. The two of them against the world.

But then Soleil died, their girl, their charge, the future queen they all would have been happy to serve. And even if Jericho had tried to go anywhere, she never would have made it out; the title of Heir fettered her irrevocably to Atlas.

Luckily for her, Heirs could marry whomever they liked. Ramses himself had been a fisherman before he was king. But even with Vaughn at her side, Jericho had never really shaken that old dream from her soul. Sometimes Kallias caught her watching the trade ships that left their harbor with a wistful, aching look on her face.

In fact, until he'd seen Soleil in that valley, he'd been inches away from bribing Jericho into doing exactly what she wanted to do, convincing her to take Vaughn somewhere he could find a cure. To go and have her adventure.

Leaving Kallias as the next best Heir.

Gods, even thinking it made his very bones cringe, guilt jittering deep in his stomach.

He loved his older sister as much as he loved all his siblings. But Jericho didn't *want* the throne. She didn't care for politics or wars, didn't dream of the gold sunburst diadem sitting on her brow. She resented the crown with as much fervor as he coveted it.

It wasn't about ruling. It wasn't about greed. It was about home—how Atlas was *his*, how it was buried in his bones and coursing through his blood, how he was almost certain he would die if he was forced out of it, torn away and shackled to some royal who had no use for him beyond keeping the extra throne warm.

"I'm going in the water," he said abruptly, pulling away from Vaughn. "You're sure you don't want to come?"

"I might join you in a bit. I'm going to wait and see if Finn comes back with that food first."

A nod was all he could manage, that anxious buzz running over his skin, his chest clenching nearly to the point of pain. Even here on the open shore, he felt suffocated. Trapped.

He needed the ocean. He needed that vastness, that gentle infinity with a million and one ways to go. Every wave was a new path he could take, and just now, he needed to be able to choose *something* for himself.

It wouldn't be long until he didn't have that option any longer.

CHAPTER 24

FINN

*W*hat happens now that the Heir is back from the dead?

He was so foolish. So gods-damned foolish and ignorant and *foolish*.

How had he not realized it? How had he not even *once* thought about the fact that Soren was technically the true Heir? Could that be her play, assassinating her way through the palace until only she was left, claiming the throne for herself? For Nyx?

He hadn't gotten that impression from watching her lately—not that it meant much. She was a good enough actor to fool the rest of them completely. But she did seem to be making a genuine effort to get to know them, exploring the palace, even going as far as staying in her old room. Which happened to be right next to his, so at least if she did decide on the assassination route, he'd be the first to know.

Not that it would do him any gods-damned good.

In any case, he'd needed a minute to clear his head before Kallias could catch him *using* it for once. But wandering the halls barefoot and shirtless while popping grapes into his mouth was proving not to be very helpful for anything other than earning him strange looks from the staff.

He slowed when he approached his room, his eyes jumping ahead to Soleil's door. To the finger-paintings they'd done together at six and seven, giggling and shushing each other the entire time until their mother caught them and herded them to the baths.

Soleil had begged for the paint to be left, endlessly proud of the *"mathterpiece"* they'd made, her missing top teeth from a tree-climbing incident giving her a lisp that had sent Finn into hysterical laughter every time he heard it.

Without really deciding to, he found himself knocking on that door.

"Come in," called Soren.

The moment his hand closed around the knob, his throat went dry. He'd been in this room more times since the fire than the others, as far as he knew. Every year on Soleil's birthday morning, while the others went to her grave, he came here. He paid off whatever guard was on duty for their silence, picked the lock, and slipped inside, careful not to let anyone else spot him. He never moved anything, never touched anything except for one item only he knew about, and it wasn't a secret he'd ever reveal to the others. One he doubted she'd ever find on her own.

There were only two promises he'd ever made in earnest, only two he ever truly intended to keep. And that secret was one of them.

Because of that, they all thought he didn't grieve for her any longer. Kallias had screamed at him for it during what they all referred to now as "the incident," the day their family almost fractured for good. The day Kallias went from confident, outspoken prince to uncertain, desperate son trying to win back his family's favor. To make them forgive and forget.

But Finn didn't have the energy for forgiveness, and he was incapable of forgetting. So instead he buried it, setting it aside until he had need of it, a weapon wielded when Kallias got too close to stepping on the toes of his personal designs.

Finn shook all those thoughts off, forcing a harsh breath out through rounded lips. This was just a room. It *could not* break him. It never had before.

He stepped inside to find Soren hanging upside down off the window seat, the tips of her hair brushing the floor, her brow wrinkled and her eyes closed. She was wearing Atlas clothes: tangerine silk shorts and a matching sleeveless top, her muscled arms braced against the bench, her palms flat to the floor. She was scowling.

Finn paused. "Um. I'm a bit afraid to ask, but what are you doing?"

"A Nyxian ritual," she said without opening her eyes. "I'm cursing Seamus and his family for the next thousand years."

"Fun. Can I help?"

"Do you know where I can get a liter of goat's blood and some relics of Mortem?"

"Unfortunately, I'm fresh out of goats. Would a jellyfish work?"

She heaved a sigh. "No, I don't think so."

"Pity. Then you might as well tell me what you're actually doing, hm?"

She was quiet for so long, her eyes closed and her lips just slightly parted, that he thought she might've passed out. Then, with another sigh, she said: "Thinking."

"Trying new things is always good," he said, and she snorted—a promising improvement from snarling and baring her teeth, at least. "About what?"

She shrugged, the movement nearly upsetting her balance, but she caught herself. "This room. All of you. Just . . . trying to remember."

He almost, *almost* smiled. But he cleared his throat instead, leaning against the door to close it, swishing a grape around the inside of his mouth while he watched her. Talking with his mouth full was one of the best ways to keep people from looking too closely at him while he was lying. "I don't think hanging upside down is going to help you any."

"My moth—the woman who looked after me in Nyx, she always says the brain works better with more blood in it."

"Yeah, maybe, but the rest of your body isn't going to feel so great." He strode across the room to sit beside her on the bench, offering her a hand. "There are easier methods. Trust me."

To his surprise, she took his hand, tugging herself up in a single quick motion, grimacing at what he could only assume was a rush of dizziness. "Did you get bored of Kallias torturing you?"

He blinked. "Were you spying on us?"

"Not spying." She gestured out her window, hugging her knees to her chest to keep herself balanced on the bench. "Just watching."

"You could have joined us."

Her body stiffened slightly. Fear, he thought, not defensiveness. "I don't know how to swim."

"You mean you don't remember."

"I don't see how that's different."

He wished that wasn't such a blow. Soleil had loved swimming, almost enough to rival Kallias. She was out there with her waveboard every spare moment she could steal between her studies. "Come on. You can't be serious. Nyx has rivers, doesn't it? Lakes? Other inferior bodies of water?"

Soren gave him a look that made him feel the way their garden plants looked after a boiling-hot summer day. "They were frozen most of the year. And I was never taken to them when they were thawed."

Hm. Unsurprising, if they were worried about triggering her true memories. "So if I ask you if you want to go out now . . .?"

Her arms tightened around her legs, and she buried her chin against her bare knees. "No thank you." But still she gazed out at Jericho and Kallias and Vaughn, watching them with a tilt to her mouth that didn't look angry, or uncaring, or cocky. She looked . . . sad.

And gods, he didn't know what was wrong with him, but he said, "What if we went somewhere else?"

She turned to look at him, frowning in earnest now, leaning back a bit. "Like where?"

"Have you explored the palace at all since Kal brought you home?"

Soren gestured around the room, a glimmer of irritation coming back to her eyes. "I haven't exactly been free to roam, have I?"

He was being a fool. For a thousand and one reasons, not the least of which that he was risking everything on his faith in his ability to keep her from running off. But still, he said, "Meet me in half an hour. I think I know what might help you remember."

CHAPTER 25

SOREN

"I really don't see how this is going to help!"

Panic threaded through every word, but she couldn't care about that when she was standing on this deadly precipice, her bare toes mere inches from the promise of death. The enemy below writhed and mocked her with its gurgling laugh, reaching fingerless hands toward her, ready to drag her down.

Finn sighed impatiently behind her, along with the flutter of a book's pages being flipped. "Soren, it's a swimming pool, not a vat of acid."

That, in her opinion, did not matter *at all*. "Who cares? It'll kill me just as well!"

"You're standing by the shallow end."

She looked over her shoulder at him, fists clenched over her exposed stomach. She'd never worn anything like this, never *seen* anything like it—undergarments, more or less, but made of some strange water-shedding material. Finn had called it a *wetsuit*.

Admittedly, she looked damn good in it, the green bringing out her eyes nicely. But even her vanity wasn't enough of a distraction to keep her muscles from locking up at every lap of the water at the side of this giant tiled bathtub. "What does that mean?"

Finn licked his thumb, turning the page on his book. He was lounging in a very strange wooden chair, the top half too short and the seat part too long, the legs barely holding it a foot over the floor. "It means you're taller than the water level there. It can't cover your head unless you duck under on purpose."

His voice echoed through the vast room. The "swimming pool" was over fifty yards long, surrounded by great white columns that supported balconies fenced in by white-painted wrought iron. The pool itself was tiled in rich blue, a color so deep and intense she was half-sure it was actually filled with blue paint and not water. When she reached one toe out, brushing the very tip in the water, it was warm as a freshly drawn bath.

"I thought it would be cold," she said.

"If you want cold swimming, you can head to the ocean. The pool is for fun."

"Why do you need two places to swim at all? It seems like a waste of resources."

Finn frowned at her. "Does Nyx not have anything just for the fun of it?"

She ground her teeth against a sharp retort. "When your kingdom's winter lasts half the year, you learn not to waste anything."

Including time. Which was exactly what she was doing, wearing strange clothes and letting Finn distract her with *swimming lessons* while Elias was gods-knew-where and Atlas was preparing for their next strike against Nyx. She should be with Jericho and Vaughn, prying them for information on the Vipers. But the couple had been notably absent from breakfast, as had the Queen and King, and Soren hadn't seen any of them since.

The Queen still refused to speak to her, or even look her way, but that might be better. If Soren got in a room alone with her, she might just abandon sense and try to strike a proper blow for Nyx's sake.

She couldn't, not yet. For Elias, she had to play the long game. But gods, was it tempting.

"Soren," said Finn, and she was struck again by the strangeness of hearing her real name from an Atlas mouth. He and the King were the only ones who used it, and Finn only when it was the two of them alone. Like he, too, was pretending for the others . . . but not for her. "Get in the water before I push you in."

She almost bared her teeth, but held it in, remembering his comment about her wolfish nature. "You wouldn't *dare*."

He adjusted his glasses downward, giving her a look over them. "Try me."

Oh, she would try him, all right. Try him with a knife in her hand and a target on his scrawny little neck.

She let out a breath in a quiet huff, then drew it back in, filling her lungs with as much as would fit just in case the worst happened. She wanted to buy herself as much time as possible to problem-solve if things went awry.

Then she slid into the pool.

It really was like being in a giant bathtub. The water came up past her hips, just barely lapping at her waist, her newest scar tingling unpleasantly where the water touched it. All the scabbiness and bits of dead skin were gone now, leaving behind a ropey knot of flesh that stretched from just below her navel to just above her heart. Easily the most impressive of her many marks, and definitely her least favorite.

Her favorite had to be her crooked nose, the bend in it the result of many, many fights she'd picked. She'd *earned* that imperfection. Elias didn't care for how enamored she was with it—mostly because he was partially responsible for it.

"See?" Finn said, that infuriating lilt to his voice making her want to jump right back out. "Not so bad, is it?"

"It's fine," she muttered curtly, silently marveling at how slick the tile felt beneath her toes.

"Good. Now try wading in deeper. Up to your chest."

She squeezed her arms tighter around herself. "I'm good right here, thank you."

"You'll never learn anything if you stay in the shallows. You have to trust the water."

"I *trust* that the water is going to drown me the first chance it gets."

His chuckle was not the least bit reassuring. "Just try it."

Inch by reluctant inch, she toed her way forward, the water gently swishing with her movement until she was submerged to her jawline, only able to touch the bottom by standing on tiptoe. She stretched her neck higher, the brush of water on chin such an unfamiliar sensation that she almost panicked and stumbled back to safety—but not quite. Not yet.

Her legs were weightless, her toes trying to float away from that grounding tile, but her chest was so weighed down with pressure she could hardly breathe, even with her head above water. The water cocooned her and smothered her, held her and hung her, coaxing her deeper still. Like a friend whispering from the shadows.

Come here, it said. *I remember you.*

In a burst of boldness, she flexed her toes, pushing off that last tether keeping her held down. She cut forward into open water, the floor vanishing beneath her—

And sank like a stone.

Her panicked gasp gained her no air, only more of that gods-damned water, clawing its way from mouth to throat to lungs, burning and smothering, like its dry and raging cousin, like smoke—

Oh gods oh gods oh gods.

She waved her arms and legs, trying to find the floor or the surface, anything to give her direction.

Nothing. Nothing but open water roaring dully in her ears and knotting up her chest.

"Mama, it's too deep!"

Gentle hands supported her just before her head plunged under, her mother laughing above her head. "Not so fast, Soleil! The water has slippery hands, you know. It drops everything."

Arms snagged sharply around her waist, dragging her back up toward that blessed edge of the pool. Her hands scraped against rough tile sides, and she scrabbled with all her might, clinging on and pulling herself above the surface with a hacking splutter. Finn burst out from the water moments later, soaking, gasping, and very much pissed.

"What in the depths was that?" he snapped, dragging himself out of the pool to sit on the edge, shaking water from his hair. "I didn't tell you to go *that* far, dumbass!"

She didn't have an answer. Not for him or for herself.

She bent and choked out a couple mouthfuls of water, every splash birthing new pains in her body. She hadn't known water could *burn* like this.

She squinted at Finn through a haze of water and pain, then looked over her shoulder at the deep end of the pool. "Show me."

"Show you what? How to drown yourself? I think you had that pretty well figured out!"

"No." Soren swiveled back to face him, a quiet exhilaration building in her breast, something foreign and new . . . or old. "Show me how to swim for real. Tell me what I did wrong."

Finn's irritated scowl softened at the corners. His doe-eyes followed suit, the glare dripping away with the water in his hair. He studied her for one moment—two.

"Well, for starters, don't lose the floor," he said finally. "Until you get the basics down, you need your safety net. Let's try a dead man's float to start."

She wrinkled her nose. "Promising name."

"All you have to do is lie there. Here, I'll show you." He hopped back in with her, and for once, she couldn't see that conniving look hiding beneath the brown in his eyes. He looked cautious, skeptical, but there was a glimmer of something warmer, too. "We'll have you swimming from end to end in no time, just you watch."

The rest of the day passed in a blur of water and laughter and muscles learning a new way of moving. Finn wasn't a bad teacher when he put his mind to it, and more than that, whenever he had the beginning of a thought, Soren found the tail end of it in her own head; and when she began a question, Finn was already giving her the answer.

Navigating water was a matter of push and pull, and she was beginning to wonder if navigating this trickster prince would require the same principle. There was no point in playing a fair game against him, because *he* wouldn't play fair— she'd seen that much. Cheats and charms were his strategy, and she couldn't hope to beat that.

But she had a cheat or two of her own. And judging by the way he loosened up throughout the lesson, even going as far as to give a genuine laugh at one of her jokes, she was beginning to guess which one this prince would require.

She was sitting on one of those misshapen chairs, the open air raising goosebumps on her damp skin, taking a break to breathe and stanch her dripping hair with a towel, when the sound of someone knocking came from the pool entrance. Kallias was standing just inside the door, his hair draped over one shoulder in a single braid, his grin stretched from ear to ear. And beside him, so different-looking in that Atlas uniform that her heart dropped to her toes . . .

"Hello, you," she called, in what she *hoped* was a voice full of bitterness. "Come to tackle me again?"

Elias didn't rise to her taunt, which wasn't like him at all. His cheeks were flushed with color, his eyes wide as if in pain, his mouth opening and closing like a dying deer gasping for its last breaths, and for a moment she feared he *was* hurt, or sick, or maybe having a seizure.

Then she realized *what*, exactly, his attention was focused on. And a smug, tingling delight swept away all worry.

She lazily stretched out her legs, settling her head back on her folded arms, letting him get the full measure of that glorious wetsuit she was never taking off *ever*. "Paint a portrait, sweetheart, it'll last longer."

Her battlemate's gaze snapped up to her eyes and stayed there—a very deliberate move, she guessed, biting her tongue on a laugh as she watched his throat bob in a way that looked painful.

"Forgive me, Highness," he rasped, in that Atlas accent that just barely managed to cling to his Nyxian voice. But his brows stayed furrowed, his lips tilting toward the scowl he saved for when she was being particularly heathen-esque. Or maybe he was just trying to keep all the drool in. "I was lost in thought. I didn't mean to stare."

"Play nice, Soleil," Kallias called, his voice echoing off wall and water, clapping Elias on his bad shoulder. He stiffened, his jaw clenching, and suddenly Soren didn't feel like teasing him at all. Was it really that bad already? "This is Eli Dorian, I see you remember him. I'm giving him a quick tour around the palace grounds."

"A personal tour from the First Prince?" Finn didn't look much happier than Elias, all that eagerness gone now that there was an audience. He leaned back in his own chair, hands on his knees, raising one eyebrow at Kallias. "I don't know if his services merited that much of an honor."

"He handled the situation when you couldn't," Kallias reminded him.

"Yeah, because I was *knocked unconscious*, thank you! Where was he for *that* part?"

Soren grimaced, catching Elias's gaze over Kallias's shoulder.

"In any case, Soleil," said Kallias, "Get used to seeing his face. He's going to be part of the rotation guarding your room at night."

"I don't need a guard," Soren snapped—before realizing that yes, she absolutely *did*, because that would be *perfect*. If they were dumb enough to actually stick Elias right in front of her door . . . "But if you insist, fine. He's not there to keep me in, is he?"

"Not at all. He's there to protect you—and to escort you anywhere you'd like to go."

"Hmm. All right, then, as long as I can boss him around." She gave her hair one last wring before letting it fall against her shoulder, damp ends lashing cold lines across her skin. "Care to join our lesson, Officer Dorian?"

Elias kept his gaze determinedly above her head. "I'm afraid this uniform isn't made to shed water, milady."

Oh, that wasn't fair. The way that Atlas accent pitched his voice differently than normal, the way it rumbled in his chest . . . and she could definitely get used to him calling her *milady*. "Nobody said the uniform was required."

"Okay, enough," Finn swatted her on the back of her head with his rolled-up towel, dodging her attempt to punch him in the ribs with a high-pitched yelp. "Hey! Flirting with the guards is bad form, okay? It distracts them. Don't follow Kal's example, he got caught in a storage room with one of the girls last year and Mama nearly killed him for it."

Now it was Soren's turn to avoid Elias's gaze—the two of them knew a little something about soldiers stealing kisses in strange places, thanks to a late-night game of truth or dare early on in their training. A game they'd *never* discussed since.

Kallias groaned. "For the last time, that *never* happened, and I don't know who started that rumor—"

Finn waved his hand dismissively. "In any case, he's still got half the garrison in love with him."

Kallias blushed. "I do *not*."

"Well, they definitely don't gather around to watch you train because they think they'll learn something."

Kallias frowned. "I'm a damn sight better than you."

"I didn't say you weren't." Finn tossed his towel Soren's way, and she barely managed to block it from smacking her face. "Come on, killer. Lesson over for the day. We'll start again tomorrow, if you want."

"Sure. It'll have to be in the evening, though. I have a thing with Jericho in the morning."

Out of the corner of her eye, she saw Elias stiffen. Finn merely waved in acquiescence, mock-wrestling Kallias for a moment before he sauntered out the door, his warbling whistle echoing back to them in ghostly ripples.

"I should follow him," Soren sighed. "I don't know my own way back to the main palace."

"We'll walk you," said Kallias. "This was our last stop, anyway."

And that was how Soren ended up once again between her battlemate and the prince, two different kinds of tension writhing like loose rappelling cables between them. With Kallias, it was one-sided, his unguarded back almost too much of a temptation to ignore. On the other . . .

She had no gods-damned idea what to make of that *something* stretched taut between her and Elias. No idea what it meant, if it meant anything at all.

She knew she was beautiful, and she knew Elias thought so too. At least, he'd told her so in deadpan on several occasions when she'd collapsed across the foot of her bed, bloated and in pain from her monthly cycle, moaning that she'd swollen to the size of a mammoth while he rubbed her cramping back, promising that she was "the prettiest mammoth in the tundra." But that wasn't exactly the same thing.

If he felt anything in earnest—anything more than their love as battlemates, anything different, anything passionate—he'd never said it. And if he hadn't by now, he likely never would.

But it didn't stop her from walking with a bit of a sway to her step. And it didn't stop him from holding his breath for so long she had to look over her shoulder to make sure he was still alive.

CHAPTER 26

ELIAS

That Mortem-cursed *woman* was going to get Elias sent to Infera, and he would be blushing the *entire gods-damned way* there.

He couldn't look at her the whole walk back. He couldn't *stop* looking at her the whole walk back. He couldn't breathe or think or even blink.

It wasn't the first time he'd seen her in something revealing; barracks and battlefields didn't allow for much modesty. But gods, this was different. Nyx's underclothes were thicker and longer, covering more skin than whatever *that* ensemble was. Thank the gods she was in her bathing room now, washing off the water from that strange *pool* and singing at the top of her lungs while she did so. Badly, he might add.

And gods, he was so relieved she was alive to be hurting his ears that he almost started crying again.

He rubbed the back of his neck, rolling his head from side to side to try and loosen the muscles. This was his first shift as a part of the Atlas garrison—and Nyx's first spy in the palace.

It would have been better, smarter, to keep to his post for the first night. But Soren had allowed him exactly ten minutes to try and pull himself together in the hallway, breathing in composure and exhaling whatever was wrong with him, before poking her head out and asking if he was going to huff and puff out there all night.

No, what he *planned* on doing was asking her where exactly she got off jumping into twelve-foot-deep water with one of Atlas's princes when she *knew* she couldn't swim. What he *planned* on doing was telling her that she was pushing this ruse too gods-damned far for her well-being or the well-being of his already-frazzled nerves.

He sat on the edge of her bed, grimacing as he took in this room, nearly the size of his entire home back in Nyx. All for one person, one *child*, no less, while his family of eight lived practically on top of each other, piled in bunks and shared corners, his five younger siblings and one older having no concept of *personal space* as a result.

The difference between a kingdom of wealth and a kingdom of generosity, he supposed. Enna gave much to ensure none of her citizens went without, especially in the cold months. And it was common in Nyx to see neighbor giving to neighbor, everyone holding each other up to ensure they all made it through to the next warm season no worse for the wear. There was a sense of mutual responsibility, camaraderie, people never unwilling to help folk in need of it.

Here, they gave a child a room smothered in lavish waste.

Still, he wasn't surprised Soren was enjoying it. She'd always had an eye for shiny things, ever since the very first time they'd met—long before either of them were soldiers, when she knew him as nothing but the son of the ironworker her mother often hired, sixteen and shy as a startled rabbit.

He'd heard of *her*, of course. Everyone had. The Queen's ward who'd been expected to take to the battlefield any day. But she hadn't looked like a warrior when he first met her, at the Winter Fair just before he joined up in the barracks.

Snow drifted softly from the sky, settling on Elias's hair and numbing the tip of his nose as he helped his mother rearrange their wares. The iron was so cold they had to wear gloves to keep the sweat on their fingers from freezing to the metal, but he loved it. He'd been in the forge all morning; the snow was a welcome reprieve.

The encounter he had next, however, was not.

Soren and the eldest princess were bickering in the way siblings did as they ducked around the merry crowd, every sharp comment on the verge of a laugh. Yvonne was dressed in a sharp black dress with silver detailing, what everyone would expect from a princess of Nyx, but Soren apparently wore whatever she liked, because the bright gold dress and sparkling cloak stuck out like a sore thumb in the sea of Nyxian black.

Her hair blended no better, lit up like sunfire and sprinkled with bits of crystal. Her pale skin gleamed with some kind of cosmetic item, like someone had stroked her cheekbones with gold-dusted fingers, and her lips were colored red as blood.

Elias loved her from the moment he saw her to the moment she opened her mouth.

"What are these *supposed to be?"*

She regarded his goods with an air of incredulity, as if she couldn't believe they could possibly be worth Yvonne's attention. A spoiled, outspoken princess. Elias apparently looked offended by her tone, because she gazed at him with what he now knew was the look she reserved for the most idiotic of people. "What're you scowling at?"

Elias only just managed to keep a leash on his tongue. "Pardon me, milady?"

Soren blinked, smiled, and showed her teeth like a snow leopard—the first flicker of danger he'd seen in her. "Oh, milady*. I like that. Vonnie, did you hear that? He called me milady." Yvonne only waved impatiently in her direction, so Soren's attention went back to him. She leaned in close as her smile turned taunting. "You have a little something on your cheek, steel-for-brains."*

Elias, face burning, rubbed quickly at the spot she'd been staring at, but his fingers came away clean. Soren only grinned, a tiny, cruel thing that said he was entirely too gullible.

Elias didn't often make a habit of hating royals, but she was testing his resolve.

"I want that," she suddenly declared, jerking her chin at something behind him. "Let me see it."

Elias blinked at her, a placid smile slowly forming on his face. The mirror to the one his mother wore for particularly trying customers. "Pardon me?"

Soren scowled—an expression that somehow made her even more beautiful, even as he was busy hating her haughty tone. "I said, I want to see that ring on the shelf back there."

Elias made a show of smacking his forehead in understanding, giving her his biggest, most insincere smile. "Oh! Of course. I'm so sorry for the misunderstanding, milady. It's just that, you see, I don't speak raging *snob."*

Soren's mouth formed a perfect little O, and Elias took a moment to accept his oncoming death.

"Elias!" his mother snapped, her eyes wide in horror. But before anyone could do anything else, Yvonne saved him by doing one simple thing: she guffawed.

The Crown Princess doubled over, hands on her knees, her laughter booming out across the snow-laden streets. "You deserved that," she said to Soren, absolutely beaming. "You completely deserved that."

Soren blinked once or twice before waving his mother off, mumbling out something about how it was all a joke. His mother looked skeptical, but she turned away after leveling one last wide-eyed glare at him, leaving Elias shockingly un-murdered.

When he turned back to Soren, he found her staring at him—not with rage anymore, only curiosity. "Elias Loch. You're joining up this harvest season, right? Some of the captains have been talking about you."

He hardly dared give her a truthful answer, but he offered one stiff nod, unsure whether to glow at the fact that she'd heard of him or to beg for her not to tell his eventual captain about his behavior.

She gave him a quick once-over, repeating his name quietly under her breath. Then, with what he could've sworn was a hint of respect, she said, "I suppose I'll see you on the battlefield, Elias."

He only just managed a nod, some of the adrenaline fading from his limbs.

"And just so you know," Soren added, turning treacherously bright eyes back to him, "you haven't seen my raging anything yet."

He *really* hadn't. Until the day they were forced together as battlemates, both hurting and grief-stricken and revenge-hungry, he hadn't known true rage from Princess Soren Nyx.

They'd nearly killed each other that first day. Not because of anything the other did, but for the simple sin of not being Jira or Kaia. For not being the battlemates they chose for themselves.

That damned ring. He still had it, his little luck symbol, tucked away now in his pack. A reminder that he'd faced down a princess and come away unscathed— the first time, anyway. She'd gotten her revenge through many of their subsequent encounters.

The bathing room door banged open, and Soren emerged in a cloud of steam, wearing what he guessed passed for nightclothes here: a periwinkle silk top with sleeves thinner than his bootstraps and matching pants that seemed to have been cut off at mid-thigh. Now whether that was the style or whether she'd done that herself to try and get another rise out of him, he wasn't sure . . . but either way, Mortem curse him, it was working.

"You're wrinkling again," she sighed, long legs eating up the distance between them in three quick strides, a towel over her shoulder and a brush in her hand. She pulled his brows apart with her fingertips before handing him the brush and sitting on the floor between his legs, back settling against the bed, her hair in easy reach. "Go easy, okay? It's all tangled up."

He heaved a sigh, taking a section of her hair and starting to brush, slow and steady, working out any stubborn knots with his fingers. "I shouldn't be in here."

"Neither should I, but here we are." She let her head fall back, green eyes searching out his, an uncharacteristically serious look on her face. "How's your shoulder?"

"It's fine." Throbbing and burning like Infera, but fine. "You're *sure* you want to go through with this?" He held his hand out beside her face, and she reached up and handed him the strip of leather she used to keep her hair back. "Braid or ponytail?"

"Have you ever seen a woman sleep in a ponytail, Elias?"

Braid it was, then. He got to work, sticking the leather between his teeth while he twined the sections of her hair together.

"And yes," she said more quietly. "I'm sure. Tell me how your shoulder is, without lying this time, jackass."

Elias gritted his teeth, silently cursing. "Fine, smartass. It's . . . a little painful. But nothing dangerous yet." At least, he hoped not. He'd been avoiding looking at it ever since that night in the barracks.

Soren's shoulders didn't relax, but she didn't push him further. Instead she cocked one knee up, leaning further into the bed, letting her head loll sideways to brush against his knee.

"I'm glad you're here," she whispered, exhaustion weighing down her voice, a soul-deep tiredness that tugged at his heart. "Really."

He swallowed down the lump in his throat, running his hand briefly down her hair before remembering himself and snatching it back. "I'm glad I'm here, too."

When had this become so difficult? When had touching her started to fill him with ecstasy and terror and a pain so sharp it was almost pleasant?

His palm practically sang with burning warmth where he'd stroked her hair. His knee pulsed where her head rested. His throat was dry as an abandoned well. He hadn't felt anything like this since they were paired up as battlemates . . . at least, he hadn't *let* himself. There'd been no room left for his *silly little crush*, as

Kaia had called it, smacking him upside the head every time she caught him staring too long at the princess who found her joy in torturing him. There'd been no room for thrills and blushes and *gods-damn it how can one person be so awful and so pretty all at once.*

So whatever had reverted inside him, he needed to get it back in check. There couldn't be any tension between them if they were going to make it out of this alive.

He couldn't be thinking of how nice her hair smelled, rose and peach staining his hands sweet. Or how much he wanted to take that smug face of hers in his hands and—

He shook his head with the ferocity of a wet wolf shaking itself dry. No more of that. *Absolutely no more* of that.

"You should get some rest," he rasped. "You had a long day."

"I will," she agreed softly. "When you have to go."

He heard it then—the quiet loneliness in her voice. The same missing that had dogged him from Nyx to Atlas, leaving him sleepless, praying through each night like a dying man who'd sinned every day of his life.

"All right," he murmured, reaching down to squeeze her shoulder. "I'm with you. No matter where this takes us, it takes us together. You hear me, smartass?"

She reached up and covered his hand with hers, clinging so tightly that her knuckles went white. "I hear you, jackass."

Something catastrophic and quiet rumbled to life in his chest, and it was all he could do to swallow back the tangle of words that rose with it.

No more of that.

Not tonight.

Not like this.

"Hey, Dorian. Get up."

It took Elias half a heartbeat too long to remember that was *his* name now, and he sat up too fast, crashing his head into the bunk above his, stars exploding as his skull sang with pain and his teeth slammed into his tongue. Eyes smarting, he blinked away tears to find Seamus glaring at him. The captain was dressed in his full uniform, all turquoise and gold and shiny buttons that would've gotten him mocked relentlessly in Nyx, blond hair combed and gelled with precision.

"What is it?" Elias asked groggily, tasting blood on his tongue. It felt like he'd only just been relieved of his post by another guard. It couldn't be morning already.

Seamus tossed him a clean uniform that, unfortunately, looked less like the simple one he'd worn earlier and more like the one he'd just been silently making fun of. "Suit up. The prince needs an escort into the city."

Elias blinked blearily at him, trying to read that glare through the pitch-black of the stuffy room. He guessed from Seamus's tone it wasn't the usual authority-figure-giving-an-order glare, but something more personal. The captain hadn't exactly been pleased when Elias had showed up at his doorstep, sweating and claiming he'd been sent there by the gods-damned First Prince of Atlas, of all people, praying to Mortem that they didn't bother to question it too deeply . . . or demand to search his pack first.

Luckily, it seemed Kallias's name held particular sway in this garrison, likely because he was the only royal who followed them on and off the battlefield, the only one who got his own hands bloody. Thanks to that, no one had bothered Elias yet, which worked just fine for him.

He eased himself off the bunk, dropping onto his heels, bending his knees slightly to take the impact. Even so, his shoulder throbbed with heat, and it was an effort not to wince.

At least the Atlas uniform had long sleeves.

Though he felt exposed without a blade at his belt, it was a relief to leave the dank room and its snoring occupants, the sweat on his neck and back cooling at the touch of fresh air from the open windows. Moonlight drowned the hall— so it *was* still night, then. The smell of brine and salt made his tongue curl in his mouth, made him want to gag, but at least the humidity had waned. He already missed the sharp sting of Nyxian wind, the clean scent of snow and cold so deep it bit his bones and woke every sleeping part of him. He wasn't born for heat and humidity and *fish*.

"Did the prince say why he needed an escort?" he asked as casually as possible, fussing with one of those ridiculously shiny buttons holding his uniform shut. It was a bit snug in the chest and shoulders, and he would've undone one or two if he could, but something told him Seamus wouldn't care for that very much. "In the dead of the night?"

Seamus cast him a warning look. "In this garrison, we don't question the royal family. They say jump, we ask 'How high?'"

"Understood. It just seems like an unnecessary risk, that's all. Isn't Port Atlas dangerous at night?" Yes, good—that sounded like something a fresh face from some backwater Atlas town might ask.

"Yes, it is. Which is why he needs an *escort*. You got seawater where your brain should be or what, Dorian?"

You have a brain in that pretty head of yours, or is it all verses and prayers?

"It's been suggested before," Elias mumbled.

"Shocking." The sarcastic bite in the guard's voice reminded Elias briefly of Jakob, though Seamus certainly lacked the good humor of the Nyxian captain.

Gods, what he would've given to have his company at his back.

The two of them made their way to the main foyer, an ostentatious space Elias had instantly hated when he first laid eyes on it. The ceiling soared high above their heads, culminating in a frosted glass dome with clear strips to let the sunlight through. The walls were a shade of blue he'd never seen elsewhere, rich and dark, accented with streaks of metallic gold, and there were three sets of alabaster staircases that led to the various levels of the palace: one to the left, one to the right, and one in the center.

Seamus went to the grand doors at the far end, saluting to the guards there with a quick tap of his fist over his chest, an action Elias quickly mimicked. Then they were out into the courtyard, a round space pathed with cobblestones and surrounded by a forest of palm trees and tropical flowers and strange berry bushes. Kallias was waiting for them in the shadow of the iron gates, a cloak shielding his hair from the tattletale moon, his mouth twisted downward as he stared at his shoes; boots this time, not the abominably loud shoes Elias had recently come to discover were called *sandals*. A sword sheath hung against his hip.

Hopefully that wasn't meant for him.

When Seamus halted and bowed, Elias followed suit, even though his spine rebelled against the idea of bowing to this Atlas prince, this captor, this murderer. It was difficult to even look him in the eyes, to speak with some semblance of civility, knowing what he'd done to Soren, to Jira . . . to so many of Elias's people.

"Highness," Seamus said, head still lowered.

Elias felt the prince's eyes giving him a long once-over. "You brought the new one."

"I thought it would be a good chance to test his skills." Seamus didn't say anything further, but Elias heard the implication well enough. *I thought it would be a good chance to get him kicked back onto the page staff.*

"If you think so," Kallias sighed. "You two can stop bending in half now. You're going to pull something."

Elias clamped his teeth down on the inside of his cheek against a retort, and his abused mouth protested; he'd been doing a bit too much biting back lately. "May I ask why we're out here, Highness?"

Seamus shot him a look that promised his days of going un-hazed were about to be over, but Kallias simply said, "Follow me."

The gates groaned as he pushed them open, and Elias frowned as they walked through them. "You've got rust issues."

Kallias paused, turning to look at Elias over his shoulder. "Excuse me?"

Gods, he needed to shut up. "It's just . . . your gates. The iron's rusted."

"That's what iron does," Seamus said condescendingly. "Can we keep moving?"

"Have you ever cleaned these?" Elias ran his hand over the gate, wincing. Their condition was appalling. "A little salt and lime will do wonders."

"For what? Making drinks?" Seamus snorted, but Kallias narrowed his eyes.

"How do you know?" he asked.

Elias hesitated, but this bit of truth couldn't hurt. "My mother is an ironworker. My sister's a bladesmith. My father was in the trade too, before his death. I know a thing or two."

Kallias cocked one eyebrow. "Where did you say you were from, again?"

"Nowhere you'd have heard of here, Highness."

He seemed to accept that answer, though curiosity still shone in his eyes. "Let's keep moving."

Dry thunder rumbled above and around them, heat lightning streaking between the clouds, igniting their path through the winding streets and snow-white houses with colorful doors and roofs that definitely weren't built for snow and cold. Traces of sand were buried between the stones of the street, odd little rocks shaped like fans and curls scattered around them. He plucked one from his path as they walked, studying it with furrowed brows, running his fingers over the grooves, the glassy surface, the oddly bright colors.

"Keep up," Seamus barked over his shoulder. "What, you've never seen a shell before?"

Elias blinked. "Well . . . no, actually."

Kallias *did* stop then, dead in his tracks, so suddenly that Elias almost thought he'd run into something. "Wait, are you being serious?"

Mortem save him. He was terrible at this. He swallowed, deepening his Atlas accent just a little. "My town's not exactly close to the sea, Highness. We've never been able to afford the trip out here to see it."

"You've never seen the ocean?" Kallias sounded as if he couldn't imagine a fate worse.

"Highness," said Seamus. "With all due respect, don't we have something to see to?"

"On task as ever, Seamus." The prince started walking again. Didn't seem like he had much in the way of a backbone.

It wasn't like Elias had any solid expectations of where this outing was going to lead them—unless they'd discovered his identity and planned on making sure his first real glimpse of the sea was also his last—but somehow, ending up at a cemetery wasn't even on the list.

Alabaster headstones were arranged in neat, almost obsessive rows, the grass brighter green than Elias had ever seen before, damp and lush beneath his boots. The cemetery was filled with flower beds and hedges and stone fountains, all perfectly groomed, all flawlessly maintained.

"It's . . . pretty," he said in surprise. Nyx didn't have cemeteries anymore; they had marble mausoleums to entomb the dead who weren't burned on pyres, their coffins kept behind lock and key. Old superstitions from back when necromancy was legal and cults of its wielders would terrorize the kingdoms, that addictive magic eating away at them until they were little more than corpses themselves.

Kallias shook his head. "Not every part of it."

Together, they picked their way across the cemetery until they came to a stop at a space that didn't match the rest. Seamus swore under his breath and horror chilled Elias to the bone; it took effort to choke back a prayer to Mortem as he stumbled back a couple steps from the travesty before them.

The grave had been *desecrated*. There was a gaping hole in the ground, yawning open like the maw of some unholy creature, shards of splintered wood scattered in the piled-up dirt. The top of the coffin—wooden, simple—was torn up, like someone had burst in.

No. Like someone had burst *out*. The sides of the hole in the coffin were curled outward, not inward, shoved open from the *inside*.

Elias was going to be sick.

"Grave robbers," Seamus said like a curse, not seeing what Elias had, disgusted by an entirely different idea. "I thought we put an end to this."

"Not grave robbers," Elias croaked. "Necromancy."

The prince and the captain both looked to him, eyes sharp. Kallias spoke first, gesturing to the grave. "You know something about this?"

He was going to have to get better at lying if he was going to keep putting his foot in his mouth. "I've done a lot of reading," he said lamely. "And my mother was a girl when the last dregs of necromancy were being eradicated. She's told me stories."

Stories about the dead clawing free of their graves, of skeletons and half-rotted corpses terrorizing farm and village, city and homestead. Of their shambling walk and their unearthly cries. How their wielders hadn't been much better, skin and bone feeding on skin and bone, their hollow eyes lit with sick relief as they played puppeteer with lifeless marionettes. Elias *still* had nightmares of bony hands grabbing him by the ankles and dragging him from his bed.

Kallias crossed his arms, that thick black cloak swirling around him like a pet shadow. He jerked his head to the ghastly sight before them. "Tell me what you see, Eli."

Elias swallowed, the muscles in his legs practically bending backwards as he tried to approach that grave. His very blood resisted its nearness, soul-deep sickness flooding his gut like a burst pipe. But he forced his feet to the edge of the hole, crouching before it, dirt crumbling from the edge and falling into the broken coffin with foreboding thumps.

"Look at the coffin," he said after a moment. "Grave robbers would have broken the clasp and pried it open by the lip. Who would go to trouble of breaking through solid wood if they didn't have to? And here, see all that debris? If someone had broken in, the pieces would be inside the coffin, not outside. Someone broke out. And I've never known dead bodies to spontaneously decide they're tired of their graves, have you?"

This time, even Seamus didn't have a nasty retort. The two men simply stared at the grave, brows furrowed; slowly dawning horror on Seamus's face, resigned dread dragging down Kallias's.

Elias's shoulders tensed. "You already suspected."

"I hoped I was overreacting." Kallias rasped his hands down his beard, studying Elias too closely for comfort. "How much would you say you know about this sort of thing?"

Thanks to his priesthood, he knew far too much about all magics, even illegal ones. "Enough. More than most."

"Good. Consider yourself hired."

"What?" Elias and Seamus said at the same time, Elias's voice tinged with barely-contained panic, Seamus's with outright disbelief.

"I don't exactly have any kind of experience in this area. My sister might know more, but she . . ." The prince hesitated, and Elias's ears pricked. A fissure in the family, perhaps? "She's busy with the day-to-day of ruling. This stays between the three of us. I want a full investigation launched."

"The two of us can't manage a whole investigation on our own," Seamus protested. "Especially with Eli so *new*."

"I may be *new*, but I still saw more than you," Elias reminded him coolly.

Seamus's jaw ticked. "Be that as it may, two bodies won't be enough."

"Then take on a couple more, but no more than three. The more minds that hold a secret, the more mouths there are to spill it."

"You're not going to tell the Queen?"

Kallias's gaze flickered. "Not until there's something concrete to tell her. She's preoccupied with war work right now."

That wasn't the whole of it. Even as little as he'd been around this prince, Elias knew that subtle shift in his tone, the odd angle his words struck at. It was the same tone Soren wore when she lied.

He shoved that thought away, silently cursing himself. They couldn't *both* start going down that road. One of them had to hold to reality. "I'm happy to serve."

Kallias smirked faintly. "Good answer. In the meantime, let's get this grave reburied. Don't want anyone stumbling across it and panicking the whole city."

Elias nodded, even as fear tugged at his gut. He was already sick of this kingdom, every part of it: its strange magics, its murderous and lying royals, its fishy smell and heavy air. But it had its claws in his battlemate, and its teeth in his arm, and until they figured out how to extricate them both . . .

He caught the shovel Kallias tossed him and began to dig.

CHAPTER 27

KALLIAS

There were only two duties as First Prince that Kallias truly hated. The first was the arranged marriage, of course, but he didn't want to dwell on that just now. And the second . . .

"I am telling you," Finn snapped, more cross than Kallias had heard him in a while, his hands splayed like he wanted to strangle their older sister, "you *cannot* set off fireworks in the courtyard!"

"And I'm telling you," Jericho fumed, her voice bordering on a shout, her cheeks flushed with fervor and her painted nail an inch away from Finn's nose, "that you can't set them off on the beach! It pollutes the water and dirties the sand for *weeks*—"

"And if you set them off in the courtyard, we're going to end up having to rebuild the palace for the second time!"

The second thing that Kallias hated, hated, *hated* was event planning. He'd go live in the bug-infested forest with all seven of his wild Arborian cousins if it meant he never had to plan another gods-damned festival again.

Kallias and Vaughn sat on one of the many sofas and couches in the palace center, passing a bag of saltwater taffy between them and watching Finn and Jericho bicker. Vaughn's appetite had woken with a vengeance this morning; Kallias hadn't seen him stop eating since breakfast. His eyes were brighter, and for once his cheeks had some color in them. Kallias would have been far more annoyed by the fight if he hadn't been so relieved to see his brother-in-law having a good day.

"Look," Jericho finally interrupted her own rant about sea turtle health, waving to get their attention. "Forget the fireworks. What if we look into what Nyx does during their celebrations and incorporate a few of those traditions? It might make Soleil feel more at home."

"That's the *opposite* of what we want to do," Finn protested. "We're trying to get her *away* from Nyx."

Jericho scowled. "I know that. But gods, haven't you seen her face? She's *sad*. Not just angry anymore, but *sad*. She misses home. Maybe if we bothered to show a little compassion—"

"It's not a bad idea," Kallias interrupted before Finn could jump down her throat again. "But it would have to be subtle. Mama will have a fit otherwise."

"Good luck with that. They probably make sacrifices on altars and decorate the castle in blood," Finn said glumly, earning a kick from Jericho.

"You're awful," she scolded him. "They probably say the same of us. War breeds monsters in the minds of every side, but the truth isn't often that grisly."

Kallias grimaced, flashes of the battlefield playing hide-and-seek in his head. "Said like someone who has yet to taste someone else's blood in their mouth."

"I knew it. I *knew* you were a vampyre," Finn said, nudging Kallias's shin with his shoe. "All that brooding had to come from somewhere."

"Vampyres aren't real, Finn," Kallias, Vaughn, and Jericho chorused, their tones ranging from tired to outright annoyed.

Finn jabbed his finger at them. "You'll see. One day, you'll all see. I'm *telling* you, Old Lady Agatha down on Conch Street, she's too gods-damned creepy to be of this world."

"She's ninety years old, Finn. And she's very nice," Vaughn said. "She makes good cookies."

Jericho gaped at her husband. "She gave you cookies?"

Vaughn's smile, small as it was, turned smug. "She says I'm a very sweet young man."

"Teach me your ways," said Finn. "Last time I passed her place, she threw a broom at me."

Jericho gave him a look. "And what were you doing while you passed her place?"

Finn scowled. "According to her, I was skulking like a ruffian."

"And I bet you were," Vaughn said, holding his arm out to his wife. Jericho came over and sat beside him, nuzzling into his side, planting an absentminded kiss on the corner of his jaw. Kallias caught the worried look she flashed her husband's way, her silent question answered with a calm smile and a kiss to her brow that smoothed the creases there. There were shadows under her eyes, marks of the fervor Vaughn had mentioned, the desperation to save him from the silent monster eating him away from within. None of them knew how long Vaughn had left, or how this sickness would progress.

He would have to help Jericho in her search once everything was sorted with Soleil.

Just as that thought had crossed his head, Seamus entered the parlor, picking his way around laughing and lounging palacefolk to stand before them, one arm held behind his back. He gave a shallow bow. "Highnesses. Your parents have summoned you to the dining room."

"Do you do anything around here besides summoning people places?" Finn asked.

"Can't you tell them we're in the middle of something?" Jericho pleaded, shooting Finn another glower.

Seamus's mouth twitched. "It's about Soleil."

Kallias's chest tightened, and he pushed himself from the couch, already tensed for a fight. "Did something happen?"

"We're on our way, Seamus," Jericho cut in before Seamus could answer, flashing Kallias a warning look. The buzz of conversation around them had hushed, palacefolk staring while trying to make it look like they weren't. Kallias swallowed down the rest of his questions, gritting his teeth against the snippy retort that wanted out.

He couldn't argue with the Heir in public; it wouldn't be seen the same way as Finn's bickering. But he didn't think a question or two was out of place.

Vaughn got up first, a spring in his step as he took Jericho's hand and twirled her up from the couch, meeting her startled laugh with a kiss that *quickly* turned uncomfortable to watch. Kallias groaned in protest, Finn outright gagged, and they both hurried toward the hall, leaving the lovebirds behind for the time being.

"I see Vaughn's feeling better," Finn said with a gag as they walked, shoving his hands in his pockets. He was wearing a thick, long-sleeved gray shirt today, more muted than what he normally liked to strut around in. "That's good. With gross results, unfortunately. But good."

Kallias chuckled. "I'm surprised he waited that long."

"Where do people get off chewing on each other's faces in *public*? It's embarrassing!"

"I honestly don't think they realize other people are even *there*."

They paused for a moment when they reached the dining room door, both glancing at each other out of the corners of their eyes.

"Good or bad, do you think?" Kallias asked quietly.

Finn snorted, but there was no amusement in his voice when he said, "If the pattern holds, we may never get good news again."

Either someone had died, or someone was about to.

One glance at the table was all Kallias needed to deduce that, because for the first time in gods-knew how long, his parents were seated next to each other instead of across from each other, side-by-side at the head of the table. His father's chair was angled awkwardly inward, his elbows on his knees as he leaned forward, whispering urgently to Adriata under his breath. For once, she seemed to be paying her full attention, green eyes locked on her king with a look softer than Kallias was used to apart from special occasions. Their hands were intertwined, resting on their touching knees.

Oh, someone was definitely dead.

They didn't have any grandparents left. Their uncles on their father's side were sailors, so maybe there'd been a wreck. But they weren't that close, and his father didn't seem to carry any grief beyond what he'd carried since Soleil's loss. And their mother's older sister was Queen of Arborius, so they would have all heard by now if *she'd* died. News of a royal's death, no matter the kingdom, spread faster than a plague.

He was starting to give himself a headache trying to remember all the names of their cousins who could have met some grisly fate when Soleil herself entered, Eli at her back—during the day? He must have taken another recruit's shift.

Kallias was impressed with his dedication. Usually when a new recruit joined up, it was a hassle to keep them at their post for the first couple weeks. Eli was taking his responsibilities more seriously than some of their seasoned guards. He'd be an asset, so long as he kept that work ethic. And his knowledge about their newest problem had proved invaluable so far.

The memory of the cracked-open casket whittled his head pain into a sharp point, stabbing ceaselessly into the base of his skull. Cold sweat pooled in his palms, and he absently rubbed it off on his pants.

Between finding Soleil again and necromancy making a comeback, it seemed Mortem wasn't feeling very committed to her craft lately.

"All right," Soleil announced in that breezy voice he was beginning to recognize as her being tense and hiding it, "what's the big news?"

She fell into the seat between him and Finn, propping her elbow on his shoulder and her ankle on Finn's leg. Shock stuttered through Kallias at her casual touch, something so similar to Finn that he actually had to check and make sure his brother was indeed sitting a chair away, that this wasn't some trick his stressed mind was playing on him.

Finn himself seemed unbothered, barely giving her intruding ankle a glance before looking down the table at their parents. "Yeah, let's get this suspense out of the way, please. Who died?"

"We'll explain in a moment," Adriata hedged, sitting straight-backed against her chair, mouth pinched, carrying the strain of the moment in every line of her face. Whatever this was, she wasn't happy about it. "Let's wait for Jericho and Vaughn."

Kallias's back tensed, bracing for a blow. Even the air felt charged, a storm about to break, lightning held captive between his mother's pursed lips.

He'd had just about enough of surprises lately.

Jericho swept in with Vaughn trailing her, but even she seemed apprehensive, fists curled around skirts, chin raised like a weapon. The gloss on her lips was smudged, but she didn't seem concerned about fixing it.

"Thanks for waiting," she said, sitting on the other side of the table across from Soleil. Vaughn took up the seat across from Kallias, briefly making eye contact. Kallias tapped subtly at his lip. Vaughn, flushing, quickly wiped at the streak of gloss left across his mouth, flashing a grateful smile.

"I'll make this quick," said Adriata, placing her hands palms-down on either side of a stack of papers. Rather official-looking ones. "We brought you all here to discuss what happens now that Soleil is . . . here."

Soleil stared at their mother, a slight frown digging a dimple into her cheek. "What do you mean, *what happens?*"

Adriata's jaw twitched. "I'm not sure if you remember this, but in Atlas, the line of succession begins with the youngest daughter. This would, in the traditional sense, make you our Heir."

Ice locked every one of Kallias's joints.

No. They couldn't possibly be about to have this conversation.

Vaughn lost all the color he'd regained in the past few days, lips parting slightly as his eyes darted to his wife, who merely stared at her folded hands on the tabletop. Soleil's ankle fell from Finn's lap, and Finn gripped the edge of the table, his expression unreadable. No sparkle in his eyes. No smirk on his face. Nothing.

"Oh," said Soleil. And that was all.

"Currently, Jericho possesses that title and has performed those duties for the ten years you've been . . . gone." Ramses carefully studied Soleil's reactions, his hand tight around Adriata's. "But we've discussed it at length, and provided you're amicable . . ."

"We'd like to reinstate you as our Heir," said Adriata—and Kallias's head howled as he watched her finally give Soleil a gentle, *motherly* look. As he watched her pick up that privilege, that freedom, that key he'd coveted and longed and nearly bribed for . . . and move it permanently out of his reach. "Jericho will guide you through your duties, and she'll be at your side until you're ready to stand on your own. If you feel ready to take it back."

In the silence that dropped down the center of the room like a guillotine blade, Kallias heard Eli's back hit the door. He heard Soleil's sharp intake of breath.

And most importantly, he heard absolutely nothing from Jericho.

"*What?*" Finn and Vaughn both said at once, the flattest he'd ever heard Finn's voice, the angriest he'd ever heard Vaughn's. Both men stood, and Kallias followed suit; he had no idea why, or what he thought he could do, but sitting and taking this felt just as wrong. He needed to fight this, to talk sense into them, to . . . to do *something*, gods damn it, because this couldn't be right. They'd made this decision without him, without asking for his counsel. Without even *warning* him.

"Mama, it is *far* too soon—" he tried, but Finn spoke over him.

"You have to be kidding! Mama, that's *insane*. You can't be serious. Jericho, tell me she's not serious!"

Jericho did no such thing. Instead, she jerked to her feet, shaking off Vaughn's hand when he tried to hold her, ignoring him when he tried to call her back. She pushed past Eli without even a backward glance, the door slamming so hard into its frame that dust shuddered free from its hinges.

Ramses and Adriata exchanged looks. Finn, still gaping at their parents in disbelief, shoved back from the table and hurried after their older sister. But Kallias stood frozen, palms cold, knees knocking, his mind spinning like a funnel cloud.

Soleil, too, seemed stuck. And for the first time, she looked small, trapped, clinging to the sides of her chair while she watched him and Vaughn tower over the table.

"That went well," sighed Adriata, rubbing her temple.

And Kallias had no words to ask her what exactly she'd expected. No words to ask her why, if it had always been an option to change the Heir, she hadn't given Jericho what she wanted all those years ago . . . and picked him instead.

CHAPTER 28

FINN

"Jericho!"

Finn chased his older sister down the hall, but she only quickened her pace, pastel green skirts swirling with every brisk step away from the room. Her hair flowed freely down her back—no tiara to pin it back today.

He should have known—should have *seen*—

"Jericho!" he snapped again, gripping her shoulder the moment he was close enough, turning her around to face him. "Jericho, come on, this isn't right, they can't do this to you—"

He broke off when he finally got the full view of her face. She was crying, heavy tears that dripped off the edge of her chin in fully formed droplets.

"Jer," he whispered, one soft piece of his heart hardening. "I'll talk to them. Me, Kal, Vaughn, we'll all get them to realize how ridiculous this is, they can't take the crown from you—"

"Finn, stop." She took his hand, folding it between both of hers, and drew in a slow, trembling breath, strands of her hair stuck in the tear tracks on her face. "They didn't make this decision. I did."

The floor dropped away beneath Finn's bare heels. "*What?*"

"They asked me for my counsel. They planned to leave everything as it was. Tradition demands the youngest girl is named Heir, but with Soleil's extenuating circumstances, they didn't feel ready to give the title back to her."

"Yeah, because it's the worst idea I've ever heard—"

"I *told them to do it,*" Jericho interrupted, more sharply than she usually spoke, "because I am no longer fit to fill the position. My . . . my focus is divided. Has been for a long while. I need more time to help Vaughn. More time to find a way to save him."

"Jer, you don't have to turn the throne over to *her* for that. We can help, we can all split the load, I have sources—"

"Finn." She let go of his hands and held his face instead, giving him a look stamped with more pain and exhaustion than he'd thought was allowed to live in the Sun Princess. "An Heir must love her kingdom before all else and all others. But Vaughn . . ." A small tremor ran through her hands, a quake before collapse, a cave-in waiting to happen. "Vaughn is my kingdom. Vaughn is my home. And he needs me more than Atlas ever has."

How was he the only one that could see this? His family wasn't foolish, only when compared to him. "You think Soren is going to do any better of a job? Gods, Jericho, this is insanity, she's still *theirs!* Give it to *Kal* if you're so desperate to be rid of it, gods know he wants it!"

"*Soleil* is coming back to us," Jericho snapped. "Slowly, but she is. I see it. Kal sees it. She *will* remember us, Finn. I believe it. And maybe taking on some of her old duties will help tug that memory. In the meantime, I've made my choice, and you have to respect it. Whether I'm Heir or First Princess or whatever I am now, I'm still your older sister."

Finn swallowed hard. "You swore a vow when you took that crown." Not that he'd ever cared much for vows or crowns or any other chains a kingdom tried to thrust on its princes and princesses. He'd shrugged off his own long ago. But this was different. This was *madness*.

"And I swore a vow to my husband when I took his ring. I intend to keep both to the best of my ability, and right now, that means my stepping down."

"Vaughn didn't know?"

"It wasn't his decision. And he would have fought it, anyway." She balled her skirts in her fists. "He doesn't think his life is worth me setting aside my position for."

"And you don't agree."

"His life is worth whatever price I must pay for it. You know how that feels." She started walking again. "I heard what you prayed for after the fire."

Shivers ran hot and cold down Finn's spine, but he didn't chase her down this time. He watched her leave—*flee*—and grudgingly resigned himself to the fact that he was going to be spending the next few nights out in the city. And possibly the days too. This news wouldn't go over well with the people. He and Kal had done far too much work to endear Jericho to the general populace, to coax them into loving a new Heir after they'd invested so much in the first one.

Back when Soleil died, most people had guessed Jericho had no plans to stay in Atlas. The rumor mill had run on her dalliance with Vaughn for months *after* the fire, even after they'd wed, when it shouldn't have been scandal-worthy any longer. And as time crawled by without the two of them conceiving an Heir of their own, the rumors became crueler. Louder. Reaching past the city's underbelly and crawling into palace halls, whispered from the mouths of palacefolk, echoing to Jericho's ears.

That was the rashest action he'd ever taken, the most merciless he'd ever been while stepping in to quell an unsavory opinion of the public. He'd called in every favor he'd saved up, had wielded every bit of blackmail he had in his possession to get that gossip killed—*fast*. Negative attention was nothing new when it came to royalty. Some things had to run their course. But he drew the line when those things broke Jericho's heart.

All time wasted, now.

He folded his hands over his face, taking in a long, steadying breath.

This was fine. It was fine. He would adapt. He always did.

But that didn't mean he had to like it.

CHAPTER 29

SOREN

Soren couldn't sleep. Every toss and turn felt like a mimicry of waves, an acceptance of what they were turning her into. Every pound of her heart felt like a betrayal, every blood-beat whispering *Heir, Heir, Heir,* diluting the stardust in her blood with seawater.

Heir of Atlas.

This was either her most brilliant accomplishment or her maddest stunt, and she and Elias had disagreed—loudly, and for several minutes—over which. Luckily, he'd been dismissed from his shift and replaced with Alia, a girl half Soren's size who was nowhere near as inclined to talk to her, so she'd been left to stare at her ceiling and count an infinite amount of mountain rams in silence.

Well. Not quite silence. That monstrous gossip outside her window never seemed to stop chatting, the heave and ho of waves her constant companion no matter which room she walked into.

Soren tugged one of the pillows from her small mountain and jammed it over her head, clamping it hard over her ears and burying her face in a second pillow. Still the ocean roared.

A groan rumbled out of her and into the cradle of cloth and feather, and she shoved backwards out of her pile of pillows and blankets, rubbing the bleariness from her eyes with the backs of her hands.

This was no use. Dawn was approaching, anyway. She needed to move. She needed to *walk*.

She rolled off the bed, landing lightly on her heels, snatching up the peach-pink silk robe draped over the footboard and throwing it on. It brushed strangely against her scars, not quite unpleasant but not quite soothing. She was so desperate for the touch of something familiar that she'd almost begged Finn to let her steal one of his sweaters before remembering that showing weakness to that particular prince would probably dig her even deeper into a pit than she already was.

At home, she would've slept in one of Elias's shirts. But that obviously wasn't an option, either.

He was acting strange; she was trying not to read too deeply into it, but he seemed nervous around her now. He'd nearly leapt out of his skin that morning when she'd left the room and brushed her fingers against his back in passing, a silent reminder that she was with him, that they were all right.

Maybe not as all right as she'd *thought,* if he was going to act like a rabbit caught in a trap every time she touched him. Maybe he was doubting her again. Thinking she'd let them too far into her head.

And gods, maybe he was right. What was she thinking, indulging in swimming lessons and family dinners? She had a *mission* to complete. Elias didn't have the time to spare.

Determination hardened her heart. She could prove to him that she still had her eyes on the prize . . . and she knew exactly where to start.

When she left her room, bare feet brushing against the polished floor, she went toward Jericho's office. Lamps were lit inside, a soft golden glow haloing from the crack beneath the door, softening the edges of the hallway beyond. Soren's heart pounded as she drew closer, the muscles in her stomach tightening, every inch of her humming with adrenaline.

When she raised her fist to knock, the light beneath the door brightened, harshened, then snuffed out.

The door opened away from her poised fist, and Jericho appeared, rubbing her eye with the heel of her hand. Exhaustion had settled in the slope of her shoulders, the downward angle of her mouth, the droop of her eyelids. But when she saw Soren standing there, fist still raised, lips parted halfway to an explanation or an excuse, she straightened up and forced half a smile onto her face.

"Couldn't sleep?" she asked, gently shutting her door behind her. The smell of hibiscus and something sourer drifted out after her, something medicinal maybe.

"Not a wink."

"Need some company?"

Soren shrugged, and Jericho fell in beside her, leading her back up the hallway. The Heir—no, First Princess now—wore a simple green nightdress, her poisonberry hair loose down her back, the shadows stamped under her eyes beginning to rival her sickly husband's.

"What are you doing up at this hour?" Soren asked in what she hoped was a casual voice. She wasn't good at being anything but blunt. "You look like you need sleep more than I do."

Jericho smiled, but it was a flimsy thing. "And Vaughn needs a cure more than I need sleep."

Soren's stomach twisted uncomfortably. Those words could have come straight from *her* mouth if she swapped Vaughn for Elias. "So the gossip I'm hearing is true?"

Jericho's jaw flexed. "The gossip about my giving up being Heir or the gossip about him dying?"

Ah. Awkward. She hadn't expected that sort of frankness. "Um . . . both?"

"I can't serve my kingdom and save him at the same time." Jericho slid her hands beneath her hair, twining her fingers behind her neck, bending it side to side until it cracked. Soren tried to ignore how familiar the action was, how often she did it herself, how often Elias jumped at the sound and cursed her soundly for trying to break her neck. "And that choice is *always* going to be him."

Tattooed shoulders. Dark hair. Sleeptalking. Sleepy grins. Hands braiding her hair. "I know something about that."

Jericho looked at her out of the corner of her eye, and sweat began to gather on the back of Soren's neck. "You're still hoping to save your friend?"

Lie. Lie, you gods-damned fool.

"Yes."

Damn it, Soren.

Jericho was quiet as they slipped out of the hallway and entered the common area of the palace. Somehow it was so much spookier with only the moonlight to guide them, melting every edge of the space to quicksilver. Then: "Even knowing what Nyx did to you?"

"He wasn't responsible for that. No matter what they did, he's a good man. The best. He doesn't deserve to die. I . . . I can't let him die."

She hadn't meant to give that much, to be quite that honest. But there it was.

But maybe that was exactly what she should do, she realized when something in Jericho's gaze softened.

"I owe him my life," she continued, allowing in a twinge of the desperation that riled in her whenever she pictured her life without Elias. "Many times over. And he owes me his. We are . . ." They were something she had no idea how to name. Not just friends. Not just battlemates. Something precious and perfect and terrifying, and if she lost it, she didn't know what she'd become.

They were campfires and shared shirts and stolen socks. They were elbows in ribs and broken noses and headlocks. They were promises whispered in the dark. They were *jackass* and *smartass*.

"He is my best friend," she finished softly. "And even if I never see him again, I will never give up on saving him."

Jericho's hands gathered in her skirt, her knuckles whitening. "I hear you. That's Vaughn for me."

The sisters walked in silence for a moment. Step for step. Ache for ache.

"I have contacts in Arborius," Jericho said finally. "Some family. Obviously things are too tense right now, but maybe eventually . . . maybe we can find a way to arrange passage for your friend. Or we can send someone from Arborius there."

Soren's heart fell to her toes. "Why not just—"

"Soleil, there isn't..." Jericho broke off with a soft sigh, fussing with a lock of her hair. "Do you really think Mama will let me just hand over the antidote to the Viper venom? She won't care what this boy is to you, only that he's Nyxian."

Soren swallowed down her anger. "I thought you—*we* were winning this war. What does she care if you save the life of one Nyxian?"

Jericho's eyes burned; for a moment, Soren could have sworn they flashed with green light. "No one is winning this war. We take more ground, they take it back. We kill, they kill. We're just going to keep fighting, turning over new blood until it runs out. We'll either go on forever, or we'll destroy each other."

Soren didn't like the vicious cut to Jericho's mouth when she said those words. Or the way that she sounded so sure, so beyond hope for an end.

An idea began to tingle in the back of her mind. Such a wild, wishful idea that she immediately kicked it back into the abyss where her worst ideas came from.

Still. There was more than one way to end a war. And if she couldn't kill her way through, maybe she could try something else. She was the Heir to the Atlas throne now, after all. There was no telling where that could take her. What it could offer her.

"Are you ready to start your lessons tomorrow?" Jericho interrupted her thoughts, looking at her with the smallest possible smile. "Heirship comes with responsibilities, you know."

Soren wrinkled her nose. "Like what?"

Jericho grinned in earnest that time. "Like planning the Saltwater Ball."

Oh, *gods*. Not another party. "Why don't you just kill me now? I'm sure Finn can help you make it look like an accident."

Jericho laughed, nudging Soren with her hip. "Oh, relax. It'll be fun. You'll be good at it, I bet. You've got a good eye for color."

Oh. Did she?

"Fine," she mumbled. "But we might as well get a head start now. I don't want to look like a fool in front of the others."

Jericho's eyes gleamed the same way Elias's had the one time Soren made the mistake of asking him to explain something religious to her. "Follow me."

Hours later, the sun doused the common area in pink-tinted dawn light. Books lay strewn about on the various couches and chairs. Palacefolk were just beginning to disperse to their duties, breakfast plates empty and bellies full. And Soren still hadn't slept.

"The Saltwater Festival was established two hundred and four years ago to celebrate the end of the year," she recited, pacing back and forth across one of the couches, feet sinking haphazardly into the cushions with every step. "Vendors leave their shops to set up booths in the streets, the entire city joins in to decorate, and games are played on the beach. Tournaments are set up and the winners are given awards by the royal family themselves. People travel from all around the kingdom to visit for the week-long festival, beginning with the Saltwater Ball and ending with a performance by . . . I don't know, pyromaniacs—"

"Pyroperformers," Vaughn corrected her, nose buried in a book.

Soren waved her hand at him, irritation burning at her joints. "Whatever. They play with fire, which feels ironic coming from the kingdom that got its palace burned down—"

"Nyx's fault," Jericho interjected from her chair, gnawing on a pen while she absently twined a strip of green light between her fingers.

"Semantics. And during the week, presents are exchanged, people visit family, etcetera, etcetera." Soren spread her arms out and gave a sweeping bow, wobbling forward, barely managing to catch her balance. "Have I passed your test?"

"Anima help us, you're really starting to sound like Finn," Jericho groaned, but she was smiling, which Soren guessed was a good sign. "You only forgot one thing."

"And what's that?"

"They'll announce your Heirship officially at the ball." Vaughn looked up, adjusting his reading glasses. He seemed more tired today, his gaze duller, that bright-eyed energy he'd been radiating yesterday already faded to nothing. And she guessed the pipe between his teeth wasn't helping, smoking some sweet-scented thing that made her own head feel a little fuzzy. She guessed it was some sort of pain-killer. "And you'll officially be home."

No, home was miles away. Home would be readying for the Winter Fair, something actually quite similar to this celebration, if somewhat less grand. No balls thrown or fireworks set off, but bonfires lit and s'mores made, cookies baked and sweaters knit. She would've been working on Elias's gift if they'd been home. He probably would've been making her a new set of armor, since Atlas ruined the set he made her last year.

She'd *cried* when he gave it to her. She'd loved it so much that she'd almost felt guilty giving him that horrifying hand-knitted blanket. But then he'd slept with it every night after, and she'd felt a bit better.

She had very little in the way of a bucket list, but making Elias admit he hated her handmade presents was at the very top. Every holiday she managed something uglier than the last, and every holiday he managed to act *more* grateful, *more* thrilled. He'd worn the sweater she made him two years back until it literally fell apart.

She *would* break him. It was only a matter of time.

"Right," she croaked. "Home."

"I can't believe it snuck up on us like this." Jericho dismissed her tendril of magic with a wave of her hand. "I haven't even started my shopping."

Vaughn took a puff of his pipe, closing his eyes. "I've been done for two weeks."

"I told you to wait for me! Now I have to go alone."

A sudden thought set Soren back on her heels, hope blazing through her. "Could I come with you?"

Jericho and Vaughn both stared at her like she'd grown antlers.

"You . . . want to go?" Jericho asked slowly. "With me?"

Soren cleared her throat, reeling her enthusiasm back in as quickly as she could. "I mean . . . if you wouldn't mind. I'd like to. I don't have money, but—"

Jericho lit up like the gods-damned sun, her grin almost stretching to either ear. "Of *course* you can come! Don't worry about money, I'm sure Mama won't mind if we give you a little something for the sake of the holiday." She hopped to her feet, tossing aside her things, babbling at the speed of an overfull bobsled set loose at the top of a mountain. "This'll be so fun, it'll be just like when you were little—oh, should we invite the boys? No, never mind, they'll ruin it. You really want to come with me?"

She hadn't expected Jericho to be quite *this* excited. But honestly, it was nice being wanted that much. Even if it was by a terrifying Atlas witch.

"Yeah," said Soren, surprised to find that she really meant it. "I want to. It'll be fun." It would help her appearances to be seen out in the city, shopping and laughing with her older sister. And beyond that . . . she might just be able to get a gift for Elias after all.

Jericho snagged her cloak from a hook on the wall, quickly doing up the clasp and tossing the hood over her hair. "This'll be great. If we're lucky, we might even find you an escort to the Saltwater Ball!"

Soren's heart slammed to a halt. "A what?"

"An *escort*. The Heir always brings someone with her to the ball, it's tradition!"

"Does that mean I'm off the hook this year?" Vaughn asked hopefully.

Jericho shot him a withering look. "I'm still *going*, you limp piece of seaweed."

In response, Vaughn gave her a loving smile, his eyes sweet and pleading. "You know I'd never pass up a chance to dance with you, my love."

Jericho grumbled under her breath. "Flattery will get you nowhere."

"What about flowers?"

"Maybe."

"Chocolates?"

"Now you're speaking my language, handsome."

Soren had to fight the urge to snort. At least they'd moved on from the subject of that *tradition* she'd just have to be the first to break. "If you two are done flirting, can we get going? I already missed breakfast because of you, and I'd rather not miss lunch too."

Jericho planted a quick kiss on Vaughn's cheek and squeezed his shoulder before walking her toward the front entrance of the palace. "You're in a rush. You must have something big planned."

A smirk played with Soren's mouth, and she stretched, her shoulders popping with the movement. "You have no idea."

CHAPTER 30

KALLIAS

Kallias was burning alive.

Unbearable heat pressed against him, walls of fire inching closer and closer with every panicked breath knifing into his chest. He scrabbled backward, palms scalding against the floor—not a floor. A pit of pulsing coals that gnawed through the soles of his sandals, spurring tiny blazes to life on his pants and tunic.

There had to be a way out, a gap, a sliver, anything. But he couldn't see it, saw nothing beyond flame and coal, a box of fire that had no lid and no door.

He couldn't die, not here, not yet. He had to find Soleil. She needed him, she needed him . . .

Every breath felt like a weapon itself, oppressively hot, and it was like he was being cooked from inside and outside, his skin melting, his shoes smoking. Everything was terror and sweat and smoke, and he—he—

He wasn't going to find her.

Not again. He couldn't fail her, not again.

Cold, crystal-clear fury burst to life in his chest, fear honed to rage, and he roared *with the force of it, defying flame and coal, defying death and doom.*

Kallias Atlas did not belong to this devouring thing. He belonged to sea and surf, to sky and storm, and he refused *to die here.*

When he dug his fingers into the red-hot coals beneath him, they did not burn. Instead they hissed, smoke wafting from them as they went dark, put out by his touch. Something burned in his hands that wasn't fire, something slick and strange and cold.

Instinct took over, and when Kallias flung his hands out toward one of the walls of fire—

His scream rent apart the darkness as he flung himself upward out of dreams, feet hitting the floor before he even realized he was awake, the momentum sending him staggering forward. He caught himself against the wall, fingers splayed, head ducked and chest heaving, awful shakes threatening to collapse every flimsy structure that held his frame together.

His forehead fell against the wall, a quiet breath escaping him as the cool paint soothed the feverish heat from his face.

I'm home. I'm home. I'm okay.

Everything was as it should be. The smell of the sea laced in the cool breeze coming through the window, the chill in the air promising that winter was finally here, that soon the beach would be his alone to brave and he could swim off the heat of his nightmares rather than relying on a wall that took on his body heat too quickly to comfort long.

Only . . . the wall wasn't warming beneath his skin. Instead it grew colder, colder, until it was no longer comforting, until it stung.

Kallias looked up to find his own face reflected back at him from a sheet of ice.

"*Depths!*" he swore, staggering back from the wall, his eyes struggling to take in the sight before him, his mind refusing to comprehend what he was looking at.

A thin, perfectly clear layer of ice smoothed over the wall, only just visible in the gleam of the morning sun shining from the window behind him.

He blinked. Swore again, like that might help. Rubbed his eyes hard with the heels of his hands, hard enough that his vision blurred for several seconds before he blinked it clear.

The ice was gone; only some droplets glimmered where it had been, or where he'd *thought* it had been, condensation sparkling cheerily against the deep blue paint.

Kallias took in a slow, shaking breath and let it out in a whoosh. Clean—no smoke, no frost, nothing strange left to taunt his senses. The only thing he smelled now was his own morning breath.

He snatched up the shirt he'd discarded last night, balling it around his fist and using it to wipe the moisture from the wall. Still, every hair on his body stood on end, his knuckles clenching every so often, remembering the sensation crackling deep inside them . . . a pressure that felt like *power.*

Hallucination, definitely. Stress was getting to him, messing with his head in ways he couldn't afford with a necromancer on the loose and a new Heir to get caught up to speed and a ball to attend.

A groan ached in his tight chest.

Oh, depths take him. The ball. He was late to meet the others for their fittings. He'd promised Finn he'd be there so he wasn't the only one looking like a stuffed peacock, and gods knew he was never going to hear the end of it if he didn't get there in time.

Throwing on a thick knit shirt and whatever pair of pants his hands touched first, Kallias left his room hopping on one foot, pulling on his boot, swearing under his breath when the other caught on a loose bit of flooring and almost pitched him to his knees. Thank the gods the hallway was empty, only thin sunlight to greet him and remind him exactly how late he already was.

He could feel Finn's irritation building from floors away, pushing against his heels until he was running like he was fourteen again, late for his lessons with his swordsman uncle who thought being forced to run laps on the sunbaked beach with bare feet was a proper punishment for tardiness. The day Uncle River left to sail the world was the biggest relief in Kallias's life, even if he'd missed him a little once he was gone.

His siblings were already waiting at the door, as expected: Finn sitting cross-legged on the floor, scribbling in a notebook; Soleil propped against the wall, playing cat's cradle with a bit of yarn; Jericho and Vaughn having a competition to see who could balance the most almonds on their nose. As Kallias ran up to them, limping from a stitch in his side, Vaughn shot his hand out to tickle Jericho's stomach, startling a squeal from her that could have shattered glass, almonds flying every direction.

"I'm so sorry," Kallias panted. "I slept late."

"Unbelievable news!" Finn said in a faux-perky voice, not looking up from his notebook. "Man who is always late to everything is astoundingly *also late* to his newest commitment! He just keeps on surprising us."

Jericho tossed an almond at Finn. It bounced off his head. "Don't be sour." Then, to Kallias: "We just dragged Soso out of bed, anyway."

She certainly looked it. Her brows were drawn in tight, her scowl a death-promise, her hair poofed out like the manes of one of the mountain cats that prowled the outskirts of Tallis. "They didn't even let me fix my hair."

"I'm sure you'll survive." Kallias reached out to muss her hair, but at the wide-eyed glare she leveled his way, he slowly lowered his hand and took a step back. Maybe a few.

"I missed this," Vaughn announced suddenly, grinning from ear to ear. "The four of you fighting. I didn't realize how much till just now."

"Glad you're entertained," Soleil grumbled. But there was a softer edge to it now; even she couldn't find it in her to be cruel to Vaughn.

"Well, let's get going before it turns into a wrestling match. Soleil's hair will really suffer then," said Finn, heaving himself to his feet and snapping his notebook shut. "Jericho's a hair-puller."

Jericho fluttered her eyelashes innocently. "Please. I outgrew that ages ago." She gave Soleil a once-over, frowning. "Are you really sure you want to wear that out?"

Soleil blinked, then looked down at her ensemble: a sleeveless goldenrod-dyed tunic tied at her waist and dark leggings cuffed at her ankles. "Is something wrong with it?"

"You might be a bit cold, is all."

Soleil and Finn both leveled Jericho such similar looks of condescension that Kallias blinked again, wondering if he was seeing double. But when he opened his eyes again, only Soleil still wore the look. "I'm from Nyx. Your winter is warmer than our summer. I think I'll manage."

That settled the discussion, so they made their way out, Kallias tugging on his own jacket as they walked into the brisk air. The courtyard was filled to the brim, people bustling about with garlands and lanterns and crystal strings in hand, excited chatter rising and falling like an invisible tide. Jewel tones and joyful grins flashed wherever he looked, the holiday already in full swing even before it had officially arrived.

The city, too, felt different—no longer waiting with baited breath for news from the war. Instead, people smiled at each other, calling out greetings and asking after each other's partners and children and grandparents, offering spare treats and laughing at bad jokes. Mr. Hargreeves was setting up his kite stand already, proudly painting a new sign proclaiming him as the longest-serving vendor of the Saltwater

Festival. The Kilgrave brothers were helping him, their own weaponsmith stand already set up. The owners of the bakery stand next door, Jemma and Erica, were too busy practicing a waltz in the middle of the street and giggling at each other's clumsiness to get much work done.

The tightness in Kallias's chest finally eased as he breathed in the familiarity and breathed out the lingering dissonance from his nightmare. Bad dreams had nothing on this: seeing his people happy, his home vibrant, everything finally beginning to fall back into place.

Out of the corner of his eye he saw Soleil drift forward, slowly taking everything in.

"What do you think?" he asked. No answer. Frowning, he touched her shoulder. "Soleil?"

She jumped like his touch sent a shock through her, a quiet curse hissing just under her breath. "Gods, Kallias, what?"

"I was just wondering—what's wrong?"

"Nothing." Her gaze seemed off when it wandered away from him again. "I just . . . I think . . ." A shudder quaked through her shoulders. "I think I remember this. More than I thought."

Excitement lit him up like a firework, and he let go of her immediately, not wanting to pull her away from wherever her mind had taken her. "You do?"

"A little."

"Hey, Kallias!" called one of the Kilgrave brothers—Maleko, he thought, based on the cocky grin. The older of the twins leaned against Hargreeves's stand, giving Kallias a quick salute. "You'd better be saving a dance for me at the ball."

"Always do, Le," he called back, offering a dramatic bow. "Should I save one for Makani too?"

"Not this year, Highness," called Makani, his eyes gleaming as he popped up from behind the stand. "I've got a date."

"You and Lira finally gave up on torturing each other, huh?"

Makani blushed, and Maleko burst into laughter, patting his brother on the back. "Told you. Everyone knew but you two."

"Well, we know *now*," Makani grumbled.

When he waved goodbye to them and turned to check on Soleil, he found her already staring at him, her eyes narrowed. "You know all their names. You say hello to them all."

Kallias's ears burned. "Is something wrong with that?"

"No." But she didn't look pleased, and though he knew there was no way to unravel that look, he still wished he could try.

The siblings wove through the crowded, spice-scented streets until they reached the tailor, the door propped open as if expecting their arrival. Fine gowns and suits gleamed in the window, and Jericho whimpered in envy and delight. Even Soleil blinked away that haze in her eyes, something hungry replacing it when she saw the piles of cloth and shimmer and shine.

"All right," she said. "I might be able to get on board with this."

"Too late to run now, anyway," Finn sighed as Jericho pushed him inside and dragged Vaughn in after her. He met her squealing enthusiasm with his usual patient smile, letting her plunge them both into the racks with only a brief helpless look thrown Kallias's way.

It didn't take Kallias long to find something he liked—a fine blue brocade jacket, laced with gold lining and shining buttons. Finn, miracle of miracles, actually begrudgingly agreed to something similar, though his ensemble was a vivid shade of purple. Vaughn, per usual, wore the plainest thing he could get Jericho to approve of, and Jericho seemed to have forgotten that she was no longer the Heir, that not every eye would be on her this time. Her gown was a dark, rich green, the ruched sleeves resting off her shoulders. The bodice was embroidered with pastel flowers and vines that crept down toward the taffeta skirt that swished and twirled with her when she moved, her laughter bubbling like uncorked champagne as Vaughn helped her test it in the middle of the shop, twirling her so elegantly people on the street stopped to peer inside and applaud.

Soleil had yet to make her exit from the fitting room where she'd disappeared with a mountain of gowns in all sorts of colors and cuts. Kallias had no idea what to expect from her.

"Soleil!" Finn rapped his knuckles against the door, already back in his pants and sweater, a pout on his face. "Come on, kid, I'm starving. We already missed lunch."

"This is my first royal ball as an Heir that I can remember," she called back, "and I want to make sure I get it right."

"There's no way to get it *wrong*! It's just a dress."

"First impressions are *important*!"

"Let her be, Finn," Kallias said, quietly enough that Soleil wouldn't hear. "This is the first time I've seen her having fun since she got here."

"Kal, if I don't get a fried fish sandwich in about thirty seconds, I'm going to shrivel up and die."

"A shame," Soleil deadpanned. "Move over, you dramatic asshole, I'm coming out."

When she stepped out of the dressing room, the whole shop went quiet, filled with the silent echo of jaws hitting the floor.

"Well?" Flushing, Soleil brushing an invisible piece of lint from her skirt. "Will this work or not?"

Finn composed himself first, letting out a dark, delighted cackle. "Oh, that new guard is going to have a *stroke*."

CHAPTER 31

ELIAS

The first thing Elias had learned as a young acolyte was that there was an order to things, a natural pattern that must always be followed to the letter: birth, life, death. And nothing more after. Not in this world, anyhow, and the matters of Infera and Arcaea were far more complicated. But those didn't matter here. In fact, according to Seamus, who seemed determined to prove Elias was entirely useless, none of his knowledge was helpful at all.

Which wasn't true, of course, unless Seamus had *also* spent eight years of his life trailing behind priests and priestesses, staying up well into the night reading any piece of divine lore he could get his hands on, or had grieved his lost father at sixteen and been possessed with the singular need to *know* what happened to the dead after their souls departed their bodies. Or if his mother had also experienced the scourge of necromancy as a young girl.

All of which Elias found highly unlikely.

"This is useless," Seamus announced, tossing aside his third book in as many hours, rubbing his temples like there was actually something working behind them. "There's nothing in here that isn't common knowledge. Nothing to help us *find* this monster and get them locked up."

"I already told you," Elias said, his patience wearing thin, his teeth tasting strange from being ground too hard, "we're looking in the wrong places. The public libraries won't have anything useful on display. Books on necromancy were gathered up and hidden away long ago. We need to be looking for private collections."

He wished Kallias hadn't agreed to have both of them working on this problem. Ordinarily he would have thrived on hunting down someone who was undoing Mortem's work. But when it came with a bumbling blond babysitter, it felt considerably less worthwhile.

As if summoned by that thought, Kallias ducked in moments later. He looked harried, his hair tied up in a messy knot instead of his usual neat braid, his lips chapped from being chewed on, just like Soren when she was stressed about something. "Any progress?"

"No, Highness," Elias and Seamus chorused. Elias hated when that happened; his paranoia piqued every time, convinced Seamus's legitimate accent made his sound clearly fake.

Kallias breathed out a curse, rubbing the corners of his eyes. "Forget it, then. Seamus, take Eli and head to the usual gossip spots tonight. See if anyone's whispering about grave robbers. I want this dealt with by the Saltwater Festival."

"Yes, Highness," Seamus said, alone this time. Elias didn't feel like genuflecting too much, mostly because he wasn't a kiss-ass . . . though Soren might have disagreed.

"And go quietly," Kallias added. "Until we have an idea of who's responsible, anyone is a suspect. I don't want them realizing we're on the hunt and fleeing somewhere else in the kingdom before we can catch them."

Not just that; Elias had gathered that Kallias didn't want the Queen to catch wind of these incidents either. Whether because it was Kallias's responsibility to deal with or for some other, stranger reason, Elias didn't much care. All that mattered was that it signaled another potential weakness in the Atlas family.

"Highness," Elias said carefully, "if I can ask . . . what exactly is the Saltwater Festival?"

Kallias and Seamus both looked at him like he'd spat out feathers. "How small is your town, exactly, Eli?" Kallias asked.

His cheeks burned, and he rubbed the back of his neck, giving a one-shouldered shrug. It seemed reasonable to be bashful over his ignorance in front of a prince. "Small enough that *town* is a bit of an exaggeration."

He was saved from any further struggles by a knock on the door, and Alia's head poked inside, her dark eyes fixed on Kallias. "Highness, your sisters want you to join them in Princess Jericho's room."

Sisters. Sour fear tanged across Elias's tongue. He'd promised Soren time, but every day they spent here seemed to pull her further from him, unraveling her bit by bit, pulling her deeper into the fold of Atlas.

He'd thought he'd known what torture was. He hadn't expected it to be as simple as watching his battlemate slowly lose herself to these liars for his sake. Whips and saltwater and chains, he could have borne. But seeing his confident, brash, smartass battlemate looking so *lost* was going to kill him well before this poison did.

He swallowed down that fear, bracing himself against the taste like taking a shot of strong liquor. Soren knew what she was doing, always had, even when they found themselves up against impossible odds and unforeseeable circumstances. She thought on her feet, bobbing and weaving around the blows thrown at her, always ready with a sharp right hook.

She was a survivor, that was all. She was doing what it took to endure, and as helpless as he felt, he wasn't helping anyone by wallowing in worry. Right now, the best way to help Soren was to continue proving himself, even if he'd rather shove his beads down Kallias's throat and say a halfhearted prayer to Mortem for the prince's soul.

"Great," sighed Kallias, but the smile on his face contradicted his irritated tone. "Wonder what they're up to now?"

"We'll handle this, Highness," said Elias, earning himself another bitter look from Seamus. "You go ahead."

Gods, this was going to take some getting used to.

It wasn't until he was sitting alone, far from the palace and the bustle of the city that had lasted well into the night, that Elias figured out what was causing the jagged ache in his chest, a sensation like he was being gnawed away at. A pain that hadn't faded in days even when he tried massaging it away or loosening the muscles with a warm shower, even when he hugged a pillow against it to try and brace whatever had been knocked loose.

He was homesick.

He missed the castle kitchens, sneaking in with Soren when the staff had all gone to bed, trying to bake cookies while keeping her from eating the entire bowl of raw dough instead. He missed his mother, her warm smoke-scented hugs and her cooking lessons and her stern, steady way of letting him know he was loved beyond measure. He missed his siblings, their laughter and racing feet pounding against their little house until its windows shook in their frames, their weight dragging him down to the floor when they all tackled him at once.

This holiday wasn't helping. Back home, they'd be close to the Winter Fair, and the similarities were almost too much to bear. Between the street vendors and the mouthwatering smells of baked goods and the palpable joy in the air as he walked from the palace to this tavern, it was enough to make him want to drag Soren out and take her home now, all her clever plans be damned.

He didn't even have a present for her this year. Nothing besides the fact that he was here, anyway, and that didn't seem like much of a gift.

Well. There was the ring in his pack. But that would open a whole new realm of jokes from her that, for once, he wasn't sure he could endure.

He swung his pack off his back, rifling around until he found the ring. He slid it over the tip of his second finger, spinning it absentmindedly, watching it sparkle in the light of the tavern's surprisingly nice chandelier that told him this was the place to go for gossip. A tavern that could afford to be decorated that nicely was getting paid off by more than one person to keep their secrets, and there was no need to keep secrets in places where they weren't being told—and sold.

And he wasn't the only one with his ears open tonight.

He wasn't sure *how* Finnick Atlas was fooling everyone here with a scarf and a slightly deepened timbre to his voice, but damn if he wasn't. He'd finagled his way into a card game that Elias had already failed to join, and if Elias was seeing right, he appeared to have an entire deck of cards stashed in various places on his person.

And he definitely knew Elias was watching him.

So Soren was right, then; Finnick was the dangerous one, the one who would catch them when their luck ran out. And risking that out here, when he was too far from Soren to warn her, wasn't worth confronting him now.

So Elias sipped his tangy, too-sweet drink that made his tongue curl and left an aftertaste of rotten fruit, listening for any whisper of unholy dealings.

It didn't take long for something to stir his attention; a murmur here, a quiet curse there. But it wasn't anything to do with necromancy.

"Damn Nyxians," muttered a man who wore an Atlas army uniform, eyes haunted by ghosts that visited Elias most nights too. "They've gone over a year without initiating an attack. What in the depths possessed them to try it now?"

It was only by the grace of Mortem that Elias managed to catch himself before he could show an obvious interest. Still, shock set his finger tapping lightly against the side of his glass while he tried to listen more closely.

"We've held Delphin for five years," snarled the grizzled soldier, slamming down his shot glass, "and they take it back in an afternoon? I don't like the smell of that. Something changed. They've got better strategists, or better weapons, maybe a new ally—"

"Oh, they have a better weapon, all right," scoffed the young man who poured the old soldier another drink. "We let one of them right into the palace and handed her a crown while we were at it. Word is that the soldiers who took Delphin were screaming her Nyxian name. *Soren, Soren, Soren—*"

"Hush," snapped the barkeep, her nervous eyes darting to Finnick before fixing themselves firmly on the counter in front of her. "That poor child had no choice in where she was raised, thanks to those Nyxian pieces of filth. It's a gods-damned miracle she was brought home. I'll not hear ill being spoken of a victim in my tavern, Wes, and you best remember it if you want to keep that apron you're wearing."

The young man's cheeks colored. "Yes, ma'am."

Chills of dismay rode up and down Elias's back, hearing Soren being spoken of with such venom in this kingdom that supposedly loved their dead princess so much they'd been willing to war Nyx into the ground to avenge her. But beneath that, there was a thrill, too. Delphin used to be the most important of their border cities, the fortress that kept Atlas from pushing them back for the first five years of the war. It had taken a months-long siege for the Sun Kingdom to force a surrender.

And now Nyx had taken it back. In a *day*.

The old soldier was right on one count—someone must have given Nyx something useful. It hadn't been Soren, and it certainly hadn't been him, so another spy in the city must have stumbled across something truly mountain-moving.

That was fantastic news for Nyx. It was considerably less fantastic news for him and Soren.

If public opinion was already turning on Soren when her appointment as Heir was barely even a rumor yet, it was only going to get worse if Nyx started making real headway. And scrutiny toward the palace staff would double, that was for certain.

His fingers tightened on his pack, and he slid it back over his shoulders, taking his time pretending to finish his drink, lingering just long enough for the gossip to flow down different streams, to not seem like he was being driven out by that particular subject. And when he felt the time was right, when Finnick was looking the other way and the other patrons were lost in their own drinks or conversations, he quietly slid out the door.

He barely made it four steps before something sharp twinged the small of his back.

"Evening, Eli," Finnick greeted him, perfectly casual, not a trace of malice in his tone. "Drinking on the job is generally frowned upon, you know."

Oh, he was so dead. *Mortem, take me gently.*

"Prince Kallias asked me to visit the taverns, Highness," he said, keeping his hands where the Second Prince could see them, desperately wishing he'd said goodbye to Soren before he left. A dingy Atlas alley wasn't exactly what he'd had in mind for his deathbed. "Can I ask why you have a knife on me?"

"How about we make a deal? You don't lie to me, and I won't lie to you. Can we try that on for size?" Still so pleasant, that voice. Still not matching the press of blade to back.

He swallowed hard. "Shouldn't be hard, Highness. I haven't lied to you yet."

"Mmhm. Cute. I'll let you get away with that one, but it's the *last* one, am I clear?"

"Crystal."

"Good. Now that we've got that sorted . . ." Finnick circled around to the front of him, knife gently dragging against the fabric of Elias's dark jacket with his movement, head cocked in a way that felt a bit inhuman. His eyes glittered in the moonlight, a snow leopard on the hunt, a killer who'd caught the scent of blood. "Tell me, *Eli* . . ."

Dead. Dead. He was so gods-damned dead. No, wait, he shouldn't be swearing right before dying, that wouldn't gain him any favor in Mortem's realm.

"What exactly are your intentions with my little sister?"

Elias's stomach dropped to his feet, bounced off his soles, and shot back up to slam itself into his throat. "Pardon me, Highness?"

Finn raised one eyebrow. "You heard me. You think no one can see the way you look at her? I mean, good gods, man. I know you come from a small town, but you'd think you'd know not to gawk at people that way. You're drilling holes in the poor girl's head."

Heat flared in Elias's cheeks. "I don't . . . I—Highness, I'm not sure what you're—"

"Sure you aren't." Finn sheathed the knife with one hand and flung his other arm around Elias's shoulders, and Elias had to tamp down the unbearable urge to dislocate the prince's shoulder from its socket. "Look, it's completely understandable. The Atlas royal family is Anima-blessed with good looks. Myself being the best example. But you're going about this all wrong. Soleil's not a subtle kind of girl. If you want her to notice you, you're going to have to do more than stare and hope for the best."

They could not possibly be having this conversation. He honestly would have preferred being murdered. "Highness, I have no intentions of any kind towards the princess."

None whatsoever. A reminder to himself, an order, a plea to pull it together. If this was bad enough that *strangers* could see it now, he was in deeper trouble than he thought.

Finn patted his shoulder. "I get it. Don't worry, I haven't said anything to Kal, and he's probably too dull to see it himself, so you're safe from that older-brother-wrath stuff. Now, if you want it to stay that way . . ." Finn's hand tightened on his shoulder—the wounded one—and a nauseating wave of pain radiated down his arm. That knifetip nibbled at his side again. "We'll just keep quiet about my being in that tavern this evening. Does that sound fair?"

Elias swallowed down bile and adrenaline, wishing to Mortem the prince would let go of his arm. "I'd say so, Highness."

"Great!" Finn squeezed harder, and Elias's knees quaked from the force of the retch that built in his body, but by some miracle, he held it in. Cold sweat gathered on every exposed inch of skin, sickly shivers rumbling beneath his skin alongside the pain.

Finn let go after that, stretching with all the lazy contentment of a housecat and walking backwards as he moved away, keeping his back out of reach as he left. "I so prefer when people are reasonable. It saves me so much mess." With a wink and a grin, the Trickster Prince vanished into the Port Atlas shadows like he'd always been one of them, like he'd only worn the form of a man for a short while.

And once Elias was sure he was gone, he ducked into an alley of his own to vomit.

CHAPTER 32

FINN

"That was *mean*," Luisa scolded as he swaggered into the alley they'd chosen to meet in. No readings or gossip tonight; he'd borrowed some tools from her for his Saltwater Festival gifts and needed to return them. Something mundane for once.

"But fun," he said, still grinning, smug satisfaction a much kinder companion than the headache pounding in his temples. He hadn't been able to shake it since *Eli Dorian* over there knocked him out, not even with several healing sessions from Jericho, and it was becoming well and truly annoying. He was quite fond of his head; it was more or less the only thing he had going for him, and he couldn't afford for it to be damaged.

"That poor man looked like he was going to puke on your shoes."

"*That poor man* is a Nyxian spy, and if I didn't think Soren would burn down the palace again if I killed him, he'd already have my knife in his back."

Luisa snorted. "Ooh, Finnick Atlas actually bothering to do the dirty work? Must be personal."

His scowl dragged another pulse of pain through his skull. "He broke my brain."

"Can't break what was already broken," said Luisa, stepping away before he even considered elbowing her for it. "Besides, she'd only be proving everyone right. People are starting to whisper about her again . . . they think it's her fault we lost Delphin."

"It's not. She hasn't even tried to contact Nyx." He knew this, because any pages in the palace that *could* be bought belonged to him already, and he'd been checking in with them periodically. "Neither has her friend, because he's not a complete idiot."

"Unfortunate."

"You're telling me."

"Why haven't you stopped them yet?"

Why indeed. "Curiosity," he said with a shrug. "They're not causing any harm yet. She was telling the truth about the venom, that much is for certain. That man's got a bite under his sleeve. He's been favoring that shoulder when he trains, and he almost fainted just now when I touched it."

Luisa sighed delicately, fingering the hood of her sheer silver cloak. "You're playing too many games at once, Finn. You need to put some of the players out of their misery before one of them gets lucky."

"That a suggestion or a prophecy?" Luisa merely held out her hand. Gods, that was annoying. "Can't you ever just *tell* me something?"

"You've missed your last two appointments to play big brother. I need to make up the loss in profits somehow."

Finn dredged up a sigh, but honestly, that was fair. He dug around in his pocket, dropping a couple gold coins into her palm.

"Suggestion," she answered finally, with a wicked grin. "But it's a good one all the same."

Finn wrinkled his nose. "There's more gold in it for you if you can dredge up something about what the Festival will look like."

Greed polished her dark eyes to gleaming, and she squeezed them shut, clasping her hands over her wrists and the tiny mirrors she wore there at all times, held in place by tight leather bands. When she opened them again, her eyes flashed pink, light fizzing at her fingertips, then snuffing out.

"Nothing but flashes." She sounded frustrated this time, bordering on nervous. "A dress here, a ring there, music . . . I think someone faints during the dance, but I couldn't see who. Too much to drink would be my bet. There's something after, though . . . something . . ."

A sound like cracking knuckles, like a wishbone pulled apart. Half-rotted teeth bared in eternal grins. A voice that chilled the marrow in Finn's bones.

"Finn!" Something hard shoved into his chest, pain bursting into pounding life behind his eyes. When he opened them, he found Luisa propping him up with her hands, her brows nearly touching her hairline.

"What?" It wasn't until he spoke, slow and slurring, that he realized *he'd* fainted. Only for a moment, but he definitely fainted. Maybe the timing of her vision was a little off.

"Finn, your eyes just rolled into your head, you started to fall—what's wrong? Did you drink anything in the tavern?" Her eyes widened further, and she dropped her hands so quickly that he almost staggered into the wall behind her. "You'd better not be poisoned, we agreed neither of us gets to die when the other one is the only witness!"

He barely managed to glare at her through squinted eyes past the hammering pain in his head. "Relax, moon girl. I'm not poisoned." At least, he didn't think so. "It's this gods-damned *headache.*"

Luisa's alarm cooled to caution, then suspicion. "What headache?"

Now, this was Luisa, the closest thing he had to a friend, someone he should have been willing to bring into his confidence. But he knew people too well to believe *anyone* could be beyond corruption, beyond betrayal. Everyone had a price on their integrity, and just in case hers sold to a higher bidder one day, he couldn't risk it.

"Nothing," he sighed, tugging his sleeves up to his elbows, suddenly feeling heat-flushed. "Just something left over from when that Nyxian brute hit me." Half-lie, half-truth. It was true the ache had started then, but these flashes . . . these *pictures* . . . he didn't know what to make of them, if he was concussed or confused or possibly going mad. And even if he trusted Luisa, he was too terrified of the implications to even try.

He'd never been strong and reliable like Kallias, never had grace and magic like Jericho, never had compassion and calm like Vaughn. His mind was his power, his weapon, and if it was beginning to fail him . . .

The structures of this city had been bolstered by his meddling for nearly a decade. If he started to slip, started to miss things, the foundation of Atlas might just follow suit.

Another session with Jericho, that was what he needed. Another healing and a salt bath and maybe a nap, and he'd be right as rain.

He had to be. Atlas couldn't afford any less.

"Do me a favor—a paid one," he added impatiently when she started to protest. "Start spreading rumors that Soren's feeding us information on Nyx's armies and their movements. Make sure to spread it to the bakery on Antica Street and the glassblower on Riptide . . . they have two of the better Nyxian spies employed there, so it should get back to Nyx fairly quickly. I want this martyrship they're giving her ended before it goes any further."

Luisa's eyes glimmered with doubt, with reluctance. But she nodded. "As you wish, Prince."

CHAPTER 33

SOREN

"Mercy! Mercy!"

Finn's wavering cry shattered Soren's daydreams of ice-skating and cinnamon-sugar coated pastries, bringing her back to the training room. She was curled up on the sunny window seat at the far side, her knitting half-forgotten in her lap, her backside an uncomfortable mix of sore and numb that told her in no uncertain terms she'd been sitting on it too long. Finn and Kallias were in the center of the room, performing a sad excuse for a sparring session, and she would've thought Finn wasn't even trying if not for the sheen of sweat on his forehead.

Only a handful of actual guards were scattered around the space, exercising or grappling or running drills with training dummies. Elias was among them, doing pull-ups on a bar propped on the wall, though he was woefully clothed. He always trained shirtless at home, thanks to his body's general resemblance to a furnace in terms of temperature, but here he confined himself to long pants and a long-sleeved shirt—a necessity thanks to his Viper bite. But pits, that didn't mean she had to be happy about it.

Finn flipped his sweat-soaked hair off of his forehead, gasping noisily, his chest heaving beneath his sleeveless training shirt. His sword hung limp from his hand, and he seemed perfectly content to stay on his ass where Kallias had knocked him for the fifth time.

"I give up," he announced. "We all know swordplay isn't my strong suit, Kal. Get a better partner."

"I would, but it's just so nice to win," said Kallias. "Again. And again. And again, and again—"

Finn made a grumbling, groaning noise, waving Kallias off as he hauled himself to his feet. "You're cruel."

"And you're a lazy ass," Soren called across the room.

"Aww, you noticed?"

"Hard not to."

"Well," Finn said, shooting a glare at Kallias, who merely rolled his eyes, "it's nice to know *someone* is paying attention."

"All right, all right." Kallias planted his shoe in the small of Finn's back and pushed, sending his younger brother stumbling toward the sidelines with even more complaints. "Soleil? Care for a go?"

"I'm a little busy." She lifted her knitting in demonstration. "Why don't you ask Eli?"

"Because he's scared he'll get his ass kicked," Finn said, dropping down beside her feet, stealing the sock off her left foot and wiping his sweaty forehead with it.

Soren yelped in protest, snatching it back. "That was rude!"

Finn merely gestured to himself. "Did you forget who you were talking to?"

"I'm an amnesiac, so . . . maybe. It's happened before."

Finn reached over and took her face in his hands, squishing her cheeks, staring deep into her eyes, looking oh-so-solemn. "Soleil? Hi. It's me, Finnick. Your brother? We met nineteen years ago when you showed up and stole my place as the youngest and therefore most loved child."

"And again when I tried to climb down the palace wall," she mumbled through pursed-out lips, silently reminding herself that she couldn't bite his hand if she wanted to keep up the ruse that she was becoming less wolf and more princess.

Finn grinned, his eyes igniting with a different light, a genuinely pleased one that tweaked uncomfortably at her chest. His moments of honesty were becoming more and more frequent, and it was making her . . . angry? Suspicious?

Guilty?

"I knew you'd remember," he said, giving her cheeks a quick pat before drawing away. "But really, Kal, I kind of want to see what the new guy can do."

Kallias looked to where Elias was still doing pull-ups, giving him a once-over that raised the hackles on Soren's neck. "Ehh, I think not. It's rude to interrupt someone else's session."

Elias got a lot of those looks back home, too. She'd learned to ignore them, or tease him for them—or at least, she tried to. Other times, she only managed to be grateful that he never returned the attention.

"Eli!" she called across the room, and Elias immediately dropped down to the floor, rocking back on his heels to regain his balance, his eyes finding her instantly. "Kal needs a sparring partner. Care to teach him a lesson for us?"

Teach him a lesson for Nyx, she said silently, offering him a subtle wink.

Elias's eyes gleamed, and she caught the barest twitch of his lips, the slight roll of his shoulders as he said, "I'm not sure I'll be much of a match, but I'm sure I'll do better than sitting on the floor."

Finn pouted. "I did *start* on my feet, to be fair."

Kallias and Elias eased into their match, feinting and offering halfhearted jabs, each feeling out the other as they circled. Stances shifted, eyes darted, and weapons changed hands and grips as they sized each other up. Neither made a move forward.

"This could take ages," Finn groaned. "Let's get some snacks."

Soren thought about telling him to go his own damned self, but her stomach grumbled at the idea of food. It wasn't fair that Finn had already learned her greatest weakness. "If I walk in there and find another bowl of fruit, I'm going to slaughter you."

Finn rolled his eyes. "There's cookies hidden in the closet. Marisha has a stash she sells off when Kallias isn't looking."

Well, that sounded . . . suspicious. "What kind of cookies are they?"

His brow furrowed. "Chocolate chip?"

"Okay, but what's in them?"

"Chocolate. Presumably in chip form."

Soren rolled her eyes. "Where I come from, if people are hiding baked goods, there's something in them that they don't want a barracks leader to find."

Finn's brow furrowed. "Like . . . raisins?"

Soren resisted the urge to sigh. "Yeah. We have a big raisin problem in the barracks." There was no need to tell him the story of how Lily and Raquel had once gotten the entire barracks drunk off a couple improperly made rum cakes—by complete and total accident, of course.

Scooping up her knitting, she followed him into the next room over, a private chamber with a single rack of weapons on the wall. Finn beelined for the closet, rubbing his palms together, warming up his thieving fingers. Soren hesitated, her eyes catching on something sharp and beautiful and unbelievably shiny.

"That's gorgeous," she breathed, setting her knitting aside, wandering to the weapons rack. A sword gleamed there, its blade pearlescent white, the hilt carved from rich green jade, the crossguard forming of a cage of metal that intertwined like flowering vines. "I've never seen a blade like that before."

"It's Mama's," said Finn. "Or it was, back when she was young. Our Aunt Genevieve had it made for her as a wedding present when she married Papa. A blade worthy of a queen . . . or a goddess."

Her fingertips brushed lightly against the blade, admiring the upkeep. If it really hadn't been used in years, someone had been taking very good care of it all that time. "Can I . . .?"

"By all means," Finn said, his mouth stuffed full of chocolate, presumably in the form of chips. "Gods know everyone else is too scared to."

Gingerly, she lifted the sword from its perch, testing its weight with her hands, swinging it in gentle arcs to get a feel for it. It sang through the air like a perfect violin note, smooth and weighty and sharp enough to pierce a heart. "Artem-forged?"

"No other place makes weapons that frivolously pretty, do they?"

True enough. Nyx had considerable skill when it came to weaponry, but they tended toward practicality rather than prettiness. "Will Her Majesty go ballistic if I play with it?"

Finn shrugged. "I don't see anyone around to tell her, do you?"

No, she supposed not. But she still checked to make sure the door was closed before hefting the sword and flinging herself at the nearest training dummy.

It only took a few blows for her to realize that this wasn't going to give her the release she needed; the easily landed strike of steel on lifeless grainsack was doing her no favors, giving her no challenge, no satisfaction. She needed a real body to fight.

"Heads up," she said, tossing Finn the only other weapons left on the rack: a pair of bejeweled daggers that winked at her as she threw them. Finn yelped, ducking away, letting them clatter to the floor as he curled every part of his body inward to shield his core, leaving him standing on one leg, hopelessly contorted around himself.

"What in the depths was that?" he cried.

Soren rolled her eyes. "I said heads up."

"It was almost heads *off*, shells-for-brains! By Anima and all her gods-damned tree-hugging followers, could you manage not to try and murder me for one single day?"

"Probably not. It's kind of how I show affection."

Finn scowled. "Fine." He picked up the daggers, holding them awkwardly—a man whose hands had no idea what a weapon felt like, clearly.

This was going to be fun.

Baring her teeth in one of those wolfish grins he loved to mock, she flung herself at him, sword angled to disarm—

Her sword jumped sideways, almost out of her hand. She staggered to the side, thrown by the unexpected impact, quickly steadying herself with a quick skid.

Finn blinked at her. "Did you trip?"

"I just lost my balance," she snapped. She didn't give him a warning this time, didn't go recklessly; she adjusted her stance in a blink and moved carefully, aiming just so.

Again, her sword jerked to the side.

But this time, just before it skewed away, Finn's hand twitched. A movement so quick and subtle she'd missed it at first, a pinpoint twist, an artful blocking of her blow with his little blade.

She blinked at him, chilled realization slowly dawning on her. And Finn merely smiled—a terrifying, wolfish grin of his own, a mirror to the one she loved to wear—like he'd been *practicing*.

And suddenly, they weren't sparring. This wasn't play, wasn't mocking or gentle or good-humored.

In the space between one blink and the next, this had shifted from a joke to a trap.

With a quick flick of his wrists and a toss of his head, Finn flipped the daggers, palming them in a much more efficient position. He lowered himself into a perfect stance, gazing at her over their blades, fool's gold hardening to spymaster steel. He crooked one finger at her deliberately, coaxing. Baiting. An invitation she couldn't refuse without proving herself a gutless coward.

Soren forsook all sand and salt, digging her heels into snow and ice, tasting frost on her breath. Nyxians did not back down from a challenge. Especially not *this* Nyxian.

They both moved at once—Soren toward Finn's right side, Finn toward her gut, going for each other's weak spots. Finn dodged, Soren tucked and rolled, and they both ended up facing each other again. Finn chuckled, a lazy, easy sound that had no place in a confrontation like this.

Then they were fighting, blow for blow, step for step, dodge for dodge. Soren never stopped moving, and neither did Finn. His daggers were always there to meet her sword and vice versa, both of them flying across the training room floor like falcons intent on a kill, like stags locked in a battle for dominance. Their blades were their antlers, connecting again and again and again, steel singing a sparking dirge with each blow, Soren's hand rapidly numbing from the repeated impacts.

For one long, horrible moment, she was certain she was going to lose. And she would have, too, if she hadn't gotten lucky. If, when Finn's knife finally bit into the thin sheath of skin protecting her throat, she hadn't already put her sword against his.

The world held its breath.

Prince and Princess stared at each other over their blades, panting, each drawing the thinnest line of blood from the other's neck. Each waiting, waiting— wondering how fast they could cut if the other tried. Wondering whose throat would be the first to spill. Wondering whose heart wasn't quite dark enough to do the deed, and hoping to the gods it wasn't them who would hesitate.

It was Finn who finally eased, finally smiled—not the wolf, not the trickster. A broad, gleaming grin that lit his eyes with genuine joy. "This is the first time you've really reminded me of her," he said, his voice so unbearably soft that she blinked.

"Oh, you and Soleil had knife fights often at nine and ten?"

"No. But she was the only one who could ever keep up with me."

All the adrenaline cooled, settling back to the bottom of her veins, silt waiting to be stirred if he made another move. When he lowered his blade, she held hers for a beat.

It would be so easy.

No—no. It wasn't time. Not when she still didn't have her hands on that gods-damned antidote. Silently cursing herself, she lowered the blade. "Can I ask you a question?"

He pulled an embroidered handkerchief from his pocket, dabbing the blood on his neck like one would a puddle of spilled tea. "Shoot."

"Why do you pretend with the others?"

Finn was quiet so long that it seemed like he was going to ignore her. Then: "If you promise never to ask me that again, I'll promise never to ask the same question of you."

They gazed at each other. Prince and Princess. Trickster and Decoy.

"Can I ask *you* a question?" he said, quieter.

"Seems only fair."

"Your friend . . . the one you want the antidote for. What will you do if he dies before you get it?"

All the blood drained from Soren's body to pool in her feet, leaving her cold and numb. "Have you ever had a best friend, Finn?"

His bleeding throat bobbed, his eyes focusing on her face for a moment before jumping away. "Once."

"What would you have done if you lost them?"

Finn's hands curled into fists at his sides. He didn't answer, but she saw it in his eyes; the darkness that gathered. The promise of a reckoning on his face. The pain that pulsed just behind his mask.

"Then you already know the answer," she said softly.

She could survive unbearable loss. Had before and would again. But there would be a price demanded of the world if it took Elias away. His loss would be one too many, and whether the gods he loved so much existed or not, *someone* was going to pay for the unfairness of his death.

She'd heard once that those Mortem loved were never more than one foot away from an early grave. She hadn't believed it until now.

Well, you can't have him, she thought—prayed, more or less. *I love him too, and he's staying right here with me. You keep your cold, icky hands off.*

When she and Finn put the weapons away and went back to Kallias and Elias, they told them a shelf had fallen on them and cut them both. And they never said a word about the truths revealed in that room.

CHAPTER 34

KALLIAS

Kallias Atlas did not remember his dreams from the night before the ball. He did not remember the claws of ice that sprouted from his fingertips in those dreams, or the beasts of fire that roared his name like a death sentence, or how he finally fought his way to the palace entrance only to find it locked, the ring on his finger a mark that he was now *other*, that he belonged to a kingdom not his own, that he was no longer Atlas at all.

He remembered none of that. But he did remember that they were not kind dreams. And dread followed him as he dragged himself out of bed, went to his desk, snatched up the bottle of wine he kept tucked in a drawer, and downed a glass before the sun had quite peeked its rays over the horizon.

One glass—just one to steady his nerves.

FINN

Finnick Atlas remembered every dream he'd ever had, but he wished he could forget the ones the night before the ball.

Thrones made of bones instead of gold. Revelers whose laughing faces became grinning skulls, skin rotting and peeling away as they danced, their limbs bending unnaturally with every sweeping stanza of the waltz. Cold hands wrapped around his neck from behind, a whisper like a dying breath in his ear: *You asked for one of us to do something worth worshipping, didn't you? Looks like she's answering your prayers.*

When he woke, he almost went to tell his mother to call the whole thing off. Almost told her about the secrets Kal and Soren and Eli were keeping. Almost went to Jericho to ask what it meant if he was having dreams that felt realer than his waking hours.

Instead, he told himself to pull it together. And he went to find some breakfast.

ELIAS

Elias Loch did not sleep the night before the ball.

He stayed awake all through the night, praying ceaselessly to Mortem for strength as he slid into the bathing room with his dagger and bit down on a rolled-up shirt while he cut away the dying, infected flesh from his arm. As he bandaged himself up, disposed of the evidence, cleaned his dagger, and crawled back into bed. As he reached into his pack and pulled out not his holy book, not his prayer beads, but his lucky ring and its chain.

And this time, while he clung to that ring and continued to pray, he prayed not for strength, but for restraint. For the ability to keep his selfish wants to himself.

He would *not* make Soren think that her friendship was not enough, that only her romantic interest was of value to him. Her friendship was the best damned thing in his life, and everything she gave him now was already more than he deserved.

Besides . . . judging by the state of his arm, by the slowly spreading weakness in his body, he had a month left. Maybe two.

He would not make this worse. Would not tell her he wanted more, only to leave her weeks later. Even if by some miracle she might have wanted . . .

No. No more of that.

But still, he held that ring the entire night. And was still holding it, still aching with the weight of words he would never say, when Seamus came in to rouse them all for breakfast.

SOREN

Soren Nyx—or Soleil Atlas, depending on who was asked—did not dream the night before the ball.

She slept deep and true, the exhaustion of the day before killing any ideas her body had of disturbing her slumber. When she woke, it was to the sound of Jericho knocking on her door, singing some Festival song and changing the words to tell Soren she was being lazier than Finn, and she needed to pull herself out of bed or she'd never be ready in time for the ball, which was still twelve hours away.

But even having slept deeply, even with that pleasant-ish waking, Soren felt . . . wrong. Like a part of her mind was flipped upside down and every thought was coming out half-formed, disjointed and strange-sounding. Like there was something wrong in her very core.

But she still smiled when she opened the door for Jericho. And kept smiling, even when she wanted to reach into her skull and flip that mismatched piece of her back over, even when she wanted Elias so badly that she almost threw caution to the wind and ran to find him, to make him tell her that she was still herself, still all right, still *here*.

Breathe in, hold it, breathe out. Control what you can.

She could control this. She just had to breathe.

Breathe in.

Hold it.

Breathe out.

Let's show them what an Heir looks like.

CHAPTER 35

SOREN

"**T**a da!"

Blackness lit up gold as Soren opened her eyes, confronted with a mirror shoved in her face, too close for her to see anything but the green of her eyes and a tiny smear of kohl dripped on the bridge of her nose. The stuffiness of Jericho's dressing room pressed its hands against her chest, making it hard to breathe, sending her head spinning.

Her eyes crossed involuntarily, and she tried to blink them back to normal. "Jericho, I'm going to need you to tell the mirror to give me some breathing room."

"Right. Sorry." Jericho took a step back, skirt rustling with the movement, her grin broad and bright. Her face was flushed prettily, her lips glossy and shimmering, tiny pink flowers painted across her cheekbones. Her hair was unbound, falling in perfect ringlets down her back, bits of sparkle embedded in the strands like hidden stars. And her dress . . . gods, that dress.

She looked like a garden given form—in a flowery, elegant way, not a dirt-and-earthworms way. And more than that, she was glowing from the inside out, excitement radiating from her like heat from a campfire, her heeled shoes clicking with nervous energy against the floor.

Jericho raised the mirror to her again. "Ta da! For real this time."

Soren's heart thumped to a complete, sudden stop.

Oh, Mortem's rusty scythe. She looked . . . unbelievable.

"Jericho," she said, admiring the way her red-painted lips looked forming the name, the dagger-sharp point to the kohl around her eyes, the golden shimmer glistening along her cheeks and nose and collarbone like she'd been formed from a sunray, "you missed your calling."

Jericho's chest rose and fell in a wistful sigh. "I know."

Soren delicately touched one of her curls, twisting her head to see the magic Jericho had wrought—some figurative, some literal. She'd taken two sections of her hair and braided them, forming a crown of hair around her head with her curls falling down her back between them. She'd asked what Soren's favorite flower was—Soren had told her roses, but she'd lied. She didn't really care for flowers. She just knew someone else who was rather fond of roses, and besides, they'd go well with her dress. So using her gift, Jericho had grown miniature roses and gently weaved them into the braid, crowning Soren in red and gold.

There was a light knock on the door.

"Come in, Kal!" she and Jericho both called at once, giving each other knowing looks.

But it wasn't Kallias who opened the door.

"May I join?" asked Queen Adriata. She was a vision in violet, her own hair an intricate arrangement of braids pinned in place off her neck, a tiara weaved in at the top. This time, she didn't look at Soren like she was an intruder or an enemy; instead, she looked at her like a like a child's toy abandoned on the side of the street, a thing out of place with no home. A thing to be sad for, to be pitied.

Or a thing to be missed.

Her neck straightened, her chin rising, and she gave the Queen her best and sharpest grin. "Of course. We were just finishing up."

"Actually, Mama, I need to go help Vaughn," Jericho said, giving Soren an apologetic look. "He always ends up putting some piece of his suit on out of order and I promised I'd be there to prevent a disaster like last year." At Soren's questioning look, she added, "There was a shoe situation. Punch bowl incident. He doesn't like to talk about it."

A plea rose and fell from Soren's throat, some foolish part of her trusting Jericho's clear danger over Adriata's uncertain threat. But she'd run out of excuses that didn't sound suspicious days ago.

That was the trouble with playing a long game. She'd used too many of her tools early on, and now she was facing the consequences.

The door closed behind Jericho, and then it was only her and the Queen of Atlas. The woman who had waged a war to avenge her daughter . . . and that same daughter, back from the dead.

Soren's palms went slick, and when she tried to grip the arms of her chair, they slid a little. "I was wondering when you'd finally decide to talk to me."

"So was I. May I sit?"

"It's your palace," Soren mumbled; but when Adriata continued to stare at her, waiting, she sighed. "Yes, I suppose so."

Adriata took the seat opposite of Soren's, turned at an angle. She studied her for a long time, her brow creased, her stormy gaze further away than Soren had seen a person travel into their own head before. Then, so softly she almost didn't hear it: "You died the night of the Saltwater Ball that year."

Cold jammed into Soren's spine like an icicle staked into the bone.

Smoke and screaming and the eerie siren call of a violin crooning over the chaos, wielded by a musician who hadn't yet realized why everyone else had stopped playing.

"What?" she whispered.

"You wanted to get ready with Jericho instead of with us. You wanted her to do your hair." A quiet snort sent Adriata's head bobbing, and she rubbed her temple, the creases around her eyes growing more pronounced as she squinted into the past. "Your father and I were in the ballroom when the screaming started. You four hadn't arrived yet, but everyone else had, and it was . . ."

People who normally moved aside as she walked toward them now ran toward her without any heed, feet kicking and hands shoving, a hurricane of bodies and panic and screams, so many screams her hearing dulled, ringing with the echoes . . .

"Mama! Papa!"

Soren shook her head fiercely, tugging a headache free from deep within her skull—a dull, pounding pain, like her heart had suddenly been shoved into her head and there wasn't enough room for both. "I don't remember that. Just the fire. And a lot of noise."

"Shock can do that to a person. Ramses doesn't remember much of it, either." The Queen's tone implied that she didn't share the same affliction.

Soren didn't know know what possessed her—maybe it was the fact that this woman was actually trying for once. Maybe because the way Adriata was looking at her made her miss her mother. But she said, "Queen Ravenna wasn't responsible for that attack. Her father was bloodthirsty and tyrannical, and after he died, she gave all his conquered kingdoms their land back. And she offered reparations to you."

Adriata's teeth gritted together. "Ramses already told you what happened then. And even if it hadn't, there are no reparations that can heal the loss of a *child*. My daughter was *nine*. She was bright and clever and wild, she built fairy gardens in the courtyard and woke me up in the dead of night to tell me she'd seen mermaids in the ocean, and she was always getting in so much gods-damned trouble I stayed awake at night fretting over how we would ever raise her to become a queen, but she was—she—" Adriata slumped. Her head bowed. Her hands spread in helpless grief. "*You* were everything to me. All of you were. And if I couldn't bring you back, I was going to make sure *someone* paid for what they took from us."

Soren's heart clenched and hardened all at once. "Nyx has paid *enough*."

Adriata's wet eyes jumped to hers, accusatory, *angry*. "How can you still love them? Even knowing what they did, even knowing they *stole* you?"

Soren met her gaze steadily—no backing down, no shrinking. She was neither queen nor general, but here, she was all Nyx had. Their only defender.

If they could not win with blade and blood, perhaps she could make some progress with heart in hand.

"I have a family there," she whispered. "Sisters. A mother. Friends I have fought and bled for, friends I've *buried*, friends who died on Atlas blades. You lost someone precious to you because of Nyx. I have lost *many* who were precious to me because of *you*."

Adriata stared at her, and she couldn't read her expression. Couldn't decide if it was rage or indifference or if she was really listening. But Soren pressed on anyway, the words flooding out of her like an avalanche now, drowning every other intention.

"You see this?" She moved her hair aside to show Adriata her mourning braid, that bloodstained piece of Jira's tunic still woven into it. "It's a Nyxian custom. When we graduate from training, we choose battlemates—partners to take with us on the battlefield, our spare shields and swords."

"We know. You swear vows to each other."

Soren's heart pulsed with fondness and pain, remembering angry words spit through gritted teeth as she and Elias swore their vows too early, before their battlemates' ashes had even been gathered; then again, weeks later, after their third battle together. A dark room, quiet murmurs, bandaging each other's wounds while re-swearing their vows, and *meaning* them that time. The way he'd looked at her that night . . .

"Yes," she said. "And when one dies, we take a piece of the clothing they were wearing and braid it into our hair. We're never allowed to take it out."

Adriata's eyes flickered back to her braid. Understanding dawned.

"I wear this one for Jira," Soren said softly, "who was the other half of me, killed by Kallias Atlas with his blade in her back. And when my new battlemate dies from the Viper bite in his arm, I will wear a second one."

Silence stretched taut between them—two griefs warring and clashing, one caused by the aftermath of the other.

"Nyx has paid enough," Soren repeated, her voice rasping beneath the lump she couldn't seem to swallow away. "I know. I've helped pay it."

Adriata looked away again, her throat bobbing, silver lining her eyes. "If I'd had any idea you were there . . ."

"It shouldn't have mattered. One person is never worth the lives of hundreds. No matter how much you loved them. No matter how much you *needed* them."

Adriata's jaw clenched, and she stood with a jolt, looking down at her, all pity gone. "I seem to recall you were attempting to take your vengeance on Kallias when he first found you."

Soren's face burned beneath her makeup. "That wasn't exactly what happened."

"Even so. You are not a mother. It's an entirely different grief."

Soren ground her jaw so hard that her teeth ached. "Love doesn't know the difference between losses, Majesty. And no matter who I lost, I wouldn't take that grief out on innocents who didn't get to choose their king. *Or* their queen."

She had no idea if that was the truth. No idea what she'd do when Elias took his last breath. But Adriata didn't challenge it, and as she walked out, she seemed deep in thought. A good thought or a bad thought, Soren had no idea.

But that was for later. Now, it was time for a ball.

CHAPTER 36

ELIAS

Elias just wanted this night to be over with.

His feet ached, but not from dancing; he'd been posted at the far right door of the ballroom, quiet little Alia by his side, the two of them watching as hundreds of people trickled inside in a kaleidoscope of colors and jewels and grandstanding. The excessive curtsies and bows made him want to go over and forcibly make them stand straight.

He'd never seen so much brownnosing in one place. It looked exhausting.

"Please tell me you see something suspicious so I can go arrest someone and get out of here," he mumbled to Alia. She cracked the slightest of smiles, but shook her head with an apologetic shrug, the gold buttons on her ocean-blue dress uniform gleaming, the sparkling chandelier light playing on her tawny brown skin.

She was done up much more simply than the rest of them, her dark, textured waves worn in a low ponytail, her only makeup a bit of kohl around her dark eyes. If he hadn't seen her in the training room, meticulously disemboweling a training dummy with silent, deadly accuracy, he would've thought she was harmless.

Seamus had asked her to help with the investigation for that exact reason; her wide-eyed, sweet face made it easy for her to gather information without raising suspicion of her intentions. And as much as Elias wanted to hate every single person in this palace, Alia was just so damn *nice*. She'd made cookies for the entire garrison that morning because they'd all been running themselves ragged trying to prepare for the ball and the festival to follow. She'd found new laces for Elias's boots when he ruined the first ones wading through the mud from yet another desecrated grave. And she took protecting Soren *extremely* seriously, which he was grateful for. Obviously he preferred when *he* was the one guarding Soren's back, but strangely enough, if it couldn't be him, he at least trusted Alia to keep her alive.

More than the others, anyway; more than the ones whispering about the Delphin battle with increasing bitterness, their voices soaking Soren's Atlas name in suspicion, the ones beginning to think that she was funneling information back to her "kidnappers" to aid with the war effort.

They were wrong, but close enough to being right that it wouldn't help matters if Soren was caught based on that accusation.

Still . . .

"Many of the Nyxian soldiers that attacked Delphin were wearing braided cords around their wrists," he'd heard Seamus telling Kallias in hushed tones. "We're guessing it was symbolic of their mourning braid custom. And they were shouting her Nyxian name. Screaming it like a battle cry."

Kallias had cursed. "They're turning her into a martyr."

"The army captured one of them, briefly, before she died of her injuries. Said her name was Lily, a friend of Soren's, and they would take every wound we dealt her and increase it tenfold. That we made our last mistake when we took her away."

Elias's heart clenched just as hard remembering it as when he'd first heard it, pride and grief and homesickness brewing painfully in his stomach.

Their company had taken Delphin back. Jakob, Varran, Lily, Raquel, Frigga . . . all of them. And they'd done it for Soren, for their princess, their friend.

The news of Lily's death had rendered him sleepless again, remembering her teasing grin, her constant ribbing and flirting with everyone in their company, the fierceness with which she'd protected her friends. He'd miss her . . . and gods, he didn't even want to think about how Raquel was coping. First her sister, then her battlemate, and with no one to pull her out of that hole this time . . .

She was strong enough to do it on her own, he knew that. But whether she would or not was another question entirely. He hoped she would—and that when it came time for Soren to go through the same, Raquel's loyalty to her late sister would push her to help Soren through that loss as well. That *someone* would be there to watch her back when he couldn't.

As if in response to that thought, his shoulder gave a harsh, sudden throb, tingles of painful heat crawling up and down his arm. Fighting a wince, he adjusted his stance, gripping his elbow to support it as his arm went numb. These strange fits of pins-and-needles were getting worse, and spreading. Last week they'd been isolated to the wound itself. Now it prickled all the way from his fingertips to his collarbone.

It was time for them to leave. He had to tell Soren the truth, that they were out of time. *He* was out of time.

After the ball, when he escorted her back to her room, they would have that conversation. As much as he hated it, as much as it broke his heart. As much as the idea of leaving Soren dug a pit in his gut he could never hope to climb out of.

Without meaning to, he'd actually begun to hope that Mortem had granted him mercy, that Soren would be able to pull off a miracle with nothing but sheer stubborn will. But if Mortem willed him to her realm, he had little choice but to accept her invitation.

He knew where he was going. He was not afraid. Worried for Soren, yes. Already grieving the years they would never have, yes. But not afraid.

The music dipped into a lull, and in the quiet, approaching footsteps behind him pulled him out of his mind. He stood straight, doing his best to look like a guard who actually cared about keeping his job.

Kallias passed first, his ensemble predictably blue, his hair bound in a neat bun. Behind him swaggered Finn, who'd actually bothered to wear something prince-like instead of that ragged sweater Soren loved to complain about; then Jericho and Vaughn, the former looking like a vision formed by Anima herself, the latter looking . . . tired. He smiled, showing off his wife with a gentle twirl and a dip, but Elias caught a bead of sweat running down his forehead just from that simple movement. Jericho put her hand on the small of her husband's back as they walked away—firm, careful, like she was ready to catch him if he started to fall.

"Ahem."

The corner of Elias's mouth turned up; he knew that voice. "Hello, Princess."

"Hello, Eli." Oh, gods, he could hear the flirty smirk in her voice already. She must be wearing something pretty. "Aren't you going to turn around?"

"Tonight, my job is watching the room, Princess. Not you."

Now the smirk turned into a pout. "You're hurting my feelings."

"Oh, my apologies. I didn't realize you had any."

Her snort was followed by the brush of skirts against his leg. He saw fiery curls first, then roses, then—

Oh.

Oh, pits.

The sight of her kicked Elias's breath out of his chest. She'd worn roses in her hair—Mortem's flower, hardly welcome here in Atlas. Her makeup was fierce and sharp-edged, painting her as a warrior even in her finery, a blade herself, lovely and piercing. And her dress . . .

Gold like the day they'd met, made of some strange material he didn't have a name for, embossed with floral designs over the entire gown. He'd never seen her in something so unbearably elegant, entirely sleeveless with a skirt that billowed gently to the floor, her shoulders and collarbones bare, showing off every freckle and scar that decorated her body. Her eyes gleamed. Her stance was strong. She looked ready to conquer a kingdom with her bare hands.

She was not just a princess. She was a force, a vision, a newborn goddess in all her glory. She was ruining his entire life with that dress, and gods, he never wanted her to stop.

Her smirk, smug and knowing, softened when she met his gaze. Knees threatening to collapse, to bow him before her, he met her gaze with no idea what she was seeing on his face, no idea what truths he was revealing with his eyes.

For you, jackass, her look said.

Still with him. Still fighting. Still *her.*

Swallowing the lump in his throat and every gods-damned foolish thing he *wanted* to say, he put his hand over his chest. A silent salute. *Thank you, smartass.*

She blew him a mocking, playful kiss before sashaying after the rest of the Atlas family.

Alia's hand thumped solidly into the small of his back. "Breathe, Eli."

He obeyed her, sucking in a breath so fast it hurt, the tightness in his chest only worsening as he watched his brash, beautiful battlemate throw her arm around Finn's shoulders, faking a laugh at some joke Kallias was in the middle of. What had felt like a small eternity to him had been mere seconds to everyone not caught in the pull of Soren's eyes.

"Thanks," he rasped to Alia. "She's just . . . so gods-damned annoying."

Alia smiled kindly, and he knew she wasn't buying it for one second. "Of course."

Restraint, restraint, restraint. That was his new mantra. That was his new gods-damned life philosophy.

The ball commenced in earnest now that the royals had arrived, music swelling to a near-unbearable volume as people began to dance. An hour crawled by on limping feet, every second dragging its heels on its way out, and still Elias couldn't get his breath back. He was only just beginning to recover his senses and remember that he was supposed to be watching out for anyone who looked suspiciously like a puppeteer of dead bodies when Soren broke back through the crowd, sweating and smiling, her eyes gleaming with a challenge he already knew would cause him a whole mess of trouble.

"Dance with me." She approached him with one hand out, chin raised.

Elias stuttered for a moment. "Um . . . pardon me, Highness?"

"You heard me, jackass." Adrenaline shot through his blood at her loud, insistent use of their private joke. It felt so out of place in this palace, in this room, in this *crowd*. But no one seemed to be paying attention; even Alia had relented her post for a moment to dance with Seamus, giving him an update on what they'd gathered, which was exactly nothing.

"Soren," he said in a whisper that barely existed among the instruments and guests chattering, "that's not a good idea."

"Come on, Kallias is giving every guard a dance," she moaned, gesturing back to the crowd, where Kallias was indeed dancing with one of the women Elias shared a guard rotation with, laughing and chatting with her before partners switched and one of the other guards pushed his way into the spot left behind, while a group waited just beyond for their turns. "I've already danced with half of them, too. No one is going to notice the difference."

Elias frowned. "Why do they all get so giddy over him? He's not that handsome."

One look at Soren's grin told him he'd made a mistake. "What, are you jealous?"

"Not for one gods-damned second." He would rather die right now than have to dance with anyone else in this ballroom.

"You can go ask *him* for a dance, then, if you're feeling so left out."

Elias sighed. "You're not going to let this go, are you?"

"No, sir." She held out her hand once more. "Dance with me. Your princess commands it."

He gave her a look.

"Please," she added, so softly his heart cracked. Before he knew it, he'd put his hand in hers, and she'd dragged him onto the ghastly battleground some people called a dance floor.

Only once they were in the thick of it did a sudden, horrifying thought occur to him. He dug his heels into the slick floor, his boots squeaking, jerking Soren to a halt and ignoring her noise of protest. "I don't know any Atlas dances."

"Neither do I. Who cares?"

"I think the *entire Mortem-cursed Atlas population* is going to care very much when we dance a Nyxian waltz in the middle of their ball!"

"It's not the *entire* population, you absolute drama queen," Soren sighed, far too blasé about a whim that was shaping up to be the undoing of her entire plan.

"Don't be a smartass about this."

"I'm a smartass about everything." She thought for a moment, then grinned in that wicked way that normally told him they were about to have a fight on their hands. "We'll just wing it."

"This is *definitely* not one of those things you can *wing*—"

"Watch me," she said simply.

Gods, it wasn't like he had a choice.

The music shifted as she adjusted her grip on his hand, sliding her arm around him, pulling him closer with gentle pressure against his back—a slower song, a loving murmur of violin and cello and pianoforte that sent shivers down his spine. Or maybe that was the way her fingers pressed against it, bracing, brave.

"Hey," she whispered. "Look at me. Not at them, at me."

"They're going to know," he breathed, but she shook her head, her fingers pressing harder against his back like she was trying to hold him together.

"They won't know a thing that I don't want them to know. And right now, I want to dance with my jackass of a battlemate, because if I have to listen to another one of these people gush about how poetic it is that I'm being announced as Heir on the anniversary of my death, I'm going to puke all over this dress, and Jericho's going to be too pissed at me to keep helping me figure out how to get you the antidote."

"You've been talking to Jericho?"

"Not important right now." She caught his chin with her thumb and forefinger, forcing him to look her in the eyes. She smiled at him, the corners of her eyes crinkling. "Just you and me. Follow my lead."

Heat flooded his core, and he hoped to Mortem she couldn't see the way it blossomed in his cheeks. *Restraint, restraint, restraint.* He kept his hand respectably high on her back, but not so high that he touched bare skin. *Restraint, you Mortem-cursed bastard.*

And they started to dance. Soren moved confidently, as she did in everything, and as always, he tried to keep up. Whenever he started to lose her rhythm or missed a cue, she would tap on his spine or tilt her head or squeeze his hand, silent signals to tell him what to do. Before long, they'd found their stride, until she no longer had to lead, until they were moving in perfect tandem.

"There you go." Soren's voice was warm with pride and mischief. "See, it's not so bad."

"When we get home," he said into her ear, "remind me to kick your ass for making me do this."

"Oh, please. You're having fun. And you look very handsome in that ridiculous uniform." She let go of his hand to playfully tug at his collar, and he gently swatted her away.

"I feel like a stuffed scarecrow."

Soren burst into laughter, the snorting, undignified kind he loved so much. "Gods, you're ridiculous."

Her hand slid from his collar to the back of his neck, playing with the hair at his nape, and every inch of him caught fire. His heart thudded with such a violent lurch that he was half-sure a rib had broken. *Something* definitely had, because suddenly, restraint was the last thing on his mind.

Her hand on his neck and her nose-crinkling grin and those roses in her hair . . . something snapped open inside him, flooding him with molten steel. Making him brave. Making him defiant. Forging him into something new.

"I have to tell you something," he rasped, and she rolled her eyes.

"Then say it, jackass. No need to make an announcement."

He couldn't even muster up a proper *smartass* in return. Not with the emotion threatening to spill out from him in an avalanche he might never be able to dig his way free from.

If he confessed this here, now, there would be no coming back from it. But maybe that was all right.

"I love you," he croaked.

She rolled her eyes. "Yeah, I know. I love you too. Was the dramatic pause really necessary?"

"No, I don't mean—I mean, I do mean that, also. But that's not—what I'm trying to say is that I—"

Oh gods, he was fumbling this. How did he explain that what he was feeling wasn't just love, wasn't *just* anything, it was something so devastating that it *frightened* him, that he'd lain awake some nights wondering how he was going to force it out of him, how in Mortem's name he was going to resign himself to the fact that she didn't want him in the same way?

How did he say it in a way that didn't make her think he was discontent with her friendship, without making her think that *he* thought he deserved more than what she'd already given him? What they already shared was the most precious thing he had, and if she never gave him another inch, she'd already given more than he deserved. But ignoring his feelings for her was killing him slowly, a gentler kind of poison, a worse kind, and he couldn't bear it one second longer.

But before he could try again, before he could even begin to find the words, the music changed again. And something shifted in Soren's eyes.

Mischief faded. Her grin vanished. Her face darkened, dimmed, like a moon eclipsed. Her hand fell away from his neck.

Alarm bells rang through his skull, and he let go of her other hand and waist to grip her shoulders. "Soren?"

She pulled away from him, sharply, like his touch had burned her. "I have to . . . I need a drink," she said in the tone of a dreamer, in a distant way that scared him.

"Soren," he hissed, but she was already leaving, drifting away from him, and at a concerned look from a nearby pair of dancers he snapped back to himself. Snapped that floodgate inside him firmly back into place.

There would be time to confront all that later. Something bad had just begun, and he didn't know what, and Soren couldn't afford for him to be distracted like this.

He couldn't chase her. Not here, not with this many eyes. But he could follow her—carefully, at an excusable distance.

So he did, navigating the crowd at a leisurely but focused pace. But even with that gate firmly slammed shut, holding back that terrifying rush of feeling, bits and pieces leaked out—a pain that had nothing to do with the wound on his arm.

CHAPTER 37

SOREN

She was real and not real. Here and not here. Alive and dead.

She couldn't remember her name.

Elias had said it, he'd just said it, but her mind was lost at sea and her blood was the wrong color and her body was separating from her, her soul tearing away from its earthly anchor, and nothing made sense and nobody was where they should be and everything was *wrong, wrong, wrong.*

Why couldn't she remember her name?

That music had started and something had . . . turned on. Or turned off. Something had changed, because—

"Hey!" Hands slammed down on her shoulders, shaking her, and she blinked to find Kallias's beaming, bearded face in front of hers. Blurry around the edges, and swaying side to side, but still Kallias. Whether *he* was the one swaying or if she was just dizzy . . . "Looks like you found a date to the ball after all, huh?"

"What?" Gods, she couldn't even feel her tongue.

"I saw you and Eli. He's a good one, from what I can tell. Unbelievable work ethic, I swear he never sleeps. I—hey, are you okay? You look like you're going to be sick." His hands turned from gripping to bracing, concern coloring his eyes in sea glass shades of green. *Sea glass? What in the depths is that?* "Did you have too much to drink?"

Maybe. Maybe. She hoped that was it.

"I know this song," she breathed, and his hands tightened on her.

"What? Soleil. You're scaring me a little. Come sit down, okay? Jer! Where's Jericho, can someone . . ."

She closed her eyes to the rapidly twirling world. Every part of her was numb and buzzing, a sound in her head like roaring, like popping, like—

Fire.

Soleil wriggled in her chair, eyes fixed on the fireplace in front of her, impatience dancing in her fingers as her sister yanked at her hair. "Jericho, hurry up, we're already late!"

"I'm going as fast as I can, Leia. It would help if you stopped all that fidgeting!"

"It helps with the pulling."

"No, it only makes my fingers pull harder. Now sit still, or I'm going to call Kal and make him do it instead, and you know how terrible he is. He'll stick your head full of pins and call it a day."

Soleil scowled, slumping in her seat. "All the good dances are going to be over when we get there."

"Count to five."

"What?"

"Count to five," Jericho repeated. "And hold still while you're at it!"

Soleil squeezed her eyes shut, crossing her arms tight, wishing her sleeves weren't so long. She was getting too hot in front of the fireplace. "One . . . two . . . three . . . four . . . five."

"There!" Jericho's hands lifted away from her head. "All done!"

"Looks perfect to me," said a voice from the door, and the two sisters turned in tandem, Jericho's face lighting with barely-contained love, Soleil squealing as she hopped off her chair.

"Hi, Vaughn!" She ran to her sister's friend and gave him a tight hug. "I didn't know you were coming!"

"Your sister invited me." Vaughn's eyes settled on Jericho, a smile softer than Soleil's favorite pillow on his face. "Hello, Princess. You look . . . very nice."

Jericho's eyes smarted with secrets, and she crossed her arms, her pink chiffon gown shifting with the movement. "Hello to you as well, sir. And I look much better than nice.*"*

"It's okay if you wanna kiss her again," Soleil offered. "I won't tell anyone."

"Hush!" Jericho moaned, but she bit her lip on a grin as she looked up at Vaughn, who had gone slightly pale. "She saw us on the stairs last week. It's all right. She knows how to keep a secret when properly motivated."

Soleil nodded solemnly. "She's paying me to keep my mouth shut."

Jericho gently swatted the back of her head, and Vaughn relaxed a little, crouching down to Soleil's level. He tipped her chin up with his finger, giving her a wink. "I appreciate your discretion, Princess."

She giggled, giving him a perfect curtsy. "Of course, Mr. Vaughn."

"All right, you." Jericho steered her toward the door. "Give me and Mr. Vaughn a moment alone, if you don't mind."

Soleil scowled. "If you insist.*"*

She left her sister and her secret behind, dragging her heels the whole way, half-hoping Finn would jump out to walk with her. She knew he hadn't left his room yet. But no one came; the hallway was entirely empty, everyone gathered in the ballroom already.

Soleil found her way to the ballroom alone, her tiny heels clicking on the floor. She spun around once or twice on the way, just to test out the twirl of the skirt, pleased to find it passed with flying colors.

It took both her hands to tug open the door to the ballroom—the attendants must have already gone inside, but that was fine. She liked having to heave at them, it made her feel strong. Like she was almost ready to join Kallias's swordplay lessons with Uncle River, even though she was still "small for her age."

As she'd been afraid of, everyone was already dancing, and absolutely no one was paying attention to the entrance, which meant no one was there to oo and ahh at her twirl-able skirt. Pouting, Soleil let the doors shut behind her, searching for any sign of her family.

Guests spun in circles about the dance floor, skirts fluttering like butterfly wings, cravats perched around necks like nesting birds. The music was bigger than its instruments, filling the room so well that Soleil almost could feel it—the Atlas anthem, a song she heard at every event, every holiday.

Her family didn't seem keen on being seen. Jericho was missing, of course, and it seemed Finn and Kallias hadn't arrived yet either. But she thought she caught a glimpse of her mama and papa, dancing near the far doors across from her. She certainly heard *them, both laughing so loudly even the music couldn't hide it.*

She was halfway across the ballroom when the screams started.

"Fire! Fire!"

Then the ball became a stampede—smoke and screaming and the eerie siren call of a violin crooning over the chaos, wielded by a musician who hadn't yet realized why everyone else had stopped playing.

Panic froze Soleil in place for a moment, her feet anchored to the floor, staring as people bolted for the doors, as the musicians finally fled, as fire crawled up the drapes in the back of the room, eating away at the wall and wainscot. Then, with a jolt like being shoved in the back, she started running in the direction she'd seen her parents.

People who normally moved aside as she walked toward them now ran toward her without any heed for who she was, feet kicking and hands shoving, a hurricane of bodies and panic and screams, so many screams her hearing dulled, ringing with the echoes . . .

"Mama! Papa!"

She ducked down, curling into a ball, covering her head with her hands and wailing *as loud as she could. But she was only adding to the cacophony, her shouts mingling with hundreds of others, parents searching for their children, sisters for brothers, partners for partners.*

By the time she looked up again, the ballroom was empty, the doors shut—only a few people left, lying prone on the floor, none of them moving.

A quiet whimper escaped from Soleil's throat, and she took in a breath to scream again, but it only pulled in smoke, her scream coming out as a cough instead, a hacking thing that hurt.

She turned to find the fire had spread, devouring the entire wall now, climbing rapidly to the others, creeping its way to the doors, down to the floor.

She was about to be trapped.

"No!" She scrabbled up and bolted for the door furthest from the fire, her little heart pounding in her chest, uncontrollable sobs already shaking her body. She grabbed the handles and pulled.

Nothing.

"No, no, oh no no no—"

Soleil tugged again, again, her tears coming in earnest, panicked sobs robbing any clean breath she had left. Behind her, around her, heat began to gather—not at all like the fireplace, not at all like the ovens in the kitchen. This was a hungry heat, an angry one, and it was coming for her.

"Please! Someone help, I can't—I can't move the door, please—" She shouted until her voice died, screamed until nothing but a pale imitation of a croak would rattle out of her abused throat. "Help!"

But no one did. No one came.

"Soleil?" he said, like it was a question, like he wasn't *sure*.

"Obviously! Finn, where is everyone? Why are we back inside, we have to get *out*!"

"Is she okay?" Another voice joined in the frantic chatter above her head, and a face appeared—a dark-haired guard, his eyes black as the kohl Jericho liked to wear, looking just as worried as Finn did. He reached toward her face. "What happened?"

"Who are you?" It came out wobbly, embarrassing, nothing like a princess should sound. "Don't touch me, please . . . Kal—" She twisted away, hiding her face against Kal's chest, shaking so hard she could feel her teeth chattering, her stomach sloshing like a storm-tossed ship. She didn't want to be sick—she hated being sick.

Kal's hand covered the back of her head, stroking her hair gently, murmuring into her ear until her shakes eased. And once hers stopped, she could feel *his;* his hands were trembling against her head.

"Eli," he said, "go get my parents. And find me Jericho—*now*. I don't care what she's doing, get her in here." A pause, then Kal barked, "Eli, I said *now! Move!*"

When she looked up again, the guard was gone—and she was being stared at.

"Kal, we should get her to her room," Finn said.

Soleil reached out her hand to him, and he took it, even though he looked at it with his brows furrowed, like he was confused by it, like something was wrong with her. She didn't like it. Not one bit.

"Finn," she said desperately, "what's going on? Why is everyone looking at me? Where *were* you?"

Finn's eyes flashed to hers, widened, and his jaw clenched. Like there was something he wanted to say, but couldn't. He squeezed her hand tightly, offering her a smile that *almost* looked right, almost looked like him. But it was too small, and too sad.

"You're okay," he said. "Hey, listen to me. Everything's okay. I'm sorry I wasn't there, but I am now, okay? I'm here. And I'm not leaving."

A leftover sob unraveled her, and she flung herself out of Kal's arms and into his, burying her face against his shoulder. After a second that felt like an eternity, Finn wrapped his arms around her in a crushing hug that almost hurt. "I'm here now," he choked against her hair. "I'm right here."

"Is the fire out?" she whispered.

He blew out a long breath, laughing shakily. "Oh, yeah, kid. The fire's long out, believe me."

CHAPTER 38

SOREN

It took two hours for her to remember her name. Two *hours* of only Soleil existing in her head. Two hours of her demanding answers and being given none, of worried whispers exchanged between her parents and her brothers and Vaughn, two hours while Elias was gods-knew-where thinking gods-knew-what about what happened to her.

Mortem damn her, she'd looked him in the face and asked him who he *was*.

She had to find him, and soon, before he did something truly foolhardy to try and get to her himself. But right now, no one was keen on letting her out of bed, let alone out of their sight.

"For the last time, I'm fine," she moaned, when Kallias tried to insist—*again*—that she should let Jericho give it one more go. But she'd already spent hours with Jericho's unnerving magic buzzing through her head, and she needed a break. "Really. I'm sorry I ruined the ball, but I'm all right now. You can go back and dance."

"Not happening," Finn, Vaughn, and Kallias all said at once, in tones that varied from worried to outright fussy. But even though Kallias sounded the most worried, it was Finn who was doing the hovering; he hadn't left her side, and only let go of her hand when she told him she'd bite it if he didn't.

"We're fine exactly where we are," said Ramses, far more diplomatically. But even he was unable to sit still, shifting his weight from foot to foot, his eyes fixed on her with a focus that rivaled a hunting hawk. "Jericho?"

"It could have been anything," Jericho said with a shrug, adjusting Soren's blankets with a practiced hand, perfectly groomed nails gleaming in the pale lamplight. "The wine, the music—"

"She did mention the music," Kallias offered.

Soren glared at him. "*She* is right here."

"*She* seems just fine now," Jericho added dryly. "She should rest for a while longer, though."

Soren gestured to her in demonstration. "Thank you! See? I'm fine. I just have a headache, and I desperately want to sleep, so if you all could please give me a little space . . ."

Finn, Kallias, Vaughn, and Ramses all exchanged looks. Not one of them moved.

Without meaning to, without even thinking about it, words leapt from Soren's mouth: "Mama, will you *please* talk some sense into them all?"

The second the words left her mouth, all breathing stopped. Hers, Jericho's, everyone's.

Adriata burst into tears.

Soren wanted to take it back, to catch the sentence in her hands and shove it into her pockets, where no one could remember it had ever been said. But it was too gods-damned late for that now.

"I'm . . . I'm sorry," she began, but Adriata was already leaving, vanishing out the door in a swirl of violet dress and passionfruit perfume. Ramses started after her, but paused to catch Soren's head in his hands, planting a quick kiss on her forehead.

"She'll be all right," he assured her. "You did nothing wrong, Soren."

She wished he'd stop calling her by her Nyxian name. It was making it harder and harder to remind herself that he was still the enemy—they all were.

But gods, it didn't feel that way. Not now. Not after she'd *remembered*.

Waking up from that memory had been like waking into a different life: one where Nyx had never existed and Atlas had been her only home, the time between nothing but a dream. Now, she had Nyx back, and Atlas was gone again, but not all of it. Not enough.

She couldn't deny it anymore. No matter what she pretended, she *was* Soleil Marina Atlas—had been born her, at least. And that made everything so much harder.

"I think it may be time for me to rest as well," Vaughn croaked, taking a step forward—then buckling to his knees.

Jericho's shriek dragged a groan out of Soren as her head pulsed against the noise. "Vaughn!" All three standing siblings rushed forward to catch him, and Soren sat up too, Soleil's little heart lurching in fear.

"I told you not to push yourself so hard," Jericho scolded, but there was no real anger there, only fear, such a familiar sort that Soren had to look away, refusing to think of wounded shoulders and prayer beads—but also, a little bit afraid not to. Afraid that pushing them away would shove them out of her reach and make her forget again.

She didn't care if Soleil's memories were gone. She would *not* pick her over Elias.

"I'm all right," Vaughn gasped, very clearly not all right. Dark circles cut deep into his eyes, his face was coated in a sheen of sweat, and he couldn't seem to keep his legs under him. "I just . . . I need to rest. That's all."

"Help me take him," Jericho choked, and Kal nodded, lifting with her and helping Vaughn stumble out of the room. But Finn hesitated, hovering by the door, his hand braced against the frame as he looked at Soren.

"Tell me honestly," he said. "Are you all right now?"

"No," she mumbled. "But I will be. Go help Vaughn."

Finn nodded and ducked out.

"Finn, wait!"

He stuck his head back in. "Yes?"

Soren swallowed her pride, her fear, everything, and forced out the words burning on her tongue: "Thank you. For coming when I . . . when she needed you."

Finn gazed at her for so long, with those unfathomable eyes he kept hidden under his mask, that she started to squirm. Then, so quietly she almost didn't hear him, he said, "Always."

Then he was gone.

The door hadn't even finished swinging closed before an Elias-shaped shadow took Finn's place. He leaned against the frame, watching her with his lips pressed together, his expression utterly calm. Waiting. Watching.

She leaned back against the wall, letting her exhaustion flow through her, going limp as a dead deer. She let her head loll sideways to look at him, forcing whatever smile she could manage. "Hey, jackass."

Elias's breath exhaled in a slow, shaking whoosh, and he closed the door behind him, crossing the room in two long strides, his arms around her before she could even muster the energy to lift her own. "Never," he said against her hair, voice raw and scratchy, "and I mean *never, ever* do that to me again, smartass."

"Sorry." She paused. "I mean . . . it wasn't my fault, so not *that* sorry—"

"We're going home," he said, pulling back, brushing her hair out of her face with a trembling hand. "Tonight. Now. That . . . that was it, all right? That's where I draw the line. If they can make you forget me, forget *yourself*—"

Soren sighed. She'd guessed he'd take this stance and had already prepared her argument. "Elias, it wasn't their fault either. And for the last time, we are not leaving here without that antidote."

"No, I'm done. Soren, I gave you time, I helped you, I've lived in their gods-damned garrison for weeks, I've trusted you to know when it was time to say enough. But I'm done. This is taking too long, and it's too dangerous, and we need to go *home!*"

"Elias, it's more complicated than that—" she tried to say, but he cut her off again, shaking his head, already wearing a wildness on his face that she'd only seen in him when he was well and truly scared. Or angry. Or both.

"Soren," he said, sitting on the edge of her bed and taking her shoulders, "this isn't a joke. You *forgot* me. Do you know how that felt?"

"Like Infera, I imagine," she mumbled, guilt prickling gently in the depths of her gut. She tried to reach out to pull his brows apart, but he caught her hand, his teeth gritting together like he was trying not to shout.

"Worse than Infera," he said. "Do you know how out of my mind I've been? I couldn't see you, I couldn't find out if you were okay, I didn't even know if you *remembered* me! Or if you ever would! I wish we could get a cure, I do, you have no idea how much I do, but they've been too stingy for too long and gods damn it Soren *I will not lose you to Atlas too!*"

His voice built from a plea to a shout, desperation lighting his eyes with wild light, and she guessed it was only the blessing of Mortem that kept someone from coming and peeking in on them, but it didn't matter, not now. Not when he was looking at her the way he'd looked at Kaia's pyre, like she was a dead thing not yet buried, like he was a boy grieving before the wake had even begun.

Everyone knew the story of Kaia's death. Elias and his first battlemate had separated to take down an Atlas ground cannon, a contraption that could wipe out a whole squadron in minutes. They'd succeeded, and Elias had run back to meet up with Kaia . . . but an Atlas soldier got to her first.

"Kaia made her choice," Soren said softly. "You two saved hundreds of lives. People still tell that story. You supported her plan—I need you to support mine now."

Elias bit down on his lip, another harsh breath wobbling from his throat. "If I'd known her life was the asking price, I wouldn't have done it."

"I know."

"What does that make me? Selfish? Horrible?"

Typical Elias, always looking for a sin to atone for. She offered him a wry smile. "It makes you just like every other battlemate, jackass. We all have someone we'd trade lives for."

He swallowed. Looked away. "I can't lose you too," he whispered.

"Elias," she said, and though her voice was quiet, there was steel beneath. "Elias Loch. Look at me right now."

He did not obey.

"*Elias.*"

He raised his eyes slowly, and her heart crunched like broken glass when she saw the tears there.

"You didn't know me," he breathed, one of those tears escaping, rolling toward a tiny scar on his jaw. "I've never been that *scared*, Soren."

She thumbed the tear away, planting a tiny kiss on the scar it brushed. "I know," she whispered against his cheek. "I'm being an ass because it's easier, okay? I was scared too. Terrified. And the moment I came out of it, all I wanted was to go find you."

His breath stuttered, warm against her cheek. She hadn't realized exactly how close her lips were to his mouth.

Her ears went hot, and she pulled back quickly, clearing her throat. "But I'm fine now. We're fine. That won't happen again, and we've come too far to give up now. If we leave without the antidote, this whole thing was pointless."

Elias searched her face for several moments. Then he said, "If you can answer all my questions, we'll stay. Deal?"

Seemed fair. "Deal."

Elias shifted so he was sitting beside her instead of in front of her, his uninjured shoulder brushing hers, his hand sliding into hers and clinging on just a bit too tightly, like he thought he could hold her in place with his will alone. "What's my middle name?"

Soren moaned, knocking her head back against the wall in frustration. "Are we really going to do this?"

"Oh, we are definitely going to do this. Can you answer the question?"

"Tiberius," she grumbled.

"What do you always steal from me?"

"Socks. And cookies, sometimes, if you're taking too long to eat them."

"How did we meet?" he asked, leaning forward—too close again, his nose inches away from hers, his eyes probing hers for hesitations or gaps.

Soren didn't fight the smirk that stretched up one side of her mouth. "You called me a snob."

"You deserved it."

"Certainly did."

"How'd your nose get crooked?"

There were plenty of fights that had contributed to that, but she knew which one he wanted, and it wasn't a story she was particularly proud of. But still, she grumbled, "You broke it because I told you Kaia was better off where she was than with you as a battlemate. How did you get that scar on your chin?"

Elias narrowed his eyes. "Do you not remember or are you trying to take power back here?"

"Honestly, I'm hoping *you've* forgotten by now."

"You *bit* me, you heathen. When you couldn't get out of a hold we were practicing."

"One more question," she said softly.

"If you have to."

She squeezed his hand, resting her head against his, breathing in the smell of fresh-pressed laundry wafting from his uniform and the rosemary-and-lemon scent from his hair. Unfamiliar, not his usual Elias smell of baking bread and weapon polish and iron, but still comforting—if only because he was the one wearing them.

"You still trust me?" she whispered, gazing at their intertwined hands instead of his eyes.

He gripped her hand in return, breathing out slowly. "With my life. Just not with your own."

She would have loved to kick him for that. But with her current track record, she couldn't exactly blame him for that pinhole of doubt. "Trust that I'm not leaving you. Trust that I never will."

His laugh, low and pained, wasn't one she'd ever heard him use before. "I'm trying. But I'd be lying if I said I didn't wish we were home for the Winter Fair right now."

Soren gasped. "Oh gods, I forgot!"

Elias turned to her so fast he nearly bashed her skull with his, his expression already contorted with terror, but she waved him off impatiently. "Not like *that*, jackass. Go to the dresser and open the third drawer down. Get the one out that's wrapped in black."

Elias pressed his hand to his chest, groaning, "*Mortem damn you*, you're going to be the death of me."

"Honestly, if I beat out the poison, that'll be impressive on my part," she mumbled. "Just open the drawer."

He obeyed, frowning down at the drawer where eight packages were nestled in crepe paper. He pulled out the black one as ordered and came back, crawling onto the bed and offering his arm, letting her nestle her aching head against his chest. "Is this for me?"

"Mmhm. Go ahead, open it."

Elias did as she said, already poised with a grin, but it faded in an instant, his eyes widening when he took in the gift inside.

"What are these?" he asked, perfectly calm.

Soren peered over just to make sure she hadn't accidentally given him Jericho's present; he probably would've been confused if she'd given him slippers pinker than the taffy they sold down by the docks. But no, he had the right parcel, so she said, "Um. What do they look like to you?"

Gingerly, as if he was afraid touching them would make them disappear, Elias pulled out a set of double daggers, their metal so black they seemed wrought from the void, from the depths of Infera itself. She hadn't even had to think before buying them for him; they couldn't have been more made for him if they had *Elias* scribed on the hilts.

He stared at them for a long moment, blinking. Just . . . blinking.

Soren crossed her arms. "Seriously, Elias, I didn't think amnesia was contagious. They're *daggers*."

"I know that, smartass. Where's my sweater?"

Soren squawked in fury, throwing her hands to the sky. "These are Artem-forged daggers! They're made of the finest metal you can mine, they cut through bone like *butter*, and you're sitting here asking me about a sweater?"

Elias pouted a little. "I like the sweaters you make me."

He *had* to be joking. "Oh gods, will you give it up already? You hate those ugly things!"

"What? No I don't! Soren, I love those sweaters. I wear them all the time! What are you—" He paused, eyes widening, jaw dropping indignantly. He pointed at her with one of his very fancy, very *expensive* new daggers. "Wait. Have you seriously been knitting me those things all this time because you thought I was *pretending?*"

Soren gaped at him. "You actually like them?"

Elias blinked in confusion. "Well . . . yeah. You made them for me."

Oh, come on. That wasn't fair. Now she *really* felt mean. "Elias?"

"Yes?"

"You're too good to me."

Elias finally, finally cracked a grin, and the sight of it threatened to make her swoon with relief. "I know."

"But if you don't start acting *incredibly* grateful for those daggers I've been salivating over for days, I *will* shove one of them into an unsavory place, and I will keep the other one for myself."

"Thank you," he said hurriedly, kissing her temple before lifting the daggers to the light to admire them. "Really. They're . . .I mean, gods. They're breathtaking."

"I know," she said softly, her eyes catching on his smile, on the crinkles by his eyes, on that scar she'd left on him back in her more feral days.

After several seconds of him admiring his gift—and her admiring him, which she decided to blame on leftover dizziness or amnesia-madness or something—Elias started to get up. "I guess we're staying, then?"

"Looks like it," she said. "I'm not letting you go that easy. Mortem can wait. You're stuck with me for a while."

"Then I should get back." He rubbed the back of his neck with an unhappy scowl. "Seamus gets pissy when people come in after curfew."

"Is Seamus ever *not* pissy?"

He smirked. "True enough."

But when he faced the door, when all she could see was his back, fear suddenly gripped her in painful talons. "Elias, wait."

He looked over his shoulder, brow already furrowed again, but she couldn't reach them this time. "What?"

Soren swallowed hard. This wasn't smart. It wasn't even excusable, really. But she still said, "Stay here. Just for tonight, okay?"

His throat bobbed. "Soren, that's not . . ."

"Please." The word broke out of her like shattered pottery. "I don't want to be alone if I forget again, okay? Please."

She didn't have to ask again. Ten minutes later, Elias had shed his uniform in the corner, leaving only his underclothes, and she'd changed into pajamas that came *just* past her knees—no need to torture him any further tonight. And with the familiar sound of Elias's nightly prayers in her ear, with his heartbeat thumping a steady rhythm against her cheek and his hand on her hair, she slept better than she had since Kallias saw her on that damned battlefield. Before she'd been given a different name, a different family, a different life. When she would have killed these royals on sight instead of choosing the shelter of their arms over her battlemate's.

She was in such awful, awful trouble.

But it was trouble that she would have to face in the morning.

CHAPTER 39

FINN

Finn didn't sleep a wink that night.

Soleil's voice kept echoing in his head, over and over and over, the memory of her terrified scream cutting across the ballroom and waking some primal thing in him he hadn't known still existed—something that would never ignore when his little sister needed him.

It hadn't been for long . . . nowhere near long enough. But she'd yelled for him; when Kal was right there, when Eli was right there, she'd yelled for *him*. She'd looked at him, eyes wide and fierce and frightened, arms reaching for him . . . and he'd known her. Instantly.

Soleil.

She pressed her forehead against the door, hysterical tears streaming down her cheeks to drip onto her skirts, and she sobbed into the immoveable wood that had made her feel so strong earlier. Now it only told her of her weakness. Now it had trapped her.

Someone had locked her in.

"Mama! Papa!" Nothing.

"Kallias! Jericho!" Nothing.

Nothing.

One last scream built in her chest—one last try, her failsafe, her one certainty. "Finn!" she shrieked at the top of her lungs, with every ounce of her strength, with everything she had left. "Finn, I'm in here! Please, please find me, please find me Finn I'm in here please please please—"

If she was going to be found, it would be by Finn. He never let her stay hidden for long, and he always came when she called. Always.

But not this time. This time, the door didn't open.

She buried her face against the wood and waited for the fire to find her.

Soleil jerked awake with a hoarse, horrified scream.

Arms were wrapped around her—Kallias. She heard him somewhere above her head, shouting at someone to get a healer, shouting for someone to find Jericho.

Were she and Vaughn still down the hall? Oh gods, had anyone gotten to them before the fire? And where was Finn, where was he—

"Finn?" she sobbed, and Kallias's face appeared over her—older, strange, not the same, but definitely her Kal.

"Soleil, it's okay," he soothed. "You're okay, you just fainted—"

"Where's Finn?" she demanded, gripping his hands in hers, her voice wobbling. If they hadn't gotten him out in time . . ."*Finn?*"

Footsteps sounded nearby, and Finn landed so hard next to her that she heard his knees crack against the floor, skidding to a halt until he was right at her side. He gripped her face and turned it toward him, his expression urgent, his eyes aflame, searching for what was wrong. He looked different, too. Older, too old, but it was *him*, she knew it was—

"What is it?" he demanded, brushing a strand of hair from her face, bracing her head with both his hands. "Soren, what happened?"

Soren? "Why are you calling me that?" she snapped—gods, everything was so *hazy*, she'd closed her eyes to fire and woken to this *nightmare*. "Finn, are you okay? Did they put the fire out?"

Finn's face dropped, and he looked up, meeting Kal's gaze over her head.

For two hours, Soleil was alive again. His sister was *right there*, her arms around him, her voice begging him to stay, to tell her honestly if they were all safe.

He thought he'd buried that grief, smothered it in so many layers of schemes and lies and games that it had suffocated, that it could never do more than raise its ugly head every once in a while to remind him that there was something missing he could never replace.

He'd never been so, so wrong. Because that grief was back, stalking in his chest, sinking clawed feet into the very core of his being until he bled. And when he couldn't bear the pain anymore, he rolled out of bed and wandered into the room next door, so tired he didn't even think to knock.

But the sight within woke him up. *Fast.*

Soleil was passed out on her bed, lying on her side, remnants of kohl smeared under and around her eyes, her hair a tangled mess. Her mouth hung open, a bit of drool on the corner. And beside her, his arm around her waist and his face buried in her hair, snoring and *shirtless*, was Eli.

Finn was so taken aback by their sheer foolishness that he forgot to catch the door, and when the knob banged against the wall, both of them flung themselves upward—Soleil instantly coming to her senses, her sharp eyes taking him in with wide-eyed surprise. Eli was slower, mumbling as he pulled himself up, rubbing one of his eyes, freezing when he caught sight of Finn.

For a moment, all three of them just stared.

"It's not what it looks like," Eli finally choked out.

"It's exactly what it looks like," Soleil disagreed, sliding her hand over Eli's shoulder. He batted her away.

"We didn't do anything," the poor man tried weakly.

"We did *everything*."

Eli flushed redder than Kallias's hair, glowering at her in a pleading way, like she was embarrassing him. Poor man. Soleil clearly didn't realize he was hopelessly in love with her . . . or else she was considerably crueler than he'd thought.

Finn pinched the bridge of his nose. "If you're going to be idiots, at least get your gods-damned stories straight, will you? You're lucky I came to get you and not Kal. Eli, go get yourself presentable. You're escorting us to the Festival today."

Elias blinked. "I am?"

Finn sighed. "I'm going to count to three. If you aren't out of my sister's bed by the time I say three, I'm going to frame you for murder. Ready? One—"

Eli was out the door in a blur of darkness, snatching up his uniform on the way out, barely taking the time to pull on his undershirt before he shut the door behind him.

"You two seem . . . cozy," Finn remarked.

Soleil shrugged, settling back on her pillows, crossing her arms behind her head nonchalantly. "Turns out he's pleasant company when he's not pinning me down." That wolfish grin flashed. "And even when he is—"

"Gods, please don't," he moaned. "First, ew. Second, I know very well nothing happened last night, I live next door to you. And third, *ew.*"

"Whatever. Are we all invited on this Festival trip, or am I still on bed rest?"

"If we tell you to stay, are you just going to sneak out after us?"

"Probably."

He'd figured as much. "Then you might as well stick with me and Kal. At least then we can keep an eye on you."

Soleil frowned. "Jericho and Vaughn aren't coming?"

"Vaughn's too sick to get out of bed." Sicker than Finn had ever seen him, actually, and he was trying not to think about it. When he'd left last night, Vaughn had been curled on his side, wracked with shivers, soaked in cold sweat, Jericho's ministrations barely taking the edge off his fit of pain. He was half-afraid they'd come home today to find that Vaughn was . . .

No. He couldn't think like that. Vaughn had bad days all the time. He'd come out of it; he always did.

He waited in the hall while Soleil got dressed, tired eyes fixed on the wall in front of him, eyelids heavier than the guilt he'd been struggling to push off. If he hadn't spent the night with his ear pressed against the wall, listening to her and Eli arguing quietly in the night, their Nyxian accents bleeding back in without an audience, he would have gone in there himself. He wouldn't have left her side until he knew she was really all right again.

When she came out of her room, he was surprised to see her wearing a huge sweater, bright scarlet, so long it nearly fell to her knees, the sleeves reaching nearly to her fingertips. She looked utterly delighted.

"Where did you get that?" he asked.

"Found it."

Right. And he was Anima's uncle. "You stole it."

"Borrowed."

"Borrowing without permission is still—"

"If you keep complaining, I'm not going to give you your present."

That stopped Finn dead in his sass. "I . . . my what?"

She offered him a parcel wrapped in brown crepe paper. "Happy Salty Day, or whatever we're celebrating."

"You know what it's call—ugh. Fine." He took it, frowning as it changed shape under his hands. "It's not alive, is it? Wait—it's not *dead*, is it?"

She bit her lip on a grin. "Neither. Just open it. No guessing."

Yeah, that *really* didn't comfort him. But he did as she said, sliding one finger under each folded edge until finally, cautiously, he folded back the paper.

Everything went still. He stopped breathing. Stopped thinking.

And for the first time in his life, he forgot.

He forgot he was supposed to be keeping her at arm's length, at swordtip. He forgot that they were playing a game, and this was probably her next move in it. He forgot that she wasn't his Soleil anymore, not *enough* of Soleil.

He forgot all of that. Because in that package . . .

His fingertips stroked the lumpy, knitted thing like it might jump and bite him. "You made me a sweater?"

Oh, Tempest take him, his voice *cracked*. He coughed quickly to cover it up.

Soleil, thankfully, didn't hear it—or didn't feel like mocking him. If he didn't know any better, he would've said she looked nervous, shifting her weight between her feet while he studied his gift. "Well, that dingy thing you've got on is about to fall apart, and Kal told me I'm the one that bought it for you way back when, so . . . I figured it was only fair that I replaced it."

His laugh caught against some jagged thing in his throat. "You bought it way too big. It used to come down to my knees."

Her eyes twinkled. "Doesn't look like you ever grew into it, huh?"

He blinked down at his old brown sweater, then at the dark purple one in his hands, eyes burning, throat aching. Maybe he was allergic to it. "You made me a sweater."

"Are all men slow on the uptake, or is it just most of you? Yes, I made it, and I didn't even make it as ugly as I normally do. You're—"

He cut her off by throwing his arms around her. "Thank you," he mumbled, giving himself one last moment to be a fool. One last moment to pretend he was allowed to hug her, that she wouldn't have plunged a knife in his back for it if she were armed. "I love it. Honest."

To his surprise, she wrapped her arms around him—hugging him back, tightly, without hesitation. "Good. I expect you to wear it everywhere."

Another laugh jammed against the first one, still stuck in his throat. "If I have to."

Gods help him. This wasn't good.

He hadn't thought he could love anyone more than he loved the memory of his little sister—his twin born a year late, his best friend, the little girl who'd skipped headfirst into trouble with him, the one gods-damned person in the world he would have bowed to if she'd ever had the chance to be queen.

But this absolute minx of a girl with a wit half a second slower than his and a scheming grin he'd only ever seen in a mirror . . . *this* sister, who had somehow gotten to know him better in a couple short months than his entire family had managed in ten years . . .

This sister, who'd knit him a sweater because she saw how much he loved his old one.

He adored her, and that was incredibly dangerous. Because as far as he knew, she still very much wanted to stick a knife in his neck.

"We should go," he rasped, finally pulling away. "Kal's waiting."

She grinned. "All right. Let's go see what all the fuss is about."

CHAPTER 40

KALLIAS

Kallias was freezing.

He was wearing three layers—an undershirt, a tunic, and a thick coat—and still he shivered. Eli, meanwhile, was barely even dressed, his pant legs shoved into his boots and his shirtsleeves rolled up to his elbows.

"Aren't you cold?" Kallias asked.

Eli shrugged, his unbelievably broad shoulders straining against the fabric of his shirt. "I run hot."

"I'm sure you do," Kal muttered, eyeing his shoulders for a moment before tearing his gaze away to scan the crowd in the courtyard. Everyone was a little quieter today. Soleil's strange, terrifying episode at the ball last night had shaken the people a bit. But still, merriment reigned over worry.

"What are you looking for?" Eli asked, following his line of sight.

"I don't know. I just . . . I have a bad feeling."

Eli grunted, tapping his fingers against his bicep. "There hasn't been an empty grave in a few days. I hate to say we're due for it, but . . ."

"That's what I'm afraid of." If a dead body rose during the day—during the *Festival*, no less—it was going to be a lot harder to hide it from his people. And his mother. He needed to solve the problem *before* she caught wind of it if he was going to use it to prove his usefulness hadn't yet run out.

His head ached, and he grabbed his canteen and took a quick swig, the sour tang of wine comforting on his tongue.

Just a little, he reminded himself—just enough to warm him. Nothing excessive. As long as he kept to his limits, he was fine.

Eli tracked the motion with his eyes. "That didn't look like a drink of water."

Kallias's knuckles whitened around his canteen, and he resisted the urge to hide it. "It didn't look like any of your business, either."

Eli put his hands up. "I'm not judging. It's a festival. But it looks to me like you're drinking your stress away, and that's a road you don't want to roll your carriage down."

Anger lashed cold whips over him, then warmed as he slumped against the gate, rubbing at the bridge of his nose. "I know. Gods, if anyone knows that, it's me. I just . . . last night was terrifying, and this morning Vaughn's unwell, and my parents have hardly been seen all day. Nyx is taking back land we've held for *years*, their people are trying to turn Soleil into *their* new war cry, and then there's this." He flashed his golden band at Eli before tucking it back under his opposite arm, scowling at his shoes.

"You've been claimed?"

"Not yet. But soon." Gods only knew how soon. His parents hadn't brought it up since before Soleil was found—and maybe that was a good sign. Maybe his bringing her home had convinced them to reconsider. "What about you?"

Eli tensed, his fingertips digging into his sleeve. "What about me?"

Kallias forced a smirk, elbowing the guard lightly in the ribs. "I saw you dancing with my sister. Looked like you two had a connection. There's no rule against it, you know. Heirs can court whomever they please." A privilege not afforded to the others in the royal line.

Eli snorted, but his cheeks colored, his eyes flitting away as he scratched at his shoulder. "The only connection she wants to have with me is her fist against my face," he said nonchalantly, but Kallias thought he could hear sadness hidden beneath, an eel peeking out from beneath a shelf of ocean rock.

"Eh, give her time. That's how she was with all of us at first, and look how that's changed. She's still settling in here, that's all."

Eli's scowl deepened. "Maybe." His gaze shot up a moment later, and that scowl wavered toward something lighter. "Speaking of your sister."

"Sorry we're late!" Soleil called, she and Finn sauntering in with eerie symmetry—both with a swagger in their step and a cocky tilt to their heads, both wearing colorful sweaters, standing at nearly the same height. Finn knocked Kallias on the back, and concern rose and fell in him as he took in his brother's slightly damp eyes, trying to decide if he'd been crying or if they were simply watering from the cold breeze.

"Are we ready to go?" Finn asked, reaching out to pull Eli into his grip, keeping one arm around both him and Kallias. He grinned at Soleil easily, though something still seemed off about it. "I, for one, am ready to eat an ungodly amount of taffy."

"You had me at taffy," Soleil said, ducking between Finn and Eli's arms, completing their chain.

"That was the *very last* word," Finn said, at the same time Eli dryly added, "I would've guessed he had you at *ungodly*."

Soren pinched both of their sides, eliciting yelps of protest. "Don't you two start! Let's just go. I want sugar."

Some of the weight eased from Kallias's chest, a warmth blooming there that had very little to do with the alcohol.

He could get used to this. It was strange, and new, and it would take some adjusting, but . . . he thought he might like it.

CHAPTER 41

SOREN

For a few shining hours, with Finn's arm around her shoulders and Elias's around her waist, she didn't feel so much like a girl torn in two.

Admittedly, Atlas's capital city was beautiful, especially decorated for the holiday: gold and green garlands hung from the streetlamps, bits of enspelled crystals strung and sparkling around merchant stands, and painted shells jangling around the necks of laughing children as they bobbed and weaved through the festival crowd.

Still . . . her heart ached for Nyx. If they were home, Elias would be helping his mother at their metalwork stand, and Soren would be baking cookies in the kitchen with Auralee. Emberlyn and Yvonne would be stealing bits of dough, Enna scolding them—and then stealing some herself. Elias and his family would come in halfway through the evening, red-cheeked and chapped-lipped, ready to devour whatever hadn't been stolen before it could be baked.

Elias's hand touched the small of her back, warm and bracing.

"I know," he said, so quietly that no one but her could hear, gazing out at it all with a glimmer of grief in his eyes. "I know."

Soren slid her arm across his back, her fist clasping his shirt tightly, and together they walked through the city of their enemies toward the crowded bakery where Kallias and Finn had disappeared, promising to bring back treats.

"We'll have to find you some shears out here," she said, fingering his hair playfully. Thankfully his mourning braid was so short that he'd been able to pin it easily beneath the rest of his hair; even Kallias wasn't dull enough to miss something that clearly Nyxian.

Elias swatted her away, scowling, but his eyes glowed. "Hands off my hair."

"Don't tell me you like it that long." She knocked her hip against his as they walked. He half-stumbled at her blow—she'd gained weight and strength since arriving here, with all the rich Atlas food she was admittedly beginning to love, whereas he could probably be blown away by a stiff wind. He was still tall, still broad and intimidating, but . . . he'd lost weight. Gained weakness.

Some of her mischief dimmed, and she caught his sleeve, steadying him. "Sorry."

"Just a loose cobblestone," he lied. "It's okay."

She let him have that one. "Fine. But really, you do need a haircut."

"I think it suits me. Besides, if you insist on coming up with more suicidal schemes, I'm going to need it long enough for another braid."

"Jackass."

"Smartass." But his smile was softer than she expected. She looked away quickly.

Kal and Finn caught up with them a couple stalls later, both with their hoods up and scarves pulled over the lower halves of their faces. Soren only knew it was them because Finn introduced himself by tugging on her hair and kicking Elias's ankle.

"Enjoying it so far?" he asked casually, as if he hadn't almost gotten himself smacked.

"It's lovely," Soren said, surprised to find she meant it. It was so similar to the way they would celebrate in Nyx that it made her heart hurt. "When does the tournament on the beach start?"

"Late afternoon," Kallias said, squinting up at the midmorning sky. "We have plenty of time."

And so they did. They spent the afternoon trailing from stall to stall, laughing and eating and playing carnival games until even Elias began to relax and Soren forgot for a moment that they didn't belong here.

The sky was just beginning to redden, the chill in the air sharpening enough that even Soren shivered, when the noise started.

Elias came to a sudden halt, his hand sliding away from the small of Soren's back, the sudden cold jerking her to attention. "Eli?"

Her battlemate turned slightly away from them, his expression severe—a look Soren knew too well.

"Trouble?" she asked, echoing his movement, her hand going for a sword that wasn't there; but before he could answer, she heard what he had.

Screams in the distance, back at the edge of the festival, near the palace. Screams . . . and an unearthly howling. Not dogs, not people, but . . . something. Something awful.

The hair on Soren's neck stood on end, and the scar on her stomach pulsed with a quick, hot pain. "What in the pits was—"

Another earsplitting wail—worse than mourning, worse than the sounds of battlefield wounded—finally brought the entire crowd to a standstill. A quiet *oof* escaped Soren's throat as a second, sharper pain tore across her gut, like she was being ripped open all over again. Elias whipped to face her, eyes stern, mouth poised to ask a question that was going to get him in trouble.

"I'm *fine*," Soren said quickly. "Stop looking at me like that."

He seemed reluctant to obey, but he did, looking to Kallias instead, who had gone so pale she was half certain he was going to faint. "You don't think . . . ?"

Elias only swallowed. His hand went to his chest like he was searching for something to squeeze, then fell again, empty.

"We need to get home." Finn's voice sharpened with urgency, and he tugged his scarf down with one quick movement, his breath coming out in a soft white cloud as the knit cloth settled around his clavicles. He looked toward the palace with furrowed brows, his doe-brown eyes uncharacteristically hazy. He blinked once, twice, as if trying to clear his head.

"Finn?" Soren prompted, unease swelling as another unearthly cry cut across the festival.

Finn gave a quick shake of his head, rubbing the bridge of his nose as if rubbing away a dream. He swayed to one side, and she quickly braced him. "Kallias!"

Kallias rushed over and caught Finn's other shoulder. "Let's go," he said, voice dark, the warrior creeping back in. It made Soren's scar twinge again. "Now."

But that was when the screaming grew louder. The sound of innocents being slaughtered.

Soren and Elias met each other's eyes—and together, with one mind, made a decision.

"Finn," she said again, a demand this time, a request he somehow immediately understood. He blinked himself back to sense, reached under his sweater, and produced not one, not two, but three daggers of varying sizes, tossing one to Kallias and keeping one for himself. He put Soren's in her palm, clasping her hand and the handle for a moment.

"Please don't stab me in the back," he said, his eyes earnest and endearing.

Soren had to bite back a grin as she put her opposite hand over his. "No promises, Nicky."

Finn gasped. "Jericho told?"

"Not now," Kallias said tensely, with another grim look at Elias. "Let's go."

CHAPTER 42

SOREN

Soren had not prayed as much as she should have in her life, and she regretted it the moment they reached the site of the screaming.

She had seen plenty of dead bodies before—pits, she knew how it felt to survive the touch of Mortem's cold hands herself. Between war and loss, between Elias's preaching and her own experience a few weeks ago, she was intimately familiar with death and the way human bodies took to it.

She'd never seen a dead body walk.

Finn and Kallias both swore. Elias breathed out a prayer that shook on poor foundations, a lame thing that named no specific god, just in case the Atlas men were still listening.

The palace gates were blocked by a wall of the standing dead.

Their eyes were not eyes, but neither were they the empty pits of long-dead bodies—a translucent mockery of eyeballs glowed inside the sockets, milky white light leaking from them like tears, red irises and pitch-black pupils sending a cold spear straight into Soren's belly. She had to swallow back bile, her hand tightening around Elias's, trying to ground herself. Her scar hurt.

Their clothes hung from them, some in tatters, some of much finer make, perfectly intact. Their skin was not skin but another ghostly charade, different shades of shadow mimicking their flesh tones from life. Bits of bone stood out from holes in the illusion, stark and sickening, a glimpse into the human body that the living weren't meant to see.

Bodies—unanimated, normal ones—littered the floor before the undead, encased in Atlas guard uniforms, the blue and gold gleaming dully in the soft winter sun. Throats torn out, arteries ripped into, guts shredded apart.

Soren was not the sort of person to swoon at blood and gore. But this was different. The dead killed like beasts. Like *animals*.

One of the dead met Soren's eyes and gave her a cruel, bony smile.

The world tilted to one side, her knees going weak, and she couldn't even muster a protest when Elias caught her, bracing her against his side. Her scar began to burn, to pulse, as if she was back on that battlefield, back in Mortem's embrace—

"Soren. *Soren*," Elias whispered urgently in her ear, his hand touching her stomach, her face, searching for a wound to stanch. But there was none—nothing physical for him to fight.

The undead that held Soren's gaze stepped forward. Nausea struck her to the core at the cricking noise the unholy thing's stiff bones made as it moved, as if every inch forward fractured a bit of its frame. It was one of the . . . *fresher* bodies, its clothes intact, hardly a smudge of dirt or decay marring the unremarkable outfit. Dark hair fell in lifeless, limp waves, cobwebs tangled in the strands, the perhaps once-pretty face disfigured by the cruel ministrations of death. Her throat was torn open, flaps of skin hanging loose. Decay had rendered her unrecognizable, but there were marks on the withered skin of her arms . . .

Tattoos.

Nyxian tattoos.

Horror turned the marrow of her bones to tar, her blood to water. This couldn't be happening. These dead, they couldn't be her people, they couldn't be—

"Traitor," hissed the *thing*, a vaguely feminine voice layered with whispers and clicks that sounded nothing like human tongues. And as she whispered, the rest of the undead joined, layers of almost-voices that left her shaking: "Sun-born. Night-killer. *Traitor.*"

The undead pinned her with its eyes again. Kept them there.

"You sold us to the sun," it whispered, a macabre grin stretching across its once-beautiful face. Something cracked in its jaw when it smiled. A giggle like bubbling blood drifted out of its wide-open throat. "What did they offer you, Princess? A throne? You had that. A family? You had that too. What more did they give you, to turn your heart from home?"

Oh gods. This couldn't be real.

"First we killed you," said the undead woman, "then you killed us. This time, we'll finish the job."

Soren jerked free of Elias's arms, palming her dagger, wishing its hilt had a better grip, wishing her palms weren't sweating. "You can try, ugly."

"This is a warning. Go back to Nyx and you may yet save yourself."

She held its gaze, bared her teeth. "I'm not finished here. But you are."

The dead thing took two lurching steps, bone-tipped fingers splayed, jaw unhinging with a sharp *crack*. Elias and Kallias both moved at the same time to pull her back—

But it was Finn who had *already* moved, a split second before the undead lunged, like he'd seen it coming, like he'd *known*.

And it was Finn whose dagger lanced through the decaying skin on the undead's face—Finn whose arm it sank its teeth into. Finn whose scream of agony blended with hers, with the sudden, primal *rage* that howled through her like a hurricane. She and Elias moved in tandem: Elias to shove the dead thing's head off of Finn, Soren to catch it by its hair and sever its head neatly from its body.

The bag of bones collapsed in a heap, a horrifying stench wafting up from it, its head hanging by its grisly hair in Soren's white-knuckled grip.

And with it went the others. Every dead body, from the barely-buried to the worm-eaten skeletons, crumbled as if the life that had bolstered them had left them just as quickly. As if their master had fled.

She started shaking so badly her fingers released the head, and seconds later, she felt Elias's arms around her. No words from him—gods, what could they have even *said*?

"Elias," she whispered, "what in the *pits* was that?"

He tightened his grip on her, his voice darker than a stormy Nyxian night. "Necromancy."

Only when Finn moaned did she snap back to herself, twisting out of Elias's grip and kneeling beside her brother. "Finn? Finn!"

Kallias was already tying a tourniquet above the wound. When Soren leaned over to peek at it, her stomach thrust its way into her throat, and she nearly gagged. A chunk of Finn's arm was *gone*, flesh torn out by teeth, blood soaking into the purple yarn of his sweater. Finn himself was pale as a mountain wolf's fur; even his lips had gone white, and his eyes were rolled into his head—

"Finn!" Her voice broke on his name. "Wake up, you bastard, now isn't the time to be dramatic!"

His body roiled with an awful shudder, something that looked too much like death throes for her comfort. His eyes, already dimming, already confused, met hers.

"I'm . . . sorry," he gasped out.

A half-hysterical laugh rattled her ribs, but it faded at Finn's next tremor. "Sorry for *what?*"

"My sweater." His chin trembled, his eyes drifting to the bloodied, frayed yarn. He groaned, a shaky, upset thing that sounded nothing like him at all. "Damn thing tore the sleeve . . . it's going to be such a pain to get those stains out . . ."

Suddenly, *violently* possessed by the need to kill a dead thing twice, she merely squeezed his hand and jerked her head around to Elias. "Does anything happen when a necromanced body bites someone?"

Elias blinked, his brow furrowed. "What?"

Adrenaline and rage pitched her voice too high, too loud, too angry. This wasn't his fault, and it wasn't his to fix, but Mortem was his goddess, death was his whole *thing*, he had to know what to do. "You're the gods-damned expert here! Does anything *happen?* Is he going to die too?"

Elias frowned like he was confused. "I don't . . . I mean, I don't think so, but it's not really my area—"

"What do you *mean*, it's not your *area?*"

"Soleil." A heavy hand settled on her shoulder, and she turned to find Kallias looking at her, stern and soft all at once, even though he looked ready to faint himself. "Eli's only got secondhand accounts and books to go off of, all right? Not like we're Nyxian. We have no idea what Mortem's magic can do."

Elias tensed. "Well, actually, Mortem doesn't—"

"Fine," she interrupted, flashing Elias a warning look. Defending his goddess here would land him in a heap of trouble she didn't have time to dig him out of. "We need to get him to Jericho. *Now.*"

CHAPTER 43

KALLIAS

"No. No. No. No. No."

It was all he could say. All he could think. All he could manage past hoarse gasps, pacing the abandoned shore, the only place he trusted to hide his weakness from the others. He'd sprinted out here the moment he delivered Finn to Jericho, bleeding and senseless, rambling some nonsense about fire or skulls and thorns, fever dreams already taking him. And no matter how many times Kallias had asked him, *ordered* him to wake up, he hadn't opened his eyes.

He hadn't stayed to watch what came next.

Every step on the sand felt unsteady, his legs shaking so badly he wasn't sure how much longer he could stand. He couldn't *breathe,* panic wrapping itself through his ribs, squeezing like a snake around its prey. His chest tightened painfully, then relaxed, then tightened again, pain spasming like a band being pulled and let go, again and again and again.

He couldn't bury another sibling. Least of all Finn.

Not again. Not again.

"Not again! Do you hear me? *Not again!*" He tilted his head back and shouted it to the sky, roaring it to the gods with all the strength he had not already given. Helplessness kicked out his knees, throwing him onto the damp sand, his hands plunging into the cold edges of the tide as he gasped and gagged and did his best to remember that Finn wasn't dead yet. Finn wasn't dead *at all,* and he wasn't dying either, because Kallias rejected it, denied it, utterly *refused it.*

"Anima, Tempest, whoever is listening," he snarled, wild beyond taming, raging beyond calm, "you tell your damned sister to get her claws *out of my brother,* because I swear by every god's name that if he dies—"

He swore what? Retribution? Revenge? What was he going to do to the voiceless, faceless gods? How was he going to fight a handful of myths? All he had to threaten them with was his unbelief—a taking away of his faith. But what did they care for one man's worship?

The thought only bolstered his rage, a buzzing whine building in his head, a pressure and pain in his chest that built, and built, and burst. He screamed out his anger and terror, slamming his fists down into the cold sand, throwing his head back to shout to the impassive sky. "Show yourselves, you selfish bastards! If you ever cared about us, if you're even there, why don't you *do something for a change?*"

In the distance, thunder rumbled, the quietest and gentlest *go to the depths* Kallias had ever heard. And that was all.

A ragged cry dragged itself out of his throat, and he crumbled, letting himself curl against the sand.

His forehead met something cold—colder than sand should have been.

Kallias froze. And slowly, slowly, he sat up, looking down at his hands. His fists were plunged into the sand wrist-deep. And all around him, in a blown-out circle . . .

Ice.

Not thin and clear this time. Thick hoarfrost that coated the beach for several feet, enclosing him in a perfect circle.

Not again. Oh, drag him to the sea and drown him twice, *not again.*

He scrambling to his feet and staggering away from the ice, from the . . . whatever it was. A sign from Tempest? Or . . . had . . . had *he* . . .

No. Of course not. That couldn't have been *his* doing.

"That was you, right?" he rasped to the sea, to the sky.

No response. Not even a whisper of thunder.

He swallowed, wishing his limbs would stop tingling—wishing he didn't feel like he'd just done something he wasn't supposed to. "I'll take your silence as a yes."

Enough of this. He was First Prince, he was Kallias Atlas . . . he was the big brother. He shouldn't be out here crying into the sand and screaming at the gods. He should be with Finn.

But even once he was safely inside, a chill trailed after him, like a winter wind clinging to his back and refusing to let go.

Like something had found him on that beach and followed him home.

"Where is my son?"

Adriata's cry cut across the infirmary, jerking Kallias up from his place at Finn's bedside as his mother pushed past grim-faced healers, Ramses on her heels, both of them wild-eyed with a learned panic. Adriata caught sight of them first: Soleil sitting with her back against the infirmary wall, dull-eyed and shaking, Finn's torn and bloodied sweater balled up in her hands; Jericho barking orders to her fellow healers, crimson-stained hands tight like a tourniquet around Finn's injured arm, a tendril of spring-green magic twining through the wound like a stitching needle; Kallias, Finn's blood drying under his nails, sand ground into the knees of his pants, one hand turned out in warning, the other gripping his unconscious brother's like an anchor; and Finn himself, flushed and frantic, agonized gasps of air escaping as he thrashed and shook with fever chills, the wound already festering from the rot that had lined the unholy creature's teeth.

At least, Kallias thought that was it. Gods forbid it was anything worse.

"Mama," Kallias rasped, but her eyes stayed fixed on Finn, tears welling in them as she half-stumbled to his bed—she would have fallen if not for Ramses, who shot his arm out to catch her around her waist just as her knee gave out. Kallias stepped away, pushing himself up against the opposite wall beside Soleil, quietly making space for them.

"What *happened?*" sobbed Adriata, reaching out for her youngest son, Ramses moving with her until they were both at Finn's head. Adriata's hand cradled Finn's face, Ramses stroking his sweat-soaked hair from his freckled forehead, the terror in the king's eyes nearly enough to crack Kallias's chest open. "Kallias, what *happened?*"

He took a breath in—then held it, the truth turning it sour.

He'd known about this. He'd known there were stirrings of necromancy, had known they were getting worse and worse—and still he'd kept it to himself.

This was his fault. If he'd told them sooner, if he'd utilized the whole guard, if . . .

If, if, if. None of it mattered now.

He told them everything, head bowed, limbs heavy with spent adrenaline and wretched guilt. And when he was finished, the look in his mother's eyes was worse than any blade that had ever been shoved under his skin, any cutting word or condescending smile, anything he'd ever endured before.

His mother looked like he'd cut the flesh from Finn's arm himself.

"Kallias?"

The cracked, quiet voice sounded so unfamiliar that he didn't realize who'd spoken until Finn's eyelids flickered, his brow knotted in confusion, brown eyes foggy and dazed. His thrashing stilled, but his eyes drifted back and forth—taking in Ramses, Adriata, Jericho, not stopping until they caught on Kallias.

"Kal," Finn rasped. "Kal, what happened?"

He was across the room again in two steps, fear and relief stuttering in tandem with his jagged heartbeats. As Ramses moved his hand to Finn's shoulder, Kallias pushed Finn's hair back, holding his palm against his forehead for a minute. Still feverish, but not burning—not as badly, anyway.

"You decided to pick a fight with a dead body," he said. "Idiot."

Finn's eyelids fluttered, a shaky sigh sliding through his teeth as he reached up with his uninjured arm, wrapping his fingers around Kallias's wrist to hold his hand in place. "Don't move. Your hand is cold."

Something tugged hard on Kallias's heart, and he brushed a bead of sweat from Finn's brow with his thumb. "I'm not going anywhere."

Jericho straightened up, blowing out a breath as she erratically waved her hand, dispelling the green coil of her magic. "You're damn lucky you got him back as fast as you did. That . . . whatever it was bit a chunk out of his artery."

"That sounds bad," Finn said weakly.

Jericho's jaw flexed, tears glimmering in her eyes. "You could've bled out."

"That sounds worse."

Jericho laughed, but the sound broke into a tiny sob, and she bent to kiss Finn's head. "Don't scare us like that again. Kal's been pacing a path in the floor."

"Is he going to be all right?" Ramses demanded, his hand tightening on Finn's shoulder.

"Yes," said Jericho, and they all let out a collective sigh. "The bleeding's stopped. He just needs to rest."

"What about the infection?" Kallias asked. "The fever?"

Jericho's brow furrowed. "That, I don't know. There shouldn't be any infection left."

"Then why is it still—?"

"I don't *know*, Kal," Jericho repeated, pinching the bridge of her nose, exhaustion weighing heavy on her voice. "I can't . . . I'm at my limit here. I've been healing all afternoon. You're not the only ones who got attacked by these monsters. I'll have to try another healing when I'm not so tired."

Movement to his right—a flicker of orange-gold hair, a blur of red and purple yarn.

"Welcome back," said Soleil, her arms awkwardly wrapped around the bloody bundle in her arms. "Glad you're not dead."

Finn smiled at her—gentler than any smile he'd ever offered the rest of them. "Likewise. You can thank me anytime, you know."

Soleil's eyes sharpened in irritation—and relief, Kallias thought. "For what? Ruining your festival present?"

Finn groaned. "You couldn't save it?"

Soleil fussed distractedly with the sweater, averting her eyes. "I'll see what I can do. But no promises."

"Understood," said Finn. His gaze was already getting hazy again, but he blinked hard, like he was struggling against it. "You okay, kid? You're not hurt, right?"

Soleil stood still for a moment. A second. A third.

Then, so fast Kallias couldn't even move fully out of her way, she tossed the sweater aside, leaned down, and wrapped her arms around Finn, squeezing her eyes shut as she hugged him.

She *hugged* him. And she didn't even snarl while she did it.

Then, just as fast as she'd bent over, she stood straight again, clearing her throat and fixing her hair with a quick toss of her head. "Glad you're not dead," she repeated in a mumble, dashing the back of her hand across her eyes before snatching up the purple sweater and marching out of the room with her head held high.

"I think maybe I'm still delirious," Finn announced, watching her go with his brow furrowed.

"Me too," Jericho said.

"Me three," Kallias mumbled, and when his brother managed to laugh, he thought it was the best sound he'd ever heard.

CHAPTER 44

FINN

Bone gleamed dully in the weak winter sun.

Finn nearly gagged, the heavy stench of death forcing its way up his nose, into his mouth. A vast field spread out before him, nothing but a stretch of dead grass and mud. Bodies—some standing, some prone, some old, some fresh—were strewn everywhere, half-buried in the mud, as if someone had torn up a graveyard. The bodies that still had eyes stared upward, their blank gazes reflecting the yellow-tinged snowclouds.

Where in the depths was he? He was just with Soleil, he was . . . what had he been doing? Was he with Soleil? He couldn't remember. He always remembered, why couldn't he remember?

He tried to run, tried to yell for Kallias or Soleil or anyone, *but something hard and unyielding caught at his ankles. The cold ground sent a jarring shock through his joints as he sprawled, and when he twisted to see what caught him—*

His stomach lurched in earnest as his eyes met empty sockets, sickening magic glowing within them, the grinning skull tightening its grip on his ankles. The stiff remains of what were once fingers slid over his leg, clutching at his tunic.

"Do you see it?" rasped the skull, its jaw clicking as it spoke. A rotting tooth fell from its smile with the movement. "Do you see what's coming, Trickster Prince?"

He did. He did.

Around him, his kingdom burned.

The palace was once again aflame, but not with natural fire. The fire was dark like the dirt beneath his knees, like the crown that graced the brow of the princess making her way toward him, bloodstained boots stepping on and over body and limb. Fiery hair flowed in perfect ringlets beneath the twisted thorn crown on her brow, and her eyes now burned gold, eyes that did not know him or love him or care for his pleading.

"Soleil," he choked out past the smoke and the rot, but his sister barely blinked. Like she didn't know that name. Like it never belonged to her.

"Weren't you supposed to be the smart one?" she laughed, a playful smile on her lips. "How did you not see this coming?"

And when she stomped down hard on his hand, the crack of his bones merely an echo of the ones that walked around him, Finn couldn't get enough breath to scream.

"For the last time, I am not *dying*, so stop fussing," Finn said indignantly, though his weak voice made it annoyingly difficult to pull off such a mood. "I just got a little piece of my arm eaten."

Jericho scowled at him, her magic wobbling around his arm, her eyes the furthest from amused he'd ever seen. "This isn't a gods-damned joke, Finn. You could have been killed."

"And yet, here I am, disappointing everyone as usual."

It had been three days since the attack—three days of being confined to his bed, drifting in and out of feverish consciousness, Jericho's magic carefully leeching out the infection the undead Nyxian's putrid teeth left in his blood.

Three days dreaming of skulls and crowns and his hand breaking beneath a boot, over and over and over again.

"Shut up, Finn," Soleil muttered from where she leaned against the wall. She looked nothing like she had in his visions; her eyes were green again, she wore no crown, and she was looking at him with something *almost* resembling worry, if he squinted enough and didn't wear his glasses. And used his imagination *real* hard. "Everyone's just worried."

"And yet, you two are the only ones here."

"Kal is talking to Mama, then he and Eli are going out to re-bury the bodies," said Jericho, with a light shudder. "And Vaughn's still recovering. Papa's dealing with the panic from the people. You might not have noticed, but there's Nyxian death-magic about."

"It's not Nyxian magic," Soleil mumbled. "Not . . . not specifically. Artem worships Mortem too."

"They told you they were Nyxian. And we're not at war with Artem."

"Well, yeah, but—"

"It's not worth arguing about," Finn groaned, his head throbbing enough already with their bickering. Besides, he hated to listen to an argument when he wasn't sure which side he was on. Jericho was right that Death was Nyx's forte, and the body had claimed itself as an agent of Nyx, and was itself the body of a Nyxian spy they'd caught a short while ago . . . but something about it still sat wrong. Announcing oneself so clearly to one's enemy was brash at best, outright foolhardy at worst, and though Nyx was losing this war, it wasn't because they were foolhardy.

Beyond that, Finn was the one who'd spread rumors of her alliance shifting from Nyx to Atlas. So if it *was* a Nyxian, if they *had* targeted Soren because she "betrayed" them, it was his own damn fault that he was missing a chunk out of his arm. It was his fault they'd tried to kill her. And he didn't really want to wear the guilt of this on his own back.

Jericho finally dropped her hands, and he sighed in relief as the pain blinked out of his arm. "You're almost there, but it's going to leave a mark no matter what I do. I can work on it more later, but I . . . I should be with Vaughn."

Finn waved her off. "Absolutely. Go. And tell him I'll forgive him for not weeping at my bedside as long as he pulls through too, okay?"

Jericho didn't even crack a smile, she simply pressed an absent kiss to his brow, then left so quickly he barely managed to say a quick goodbye. Then it was just him and Soleil.

"I'm still waiting for a thank you," he said.

Soleil snorted—then started laughing, an awful, ugly sound like someone was rubbing two graters inside her chest. She buried her face in her hands, groaning through her laughter. "Gods, I don't know *why* I bothered worrying about you."

In spite of himself, he grinned. "Were you really worried?"

She pursed her lips and dropped her hands, crossing her arms over her chest. "Shut up."

"Aww."

"I was just afraid I wasn't going to be the one to do it, that's all."

"*Awwww—*"

She hit him on the shoulder, which he was pretty sure translated to *I'm glad you're alive* in Soleil-speak. "I will smother you with a pillow."

Something warm and glowing formed in his chest. "Sure, killer."

Her shoulders rose and fell with a sigh. "So," she said. "Necromancy."

"Seems so."

"I assume you already knew."

"I . . . may have had some idea."

"Did anyone else?"

He blinked. "Eli didn't tell you?"

Soleil frowned, her brows rising. "Tell me what?"

"Well, Kal's known almost as long as me," said Finn. "He's had Eli and Seamus working the problem for weeks."

Soleil's eyes widened *ever* so slightly, her lips tightening.

Uh oh. She's pissed.

He didn't owe Eli anything, and there was no reason for him to save his ass, even temporarily. But if Soleil walked out of here to go scream at him, she might not come back, and . . .

It had been a long time since he had a friend. A real one, not like Luisa who he could never trust, not one like Kallias who only saw what he *let* him see, but one who saw through every mask and deception and still cared to speak to him. Who saw every dangerous angle he played, every weapon he wielded, and still wasn't afraid of him.

Soleil knew he was a trickster, a shadow king, a liar who built his throne from tavern boards and card towers and blood spilled silently in the dark. And still she laughed at his jokes, and knit him a sweater, and trusted him not to let her drown even if she didn't trust him at her back. And maybe it made him a true fool, but he wasn't ready to let that go.

"I'm tired of this room," he added, throwing off the blanket and swinging his legs around, carefully testing their strength with a push of his toes against the floor. They seemed steady enough. "And I could really use a drink."

Soleil narrowed her eyes at him suspiciously. "You don't drink."

"There's more than one kind of drink. Care for an adventure?"

Soleil hesitated, and gods, it was ridiculous the way his heart hovered between beats, waiting hopefully for her answer. Finally she said, "Sure. But if I have to drag your moaning, feverish carcass back here, we're calling it even on the life debt. Deal?"

His heart finally sank into its next beat, and he pushed himself up, cracking his back with a quick bend.

"Deal," he said. "I hope that sweet tooth of yours is as sharp as you say."

CHAPTER 45

SOREN

There were many things Soren had been absolutely dead sure she would never, ever see in her life. The mountains of Tallis. The Onyx Desert of Artem. Dead bodies walking and talking.

Somehow, Finnick Atlas sitting on a rooftop and sipping hot chocolate from a wine glass was at the absolute bottom of the list.

"I didn't even know you had hot chocolate here," she said, sipping at her own drink—more sensibly cradled in a ceramic mug, but Finn insisted he had an *image* to uphold, whatever that meant. They sat cross-legged on a rooftop above the bakery, both wearing their sweaters, listening as late-night patrons filtered in and out, their feet dangling alongside enspelled crystals and lanterns several feet above the revelers taking advantage of the extended hours for what remained of the Saltwater Festival.

Adriata and Ramses must have done a spectacular job spinning the attack of the dead as a one-time incident if people were still out celebrating so boldly.

"What kind of awful place wouldn't have hot chocolate?" Finn flashed her a smirk, reaching up to pull absently at his sleeve. She'd mended it badly, and done her best to get the blood out while he was still recovering in the infirmary, just to keep her hands busy. To distract her from the horrors of that day . . . and Elias's absence.

He'd told her Seamus had him running ragged trying to track down any evidence of who might have caused the attack, but no one had turned up—he'd even spoken to the Nyxian spies he'd managed to connect with in the city and still ended up empty-handed. But he hadn't told her that he'd known about this threat days, if not *weeks* ago.

Soren tugged her sleeves down past her knuckles and cradled her mug close, breathing in the warm, chocolatey vapors with her eyes closed. "It makes me miss Nyx."

The confession hung in the air like a snowflake buoyed by the wind, not yet ready to decide how it would land.

"Do you want to go back there?" Finn asked—nonchalant on the top, quietly curious beneath. "I mean . . . if you were given the choice, if you had the chance . . . would you choose them or us?"

She hadn't expected him to ask it that plainly. She'd expected it layered in a joke and a double meaning and maybe even a metaphor, disguised so well that she didn't even know what she was answering until well after she'd already answered.

"If you'd asked me before the ball . . . Nyx," she said. "No contest."

"And now?"

"Now . . ." Now everything was so topsy-turvy and terrifying and *mad* she barely knew which way was up and which way was down, let alone which kingdom she truly belonged in. "Now I think I need something stronger to add to this hot chocolate if you're going to ask these kinds of questions."

Finn laughed in earnest, a snorting, obnoxious thing that felt more familiar to her than any other part of him. "Fine, kid," he said. "You take a turn, then. Ask me a question."

Soren tapped her nails on her mug, frowning into the swirling depths.

There were too many questions. Too many things she needed or wanted to know. So she started with the one that stumped her the most. "If you like power so much, why aren't you trying to be Heir?"

"Well, because I'm a man, for one—"

"No, I don't mean that. You're smart enough to change the opinions of this entire kingdom with a whisper, I bet you could change a law in a day. Why haven't you used that for something bigger?"

Finn opened his mouth, then closed it; then opened it again, then closed it again. His brow creased, and he sat forward, resting his elbows on his knees as he gazed down at his city. At his people. "Because . . . power isn't power if someone has to give it to you. Power is something you claim for yourself. If it's given, it can also be taken away. And the more people that have their eyes on you, the less you can get away with."

"Huh. I never thought of it that way."

"Most don't. They like the visibility, the title, the fanfare . . . the sight of themselves in a crown." Finn shrugged. "I prefer to make my own crown, my own kingdom. No one can take what I made for myself. It belongs to me alone."

"You don't care that you aren't getting bowed to, Oh Great King of the Rooftop? You seem like the kind of person who would want some bowing."

Finn smiled, but it didn't touch his eyes. "People bow in different ways. They claim their power differently, too. Jericho takes it through appearance . . . looking the part of queen while Kallias and I do the dirty work. Kallias does it through his heart, by remembering people's names, fighting their battles with them, loving them all like his family. I do it by being a sneaky lying bastard, and you . . ." He studied her for a moment, biting his lip as he thought. "You claim power through your honesty. You stake yourself in stone and hold your ground. When you believe in something, when you want something, you are immoveable. You're one of the people who refuses to bow. Those are the people that change things."

There was a lump in her throat. She cleared it away. "So how do you bow?"

"What?"

"You said everyone bows differently. How do you bow?"

Finn looked away from her, gazing into nothing—or at something only he could see. "By sharing my hot chocolate. By running when someone calls me. And by giving someone an honest answer for once in my gods-damned life."

Her eyes began to feel a bit too wet then, so she turned away, too, both of them looking out at the city he ruled with puppet strings and a pretty smile. She may have been given the title of Heir, but she knew better than to think that made her claim to these cobblestone streets stronger than his—or any of theirs. Kallias had the hearts of the people, Jericho their worship, and Finn had their secrets, their sins.

If they'd only take a moment to look side to side instead of straight ahead, they could become something entirely unstoppable.

"Next question," she said. "If I never remember anything else, what's the one thing about Port Atlas I need to know?"

Another laugh from him, and he shook his head. "There's no way I can pick just one."

"All right, then." Soren stood and stretched onto her tiptoes, her legs uncomfortable from sitting for too long. "We have a few hours before sunrise, right? Show me everything."

Finn's eyes gleamed as he shoved one last pastry in his mouth and stood. "I'll show you . . . if you can keep up."

And without any further explanation or invitation, he ran for the edge of the roof and leaped off.

The next morning, all around Port Atlas, people would whisper over homemade hangover cures and leftover treats about how Finnick and Soleil Atlas ran the streets from dusk until dawn, their wicked laughter bouncing from rooftops and alley walls. They would discuss it in hushed tones, with hope in their hearts, with nostalgia burgeoning as they remembered the very same sound from a decade ago. And they would send up thankful prayers to Anima that the princess was coming back to herself.

But for now, it was not quite dawn, the chill in the air kissing Soren's cheeks, the early morning damp settling heavily on her hair and weighing down her curls, wetting the tips of her toes as she dangled her legs over the edge of a very high cliff. And for the first time since she'd arrived here, there was perfect, untouchable peace.

Finn had spent the night showing her everything—his favorite taverns, the glassblower's shop, the library. He'd even insisted on ducking into a tailor's shop with more casual, fun pieces, and they'd paired up ridiculous outfits for each other until they were in stitches laughing, Finn so amused by a particularly ludicrous hat Soren donned that he insisted on buying it for her. And lastly, he'd brought her here: to the seaside cliffs far enough from palace and port that the only sounds were the cries of gulls and the slap of waves against shore, the sun just barely beginning to peek above the horizon, checking to see if the night had finished its turn with the world.

Finn sat beside her, and in spite of neither of them having any sleep, in spite of his injury, he didn't seem tired at all. In fact, she wasn't sure she'd ever seen him so vibrantly *alive*, with no mask to dull him down. He sat with one knee cocked up, the other leg dangling beside hers, gazing out at the horizon with a look that echoed the strange peace that settled over her like a knitted blanket on a cold night.

"We used to do this all the time," he said. "With Kal and Jer. The four of us would steal breakfast from the kitchens early and hike up here to watch the sun rise. And once it was daylight, we'd all head down to get a quick surf in before Mama and Papa even knew we were up. But after you died . . ."

"Why do you all say that?" Soren demanded, turning to face him, sitting cross-legged to keep her balance. "Everything is always 'We used to, before you died.' Why did everything stop after that?"

Finn blinked. "I mean . . . I don't know. It hurt too much, I guess. Knowing what was missing. Jericho did try to get us back into it, a few times, but we just . . ." he shrugged. "It felt wrong without you."

The words hung between them, unspoken, but understood: *Everything did.*

"When I lost my first battlemate, it wasn't like that," she said. "Giving up everything I used to do with her didn't make the ache better. It just felt like losing her twice."

Finn looked at her curiously. "Like what?"

"We used to have snowcastle competitions in the city square. People would get way too into it, they'd bring things from home to decorate, some people commissioned metal brick-molds . . . the first year Jira was gone, I almost didn't do it. But I swear, I heard her voice in my head: *Are you kidding me? You're going to take the best part of my legacy and let it die just because I did? You pits-damned traitor!*"

Lips tweaking, Finn said, "I think I would have gotten along with this Jira girl."

"I thank the gods every day that I'll never have to suffer through you two meeting. That's too much mischief in one place, even for me." Soren shrugged one shoulder, twiddling her thumbs together, glancing out at the calm ocean. "I just think that whoever I was before, I wouldn't have wanted you to stop."

Finn shrugged, but he wouldn't meet her gaze anymore.

"Don't," she scolded, kicking his ankle.

Finn's eyes snapped to her. "Don't what?"

"Don't put that mask back on. The *I don't care about anything, least of all you* mask. It doesn't work on me. I still see you."

Finn blinked at her. "The others have never caught me like that."

"Well, I'm not the others."

He swallowed hard. "No. You really aren't."

They were quiet for a bit after that, both watching as the sun got its courage up enough to truly begin its rising.

"I'll help you," Finn said suddenly.

"What?"

"I'll help you," he repeated, turning to face her, the mask gone again. All the sharp things in his head were in his eyes now, an earnest determination at the helm, fervency lighting him up inside-out. "With the antidote. I'll talk to some people I know and we'll figure it out."

Her limbs went utterly numb, and it was a miracle she didn't plunge off the cliff. "What?" she whispered, afraid to believe it, afraid she'd heard wrong, afraid he was just lying a little too well for her to see this time.

Finn gave her a small smile that looked like surrender, like something changing. "I'll help you save your friend. No matter what that takes, I'll find a way to get you the cure."

Relief plunged through her so powerfully it was almost ecstasy, so dizzying she had to grip the rock beneath her to keep from swaying.

She was going to save Elias.

A broken laugh that sounded far too much like a sob escaped her, and she flung herself at Finn, hugging him so tightly she almost knocked them both off the cliff. "*Thank you.*"

Of all the Atlas siblings, Finn was the last one she would've expected to finally relent. But gods, *gods*, she wasn't complaining.

His arms wrapped around her in return, not hesitant for once. Comfortable, familiar. An embrace that a different version of her remembered clearly. "You've earned it," he croaked. "More than earned it."

CHAPTER 46

KALLIAS

Kallias had a splitting headache.

Perhaps it wasn't smart to drown his waking nightmares in wine and cake stolen from the kitchen earlier in the day, but it was better than drowning *himself*, which he also briefly considered after the reaming his mother gave him.

He'd *ruined* it. Every bit of favor he might have built with his mother, gone. Which left him here: sitting on the ground, his legs dangling inside a freshly dug grave, watching as Eli started to shovel dirt on the casket within.

They'd been tasked with reburying the bodies that walked into the city. On Eli and Seamus's recommendation—the two of them agreeing, for once—each body was placed in an iron casket, locked, the keys melted down. The graves were dug twice as deep as usual and would be overlaid with stone slabs.

"I take it the meeting with Queen Adriata didn't go well?" Eli asked, glancing up at him, eyes darker than the hole he was digging. His hair fell in sweaty clumps over his forehead, his biceps straining against his sleeves. Honestly, Kallias was beginning to consider taking up ironwork.

Still, even with those distractions, an icy flicker of fury licked at his gut at his mother's name, and he struggled to shove it back down. It was impossible to know where it came from, this tidal anger, or why it always seemed to appear when he least could afford it. "What gave it away?"

Eli sighed. "You should have let Princess Jericho take the hit on this one. It's her responsibility to catch these things, isn't it? And she probably would've gotten off easier."

Sure, maybe it was supposed to be Jericho's job. But Jericho was so busy playing nursemaid she could hardly be bothered to show her face lately. Kallias folded his fingers tightly against his palms, ignoring the cold slickness of sweat there. He caught up a bit of his cloak in his hand, rubbing the cloth absently to let some of his temper out. "So you think my mother would listen to her over me?"

Eli frowned. "Well, she was the Heir for ten years."

"In name, yes." And only that. "I don't mean to snap. You're right. She would probably listen to all of them before me."

And he had no gods-damned idea why. He was duller than his siblings, certainly, but he was better at politics. Better at war. He was loyal to Atlas with his whole heart. That his mother respected his thoughts so much less than his other siblings wasn't logical. Even their ministers and advisors looked to Kallias first when asking about matters of policy.

"Catch."

Kallias barely had time to look up before Eli tossed the spare shovel at him, the polished wooden handle nearly smacking him square in the forehead. "Help me dig," said Eli, a tiny smirk playing on his mouth, "and I'll tell you what the other guards think, for all that garrison gossip is worth."

Oh, great. So even the guards had noticed Adriata's favor seemed to rest anywhere but with him.

Kallias gazed at Eli for a long moment, debating whether he really wanted to hear this; but honestly, it couldn't do him any more harm.

He began to dig. "Go on, then."

Eli moved to stand beside him, his warm breath bursting to life as it touched the winter air, as if he was exhaling small parts of his spirit. "You almost saved Sor—Soleil, right? The night she was . . . taken?"

He jammed the shovel harder into the soil pile, ignoring how his muscles ached. Lowering the casket had been hard enough. "Yes."

He'd run back into the blazing palace, fifteen and foolish, and had almost made it back to the ballroom. But something had gone wrong, and somehow the guards that chased him found him . . . but not Soleil.

Eli shrugged. "There's a prevailing theory in the garrison. People think she blames you because you couldn't get Soleil out."

The words echoed softly, too softly, in the very core of him. *She blames you.*

She blames me.

She blames *me?*

"I was *hurt*," he barely managed to say. The ice in his gut spread, sinking spiked fingers into his heart, turning his blood to frost. "I went back in for her, and the only reason I didn't make it out was because I was knocked *unconscious*. The guards almost couldn't find me, I almost died trying to save her and my mother blames *me?*"

"Highness," Eli cautioned, his eyes on his hands, on his shovel. He didn't care.

"She blames *me*," he croaked, a bitter laugh cracking free, his hand flexing against the wood. "I was the only one who tried! And where was she? Outside cowering with the others. She ran away and left us both and she wants to *blame me—*"

"*Kallias!*" The sharp warning in Eli's voice mimicked the sudden snap of the shovel's handle.

Kallias blinked, glancing down to find the tool shattered in half. His hand was clenched into a pale-knuckled fist, blood trickling from his splinter-laden palm. The jagged edges on both sides of the shovel were lined with ice.

Oh, drown me twice.

He said as much out loud, which jerked Eli into action, immediately discarding his shovel and tearing one of his sleeves to help bind Kallias's hands.

"How did that happen?" Eli said, so quietly Kallias nearly missed it under the roar of the winter wind.

That was a very good question. And one Kallias didn't really want to answer.

He blinked dazedly at his palm, at the ice that had crept up his shovel out of nowhere, at the shape that seemed to resemble a handprint.

He hadn't slept enough. That was it. He hadn't slept, and the excess of wine the night before had gotten to him, and he was seeing things. There was no other rational explanation.

But there was ice on that shovel. And it hadn't been there moments before.

"I don't know," he whispered. "Must've been some moisture on the wood. I-It's cold. Maybe my sweat froze."

"I don't think that was it."

"You have a better explanation?"

Eli's jaw flexed. "Kallias, how long have you been—"

"It's Highness to you," he snapped. "And it happened how I said it did. Do I make myself clear, Eli?"

Misery, deep and true, clanged through him at the look in Eli's eyes; not anger, not hurt, but pity. And a curiosity that made him feel entirely unsafe, scrutinized, like a gemstone beneath an appraiser's glass—or a corpse being searched for a cause of death. "Yes, Highness," Eli said quietly. "But if you ever want to discuss other possibilities . . . I know something about strange things and where they come from."

Kallias swallowed the jumble of panic and guilt in his throat, wishing it were wine instead. At least then he'd be warm. "I'll keep that in mind. Let's just get this done. I want to go home."

But this time, that statement tasted like a lie.

CHAPTER 47

ELIAS

"Psst. Hey, jackass. Are you awake?"

Elias rubbed the sleep out of his eyes, blinking groggily at Soren, who had appeared in his bunkroom like a specter of fire, her freckled nose peeking just above the edge of his mounted cot. She gazed at him with wide, twinkling eyes— a look that always promised mischief.

He checked the clock mounted on the wall and fought the urge to groan, his muscles still throbbing from the repetitive motion of shoveling dirt in and out of graves. He and Seamus had just finished the last of the burials—not for the undead, this time, but for their fellow guards who'd died trying to defend the palace.

He should have been celebrating as the dozen Atlas coffins disappeared beneath the ground, knowing it meant fewer hands to send Nyxians to the same fate. But instead, as he watched the people he'd laughed and shared meals and trained with for the past couple weeks disappear beneath a sheath of iron, as he became the last living person to see their faces, he offered a silent, simple prayer up for each of them.

He was so tired of pointless death. Even Mortem hated to take lives that had been offered to her by human hands.

"Do I look awake?" he grumbled, and that freckled nose wrinkled.

"Your eyes are open. And I thought you outgrew sleepwalking, so—"

"What do you need, smartass?" He flicked her nose, and she yelped, eliciting groans and mutters from his bunkmates.

"Follow me," she said, rubbing the tip of her nose as she scowled toward the other occupied bunks. "I need your help."

Concern knocked on the door of his irritation, offering to take its place, but he squeezed his eyes shut against it. Soren wouldn't have that look in her eyes if it were anything serious. "Princess, my sword is yours, but . . ."

Her eyes gleamed with the promise of an oncoming innuendo. "Oh, is it now?"

His cheeks burned. "Stop it. What I'm trying to say is that I'm tired, and if it's not an emergency—"

"It absolutely is an emergency, and even if it wasn't, you'd defy your princess for a few more minutes of sleep?"

He glowered at her. She gave him an innocent grin. Somewhere below, he heard someone mumble, "Ooh, Eli's getting hung for treeeason," followed by a dull *thunk*, like someone kicked the speaker.

Seemed he didn't have a choice. "Fine. Let me down."

By the time he dropped to the floor, ankles aching at the impact, Soren had already danced out the door, trailing the smell of cinnamon behind her. Rubbing the sleep out of his eyes, fingernail fussing with the crust that had conglomerated in the corner, he followed.

It was late, but not so late that everyone had gone to bed; there were still some palacefolk wandering the halls, some arm-in-arm, some still wearing coats, having just come in from the festival. They all gave Soren nods or bows and gave strange looks to the rumpled, sleepclothes-clad guard following behind her, shuffling along like a slightly livelier version of the undead that had attacked the city.

They ended up in a quiet room Elias hadn't seen before, which reminded him of the den in his own home, except that this one was twice the size of his. A stone fireplace was set into the farmost wall, twin turquoise couches arranged in a *V* in front of it, facing toward the crackling hearth. Kallias was sprawled on one couch, looking surprisingly at ease, wearing soft pants and a shirt with a slit cut to reveal his muscled chest, wine glass in hand and his hair unbound. Jericho was propped on the other, Vaughn stretched out on it with his head resting in her lap. Jericho's face was free of makeup, and she had a soft robe wrapped around her willowy form. Finn was sitting cross-legged on the floor in front of her, slouching back against the couch, letting Jericho untangle his hair while he adjusted his spectacles and peered harder at the book in his lap. Glancing at it as he walked past, Elias thought he recognized some poison study terms from his own research.

Piles of pastries, sweet and savory alike, sat piled up on a platter in the middle of the rug—cinnamon-sugar doughnuts, cheddar and chive scones, chocolate fudge with diamond-like sprinkles of sea salt on top, puff pastry with what looked like some kind of spinach mixture in the center . . . and most importantly, none of it had scales or gills attached. Elias's stomach rumbled in desperation.

"I invited a friend," Soren announced, falling onto the left couch at Kallias's feet, picking them up and swinging them around so they were resting in her lap instead. Kallias kicked halfheartedly at her hand, but the smile on his face was warm. Elias's shoulders tensed, but he forced a smile of his own, returning the wave Kallias offered him.

"Sit," said the eldest prince, gesturing to the floor before the couch. "And take some food before Finn gives himself a stomachache."

"Take some wine before Kal gives himself a hangover," Finn shot back, though the razor edge he usually kept on his words seemed softer today, his grin gentler when he flung a pillow at Kallias's face, sloshing the wine in the prince's cup dangerously. "You're just in time, Eli."

"Just in time for what?" Besides overeating and overdrinking, apparently.

"Storytime," Jericho said with a delicate yawn, stretching her hands to the ceiling to pop her shoulders. Elias could have sworn he saw the potted plant on the hearth stretch its leaves in mirror, a glimmer of green playing hide-and-seek between its stalks. His hand twitched toward his chest—searching, not for the first time, for beads he couldn't wear without being swiftly accused of wielding *Nyxian death magic* or whatever nonsense they were trying to fill Soren's head with. "It's a festival tradition. We hide out somewhere one night a year, gorge ourselves on food and wine, and tell stories until the first one falls asleep. Then we carry them to the pool and toss them in."

Kallias scowled. "I still vote we dispel that tradition."

Finn smirked toward Soren. "He's sour because he loses every year."

"Not every year!"

"*Every* year," Jericho and Finn chorused, and Kallias pouted, taking a long draw out of his wine glass.

"Whatever," he said. "Not this year. Jericho's already yawning."

"I'm an easy yawner," Jericho grumbled, fluffing her hair. "Doesn't mean I'm an easy sleeper."

"I wouldn't worry, Kal," Vaughn rasped. He seemed to be recovering from his fit after the ball, but there was a permanent exhaustion stamping his eyes that echoed in Elias's own body. He understood where that came from—when one was fighting a battle against their own body, there was no true rest to be found. "I'm sure I'll be first to go."

An uncomfortable silence settled, and in the glances Finn and Kallias exchaged with each other, he knew Vaughn wouldn't be the one getting thrown in the pool tonight no matter what.

"Anyway," Finn said, deftly changing the subject, "who wants to start? Soleil?"

"Yeah, I think not," said Soren. "I don't have any good stories."

Elias nearly snorted, and she shot him a smug look.

"Kal?" Finn asked.

Kallias buried a belch beneath a prim cough, his cheeks flushed beneath his beard. "I need more time to pick."

"Let our guest tell one," Jericho suggested, her eyes pinning Elias so suddenly that he felt almost vulnerable, like a butterfly on display in a collector's box, tacks driven into his wings to keep them open. "I hear you know a thing or two about the gods, Eli."

The fire wasn't the only thing making his face burn. He cleared his throat, trying not to fidget beneath her scrutiny, curling his fingers into the plush rug beneath him. "Not enough to be of interest, Highness."

Her mouth twitched upward. "Come on, don't be shy. I only know stories about Anima, and the boys are bored to death by them. I'd love to learn something new."

Elias tightened his grip on the rug, sweat already pooling in the hollows of his hands. What story could he tell that wouldn't mark him as *too* other, too knowledgeable in the gods of other kingdoms to be a simple ironworker from a no-name town in the Atlas countryside?

Nothing about Mortem. Tempest was out too. But there was one story he doubted even Jericho knew—one about all the gods, but mostly about Anima.

"Once upon a time," he said slowly, sensing Soren as she shifted behind him, falling into the position he knew too well: fist supporting her chin, elbow propped on the nearest surface, watching him with a heavy-lidded look that said he was putting her to sleep, "the gods were rumored to walk among us."

It was an old story, but he remembered it as clear as the day it was told to him and his fellow acolytes, all of them congregated around Priestess Kenna's feet, cross-legged and wide-eyed, cups of hot cocoa going cold in their hands. They'd cherished those stormy nights when the priestess exchanged prayers and lessons for her rocking chair, when she gathered them around like a grandmother telling her grandchildren a bedtime story.

It was on those nights, when stormclouds hid them from the eyes of the gods and the wind drowned out her whispers, that she'd told them tales they would not find in any book or scroll. Some things, she'd said, should not be bound by ink and word—they were far too dangerous to be held by such mortal cages. This legend was one of them.

"No one knows how the gods became gods," he continued, plucking absently at a loose thread in the rug. "That story died from the mouths of mortals long ago. But the story of how gods became human . . . that one starts with Anima. Anima was a curious goddess, and above all the other gods, it was she who loved the humans the most. Mortem was a close second."

"The Death Goddess likes us?" Finn snorted. "You'd think she'd be a bit nicer, then."

"Shut up, Finn," the other four chorused at once, and Soren added, in a voice like a lullaby, "Keep going, Eli."

"Anima was a curious goddess," Elias repeated, resisting the urge to glare at Finn, who still looked skeptical, "and she longed to taste life with a form of her own. So she began to search the world for someone who could help her.

"Even with the advantage of godhood, it was decades before she found what she thought was an ideal form: a young woman named Isa. She was a gardener, orphaned and unwed, no family to speak of. She worshipped Anima with a rare passion, bringing her most beautiful plants to Anima's temple and planting them in the steps of the altar . . . a custom many Anima worshippers still follow today," he added, and Jericho nodded. "One day, when she was praying and planting at the temple, Anima came to her in a vision."

"I thought Occassio cornered the market on visions," Finn said.

"Visions of the future and a visit from a goddess are very different things," Elias said with all the patience he could muster. This was no different than guest lecturing at Mortem's temple, which he'd done more than once on Priestess Kenna's invitation despite the fact that he hadn't completed his studies before he left to join the barracks. He just needed to pretend Finn was an overeager six-year-old—and there was hardly any pretending involved there. "Only Occassio-blessed magic wielders can see visions of the future, but anyone can be visited by a deity if the deity chooses."

"And have you ever spoken to a deity, Eli?" Jericho asked, so softly he nearly didn't hear her above the pop and murmur of the flames.

He met her gaze. "Not yet. And most likely not ever. It only happens once every few decades, if not centuries. The gods rarely make themselves heard anymore."

"Yeah, yeah, fine," Finn impatiently waved his hand, sliding his glasses back up the bridge of his nose. "Sorry for asking. Just finish the story."

Elias had to bite his tongue to keep from snapping that he would *love* to, if only they would all stop interrupting. "Anima asked a favor of Isa: she wanted one day to wear the girl's form as her own, so she could see the world she ruled over. Isa agreed, and let the goddess in, giving her body over as if it was Anima's."

Kallias murmured something that sounded like it could have been a prayer or a curse, taking another sip of his wine.

"Anima's intentions were pure," Elias said, struggling to keep the distaste souring his tongue from doing the same to his words, "but this was the first time a god ever took a host. She didn't know what would happen—what had *already* happened. At the end of the day, when she left Isa's body . . ."

"Isa fell dead," Jericho murmured. Her eyes were unfocused, distant, lingering on the fire with a troubled slant to her brows. "Even a body built for godhood cannot hold two souls. The stronger soul will always win, and there's no fighting a soul drenched in divinity."

A chill buried itself in Elias's stomach. "So you do know this one."

"I don't tell it half as well as you," said Jericho with a sheepish smile. "And I've never told it to them. Besides, you're doing wonderfully. Please, finish."

"Anima was distraught," Elias said, "and tried to bring Isa back with her magic. But Isa's soul had already fled too far into Mortem's realm; she'd been dead for over a day. There was nothing to be done. So Anima went back into Isa's body—"

"Hold on," Soren interrupted, leaning forward, her jaw dropping indignantly. "She *killed* the girl and then just took her body back?"

"Why not?" Finn said with a halfhearted shrug. "The girl was already dead, right? And it's not like she killed her on purpose."

"Still. That feels . . . ugh."

"Anyway," Elias said, raising his voice above their debate, "Anima kept Isa's body and lived on as her until her form wore out beneath the weight of divinity. And when Anima's brother and sisters saw what could be done, that they could walk the earth and still retain their magic . . . they began the hunt for hosts of their own. Thus began the age of the new gods, and it went on until their borrowed bodies broke."

For several heartbeats, there was no sound beyond the purr of the fire and the quiet, stilted breathing of the Atlas royal family. In the silence, he could practically hear their minds racing, digesting the hollow echo his words had left behind.

Vaughn's soft snore finally broke the silence; the Prince Consort was out cold, his lips parted. Jericho was smoothing out the lines between his brows with her thumb, her own forehead furrowed with troubled creases.

"Depths," Finn and Soren swore in the same breath, the same tone, with the same quiet unease.

"Does that happen today?" Kallias asked, wide awake now and staring at Elias with eyes so severe he found himself remembering a broken shovel and ice where there had once been none. "Are they always . . . here?"

"No." Elias felt the tension whoosh out of the room like a sigh of relief. "It's been centuries, maybe even a millennia since the last time the gods were able to claim hosts, and even that is only hearsay. The legends say that it's so rare for a person to be born with the ability to hold a god's soul that it's only happened thrice in the entirety of time. And even then, the host must give their willing consent before a god can take their form. Only true zealots would ever choose that path."

It was a hollow reassurance, and he wished he could have said more, but even Priestess Kenna hadn't known any more details than that. The only thing she'd told him was that according to legend, Mortem had only taken a host once, and never again. No one knew the reason she hadn't followed her siblings' example.

"Well!" Finn said loudly, clapping his hands—dispelling the disquiet that had fallen over the room like a shroud, the film left behind by a story no one should be allowed to tell after sunset. "I think it's safe to say none of us are going to sleep a wink after that . . . fun? . . . little story. I bet I can eat more of these scones than the rest of you."

"Oh, you're *on*," said Soren, scrabbling down from the couch to snatch a scone out from under his fingers. Before Elias could fully shake off the tingle in his skin or the itch in his throat, laughter had taken over once again, Kallias begging Soren not to choke on a scone and Jericho loudly goading Finn into shoving a dangerous amount of dry pastry into his mouth at once.

And Elias did try to join in—tried to laugh, tried to focus on smacking Soren on the back when she did inevitably choke, tried not to blush when she fell backwards into his lap, her head pressed against his stomach and her grin flashing half-tipsy in the firelight.

But even with her hand tangled with his and cries of "You can fit more than that, you coward!" and "Finn, I swear to the gods I'll let you die if you start gagging," and the warm glow of the fire painting everything in shades of gold . . . even then, Elias felt a little bit wrong, a little bit tense, a little bit *watched*.

Like he'd been caught sharing a secret that wasn't his to share.

CHAPTER 48

SOREN

Soren stirred awake to a finger tickling at her neck.

"Elias, cut it out," she muttered, smacking his hand away, her face half buried in her silken pillow. She'd barely managed to drag herself into bed the night before after Elias's late-night storytelling, every bit of her strength drained from the countless meetings she'd been forced to attend before that, a rotating cycle of various ministers and lords and ladies from Atlas's more distant cities demanding answers. News of the necromancy attack had only just reached them, and as Heir, Soren had to attend every meeting. All one hundred and six of them.

Elias only leaned further across the bed, tugging at her braid. "Someone's grumpy this morning," he murmured in her ear, the cool touch of his breath raising the hairs on the back of her neck. The way he was speaking was like nothing she'd heard from him before. His voice was low, teasing . . . she almost would have called it *seductive.*

She cleared her throat, keeping her eyes closed, swallowing to rid herself of the sudden dryness in her mouth. If he thought she was in the mood for some kind of prank . . ."If you don't back off and let me sleep, you're going to see a lot worse than grumpy."

Elias ran his hand over her hair, cold fingers lingering on the back of her neck for two seconds too long. Her gut twinged, quivering as he leaned close, his words practically a purr in her ear. "I thought you'd like to see the sunrise with me."

Heart pounding, her cheeks growing curiously hot, she curled up tighter under her blanket. She wasn't in the mood to deal with the fact that Elias had obviously somehow lost his gods-damned mind. "I hate anything that happens before lunchtime, and you know that, jackass. Now leave me alone."

She felt Elias's weight shift, his knees planting on either side of her legs, his palms pressed down on either side of her head. "You really should get up now, Soren."

Oh, to Infera with it. If he wanted a good flirt, she would be happy to give it to him. She'd flirt him straight into a tizzy if he wanted. But if he kept insisting on doing it *now* and depriving her of her precious beauty sleep, he was going to learn how it felt to be on the receiving end of a blow from his sleep-deprived battlemate.

Bracing herself for the morning chill to rush in and shock her limbs, she began to throw her blanket off, only for a sudden thought to cause her to freeze in her tracks.

Elias hadn't slept in her room last night, and even if he had, his hands were never cold. He was always warm, even after days of marching through the highest and coldest of the Nyxian mountains.

And he always, *always* responded to *jackass* with a quick and affectionate *smartass.*

Her blood turned to ice as Elias—*not* Elias—moved his hands to her shoulders. Cold as snow. Cold as *death.*

Soren opened her eyes to a rotting smile and eyes gleaming with ungodly magic.

"Surprise," said the rotting corpse wearing Elias's voice, and he lunged.

Terror seized her with such a tight grip that her scream stopped dead in her throat, but luckily, her feet didn't have the same qualms. She kicked upward, hard, slamming her heel into the dead body's gut.

Its stomach *collapsed* beneath her foot, skin ripping like an old wineskin, half-deteriorated guts spilling out onto her bed, a horrific stench billowing out with it. And still, *still* the undead scrabbled toward her, her ankle buried in its stomach.

Its spine scratched the bottom of her foot.

She gagged and tried to get it out, but it was no use, this thing had her with its rotting teeth and hollow eye sockets gaping at her like a thing woven from her deepest, darkest nightmares—

Steel flashed, bone cut, and the undead's head toppled into her lap. Its body collapsed in a mass of limbs and withered skin, rotted juices seeping into her sheets. The scream clawing for release in her throat finally escaped then, her stomach threatening to follow suit, and she smacked the head off her lap. It fell to the floor with a dull *clunk*. Something about that sound clamped her entire body with nausea, and she staggered from her bed, retching, violent shakes rattling her teeth as she caught herself on the windowsill.

Mortem's rusty, bloodstained, gods-damned *scythe.*

"Are you hurt?" Kallias demanded, rising from his crouch on the foot of her bed. His hair was a bed-rumpled mess, his eyes stamped with sleeplessness, a slight wobble to his stance that suggested he wasn't *entirely* sober. But his eyes were bright with terror, and not of the twice-dead thing beneath him; when he hopped down from the bed and hurried to her, pushing her hair out of her face and checking her neck for injuries, that fear was all for her.

"No, I'm *pissed off,*" she choked, wishing to the gods she didn't sound so shaken, wishing cold sweat hadn't settled in a thin layer over her whole body. "How did that thing get in here?"

Kallias's eyes hardened. "Your guard's dead."

Her heart plunged. "*What?*"

"Jax," he said quickly. "Not Eli."

She didn't have it in her to feel guilty for how much gods-damned relief swept through her, turning her nearly as unsteady as her brother, whose breath definitely smelled of wine. "Isn't it a bit early to be drinking?"

"Isn't it a bit early for you to be almost getting murdered by an unholy creature?"

"Touché." She'd probably be day drinking too after this. "Are you okay?"

Kallias blinked, then smiled a little. "I . . . yeah, I'm fine. As fine as I can be."

Before she could say anything else, footsteps came pounding down the hall, and Finn and Elias skidded into her doorway at the same time, Jericho not far behind, Vaughn just behind her. All four of them were gaping and bleary-eyed, like they'd been sleeping—or hadn't slept, in the case of Jericho. And all of them relaxed when they saw her standing beside Kal.

"Gods, Soleil," Finn moaned, his eyes dragging over the mutilated corpse with disgust, "can't you go *one day* without something horrifying happening to you?"

Elias met her gaze, and she had to bite back a groan. This was going to cause another fight. "Apparently not," she said.

Vaughn pushed his way inside, followed closely by his wife. The physician, who'd seemed on Mortem's doorstep himself after the Saltwater Ball, seemed better today—his eyes alight, shoulders strong, his fingers steady as he looked over the corpse. "Another Nyxian," he said quietly. "Probably taken from one of the pyre piles near Delphin. He has soot on his clothes."

Soren swallowed, rubbing at the fear bumps on her arms, trying to flatten them. But every inch of her skin stood on alert, hackles pointed straight up, and no amount of warmth would coax them down. Slimy black decay was soaked into her left sock, already drying in inky patches on her skin, the smell turning her tongue dry and sour.

This couldn't be her people. They would *never* think she would sell them to Atlas. Enna, her sisters, her company . . . they all knew her better than that. But this could be one person. One rogue agent thinking they were on some glorious mission to avenge their kingdom, or to save it.

From her.

She shook that thought off like a horse throwing off a layer of flies. Finn would get her the antidote soon, and once the weight of Elias's survival didn't rest solely on her back, she would have time to sort out the complicated matter of her blood and her heart, time to find a way to reconcile whatever made up the different halves of her.

Saltwater and snow didn't mix. And she couldn't keep pretending that they did.

"Eli, get Seamus and search the grounds," Kallias ordered, straightening his back, and she watched as he subtly slid his hand against the wall to brace himself. "I want this necromancer found. *Now.*"

For once, Elias genuinely looked to be of the same mind. He gave Kallias a grim salute and looked at her a moment too long—promising that she was going to have some sense talked into her at the soonest opportunity—before walking out of the room.

"Well," Finn mumbled, "I guess I did ask the gods for something exciting to happen. You think they allow takebacks on prayers?"

CHAPTER 49

KALLIAS

After telling his parents about the necromancy attack in Soren's room, Kallias locked himself in his office with a bottle of wine.

He was coming down with something; the headache knocking on his skull like a relentless neighbor and the perpetual shivers rushing over his body like a rising tide told him that much. A fever would explain the ice-ridden hallucinations, too, and the fact that he hadn't slept longer than an hour or two here and there since the festival. Illness and insomnia didn't really mix nicely.

Still, he downed two more gulps of wine, completing the cocktail of misery in his gut. If he was going to be traumatized and exhausted, he might as well soften the edges somehow. The hangover was going to be a special kind of dreadful, but that was a problem for Future Kallias, the one who would eventually find the strength to pull himself together.

In the meantime, Present Kallias finished off the last dregs of the bottle, closing his eyes, savoring the musty tang on his tongue. The warm haze of alcohol slowly eased away the chills and the memory of a body collapsing like a deck of cards, dumping its guts on top of his little sister.

Somewhere in the back of his mind, in the more responsible places he'd locked up tight for this little venture into madness, the First Prince was losing his damned mind screaming that he was being a complete fool. He knew what alcohol did to him, knew it unleashed the tongue he kept in such a tight harness, knew it had almost shattered his family apart the last time he gave it free reign with the courage or foolhardiness to challenge the way they'd repaired the hole Soleil left behind.

He couldn't do that again, especially not now. He needed his control more than ever to keep quiet about all the things stewing deep in the pit where he shoved all his candid, bitter thoughts. Which was why the door was locked. And why he'd only brought *one* bottle in with him.

Limits. That was the key. As long as he stuck to his limits, he was safe.

Slowly, slowly, the wine began to lull him toward dozing, and he followed it gratefully, desperate for something more than a couple blinks of rest. His eyelids drooped . . . drooped . . .

Soleil's foot stuck in the dead body's ribcage, her eyes wide, terrified as she always looked in his nightmares of finding her smothered in smoke and fire—

A jolt of adrenaline, so intense it was almost pain, struck through him like a lightning bolt, his palms slamming against the desk so hard he heard a loud *crack*.

He stared at the ceiling, refusing to look down.

It's not real. It's not real. You're drunk, you're tired. Do not look.

But his more sensible side was drunk on the job, so who was he kidding? He looked down.

Two shards of ice were buried deep in the wood like blades driven into flesh, gleaming gently in the sun filtering in from his window.

He let out a long, slow breath as he rose to his feet, watching as the ice slowly began to melt, spreading a puddle of water over his very important, very official paperwork that needed doing.

He got up from his desk, unlocked the door, and went to find Jericho.

The marble floor dipped and swayed beneath his feet like a tossing ship. It was only through muscle memory and the staying power of sea legs that he kept himself walking straight, managing composed nods to the palacefolk he passed. Still, whispers trailed behind him like tailwinds, and he pulled his jacket tighter around himself, a chill winding its way around his body from shins to shoulders, a sea serpent claiming its prey. Still, he met every gaze. Studied every face. Ignored how blurry they all seemed around the edges.

He didn't realize until he was nearly to Jericho's door that he hadn't been searching their faces for familiarity. He'd been searching them for signs of life—checking those eyes to be sure they were real, checking every face to be sure the skin was supple, the bones strong.

His fist barely connected with Jericho's door before she flung it open. "What?" she snapped.

Kallias blinked at her. "Hello to you, too. Is everything okay?"

"Kal, we've got gods-damned corpses in the palace, my husband is only well for a few hours at a time, and Mama's not speaking to anyone but Papa now. Does any of that scream 'okay' to you?"

Most days, that scathing tone would set him back on his heels, send him slinking back to the cocoon of his office where he could bury himself in work to assure himself he wasn't a total waste of space. But thanks to the buffer of the wine, shame was no longer first in line.

She thought *she* had it bad. At least she wasn't hallucinating. At least she hadn't had to smell the fetid insides of a necromanced body. At least her shoes and thoughts and nightmares weren't soaked in spilled guts and blood that was really some viscous thing, a physical manifestation of the magic fueling their half-deteriorated insides.

He rolled his neck, cranking away that tipsy-tainted thought, swallowing the words he'd sharpened like arrows to be shot her way, letting them cut the inside of his throat instead. "We need to talk."

"Can it wait?" Jericho's fingers tapped restlessly against her arms, her eyes constantly darting over his shoulders and further down the now-empty hall. "I'm busy."

"It's already waited. I need you now." He pushed his way in, gripping her shoulder to steady himself, squeezing his eyes shut. The greenish walls of her room whooshed side to side, and nausea flowered to life in his gut, a warning that the wine was going to avenge itself fairly soon on his empty stomach. "Something's . . . something's wrong with me."

"You're going to have to be more specific," Jericho grumbled, but she followed him, shutting her door lightly behind her. The smells of burning rosemary and fresh-ground poultices tingled in Kallias's nose as it sent a gentle breeze back at him.

That wind practically curled itself along the back of his neck, murmuring words in his ear he didn't understand and didn't care to. He batted it away with an absent, erratic twitch of his hand. "I'm seeing things."

"I'd be more worried if you weren't," Jericho sighed, sinking into the chair by her driftwood desk. It seemed she'd built a tiny shrine to Anima: her door wreath had been moved there, five candles lit in the center, tiny bouquets and bits of herbs arranged around them.

Kallias narrowed his eyes at it, trying to pull the edges into focus. They only slid further apart. "Were you praying?"

Jericho's hand came down on the edge of the desk, blocking his view of her arrangement. "Were you drinking?"

Shame peeked its head back up from its hiding place beneath the pool of wine in Kallias's stomach. He shoved it back down and held it there, praying it would drown in grape-tinted darkness. "Not much. Not enough to explain . . ." What was he trying to tell her? That he was going mad? That for days now he'd felt restless in his own skin, his soul begging to be released, building pressure in his bones and blood until he was half sure he was going to explode into a chaos of ice and storm?

"I think I'm sick," he finally rasped. "I'm seeing things that can't be real."

Jericho *finally* looked at him, brows drawn together over sleepless eyes that seemed greener than they used to—but that was probably another hallucination. "Hallucinations? How much have you been drinking?"

"It's *not the drinking.* The first time it happened I was stone sober, okay? I . . . I was having this nightmare . . ."

Sea and surf, sky and storm.

He refused to die here.

He rubbed his hands uneasily, kneading his fingers until he could barely feel them. And then he told his sister everything.

To her credit, Jericho listened closely, the irritation in her eyes slowly draining away, replaced with a worry that eased the taut thread in his chest. She reached out and held his hands when he confessed his sin of screaming at the gods on the beach, of praying to Tempest when Anima was the one who had blessed their family so greatly.

And then he took her to his office. Showed her his desk, and the shards of ice he could still see, wavering in drunken glimmers before his wine-addled eyes.

"It's okay," he said tiredly when Jericho merely stared, frowning at his desk with a look like she didn't know what to say. "You can tell me I'm mad. I already know."

Slowly, tentatively, Jericho reached out her finger and stroked it down the side of one of the ice shards.

He blinked at her. She blinked at him.

The bottom of his stomach cracked open, yawning deeper than before, an abyss for his heart to drop into.

"Kal," she said, "you've got bigger problems than hallucinations."

"So far it's manifested only in ice?"

Manifested. Kallias already hated that word. Jericho had used it too much since he'd fallen weak-kneed into his desk chair, his stomach flipping in its wine bath, his mind refusing to comprehend the fact that the slowly melting ice on his desk was real, that he'd somehow *created* it—that he could do so again, if pushed, if he tried.

"So far," he rasped. "Nothing much, just . . . little bursts."

Jericho pulled the spare chair up in front of him, knee-to-knee. She held out her hands for his, and he gave them, wishing it didn't feel like a surrender. Wishing that even though his hands were twice the size of hers, hers didn't feel so much steadier. Stronger.

Maybe she'd been the right choice for Heir, after all.

"This isn't good, Kal." She pressed her fingertips into his palms, gentle green light budding at the tips of her nails. "Tempest is feared here for a reason. He's a ship-breaker—ruthless, bored, cruel. And ice? You know where people's minds will go."

To Nyx. To the ruthless kingdom of night and snow, who worshipped Mortem first and Tempest second. "How do I make it go away?"

"Kallias, it's magic. It's not something that *goes away*. I'm more worried about the fact that it's only just now manifesting, you're far too old—"

"Please stop saying *manifesting*," he groaned. "And you're older than me, remember?"

"My magic woke up at *six*. Most god-blessed have their magic mani . . . er, *appear* anywhere from as early as five to as late as sixteen. A grown man with no power suddenly waking up spitting ice from his hands, that's . . . unheard of. It shouldn't be possible."

No power.

"Right," he muttered, a laugh barking out of him like a croup cough. "Well, you are the expert in being given power you shouldn't have, aren't you?"

The words tumbled lazily from his tipsy tongue, thoughtless and bitter, and Jericho's hands stilled against his.

When he looked up, her eyes were hooked on his like an anchor sunk in sand. Her jaw was set, her gaze blazing. "What is that supposed to mean?"

He took his hands back, crossing his arms, hiding them beneath his biceps. "Nothing. Forget it."

"No, no, you don't get to throw something like that at me and then pretend it didn't happen. What do you *mean* by that?"

Every sideways glance, every shoved-down retort, every unspoken complaint rose unbidden to Kallias's lips, borne up from his gut by the bubbling swill of wine and exhaustion. That tight, thrice-knotted leash he kept himself on— he could feel it fraying, tugged on one too many times.

And he didn't care.

"I just mean that maybe if you'd spent less time playing nursemaid and more time actually bothering to do your job, Atlas would be in a better place right now."

"Is that what you think it is? *Playing?* Kallias, my husband is dying! You expect me to just ignore—"

"I don't expect you to ignore it, but gods, Jericho, I expected you to be *smart* about it! Picking *Soleil*, of all the gods-damned—"

"Oh." He *hated* the way her voice curled around that *oh*, understanding and pity gushing from it like a cut artery. "I get it. You're angry because it wasn't you."

His throat went dry, and he reached for the discarded bottle on his desk. Maybe there were some drops left. "I'm not—"

Jericho slammed her hand down on top of his, pinning it, halting his fingertips inches away from the bottle. "Well, Mr. Self-Righteous, you want to know why you can't ever be king? Why I couldn't give it up when it was just you and Finn? I'll tell you why." She let go of his hand to snatch up the empty wine bottle, dangling it in front of his face, her scowl distorted through the shield of rounded glass. "This is why. Because when things get unbearable, you and Finn can't face it. You run to a bottle, and Finn runs wherever he goes at night, and neither of you have the strength or the drive to do what you need to do to make things *better.* You can never be king until you can face the world without a hangover, Kal. And I don't see that happening anytime soon. Can you?"

"I—"

"I may have been *distracted* these past few years," Jericho seethed, tears budding in her eyes, "and yes, maybe I relied on you too much, and I'm sorry for that. But I thought that's what we *promised.* Us before all. Before politics and wars, before crowns and thrones, we were loyal to each other *first.* I didn't realize that your love was contingent on what I could *give you.* "

Not even drunkenness could save him from that blow, a gut-punch that reverberated through his whole body like a trembling gong. "No, Jer, I—that's not what I meant, I'm sorry, I'm all out of sorts right now—"

"Get out."

"What?"

"I said get out," Jericho snarled, standing to her feet. "And don't come back until you're sober enough to keep your gods-damned eyes open."

He couldn't comprehend what she was trying to say. "This is *my* office."

"Not anymore. Not until you get your head dried out. Atlas can't afford to have you in charge of anything right now."

"Jer—"

Her eyes burned with uncompromising fire. "*Now,* Kallias."

He straightened in his seat, forcing himself upright, gripping the armrests as tightly as he could. "You're not Heir anymore. You can't tell me what to do or where to go."

"No, you're right. I'm not Heir. But I am your big sister. And I'm telling you that you need to go sober up somewhere quiet, or else I'm going to kick your drunk ass straight into next *month.*"

Still, he didn't move.

"Or I could go get Mama," said Jericho lightly, as if this wasn't the worst betrayal of them all. "I'm sure she'd love to see you like this."

His tongue curled around a curse, and he shoved himself out of the chair. "I can't believe you."

She stood with spine straight, jaw clenched, hands balled in fists at her sides. "We will talk later. When you're yourself again. I can't deal with you when you're like this."

Kallias growled under his breath, but did as she said, stumbling back into the hall and somehow managing to find his way back to his room.

Sleep. Sleep would help. It always did.

But even when he buried his face in his pillow and sank into an uneasy sleep, it felt like barely a minute had passed when a page roused him with a knock on his door, informing him his parents had summoned him.

Gods, this day was going to be the death of him.

CHAPTER 50

ELIAS

The Atlas temple smelled like marigold pulp and sweet syrups, and Elias hated it.

He would have given anything for the familiar comfort of incense and rose, of beads nestled in his hand and memorized prayers on his lips. Instead, he had a white-stone tower that craned its pale neck into the sky, an altar made from pure gold, and the company of a dark-haired Prince Consort kneeling at its steps, a bouquet of fresh-cut flowers twiddled between his giant hands.

He hadn't wanted to come here. But between the mystery of the rogue necromancer and his steadily increasing homesickness and the fact that he could barely lift his mug of tea this morning, he'd needed the solace an altar brought him. And he hadn't much cared who it belonged to. Mortem would honor the prayers anyway—or at least, he hoped she would. Maybe she would count it as heresy instead.

Beggars couldn't be choosers. He'd have to take that chance.

Elias slowly came forward and knelt next to Vaughn. "What are you praying for?"

Vaughn kept his downcast eyes on the bouquet, trembling hands turned upward in supplication, his mouth carved with tired lines. "Healing. And you?"

Heat pulsed in Elias's shoulder, his fingers spasming weakly in response, and he suddenly felt very much like taking a nap. He shook it off, trying not to shudder. Those urges were getting more and more frequent, stronger and stronger—his body's command to lie down and die beginning to drown out everything else.

It scared him.

"The same," he croaked. "Maybe not the exact same sort, but . . ."

"Healing comes in hundreds of forms, and Anima is mistress of each." Vaughn's soft-edged voice did nothing to dampen the passion in his words, his love for his goddess, and it only made Elias ache for the safety of his own temple even more. "You're in the right place."

He bit his tongue. "I hope I'm not intruding."

"Not at all. I'm happy to have the company." Vaughn managed to quirk a smile. "You'd be surprised how rare it is to find someone who isn't hovering around me lately. I think my wife was a vulture in another life. She can't seem to stop waiting for me to die."

"I know how that feels," Elias said, then silently cursed himself for being so foolish. Vaughn gave him a sideways look, but didn't ask—perhaps he knew it wasn't something Elias wanted to talk about.

He'd long ago accepted that his life was doomed to be cut short. Sure, for the first week or so he'd shared Soren's fervor, both bent over forbidden library books until their legs fell asleep and their backs felt permanently rounded from slouching, but after that, he'd tried to change his perspective. To accept what was coming, to prepare for it. To prepare *Soren* for it.

He knew her like the back of his hand, like he knew every groove and chink in his prayer beads, like he knew how to pronounce his own name. Until now, until Atlas, there had never been a piece of her that was unfamiliar to him.

Soren did not do well with death or anything else of a permanent nature. She liked change; she liked having the power to take back the reins and change course for the better if life wasn't going her way. It was why she didn't care for religion, for the concept of gods or destinies . . . she didn't like the idea of inevitability, that someone else commanded her fate, and her choices were merely illusions of control.

So facing down his death had not been easy for her. And he was trying to respect that; pits, if it had been her, he wouldn't have fared any better, faith in Mortem or not. But he was beginning to feel like even his death was not his own, that she was choosing his deathbed with her own stubbornness and fear.

He didn't want to die on Atlas soil. He wanted to go *home*, to play with his brothers and sisters again, to say his goodbyes to his friends and his mother and his gaggle of cousins, to fall asleep every night in his own bed—or Soren's—until one morning, he simply didn't open his eyes again.

Peace. That was all he asked for; he wanted to greet Mortem at peace.

"Eli," said Vaughn suddenly, "can I give you a piece of advice I wish I'd been given much, much earlier?"

Elias frowned. "Of course, Highness."

Vaughn chuckled. "Please, I'm just Prince Consort . . . not even that, now that Soleil's Heir again. I'm just Vaughn." But the smile didn't last, and when he put his hand on Elias's bad shoulder, it was so gentle that it didn't even hurt.

Elias's eyes caught on Vaughn's wrist; though broad, it was bony and half-wasted, looking like it could snap if he pinched it between his fingers. A half-formed thought tickled the back of his mind . . . not quite a suspicion, but close. A memory of what he'd warned Kallias and Seamus to watch out for in their hunts through the city. But he shook that thought off quickly—a word against Kallias's brother-in-law would only buy him a permanent residence in the famed Atlas dungeons, and besides, he was hardly the right person to be flinging accusations based solely on being sickly.

"The people who love us have the right to fight for us," Vaughn said finally, bringing his mind back to the temple. "But sometimes the best thing we can do for them is to let go. Before they destroy themselves trying to save what is already beyond hope."

Elias's throat closed up, and he bowed his head—not for prayers, but to hide the tears that gathered in his eyes.

"I don't know how to break her heart," he admitted in a whisper.

Vaughn said, just as hoarsely, "Neither do I."

The two dying men sat together in silence after that, their prayers kept to themselves, not even the altar's ears allowed to hear their pleas. And though it was Anima's temple, it seemed Mortem saw fit to make herself a throne here, the shadow of death hanging low over two men who were loved so deeply that Death herself was reluctant to challenge it.

CHAPTER 51

FINN

*F*inn *dreamed of a girl surrounded by mirrors.*

She sat on a glittering crystal throne, vivid purple silk coating her from neck to wrist to floor, multifaceted violet jewels whispering in the light. Echoes of her reflected in each jagged mirror, thousands of dazzling girls, thousands of cold black eyes.

"And why would I help a heathen like you?" asked thousands of girls with one voice, thousands of smiles that curved a little too far at one edge. Her smile was a poisoned dagger, sharp and cruel and twice as deadly. "You have only ever mocked me, trickster. I've never heard your worship."

You've never deserved it, Finn thought bitterly. He tasted her name on his tongue, and was about to form it into a plea—or a taunt—when the scene before him began to shift, to waver.

The mirrors and the girl and the diamond throne vanished, the image dissipating like sea mist. He found himself leaning against an alley wall, deep in the heart of the city, the cold stone biting at his palms.

He shook his head, trying to pull himself back to reality. The city—he was in the city, and he was on his way to a meeting, and if he was recognized in this part of Port Atlas, he would be in even deeper depths than he already was.

Finn swallowed hard, quickly straightening, tugging his scarf back up over the lower half of his face. He swept his fingers over the edge of his knit hat to check that his hair was still hidden, then patted his abdomen to make sure his weapons and coins hadn't been plucked by a pickpocket while he was divested of his senses.

Jericho would have joked that he had no senses to be divested of in the first place, and not for the first time, he wished he could've brought her with him for this particular errand. But she couldn't be trusted with anything more important than who was tumbling who within the palace walls and which servants were sneaking extra portions of pudding after dinner service. Finn only gave her secrets he wanted spread.

His knuckles cracked as he flexed them, the dull ache still buried within. They hadn't felt quite right since he'd dreamed of Soren breaking them, but Jericho had assured him over and over that the bones were entirely intact. The pain was nothing but an illusion; nothing but a bit of imagination that his brain had mistaken for reality.

But it hurt all the same.

He shook himself fully back to sense, changing the way he walked, falling back into the disguise of Jaskier. It was risky to wear that one out again, but he had no real choice. A prince could not be seen consorting with fortune-tellers. It would make people nervous.

It didn't take long to find Luisa's shop. Tucked away in a dead-end alley, it would have been easy to walk past without so much as blinking. The door was plain, the sign above advertising a simple herbalist's shop.

Finn knew better.

He pushed the door open, stepping into the brightly lit shop. *"Only fakes work in the dark,"* Luisa always said, her nose scrunched up in distaste. *"So no one can see where their illusions come from."*

The shop was quaint, and *could* almost pass as an herbalist's place of business. Neat rows of wooden bookcases filled the space, swirled designs carved into the sides of each set. Only some held books; others were laden with thick swathes of herbs and flowers, others held crystals and glass balls, and still others were lined with candies and confectionaries. The entirety of the low ceiling was embedded with bits of twinkling pink crystal, casting the entire place in a warm, blushing hue. The shop smelled of mint and jasmine and crackled like the world before a lightning storm, the air charged with the anticipation of things to come.

Luisa herself was perched at the desk that served as both office and register, the surface littered with trinkets and baubles. One of her hands rested on a large glass sphere; it sat perfectly balanced on a ring of carved crystal, and she was distractedly rubbing her palm over the top as if soothing it. She had her nose buried deep in a gold-fletched book.

"Welcome to Luisa's!" she recited with mock enthusiasm, removing her hand from the glass sphere. She licked her thumb before turning the page of her book, her expression utterly bored. "We offer premium readings for five gold pieces, basic readings for ten silver pieces, and next-day-only readings are available for the low, low price of only five silver pieces! Anything having to do with romance will cost you an extra gold or silver piece depending on the level of reading you choose, and we are not responsible for any changes you cause by trying to avoid or hasten your fate. There is no guarantee the events we predict shall come to pass, as knowledge itself can be the catalyst for change, and *we do not, under any circumstances*, give refunds."

"Hmm, maybe I'll pass, then," said Finn, tugging off his hat and scarf, casually tossing them onto one of the nearby shelves. He leaned back and bolted the lock on the door in place behind him. "A gold piece for romantic advice? That's practically robbery, Lu."

Luisa looked up, her shoulders relaxing. "Oh. It's just you. I'd given up on you ever showing up for an appointment again, you know."

"I know." Normally he'd be able to muster a far more impressive apology, but not today. "But listen, I . . . there's something I need to ask you about. Something important. And, as usual, it can't—"

"Can't leave this building on pain of death," Luisa interrupted, waving him off with an eye roll. "I got it. Sit down, get the bribe for my silence ready. I'll get you some tea. You look absolutely awful."

Finn would have protested—thanks to his flawless royal genes, he knew the worst he could possibly look was *passable*—but Luisa had already disappeared into the back half of the shop that also served as her house. By the time she came back, Finn's hands were shaking, his vision beginning to blur at the edges. Of course,

Luisa's shop was set up to encourage her magic, to strengthen it. It would make sense for it to do the same to . . . whatever was happening in his head.

Jericho was always the one who had unnatural things happen to her, and Finn had always been perfectly all right with being ordinary. He hadn't asked for this, and he didn't want it, and with any luck, Luisa could tell him how to make it go away—or at the very least, how to hide it again. He struggled enough with his flawless recall of the past, and the matters he had to deal with in the present. He didn't need a perfect view of the future, too.

Luisa frowned at his trembling hands, carefully sliding the teacup his way. "Finn, really, are you all right? You don't look like yourself."

The confession hovered, half-formed, on the tip of his tongue. He wouldn't have come to her if he wasn't nearly positive she would keep this quiet. He held enough of Luisa's secrets—and was the source of enough of her gold, under normal circumstances—that she was his best bet for answers without the questions being spread to the nearest gossip. But her walls were thin, and there was an enemy of the crown afoot.

"I assume you heard about the attack?" he asked instead, crossing one leg over, resting his ankle on his opposite knee.

"The walking dead? Oh, I more than heard about it." Luisa sipped at her own tea, her eyes shining. "Easily the best thing to happen to me since the Orion battle."

Orion wasn't Nyx's capital city, but it was their largest, and it was halfway between the Atlas border and Andromeda where the royals made their home. Earlier on in the war, Atlas had ambitiously tried to send troops to subdue the city, hoping to extend their borders into Nyx. They'd been defeated . . . badly. "I wouldn't call the highest Atlas death toll in ten years a good thing, Lu."

Luisa simply shrugged. "I had families pouring in to ask after their children, their spouses. Almost all premium readings. I was swimming in gold. This . . ." Luisa plucked a coin seemingly from the air, rolling it between her fingers, the gold winking in the light. "This was even better. No one wants the future left to chance when there are dead bodies lumbering about. I had so many readings yesterday I lost my voice."

Most would think her terrible for saying such a thing, for wringing personal advantage out of tragedy, but Finn knew better. Luisa had a good heart; it just happened to also be a greedy one. Not just for the gold, but also for the security it bought her. Gold ensured that Luisa would always be able to buy her way out of any trouble that found her. And for a girl made of adventures and otherworldly magics, trouble could come fast and often. He didn't begrudge her that greed, most of the time. In fact, today, he was relying on it.

Finn slid a hand into a hidden pocket within his coat, his fingers meeting first warm wool, then a cold, smooth jewel. He slid the black diamond—barely the size of his fingertip, yet worth several readings—across the desk, letting her note the size and cut. "I like to think that we're friends, Lu."

Her eyes locked on the diamond, wide and shimmering as the jewel itself. "If you start bringing me jewels like *that*, Prince, you'll be my best friend in the whole wide world."

It took effort not to smile. "It's a Nyxian black diamond. Impossible to get since the war began . . . well, nearly impossible, anyway." He rolled the diamond about with his finger, trying desperately to cling to the casual air he wore like a shield. "And it's yours. For your friendship—and your discretion."

Luisa finally tore her yearning gaze away from the diamond, giving him a long, wary look. If he was flattering himself, he would have thought she actually looked worried. "Finn, love, what sort of trouble are you bringing to my door?"

"Hopefully, none. But it is . . . *very* important to me that word of my visit here, and the results thereafter, are not told to anyone else."

Luisa looked almost hurt. "I have never once told your secrets, Finn. And people have tried to buy them off me for higher prices than you've ever offered for my silence."

"I know that." It was why he was here in the first place. "But I trust your greed more than I trust you."

Luisa was quiet for a moment too long, and he worried for a moment that he'd truly offended her. But then she sighed, a wry smile twisting her lips. "That's fair . . . and smart of you. Fine. I'll accept your bribe."

Finn lifted his hand, letting her snatch the diamond from the table. She held it up to her window, letting the sparse beam of natural light refract off the stone, her touch nearly reverent.

"Something happened to me the day of the attack," he began, almost finding it easier to speak when her eyes weren't on him.

Before he knew it, he was telling her everything.

He told her of the day the dead came to life, strolling into the festival as if it was being thrown for them. He told her how he'd seen it before it happened, how his mind was briefly lost when he heard the screams of his people and the unearthly howls of the dead. He told her how his head had been filled with the image of dead bodies grinning at him, their barely-there forms guarding his palace like puppets with invisible strings; how it was only a flash, there and gone, and he'd dismissed it—until they'd found exactly that waiting for them at the palace. How the visions had continued after he'd been bitten, and worsened, and lengthened, until he found himself missing chunks of time . . . something he absolutely could not afford.

The whole time he talked, she sat quietly, watching him with an unusual air of patience. She didn't even interrupt when he occasionally overshared on the details, his mind focused on the tiny things that didn't matter, like the clothing the dead wore or what parts of the palace were burning in his vision. She listened to it all. Finally, when he was done, she took a moment to take it all in. Then: "By the *gods*, Finn."

"I know," he croaked, his voice nearly spent, a faint pain pulsing between his eyes. He rubbed at it, cursing silently. Every time he blinked, Luisa's hands folded on the desk became skeleton hands, and the empty glass orb became a glowing golden eye.

Only momentarily, then everything went back to normal. But it was disturbing all the same.

Luisa looked genuinely unnerved, and that worried Finn more than anything had thus far. "You're certain you weren't just delirious? Some kind of fever or poison, maybe? Have you been drinking your stress away?"

"I'm certain. The visions continued after my fever broke, Jericho checked for poison, and I don't drink." Finn counted off his answers on his fingers as he went, then splayed them helplessly her way. "They haven't stopped, Lu. I could barely walk here this morning. I'm barely keeping it at bay *now*."

Luisa leaned forward, sliding her hands over his. "I *can* sense something," she said, her brow creasing as she ran smooth, cold fingers over his palms. The ache in his head only increased as she gripped his hands tightly, a curious sensation trembling between their fingers. Like something vibrated in their twined hands.

"What are you doing?" It was an effort not to snatch his hands away.

"Testing your power. Trying to wake it up."

Finn started, an alarm bell pealing through his mind. "Wait, what *power*—?"

Sharp pink light flared, and Luisa *screamed*.

For a moment, Finn knew nothing but light and pain and noise, a chaotic swirl of images that were there one moment and vanished the next: Soleil, Kallias, Jericho, Vaughn, Eli, his parents, a throne of bones, blood-soaked dirt, a temple wrapped in thorns, a cracking noise that sounded like a vital bone being sheared,

Soleil screaming as a child, Soleil screaming as an adult, screaming like she was dying, screaming like she would never stop—

And then he was back, his hands twisted around Luisa's, their fingers twined so tightly that his were beginning to lose feeling. Luisa was gasping for breath, her eyes wide and . . . terrified, Finn realized with a thrill of his own fear. She stared at him like he'd stood on her desk, drawn a blade, and declared himself an agent of Nyx.

Slowly, too slowly, her eyes shifted to the side, and Finn followed her line of sight.

The glass ball on the desk was completely shattered.

All across the store, crystals had exploded, shards buried in the wood and carpet and even some of the books. The window wasn't quite broken, but cracks spiderwebbed across the glass.

"Well," Luisa croaked, her hands trembling in Finn's, "it seems you may have a problem, Prince. Because that kind of power isn't the kind you can just shove in a drawer."

Finn's heart sank to his feet. "You can't fix it?"

The laugh that burst from Luisa's mouth bordered on hysterical. "*Fix* it?" She released his hands, turning away to start cleaning her desk. Already the fear had left her, her composure returned, but it didn't matter. The fact that it had been there in the first place was bad enough. "I may be the best in the city, but even I only have a pinch of true power. Soothsaying isn't as rare as other gods-blessed gifts, but only one in a million of us will have anything more than a drop. Enough to see bits and pieces, enough for me to do my readings properly, but nothing else. You . . ."

She turned back to him, and he didn't like the look in her eyes at all. It was both awe and pity, amazement and sorrow.

"You may just be the first full-powered soothsayer to appear in centuries. Since the age of the old gods."

"Why do you say that like you're reading off a eulogy?" Finn asked lightly, desperately hoping she would laugh.

She didn't. Her eyes only softened further. "Because," she said, far too gently, "the mind can't handle that much of the future, Finn. It's always been that way. Full-powered soothsayers, they can only manage for so long before . . ."

The silence had barely settled before Finn broke it. "Before what? Spit it out, Lu."

But the way she looked at him . . . the way he was feeling . . . he already knew. Maybe he'd known before he even arrived.

"Before they lose their minds," she said finally. "The full powers of soothsaying come at the cost of the bearer's sanity. Occassio demands a price of those she blesses most."

CHAPTER 52

KALLIAS

Kallias could barely see straight.

The hallway rolled and bucked with every step he took, bringing to mind his first sailboat; one day, fourteen and foolish, he'd taken the boat out without realizing a storm was rolling in. After being tossed about by the waves for hours, the ocean had finally spit his vessel back on the shore, leaving him with a horrid spell of dizziness that hadn't faded for a solid day and a half afterwards.

This was worse. He wasn't drunk anymore. He wasn't ill. He didn't need to find his land legs. He was just so gods-damned *tired*.

A particularly bad wave of dizziness crashed over him, sending him lurching against the wall. He didn't even realize it was happening until the slick paint kissed his cheek, his shoulder aching from the impact.

Hurting, reeling, he slid his hand over his head to steady himself. Gods, he was going to collapse right here, right on the floor. He honestly couldn't remember the last time he'd . . . Two days? Three? He'd . . . lost his train of thought. Where was he going?

Something caught his eye—a palace staff member walking past. He reached out, already waving them off, already dismissing them, his mouth opening to assure them that he was fine—

But his eyes fell on a lampstand instead. Not a person. His mind had seen something standing and made a leap.

Oh, this wasn't good. This wasn't good at all.

Giddiness swelled in his chest, laughter threatening to escape and give way to hysteria. He was seeing things, he couldn't walk straight, and his parents—

He'd been summoned by his parents to his mother's private office. That was where he was going.

Kallias slowly slid himself off the wall only to lean on it once more, bracing himself against it, palms flat. He narrowed his eyes, breathing hard through his nose, desperately working to get his mind to focus.

One last meeting. One last meeting, and then he could sleep.

He repeated that to himself as he pushed off the wall, blinking himself back to his senses, forcing the hysterical laughter back down into his gut. One last meeting. One last meeting.

With his parents. When he couldn't even walk straight. When his emotions were swinging as wildly as his balance, from giddiness to nearly crying in the span of thirty seconds.

This wasn't going to end well.

As he turned away, he could have sworn he caught a glimpse of something slick shimmering on the wall where his hands had been—again. But he was late, and he'd thought a lamp was a person, and he simply didn't have the wherewithal to check if the shimmer was something real.

The hallway leading to his mother's office was short and nondescript: plain walls, little decoration, not many windows. Unlike the grandeur of the ballroom or the imposing threat of the throne room, Adriata wanted her office to be just that . . . her office. Her place to escape. No one would think to look for a queen behind an unmarked wooden door.

Water and storm and blood freezing beneath his nails.

"Show yourself, you selfish bastards! If you ever cared about us, if you're even there, why don't you do something for a change?"

A small decorative table collided to the ground as Kallias stumbled into it, the turquoise vase on top smashing apart with an ear-splitting crash. Kallias growled out a curse, kicking one of the fragments as he forced himself steady, his breathing coming in heated huffs.

He was in charge of his own body, and he would not make a fool of himself today. Not again.

By the time he opened the door, knees and pride smarting, his parents were arguing over whether to send someone to look for him. His mother sighed when she saw him, and he couldn't tell if it was from relief or disappointment. "You're late, love."

"Something came up." Or fell down, rather. He straightened his jacket, praying to any god that was listening that he looked better than he felt. "You asked for me?"

Ramses and Adriata exchanged a look—Ramses eyes full of pleading, Adriata's eyes sad and resigned. In her hand was a small wooden box with a finely carved design on the lid.

Twin swords and a crown of flames between them—Artem's crest.

Kallias's heart sank straight to his stomach. Weighed it down like a lump of steel.

No. No, not now. Not today. Not *now.*

"Artem's Empress has sent an offer for your hand," began Adriata. "She's offering more weapons, more soldiers, things that can cut through bone, things we need if Nyx has employed necromancers—"

Kallias was speaking nearly before she was done, his words far more rambling than he would have liked, panic spiking into his heart. "Mother, I don't think now is the best time for—"

"We've accepted their offer."

Silence.

Every noise, every thought was drowned out by the blanket of shock that settled over Kallias's mind, leaving nothing but a constant echo: *We've accepted their offer.*

"You what?" he managed, and his voice broke apart on the way out.

Adriata's throat bobbed, her eyes lined in silver. "Kallias, love, it's long past due, and they—"

"You *what?*" Kallias couldn't think, couldn't process, couldn't breathe. *We've accepted their offer.*

They hadn't asked him. They hadn't warned him.

His hands curled into fists, his mind whirling, his thoughts too tangled to fully realize that his palms were frigid cold. It felt like he'd gripped two handfuls of snow off the Nyxian border.

They had sold him. Without warning, without asking, without so much as mentioning it to him, they had sold him.

They were sending him away.

That one thought pulsed blue and burning in his mind, exhaustion freezing into rage, rage blooming into a crackling in his blood that he almost recognized.

"I don't want to go. You can't make me go," he said blankly, only realizing after he said the words just how childish they were. Of course she could make him go. He'd already *agreed*, years ago, to go wherever they sent him. And even if he hadn't, she was the gods-damned *queen*, and he was just . . . he was . . . he was so tired.

Adriata's eyes flashed, and he braced for anger; but instead, she slowly rose from her chair. "Come here, Kallias." When he hesitated, she held out her arms, her chin trembling as she whispered, "Please, love."

Maybe it was the sleep deprivation. Maybe it was how ridiculously cold he was. Maybe it had just been so long since his mother had hugged him. But the moment Adriata's arms closed around him, Kallias wept. Broken, gasping sobs shook his chest, and he could do nothing but cling to his mother as he cried, the knot of grief and terror that had been forming in his chest all these years finally coming undone.

His father's arms wrapped around them both, and before long, all three of them were on their knees, all crying, three separate griefs mingling, thickening the air with three different miseries.

"When?" he whispered. It was all he could say.

Adriata stroked her hand down his hair, her voice almost steady. "A delegation will be here in three weeks to confirm the arrangement. You'll leave with them."

Three weeks. Three weeks to pack up his life, three weeks to learn all he could about his new kingdom.

Three weeks to say goodbye.

CHAPTER 53

SOREN

There was a strange tension in the palace like the air before a storm, and it was making Soren uneasy.

Finn, Jericho, Vaughn, and Kallias hadn't been to see her in a while. Elias seemed dodgy, only spending the night in her room when Alia was on guard outside; apparently they had established an *understanding*, whatever that meant. And Adriata and Ramses had gone on a brief trip to their summer house to pack up what remained of their things and bring them back for the season. So she took it upon herself to do something for a change, and asked a page to invite all of them to the dining room that night for dinner.

Just to break the silence, she told herself; not because she wanted to talk to any of them. Not because she was bored without them. Definitely not because she *missed* them, for gods' sakes.

But it *was* a little bit strange not having anyone hovering over her for once. Like a phantom limb that itched long after it was amputated, she kept catching herself looking over her shoulder to talk to Finn, or reaching for Elias's hand, or wandering toward Kallias and Jericho's offices before her mind snapped back to itself.

She'd gotten too used to being the shiny new toy everyone was fighting over. She was going to have to break that before she went home; her sisters would never let her hear the end of it if she started following them around whining for attention. More than she did normally, anyway.

By the time she arrived at the dining room, everyone was already seated—Kallias downing a glass of wine in one long draw, not even a single breath stirring his chest. Judging by the three empty glasses scattered around him, he hadn't just started, either. Jericho watched him with eyes sharper than the daggers Soren had given Elias for the festival, her hands gripping the table edge with white knuckles, and Finn and Vaughn were seated uncomfortably in the middle, Finn fussing with a chip in the table with his nail, Vaughn studiously observing his empty plate.

Gods. If even Finn looked awkward, it must have been some fight.

"Did I miss something?" she asked lightly, slipping into the empty seat beside Jericho, across from Finn and Vaughn.

"Nothing important," Kallias mumbled, slouching in his seat, holding his wine glass up to the light, letting his head loll sideways as he stared through it. The smirk that cut across his face looked nothing like him, but suddenly there was no doubting he and Finn were brothers. "At least, Jericho doesn't think so."

"Kal, please," Jericho muttered, rubbing her temple like she was already feeling a sympathy hangover. "Not in front of Soleil."

"It's fine." She waved her hand dismissively, taking a sip of her own wine; but she watched Kallias closely, noting the way that smirk seemed even less steady than the prince himself, noting the hollowness that had carved out every proud and dutiful thing in his eyes.

She'd played the part of hurting, angry drunk enough times to recognize it from the outside. Something had happened.

"Kal," she said, "Either you tell me what went wrong, or Vaughn will."

Vaughn coughed in his water, flashing her a look of betrayal. "*Me?*"

Soren shrugged one shoulder. "I feel like you're the kind of man that doesn't know how to say no. Or how to lie."

"She's right, brother," Finn said, clapping Vaughn on the shoulder. "You're the weak link in the chain of secrecy."

"I don't know what happened!" Vaughn protested. "He won't tell me, either."

"It's not anyone's gods-damned business," Kallias muttered, finishing off his glass and promptly pouring another one, listing sideways and righting himself.

"When was the last time you slept?" Soren demanded.

Kallias blinked at her. "Um . . . four."

"Hours? Days?"

"Something like that."

Soren snatched the glass out of his hands, holding it above his head when he reached for it with a dull-hearted snarl, then climbing up onto the table itself when he stood to try and reach it again. She dangled it out of his reach, scowling down at him. "Enough drinking. And forget dinner. You need to go back to your room and sleep for a day or two."

Kallias's teeth snapped together in a visible snarl, and he shoved away from the table, jolting the wood so hard Soren wobbled and nearly fell. Finn and Vaughn's hands were all that kept her from pitching off.

"Kallias!" the men snapped in tandem, but he merely waved them off, staggering to the side, rubbing the bridge of his nose, his eyes squeezed so tightly shut his entire face screwed up.

"You don't get to have an opinion on what I need," he said to her. "You don't know me, okay? Stop playing pretend."

Soren's fingers went numb, and the glass nearly slid from her grip. "I'm not playing anything. Any idiot could see you're sleep deprived, Kal—"

"Stop calling me that!" he roared, his voice rising three octaves as he stabbed a finger at her. He launched himself unsteadily up onto his chair so he was standing face-to-face with her, his wine-soaked breath souring deep in her nose. Out of the corner of her eye, she saw Finn *flinch*, taking a quick step away from the table. "*Stop it.* It's not fair, all right? How am I supposed to accept that you remember everyone else more than me if you keep acting like you're trying to get better? Enough's enough, *Soren*. Give up the act. You don't know us, and you'll never know us . . . in fact, I'm not even sure that you don't still want us all *dead*! I mean, depths, the only reason you're still *here* is because everyone's afraid to tell you that you're chasing something that doesn't even *exist*!"

The table disappeared beneath Soren's feet. Her heart vanished from her chest. Everything turned dull and hollow and ringing, and distantly, she felt the glass slide from her fingers, shattering noiselessly on the polished wooden table. "What."

At her raw, soft whisper, Finn's hand gripped her wrist. "Soleil. *Soleil,* he's drunk, he doesn't know what he's talking about—"

"Don't even try that! Finn, she deserves to know!" Kallias snapped, a dark, broken thing searching to make more dark, broken things. The condescending, awful pity in his stare made her nauseous with terror.

This couldn't be happening.

"Even if your plan had worked on the battlefield," he added, "your friend still would have died. There isn't a cure to the Viper venom. That's the whole *point* to it. It's a death you can't outrun, can't escape, can't *fix.* Unjust death for unjust death."

Finn's hand on her wrist was burning her. "Soleil, *listen,* listen to me—"

She flung him off, twisting so fast her hair whipped against her cheeks, and anything of Soleil that had managed to encrust her like creeping crystals cracked apart, falling away—pretty bits of nothing, an illusion these Atlas bastards had smoothed over her cratered and scarred parts, someone these *liars* had tried to turn her into. "You lied to me."

Finn's eyes were wider than she'd ever seen them, and for the first time, she saw real fear there. Real heartbreak. "Yes. Every day but that one. I meant what I said, I keep my promises Soleil—"

She slapped that earnest, brokenhearted mask right off his gods-damned chameleon face.

"*Don't,*" she snarled, a guttural thing, more vicious than a cornered wolf. "*Don't you dare.*"

Jericho's hands were over her mouth, her eyes darting between Soren and Finn. Kallias looked like he was the one who'd been slapped, that drunken haze replaced with a hazy horror, his hand outstretched—the same way he'd reached for her on that battlefield. "Soleil," he whispered, vulnerable, agonized. "Oh gods, I didn't—I'm sorry, that wasn't how we planned to tell you—"

Soren couldn't breathe. Her chest was completely crushed, shards of rib and heart a jumbled, agonized mess, every beat shattering another part of her until her entire core pulsed with pain. Her back throbbed like three knives had been shoved into it, each one engraved with a different Atlas sibling's name.

She'd fallen for it. Every gods-damned moment she'd thought she was outpacing them, outthinking them . . . every moment she'd begun to wonder if they actually cared about her, if blood was truly thicker than the night she'd been raised in . . . she'd been *tricked.*

Elias had tried to tell her. She'd thought she was so *smart.*

"Leave me alone." The voice that hissed out of her ruined lungs sounded unbearably familiar, the same as after Jira's death, when she'd been so hateful and angry and *hurting* that even her voice felt useless. "Do not look at me. Do not speak to me. If you value your perfect little lives at *all*, you will stay *far* away from me, and you will pray to the *gods* that I'm gone before I decide to kill you all."

They did not stop her when she jumped down from the table. They did not reach for her when she shoved past Kallias to the door, hot tears already scalding her cheeks, half-hysterical gasps shaking that gods-awful mess in her core until she could barely put one foot in front of the other.

And though she laid on her bed with her head buried in her pillow for hours, shaking with horrified rage, unwilling to face Elias and admit to him that she'd failed . . . they did not come for her. Just like the fire, no one came—no one heard the dying screams of Soleil, buried deep in the gut-wrenching weeping of Soren, tears washing away every trace of that long-dead princess until she might as well have been buried six feet under.

Enough was enough. When night fell, she and Elias would come up with a new plan; it wasn't far to the Arborius border from here. She could still do this. She could still save him.

And she would never, *ever* admit to anyone that her broken heart had just as much to do with three redheads in an enemy kingdom as it did with her dying battlemate. She would never admit to anyone that somehow, these bastards had managed to get their hands on her heart before they'd torn it out of her chest.

That, without meaning to, she'd almost started to love them.

CHAPTER 54

ELIAS

It was the smallest mistake that finally ruined everything.

He'd gotten too comfortable here, too used to the small comfort of his bunk, too confident in the patterns of his roommates. He had forgotten that no matter how much he pretended, he was a spy in a foreign kingdom, a stranger who couldn't hope to predict the people around him.

So when he returned to his empty bunkroom after his latest errand for Seamus—yet another fruitless questioning of cityfolk to try and get wind of who might be hiding dark, addictive powers—absentmindedly, out of pure habit, he tugged his beads out of his pack.

And just when he remembered that was a bad idea here, just when he remembered *why* they had to stay hidden, Kallias barged into the room.

He was an absolute mess, half-drunk, shivering like he had fever chills, eyes red from crying and face flushed in blotches. He couldn't stand straight, listing to the side before he righted himself, sheer desperation in his eyes. "Eli, I need your help, I need you to go talk to . . ."

He trailed off, his eyes widening when they landed on Elias's hand. On the black skull with red-rose eyes cradled in his palm. At Elias's wide eyes, at his mouth half-poised to make an excuse and coming up absolutely empty.

Kallias's expression drained of all feeling. All friendliness, all pleading, *everything.*

In its place, steel. Unreadable, merciless steel. And though Kallias wobbled on unsteady feet, when the prince drew his sword and pointed it at Elias's chest, he wielded it with a surety that told Elias there would be no avoiding his strike.

"Get up," Kallias ordered.

Elias slowly put his hands up, his stomach sinking, dread flooding his throat like hot tar, slowing every beat of his heart to a terrible crawl. "Highness, please, this isn't what it—"

"Eli," said Kallias, perfectly calm, "if that even is your name . . . I will give you one chance to stop talking, and if you take it, I can promise you'll live through your questioning."

No, no, no. He couldn't have ruined it. *He* couldn't be the one to get them caught, he'd been so *careful.* "Kallias, please, I—"

Swordtip kissed jugular, and Kallias murmured, "You don't want to test my mercy today, Eli. I can promise you'll find it lacking."

Gods, no. Not this. Anything but this.

His shoulder throbbed gently, like an apology.

The very last place he wanted to die was in an Atlas dungeon.

But all he could do was stand when Kallias ordered it. And even when Seamus came skidding in—even when he took in Elias's beads with wide-eyed satisfaction, even when he'd started to blurt "I *knew* it" before Kallias shot him a look sharp enough to head an arrow—he didn't say one word.

Not out loud, anyway. But his head was a cacophony, a litany of desperate prayers thrown up to Mortem, one last attempt to be granted her mercy or her miracles.

But it seemed even the goddess he loved so much was embarrassed by his mistake. There was no answer but silence as Kallias and Seamus marched him down a flight of stairs, down, down, down into the depths of the famed Atlas dungeons. Where prisoners were flayed and drowned, where they were forced to betray everything they held dear so they would be denied even their pride when they were forced out of the world.

Elias squeezed his eyes shut as he breathed in the dank smell of seawater and mold, the air getting heavier with every step they descended, condensation rolling down the gray stone walls, cold sweat following suit on his head.

Soren was going to lose her gods-damned mind when she found out about this, and all he could do was hope that she won . . . or that Kallias's mercy was more ample when it came to his own flesh and blood.

He exhaled doubt. Inhaled faith.

No matter what they subjected him to, no matter what he was about to suffer, he knew where he was going.

He was not afraid.

CHAPTER 55

SOREN

"I f you don't get him out of that gods-damned Infera-pit in *two minutes*, I swear to Mortem and Anima and every single cloud-hopping useless deity that I will *burn this palace down* for the second time!" Soren's shout shook the walls. "Do you hear me? He is not the gods-damned necromancer, okay, he's just an ex-priest with some leftover religious angst he's working through. Believe me, if he had some sick, awful magic, *I would know!*"

Fury had nothing on what blazed through Soren's blood now. No, fury was a candle, a pretty bit of sparkle to read by at night, a pinprick of heat she could hover her palm over. What boiled in her blood today could have lit the kingdoms ablaze.

Here in Adriata's office, facing the entire Atlas family with nothing but her fists and the intention of causing a complete and utter ruckus, Soren was no longer playing princess. Everything sand and salt had been melted down into glass and polished until it was see-through, just so they could be absolutely confident she was not playing games today.

Adriata looked furious. Ramses looked heartbroken. Finn wouldn't look her in the eye, Kallias was staring at his shoes, and Jericho seemed like she would rather be anywhere else.

"I don't want to hear what this spy is and is not," said Adriata. "I want to hear the truth about *you*."

"Well, you're going to be disappointed," Soren snapped. "Because I'm not talking about anything until you *let him go*!"

"Soren," said Ramses, and she couldn't meet his gaze, couldn't look at his face, because it reminded her too much of her childhood, of the truth of her blood that she couldn't outrun. "Clearly this boy means something to you. This is not a sentencing, do you hear me? We just need to know what he is, who he is to you, and what you two were trying to *do* here."

"They were trying to win their war," Jericho snapped, but there wasn't real anger in her face. She stared at Soren with tear-basted eyes, her face flushed from crying. "Right? That's why you spent all this time *tricking* us."

"No," Soren and Finn said at once, and her eyes snapped over to meet his.

"She doesn't care about winning the war," Finn said tiredly. "*Elias* is her battlemate. He's the one with the Viper bite. She stayed to try and get him a cure."

So he had known—and used it against her. Truly the prince of fools, and she was chief among his subjects.

"A cure? There isn't a cure for the venom," Adriata said.

Finn looked away from Soren's livid glare, picking at a thread on his purple sweater. She wanted to tear it away, to ruin it, to pretend she'd never been so silly and sentimental in the first place. "She knows that now. But she didn't until tonight."

"That doesn't matter now." None of it did. None of her plans, none of her hopes, her memories . . . any of it. Soleil was nothing but a memory, and anything she'd begun to dream of was merely that. A dream. Nothing that could ever come to pass, not after this. "I'm telling you, he's innocent. Just let him go—pits, I'll stay. You can throw me down there instead, I won't even try to fight, just let *him* go home."

Adriata and Ramses exchanged looks, and in that look, Soren already knew she'd lost.

"We're not putting you in the dungeon," Ramses said, with tireless, utterly infuriating patience. "Soren, we need *something* here. You're demanding all for nothing."

"Fine," she snarled. "You want the truth? I'll give it to you, all of it. But he goes free."

"Soren, we can't let him out," Kallias said softly, his voice stumbling over her Nyxian name like it hurt to say. "It doesn't matter if you don't *think* he's the necromancer. This all started when he showed up, and he knows so much about it—"

"Because he grew up in Mortem's temple! He was studying to become a priest, and then when his father died, he—he left, but he still needed faith." Soren's voice cracked, and she cleared her throat, trying to shove the broken pieces back together. "Mortem knows I've never understood it, but that faith brings him peace. And *only* that. If you want answers, look to your own kingdom. There may be a Nyxian spy in your midst who can puppet the dead, but it's *not* him."

"How can you be sure?" Finn asked.

She held his gaze. "Because no matter what Elias is, no matter what he or I became, he would *never* try to kill me. He'd throw himself off the nearest cliff before he let that happen."

It wasn't a lie. And maybe that was why Finn relaxed, why he looked to his mother and said, "Mama, maybe we should hear her out."

Adriata looked at him, then over Kallias's head to Jericho. The former Heir simply shook her head, jaw tight.

"We will not harm the boy," Adriata finally said, and Soren's chest relaxed its iron grip on her heart, finally letting it beat again. "He is not to be touched until we can probe the matter further. But he does *not* leave the dungeons."

Soren swallowed. "Fine. At least let me go see him."

"I'm not sure you understand this, Soleil, but you are *not* in a position to be making demands—"

"It's not a demand." All the heat drained from her, leaving her cold. Leaving her tired. "I'm asking. Please let me see him. He's sick—let me make sure he's all right."

Jericho softened, if only slightly, and looked to Adriata. "It can't hurt, Mama."

"It most certainly can," Kallias disagreed, only to find himself on the receiving end of an arrowheaded look from Adriata.

"You can go," she said. "But there will be a guard posted outside the door. And if there's even a hint of trouble, we will not hesitate to do what we must."

Do what we must. Soren didn't have to be a seer to read that future.

She gave a stiff, mocking bow. "As you command, *Majesty.*" Nyxian accent on full, insulting, proud display. If she had her way, it would never fall away from her voice again.

Adriata didn't sneer, didn't shout, didn't take back her agreement to Soren's terms. But she did flinch, and somehow, that was even worse.

The walk to Elias's cell was the longest Soren had ever taken. Every footstep down the cramped, dark, curving staircase became hundreds of footsteps, echoes bouncing off every nook and cranny, surrounding Soren with the ghosts of all the Nyxians whose shoes had only touched these stairs once. Whose footsteps had only echoed in one direction. Who were probably still down here rotting, or perhaps fodder for the necromancer, speaking their master's words with tongueless mouths.

A shiver ran down her neck, a sensation like a cold finger trailing its nail over her freckled skin. She shrugged it away. She was many things, but she was not, and had never been, a coward. And today wasn't the day she was going to break that streak.

Elias needed her. Needed her strong, needed her ruthless, needed her *Nyxian.*

Soleil Atlas could not save him. She'd already tried and failed. It was Soren's turn now. And she wouldn't run because of phantom fingers and the memory of a corpse wearing her battlemate's voice. She wouldn't cringe from the ghosts of her people.

It was her fault they were dead. They deserved better than a princess who would run. They deserved a princess who would save them, or at least one of them.

Elias's footsteps would not join the eternal chorus in that staircase. Not if she could help it.

When Seamus stopped at the foot of the staircase—giving her a surprising amount of privacy, unusual for the nosy, annoying guard—she ventured into the dungeon herself, and wished there wasn't quite so much dread trying to tug her heart from her chest to her feet.

Hot, dank air pooled over her, drawing sweat from her pores like a sauna, instantly sticky and uncomfortable. Every breath tasted of brine and blood, the rust-dark stains on some of the walls a grisly reminder of how merciless Atas could be when they felt like it. The path through the dungeons was a wooden bridge-like structure, and it was soaked, like it had been underwater and was only just revealed. The cell floors were the same way, puddled with seawater and dead flicker-fish and piles of sand, and when she finally reached the only occupied cell . . .

Every part of her that had almost become Atlas, that had almost forgotten her bones were forged in iron and her veins ran through her body in their own unique paths of constellations, burst into flame.

They'd chained him.

He was kneeling on the silty floor of his cell, manacles clamped around his wrists, chains bolting him to the floor so he couldn't stand. He'd been stripped of his shirt and left with only his dark training pants, his Viper bite on full display.

Bile stung the back of her throat, and she clamped her hand over her mouth to keep from making a sound that he would never let her live down.

Gods, it looked so much worse than the last time she'd seen it, his skin marred and rotted away, dead flesh spongy and *wrong*, a blackness in the heart of the wound that suggested he had lied about how bad it was getting. But worse than that was the fact that he was utterly soaked and shivering, feverish heat flushing his cheeks, his muscles clenched tightly to keep the chills from making him seem rattled. His gaze was fixed on the floor, and she knew that look, the grit to his teeth and the wrinkle between his brows; he was in pain, and trying desperately not to show it.

"Elias," she said, and his gaze leapt from the floor to her.

"Are you all right?" was the first gods-damned thing he said. He was the one in chains, the one who had Mortem herself breathing down his neck, and still he looked at her like she was the one in danger.

Soren knelt on the damp floor, the puddle soaking her knees. She reached out to grip the bars, and Elias mirrored her. The chains barely allowed him to reach that far, and he grimaced at the effort it took to pull them, but he did it anyway. She covered his hands with hers and pressed her lips to his knuckles, that fire spreading, devouring Soleil for the second time, a wild and raging thing that knew no name but her Nyxian one.

She was going to kill everyone who had decided to put him in here.

"I'm fine, jackass," she muttered against his hands, squeezing them as tightly as she could. "But you're not."

"I don't know what you mean, smartass. I'm peachy."

"Don't." The word came out broken. "Elias, don't play with me right now. How bad is it?"

Elias's eyes gentled, and that told her everything she needed to know.

"Bad." He leaned his forehead against the bars, slumping as if the admission took the last of his energy. "It's been bad for a while, but I thought . . . I hoped . . ."

"So all that time you were trying to get me to leave—"

"It doesn't matter now," he croaked. "I assume you have a plan?"

She blinked at him. He blinked back at her.

"The plan is the same," she said. "Or, it's the old plan, at least. I'll get you out, I'll get you to Arborius—"

Elias squeezed his eyes shut. "Soren."

"No, listen," she interrupted, desperation holding a match beneath her heart, kicking it into a speed that was almost unbearable. She felt the crack beginning to form beneath the surface, a fissure she'd been carving from the day Elias was bitten, a pain that promised she would never be rid of it this time. "Elias, I can still do this—"

"No, Soren. You've done enough, you've tried enough, let's just go home—"

"*I can still do this*! Elias, you know I can, I know I messed up but I swear that's all over—"

"Soren, *I am the one who can't do this*!"

His shout in her face stopped every ragged plea, every heartbeat, even her breaths.

"What?" she choked.

Elias gazed at her, utterly gentle, utterly ruined. His shoulders bent, his eyes holding hers without mercy, a quiver to his chin that stirred tears of her own. "I can't do this. I'm tired, smartass. I'm so gods-damned tired, and I miss my mother, and my siblings, and my house . . . I miss the snow, and you stealing my socks, and waking up to you drooling on my shirt."

"I don't drool—"

"You do, and I miss it. I miss *home*." Tears slid down his face like a worshipper kneeling in piety, and when he gripped her face in his hands, every callous and scar as familiar as her own, that was when Soren shattered. That was when she began to weep. "You have to let me go, smartass," he whispered, wiping away her tears with his thumbs. "Let me go. Before this bite kills us both."

She gripped his wrists in her hands, leaning her forehead against his, *hating* the heat brewing beneath his skin. Hating the fever, hating the poison, hating every gods-damned thing that was trying to take him away from her. Every part of this wretched, unfair world that didn't care that she needed him with all her heart, with all her soul, with *everything*.

She'd thought this was a battle of stardust and saltwater. But it never had been. She belonged to no kingdom, to no blood, to no throne. She belonged to this boy, and he to her, fused together in blood and banter and broken noses, tied by vows whispered over stitches sewn by unpracticed hands and eyes locked on each other instead of their stitching needles.

When you walk, I will follow.

When you run, I will chase.

When you have no ally, I will be your army.

When you have no weapon, I will be your blade.

When you stand, we stand together,

And when you fall, I fall with you.

When Mortem takes us, she takes us.

Together or not at all.

"Don't ask me to break my vows to you," she whispered, her breath melding with his, fighting a battle she already knew she was going to lose. "Ask for anything else, just not that."

His shoulders shuddered with a sob, and he pulled back to look her in the eyes, pleading, peaceful. "When you walk, I will follow. When you run, I will chase."

A sword of her own making drove through her heart, and she bowed her head against the pain, sobbing, "Elias."

He tipped her chin up—held it there. Made her hold his gaze. "I'm not asking you to break your vows. I'm asking you to keep them. I chased you here. Now I'm asking you to walk me home."

Soren squeezed the bars between them with all her might, furious—not for the first time—that she wasn't strong enough to anchor him here. That she had no power to heal the wound he'd been dealt. That she had been born unlucky enough to lose both of the people she loved so fiercely that she thought she might break from the force of it, from the weight.

But this was Elias. And while she'd always loved to fight him, and had always loved to win . . . she couldn't deny him this.

She loved him enough to let him go. If that was what he wanted. If that was what he needed from her.

"Okay," she whispered. "I'll get us home."

And she knew exactly how to do it. But first, she was going to need a blade.

CHAPTER 56

FINN

Well. It was safe to say that everything had gone to straight to the depths. He hadn't seen Soleil since she stalked out of the room to see her battlemate, braid swinging like a pendulum counting down the hours until she brought everything crashing down on top of their heads. And knowing what he knew of his sister, there were not many of those hours left.

He should have been out there stopping her. A prince would have. The trickster would have.

But the fool found himself picking the lock on her bedroom door and heading toward the small, secret alcove hidden behind the headboard, Soleil's *treasure box* hidden neatly within. He was the only one who knew about it anymore, since she didn't remember and no one else had been privy to its secrets. And thank the gods for it, too.

This little box was the one thing that had the potential to be his undoing.

He tugged it free of its alcove: black metal inlaid with glimmering mother-of-pearl detailing, a picture of a girl with a flower crown. Settling on her bed, ears carefully attuned for anyone walking this way, he flipped the latch and cracked it open.

It was still there, safely nestled inside: a tiny leather journal with a lock on the clasp. He scooped up the tiny gold key beside it—Soleil had been too afraid of losing it to hide it properly—and gently turned it until it clicked.

That sound stirred a shuffle of memories, a shimmering deck of days he hadn't cherished nearly as much as he should have: running wild through the palace halls with his sister, taking turns dragging each other into trouble, then huddling over this journal at the end of the day to document every second, giggles muffled under blankets and pages illuminated by crystals Jericho had enspelled into glowing. Soleil snatching the pen from his hands because he was *writing it all wrong, it was cooler than* that, *Finn!* Him snatching it back because she was *exaggerating, Soleil, the spider was only the size of a button, not a dinner plate!*

His fingertips brushed over the tiny divots in the paper, his perfect cursive and Soren's blocky scrawl chasing each other in circles and diagonal lines. Pages and pages of their adventures, their pranks—and occasionally, letters to each other. On bad days when neither of them wanted to talk to anyone else, or when one of them was grounded to their room, the other would slip the journal under the door and wait for a note to be passed back.

This was why he never went to her gravestone. This was why he came to sit in her room instead. There was no body beneath that stone—never had been, even when they'd thought her dead. Nothing of Soleil lived in that white-marble slab, nothing but her name and titles that had never defined her. *Beloved daughter. Heir of Atlas. Forever missed.*

To Finn, her true titles lived here, in this leather book they'd worn down with use. *Mischief-maker. Wave-dancer. Best friend.*

Dear Finn, said one of the letters, dated three days before her death, *You were not very nice to me today, and you threw my favorite shoe into the ocean. That was not okay. I have decided to banish you. You can pay to come home. I like money and cookies. I hope you miss me a lot you mean old suckerfish.*

Not love,

Soleil (Your very mad sister)

A chuckle lived and died in Finn's chest.

The last thing she'd ever written to him. *I hope you miss me.*

He had. Unbearably. To the point he'd snuck away to the temple of Anima on Kelp Street one night, laid himself facedown on the floor, and begged Mortem to give his sister back. He'd prayed so loud and long that he lost his voice, until his forehead was pressed against the floor and his back heaving with uncontrollable sobs, until all he could manage was a whisper, until all he could say was *please give her back, I need her.*

I need her.

But his prayers hadn't been answered; or rather, they had, but far too late. He'd already put himself back together. He didn't need his sister anymore. He'd worked every single gods-damned day to make sure that he never felt that way again, that he never fell into such a bad place that he would resort to praying to a cruel and angry goddess who couldn't be bothered to keep up with the prayers being thrown her way.

Losing Soleil the first time had been enough. Losing her this time, with no one but himself to blame . . .

It was nothing. He could endure . . . he would. She'd never been coming back to them, anyway. It had all been part of her plan to save Elias, nothing else. And this was *nothing.*

He reached the last page—or where the last page should have been—and stopped.

The journal hadn't been anywhere near full when Soleil died. And sure, he'd written a letter to her every year on her birthday, but even then, the journal had been halfway full at best.

There was more writing on the next page.

Swallowing the sudden lump in his throat, Finn fussed with the edge of the page, debating. He had no idea what this could be. And he had no idea what it would do to him if he read it.

He turned the page anyway.

The handwriting was still blocky, still scrawling, but somewhat neater—adult, but still familiar. Still hers. The entry was dated just after their sparring session.

Dear Finn,

I found this when I was digging around for something to throw at Seamus's head. I hope you don't mind if I use it, but judging by the dust on it, you haven't picked it up in a while either.

I read all the old letters. I don't remember writing them, but still . . . it's the closest I can get to having those memories back, right?

I don't even know why I'm writing this, or if you'll ever see it. Hopefully not. I've been embarrassed enough for today. But tonight's been long, and you and Kallias and the others are all busy, and everything in here is so . . . empty. I guess I just needed someone to talk to.

You're not the only one who can wear a mask. I've got a few of my own. But I know this is hurting you, and—ugh, what am I trying to say? This feels wrong. I don't know. I'm just trying to say that I'm sorry I can't remember these letters, and that you've been alone all this time. I'm sorry none of the others know how to see you. But maybe now that I'm home we can figure out how to write some new letters, if you ever get tired of pretending you don't care.

Don't make fun of me for this,

Soleil (Soren. Killer. Whatever you want to use.)

Something wet fell onto the page, a perfect droplet that turned the ink in *Killer* fuzzy. He reached up and wiped at his eye, cursing soundly.

She'd been writing him letters.

More than one; they dated all the way from their sparring session to the day he'd been bitten by the necromanced body to the day he'd shown her the city. Letters about her day, about the new things she remembered or the things Jericho taught her, letters about lies he'd told her and thought she believed.

You told me yesterday that you were going to spend today in your bed, but you snuck out twenty minutes after dawn this morning. You are the Lord Jaskier I keep hearing about at the Shark Tooth Tavern, right? So many people hate him so much, it's got to be you playing some game. Honestly, I'm surprised that you haven't been murdered ages ago!

That last line ended with a sketched smiling face, and he would have laughed if he wasn't so busy weeping, his sleeve shoved against his mouth and nose to muffle the noise.

She hadn't only caught *some* things. She'd seen through *everything*—every single game he'd ever played, every trick he'd tried to pull, every lie he'd thrown at her without a second thought. Everything he'd spent ten years building, she'd torn down in a few short weeks.

And the one truth he'd given her, the one promise he'd made in earnest, she hadn't trusted. And gods, could he blame her? After everything he'd said, after everything she'd seen, she had every right to slap him, to call him a liar, to wish death and worse his way.

She wasn't some Nyxian girl Kal dragged home against her will. She was his sister—his grieving, terrified, angry sister. And instead of helping her, he'd played her, baited her, and manipulated her, and made everything even more confusing and awful for her.

No. He couldn't blame her one bit for this.

He would have wanted to kill him, too.

CHAPTER 57

ELIAS

Elias hated salt.

The taste of it coated his tongue, the sticky sea air drying his skin, pulling it taut. The sweat dripping down his face didn't help. They'd switched his chains, hanging him from the ceiling instead of pinning him to the ground—a new level of punishment, he'd thought, until nightfall came.

The dungeon level was too close to the sea, and the walls couldn't keep the ocean out. Each night, the room filled with water, rising with the moon until the tide lapped at Elias's neck, the moonbeams threatening to blind him. Fish pecked his body all night long like he was the newest in a series of Nyxian bait.

The living nightmare made it hard to meet the eyes of the guards in the mornings, especially when the ones he'd shared his bunkroom with were on shift, looking so full of hatred and betrayal he wasn't convinced he'd survive to face the ocean again that night.

All he could do now was wait.

Soren had left his cell yesterday wearing a look that he absolutely hated, and hated even more because *he* was the cause: a hollow, lifeless expression that held less animation than the necromanced corpses. Like he'd sucked the last of her determination away, and she was only going through the motions now, a hopeless girl with hopeless eyes.

But Vaughn had been right in that temple. He had to let go before she got herself killed trying to save what was already dead.

He had to let go. Because Soren never would.

Not long now, a solemn murmur told him, a voice that lived in the core of that festering wound, getting louder and louder with every pulse of poison through his body. A voice that held the cadence of a priestess and the cold of grave dirt. *Not long left, little one. Are you ready?*

Not yet, he murmured back. *Just a little longer. Just long enough to see home one last time.*

Pain struck and rippled, radiating out like a stone dropped in a well, wave after wave wracking his body until all he could do was brace every muscle and grit his teeth, refusing to scream as agony bore down on every vein and bone.

Not long now, indeed. Once the unbearable pain started, it was only days until death for a bitten Nyxian.

They had to leave soon—today or tomorrow. Otherwise, there was no guarantee he would make it back.

The loud, terrible *clang* of the prison door being thrown open distracted him from the pain—Soren had come back. He craned his neck eagerly, ready, heart lifting toward his throat as he caught a glimpse of red hair . . . then slamming down into his gut again when Kallias rounded the corner, stumbling and bleary-eyed.

"What do you want?" Elias muttered.

Kallias frowned. His braid was half-undone, long strands hanging loose, and his gray tunic sported a dark maroon-tinted stain. The smell of old grapes wafted from him in waves.

This had to be some kind of trick, some way to get Elias to lower his defenses. Kallias was nearly always poised, always in control. There was no way the prince had *actually* just wandered into the dungeon *drunk*.

"I . . . don't know," Kallias said slowly, the words blurring together, a heavy slur rendering him nearly impossible to understand. "I thought this was my room."

Elias decided not to point out to the prince—who, judging by the sway to his gait, was *very legitimately drunk*—that the royal rooms were on the complete opposite side of the palace and up a long, long staircase. "Well, it's not, so get out."

"It's my palace, dumbass, and you're a prisoner in it," Kallias muttered, but a hushed giggle ruined his scowl, his bare feet smacking against the wet boards of the path through the ocean prison as he walked to Elias's cell. The prince lowered himself down carefully, planting his palms firmly on the boards as he settled, then wrapping his arms around his bent knees. "You ruined everything, you know."

"I know," Elias said tiredly. If the prince was only here to drunkenly gloat, he was going to close his eyes and pretend he didn't exist for a while. "Look, I'm a bit busy dying, so if you don't mind—"

"I wasn't talking to you."

Elias blinked. Looked to the cell beside him on the left, then to the right. "I'm the only one in here."

Kallias made a long, dramatic gesture, twirling his finger around a few times before pointing it at himself. "No, no. I'm the problem here. Not everything is about *you*, Eli."

"That's not my name."

Kallias groaned, waving him off. "Close enough. I'm a prince, I can call you whatever I like." Then, after a pause, he added, "Peasant."

Elias scowled. "I'm not a peasant."

"Touchy, touchy." Kallias smirked, but there was nothing amused in it. He rocked back on his haunches, staring at something above Elias's head, that smirk slowly morphing back into a frown—softer, sadder. "Soleil hates me now. And I deserve it."

"You do."

"You're not supposed to be rude to the man who could kill you with a word."

"You're not supposed to lie to girls about being your dead sister, either."

Kallias's eyes sharpened past the haze of wine, and he sat forward, meeting Elias's gaze with such sudden clarity that Elias leaned back a bit from the intensity. "*That* was not a lie. That's not why she's angry."

Elias's brow furrowed. "Then why—"

"Because of you, why else? We didn't tell her the truth about the Viper venom. She was so godsforsaken bent on finding a cure, and we didn't know what she'd do if she found out there wasn't one, and Finn said . . . and I just . . ." Kallias shrugged, looking away, his shoulders slumping. "We didn't want to lose her again."

Elias's chest clenched painfully, hurting worse than his arm ever had. "You knew she'd leave if you told her the truth."

Kallias swallowed and rubbed at his eyes, the hazy look filtering back in. "Gods, I need sleep. I don't know why I'm telling you all this."

"I have one of those faces," Elias said, and the prince laughed.

"Gods, don't I know it. And Soleil does too."

Elias rotated his shoulders as best he could, avoiding the prince's gaze, trying to shove down the heartsick ache in his chest. "You don't know what you're talking about."

"I know she loves you. I know you love her."

"We're battlemates. Love is a requirement."

"But you're *in* love with her."

Elias had nothing to say to that. Admitting it felt wrong. Denying it felt worse.

Kallias's eyes narrowed. "Does she know?"

Gods, why was he even talking about this? To an *Atlas prince*, of all people?

"No," he said finally. "I tried . . . I thought about . . . but it's too late now. There's no point."

Kallias scoffed, kicking himself up to his feet, knocking his fist against Elias's bars. "Gullshit."

"What?"

"Eli . . . peasant . . . whatever," he said, "are you dead yet?"

Elias gestured with his chin to his bare, blackened shoulder. "Might as well be."

"No, that's not what I asked. Are you dead yet?"

Elias swallowed down his protests. He'd had this argument with himself a million and one times since the ball and was no closer to feeling peaceful about his answer. Not telling her was hurting him; telling her would hurt her. And when it came down to it, he would always choose his pain over hers, but . . . that didn't feel quite right, either.

"No," he said. "But I will be, soon. And how is it fair to tell her now? How is it fair to get my courage up when it's too damned late?"

Kallias leaned against the bars, letting his forehead fall against them to keep him steady. His eyes bored into Elias, twin storms brewing with lightning and trouble. "Bravery is never late. You can always choose to be braver and better than you were. And from what I know of Soleil . . . of Soren . . . she would respect your bravery more than your fear. Even if it comes on your deathbed."

"But it will hurt her."

"Yes. But she deserves to know. You don't get to decide what she can't take—we just learned that lesson, and learned it hard. Besides, what if she has things to say too? It's not fair for you to rob her of that opportunity. You two need to have an honest conversation, and you need to have it soon. It's not good to die with secrets. It weighs a soul down."

Elias blinked at him in shock. "Damn, Kallias, are you actually smarter when you're drunk?"

Kallias snorted, cracking a half-grin. "Gods, I really hope not."

Elias hated the chuckle that fell from his lips like a betrayer's whispered word. He hated that the prince was utterly, annoyingly right."Can I ask you something?"

"Why not? I'm in such a good mood."

"Your ring." At the words, the prince tensed, his right hand covering his left. "I see there's a symbol on it now."

"I was claimed," he said. "I leave in three weeks."

"Why?"

Kallias blinked at him slowly, like he couldn't comprehend even one simple word. "What do you mean?"

"You don't want to go. So why did you agree?"

"I—it's not a matter of *agreeing*. It's tradition, and it's important, Atlas needs more weapons—"

"And you're willing to sell yourself out for a pile of steel? You see that little worth in yourself?"

Kallias stood straighter, locking his spine in place; a prince's stance, a warrior's stance. "I am willing to do whatever I have to for my kingdom."

Elias gave him a long look.

He shouldn't bother helping him. He shouldn't care if Kallias thought he was only a bag of coins to be tossed from one kingdom to another. But he said, "I've seen you with your people. I've seen you work tirelessly these past few weeks to keep them safe when the rest of your family was busy planning parties and playing cards in taverns."

Kallias's frown deepened. "Wait, who was *gambling*—?"

"—and I know nothing about this kingdom," Elias continued over him, "but I know this: you are worth infinitely more to your kingdom as a man among them than as a prince apart from them. And if you truly love your people, you will fight for what they need—not what your mother *thinks* they need."

Kallias's face dropped, considering—then hardened. He pushed off the bars and moved away, raking a hand through his hair. "You're just trying to keep us from allying with a kingdom whose weapons could end this war."

"One of our princesses was apprenticed personally to an Artemisian weaponsmith long before you got the idea for an alliance in your heads. I don't care what kingdom your sorry ass lives in. Look, I'm telling you what I see, and I see a prince whose heart could never live anywhere but here. Am I wrong?"

Kallias stared at him. And stared at him. And swallowed, his throat bobbing. "No," he admitted quietly, lowering himself back onto the damp ground, unbothered by the silt and saltwater left behind. He leaned his whole weight back against the bars this time, head angled so he could keep one eye on Elias, wearing exhaustion like a masquerade mask around his eyes. "You're not. But there's nothing I can do. It's too late to stop it now."

Elias raised one eyebrow. "A very wise drunk once told me that bravery is never too late. Are you dead yet, Kallias?"

The prince's smirk was wry, irritated. "Only on the inside."

"Funny. Then I'd say you have three weeks to come up with some bravery."

Kallias was quiet for a long time, so long Elias was about to say something else, to ask another question, when a loud, rumbling snore rolled out of the man slumped with his back against the prison bars.

Elias relaxed a bit, letting himself slump forward, the chains on his wrists digging in as he swung a bit further forward.

Kallias was right. It wasn't fair of him to make Soren's choices for her. But to say the words out loud . . . to give life to them . . .

Maybe she could bear it, having it and then losing it so quickly. But he didn't know if he could.

"I want to marry your sister."

The words burned his tongue as he gave them voice, scalding with the impossibility of such a want. He had never dared whisper those words out loud. So for it to come out now, to this Atlas prince, to his enemy . . .

"I'm so gods-damned glad you're drunk," he muttered.

Kallias's only reply was another snore.

CHAPTER 58

SOREN

I t was a starry night when Soren decided to kill the Atlas king.

Or at least, she'd decided to threaten it—and if he did not comply with her demands, she would follow through. She had to. For Elias, she could not do any less.

The siblings were all gods-knew-where, and Adriata herself was too carefully watched. It had to be the king.

She didn't want to admit that she'd spent far too long trying to find another alternative—any other alternative. But he was the only one she could get to, the only one who mattered enough to the Queen that she would give in. Still, her hands shook as she paced the hall outside the war room, where Ramses was inside meeting with Atlas's generals and captains. She thought and rethought her plan a million and one times, changing the scenario just slightly every time. Still she turned to go more than once, before remembering Elias's broken eyes and pleas to go home.

Elias over all. That was the vow she'd made. Even if it broke what remained of Soleil's heart.

No one seemed to notice her when they filed out, heads ducked together in quiet conversation. When Ramses emerged, his glasses in one hand while he rubbed at the bridge of his nose with his other, Soren braced herself against the little girl she used to be. Against the teenager who'd stayed awake some nights crying for her papa. Against the woman who'd taken one look at his face and abandoned all thoughts of killing her way out of this palace.

She hadn't been desperate then—not like this.

So she braced, chanted her new mantra to herself—*Elias over all, Elias over all*—and sidled up to the king's side. "Rough day?"

"You have no idea," Ramses sighed. "They want to send your boy home in pieces, Soren. It took hours for me to talk them down."

She waited until only she and Ramses were left, lingering toward the back of the hall, only the windows left to bear witness. And their curtains were drawn— they'd closed their eyes to the coming betrayal.

In a blink, so fast she couldn't even pause to reconsider, she drew one of Elias's Artem-forged daggers that she'd found hidden in his bunk after he'd been thrown in the dungeon. "That's exactly what I wanted to discuss with you."

But before she could move, Ramses put his arm around her—pulling her closer, not pushing her away. He sighed again, eyes still focused forward, half-lidded like he was already on his way to sleep. "You used to do this all the time. You'd hide in the shadows and pounce on me when I came out of meetings. Scared years off my life while you were at it."

Soren's heart fluttered in terrified wingbeats against her chest, and she tried to pull away, but Ramses's arm held her fast. "Did I?"

"Mmhm. Well past your bedtime, I might add." He cracked a grin, nostalgia warming his eyes. "But you just had to have your story."

"Papa, tell me how you and Mama met."

Her father laughed his booming laugh, nuzzling the top of her head, his beard catching pleasantly on her hair. He smelled of cologne and spices, which meant he'd just come from a diplomatic dinner of some kind. "You don't want to hear that story again, Sunbeam."

"I do!" Soleil protested, rolling off his lap onto her bed, landing with a bounce. "I always like this story."

"You're not sick of it yet?"

"Nooo. I want to hear about Mama's dress and her hair and what you said when—"

"All right, all right!" Papa swept her into his arms, sitting cross-legged, pressing his back against her mountain of pillows and stuffed animals. He deftly plucked the soft-bristled brush from her nightstand, setting her down in front of him. "Do you want two braids or one?"

"Two," Soleil said decisively, settling herself with her legs crossed like his, her back digging against her father's knees. As he eased the brush through her thick hair—tangled from swimming in the ocean all day and still damp from the bath her mother forced her to endure afterward—he whispered a story of glittering gold and ragged shirts.

"Once upon a time, there was a queen of sunshine, and she was looking for someone to rule beside her, as she was very lonely. She threw a beautiful ball and invited every eligible citizen of the kingdom to try and win her heart. And in that kingdom lived a greedy old man, who had five sons and only loved four of them. He chose the fifth one to go and try to marry the queen, because though he was unloved, he was the best-mannered of them all. But the boy didn't want a queen. He had great plans of his own, plans to become a sailor and see the world."

"Why didn't your papa like you, Papa?"

He gently rapped her head with the hairbrush. "Remember the rules of storytime, Sunbeam?"

Soleil let out a gushing sigh, barely resisting the urge to flop forward in irritation. "No interrupting, on pain of death," she recited dramatically, wriggling her bare toes against the silken blanket.

"That's right. Now, this queen of sunshine was rumored to be beautiful, and the boy knew exactly what he would do to ruin his chance at the marriage. He would walk straight up to her in his patchy old shirt, kiss her hand, and promptly inform her that she was the ugliest thing he had ever laid eyes on."

Soleil gasped, even though she'd heard this a million times before. It never ceased to delight her, the idea of her gentle father being so wicked.

"But, as luck would have it," her father continued, sounding entirely too fond of the memory, "the rumors of the queen's beauty had undersold her—badly. So much so that when the boy first laid eyes on her, he was stunned speechless. He couldn't speak for an hour! Instead, he danced with the queen. And she was far too polite to force him to make conversation, so instead, she talked the entire time. She told him about her kingdom and herself and everything she had ever asked a wishing well for. And by the end of the hour, the boy had fallen quite entirely in love with her."

"But then . . ." Soleil squeaked out, too excited about the next part of the story to contain herself.

Papa chuckled, carefully beginning to twist her hair into braids. "But then, when they went to say goodbye, the queen leaned in and whispered, 'I threw in a wishing coin for a king last *night. I don't suppose you know anything about where I might find one?' And the boy, in a panic, reverted to the only thing he had practiced leading up to this night, which was . . ."*

"You're the ugliest thing I've ever seen!" Soren crowed with him, giggles breaking up her words until they were hardly comprehensible.

Papa groaned at the reminder of his humiliation, but laughter still weighed heavy on his words as he went on. "The boy fled the ballroom, entirely and rightfully ashamed. He was certain he'd ruined everything, that the sunshine queen would demand he be removed from the palace at once. But instead . . ."

Soleil waited patiently. Ramses finished tying her braids, planting a kiss on the crown of her head.

"Instead, the queen ran after him, kicking off her slippers just so she could catch up with him. And when she corned him, barefoot and panting and absolutely radiant, she said—"

"Any man with the stones to call me ugly to my face is surely brave enough to be king," interrupted a voice at the door, filled with laughter, love, and light.

"Mama!" Soleil jumped off the bed into her mother's arms, her braids swinging behind her. "You really weren't mad that he called you ugly?"

"Oh, I was furious. But I also knew he didn't mean it." Mama smiled, kissing Soleil's brow and shooting her husband a playful glare. "He wasn't blind, after all. And you'd have to be, to think I was anything less than gorgeous."

"Prideful creature," Papa murmured lovingly, getting up to kiss Mama.

"Honest creature," she corrected. "I know what I am, that's all."

"And I know what I am." Papa nuzzled his nose against Mama's hair, the softest of smiles gracing his lips. "Entirely in love with my beautiful, vain wife."

Mama snorted, smacking his chest with the back of her hand, though her smile—as the story had claimed—was as radiant as the summer sun. "I despise you, King Ramses."

"And I adore you, my queen." Papa kissed Mama's brow, then turned to kiss Soleil's. "And you too, Sunbeam. You have just as much sunshine in you as your mother."

"And a little pinch of darkness," Mama teased, scowling at Papa. "Did you leave out the part where you tried to steal my bracelet right off my wrist?"

Soleil gaped up at Papa. "You tried to steal *from Mama?"*

Papa blushed. "It was . . . a phase. One I expect you not to mimic, Soleil."

"A long phase," Mama snorted. "I still can't find the diamond necklace that very flattering Tallisian lord gave me a few years back."

Ramses sheepish look curved into a slight smirk. "And you never will."

She jolted out of the memory with a sharp shake of her head, but it lingered, trembling at the edges of her mind. Her hand clenched tightly around the hilt of the dagger tucked in the folds of her sleeve—so tightly her fingers had begun to fall asleep. And Ramses was looking right at her hand—right where the dagger was hidden.

"I knew," he said softly. "I knew it was an act. But I hoped all the same. Foolish of me, I know."

Soren's hand trembled as she stepped away from him and raised the blade. "I need my battlemate freed. Now. Tonight. I need . . . if you just . . . just hurry, and I won't have to—"

"It's all right," Ramses said gently, his hands slowly rising until he was holding them by his head, no weapon in sight, though he wore more than one blade on his belt. Nothing at all but the stark, unending sadness lurking in his eyes. Nothing but the grief that lined his face with creases that didn't belong there.

In her memory, he had been so young, so happy. Now . . . now he was looking at her with such sorrow she thought she might choke on it. Not like she was an enemy about to end his life, but like she was a daughter he'd lost long ago. Like she was a daughter he was losing again.

"I won't hurt you, Sunbeam," he whispered, every word rubbed raw with anguish and yet somehow laced with peace. "But I won't let him go, either. He killed my people with his magic, and I won't endanger them."

"He's not—"

"Soleil," he interrupted, so unbearably tender. "You are my daughter, and I love you, and I forgive you. If this is the choice you make for your kingdom, then so be it. But this is the choice I make for mine."

Soren raised the dagger. Ramses shut his eyes.

"My sweet little devil," Papa teased, snatching her from Mama's arms to tickle her. "I love you more than all the stars in the sky!"

Soleil shrieked with laughter, kicking helplessly at his arms. "I love you more than the moon!"

"And I love you more than the sun!"

"I love you more than the whole great big ocean and the sharks and the whales—"

Something burst free from Soren's chest, from her throat—some heart-wrenching noise that was either a sob or a scream. Maybe both.

The dagger fell from her hands. Clattered to the floor.

Ramses stared at her in surprise. Genuine, startled surprise.

Soren raised her eyes to his, unable to find it in her to be ashamed of the tears gathered there. Not anymore. Not after all of this.

"I'm sorry," she said. Then again, rambling, tearful, "Papa, I'm *sorry*, I don't know what to do I can't save him on my own—"

Ramses's face crumpled, and he barely moved in time to catch her when she collapsed into his arms, weeping. Open, messy, gut-twisting weeping. She buried her face against her father's chest and cried for the child she had been. For the childhood she'd lost . . . that had been *stolen* from her.

And worse, she cried in anger at the woman she *was*—the woman that couldn't put aside her past to protect her future.

The woman who'd chosen the King of Atlas over Elias's freedom.

CHAPTER 59

SOREN

Even when she was finished crying, even when Ramses let her go and promised he wouldn't tell Adriata what she'd almost done, Soren didn't go back to Elias's cell. She couldn't face him. Not knowing that she'd been right there, that it would have been *so easy* to march Ramses to Adriata's door, to spill his blood if they refused to comply . . . and she'd dropped her weapon instead.

She went back to her room and crawled into bed, lying in absolute dark, staring unseeingly into the abyss above and around and inside her.

She'd failed. Failed at saving Elias, failed at getting him home. Failed at everything she'd set out here to do. Atlas thought of her as an enemy again, and Nyx might not even want her back. Neither salt nor stars would welcome her now. And it wasn't like she knew how to pick one over the other, anyway.

Two different kingdoms. Two different families. Two different mothers.

Enna, soft and secretive and encouraging, never faltering in her faith, rarely ever discouraging Soren from danger or duty. When Soren had asked to go into the barracks, Enna had never fought her; she'd only ensured Soren knew exactly what she was getting herself into, that training wasn't a game, that people died on those battlefields. And when Soren had remained adamant, Enna had walked her to the armory to pick her first training blade. When Soren lost Jira, Enna and all her sisters had come into her room and piled on her bed with her—never speaking, never asking questions, only offering the strength of their arms and an echo for her own private grief.

Adriata, passionate and sharp-tongued and protective. Her vengeance had been born of love, a grief so molten and damaging it changed the very shape of her, bending her from Queen of Sun to Queen of War. She'd held a knife to Soren's throat. She'd cradled Soleil and sung lullabies to her at night. She'd wept when Soren called her Mama. She'd taught Soleil to swim. She'd lost more than anyone should and had taken more in retribution than anyone had a right to.

Raised by one, born of the other. Nature and Nurture in constant battle, waiting for her to choose between them.

Gods, her feet itched. Restlessness buzzed in her legs and arms, a harsh hum that promised she would get no rest tonight.

Her eyes flicked to the closet.

Moments later, Soren found herself creeping through the halls, barefoot and clad in a wetsuit, chanting *what am I doing what am I doing what am I doing* through chattering teeth.

The ungainly thing in her arms kept dragging her this way and that, throwing off her balance with its considerable bulk. It was bigger than she'd expected, bigger than a child should have been able to use. The Atlas people called them *waveboards*. She'd seen them out on the water, bobbing like the buoys by the docks, and up until now she'd thought they were stark raving mad. She'd seen drawings of the sea monsters that swam silent beneath those waves, giant fish Kallias called *sharks* and *whales* and *dolphins*. She wanted absolutely no part of that. No way her headstone was going to say that she'd died being eaten by a *fish*.

But there was a craving for salt on her tongue and the faintest trace of memory calling her name, and gods, maybe a little madness was all that could fix her now.

Her battlemate was going to die. She was too Atlas for Nyx and too Nyxian for Atlas. Her siblings were liars and traitors. She remembered too much about her past, but still not enough.

Something had to give. And she didn't know why this was her solution, didn't know what had drawn her from her bed to pad on calloused feet through halls silent and empty, peering around corners to check for guards before scurrying forward. But something in her soul knew, and tonight she was desperate enough to trust an instinct that vague and strange.

She snuck down to the kitchens, finding them blessedly empty, and slipped out the back door Finn always used to sneak away without being seen.

Somehow, her feet knew the way; she hadn't gone to the ocean yet, only watched the waves outside her window, and this was a far more roundabout route to get to the shore. But she hadn't wanted to chance anyone seeing her from one of the many palace windows and thinking she was trying to escape. Better to sneak and be caught when she was already in the water.

Adrenaline stiffened her muscles, every step and turn too jerky, every noise whipping her head around to search out the source. But there was never anyone behind her—even the taverns were quiet and dark tonight. With necromancy in the city, no one felt much like being out late.

Considering she was the target of those particular attacks, this wasn't the smartest move on her part, even without considering that she'd only just relearned how to swim. But she'd never been known for her intelligence.

When she reached the shore, she stopped, staring at the line between city and beach, between stone and sand. Slowly, she stretched her foot forward, letting it settle gently into the strange, rough grains.

It was cold—the chill had settled more deeply into the ground than into the air. Cold and shifty and strange, but . . .

Her feet adjusted. She knew how to walk on it, and before she could really think about it, she was striding for the thing that had mocked and called to her in the same breath when she first arrived, an ancient body that breathed and roared like a legendary beast, one of the few things that made her wonder if there really were gods living somewhere in the world. If anything screamed *deity*, it was the sea.

And she, mortal and small and smartass, was about to challenge it with a board and a halfhearted prayer.

Elias would have lost his gods-damned mind.

"Okay, Soleil," she whispered, feeling slightly foolish. But she had to try something. "Show me what to do."

Then she ran for the sea.

The water was warmer than she'd expected, but still sent goosebumps erupting over her whole body—and the moment the first wave cracked against her, fear fled without looking back.

Oh, she knew this beast. Had tamed it once, as a girl much smaller and wilder, and every part of her swelled with ecstasy, with peace, with *memory*.

Soleil laid flat on her board and began to paddle out.

Not just her this time—Soren was there, too, admiring the new constellations winking above, relishing the bite of the cold wind. There was nothing lost and nothing gained, but an even exchange—a melding of past and present, nature and nurture, girl and woman.

Soleil knew the sea. Soren knew the sky. Neither belonged to one more than the other, and for the first time, with the sea below and the sky above, her blood settled in her veins. When she spotted an unbroken wave, she swam to it and positioned herself in front of it. When she felt the back of the board lift, she jumped to her feet, knees cocked for balance—

And just like that, like she'd always known how, like she'd never stopped, she caught a wave.

Peace, visceral and so strong tears pricked in her eyes, swept through her as she rode it; not a big one, not even close, but gods, it didn't matter. The stars sparkled above her and the sea glimmered beneath her, and in their embrace she had an idea.

Maybe it wasn't Nyx or Atlas. Maybe that wasn't the choice she had to make.

Maybe the choice was war . . . or peace.

She'd died a child of peace. Been raised a daughter of war. She'd come here already at war with this family and continued to war against the two parts of herself. But there was no winner in that fight; Nyx would always be in her heart, and Atlas would always be in her blood. She could not escape or ignore either.

She didn't want to be the tug-of-war rope between these kingdoms; she'd tried it, and it only hurt everyone involved.

But maybe she could be a bridge instead.

It would mean forgiving people she didn't want to forgive. It would mean everyone in Nyx finding out that she was the daughter of their enemies. It would mean so many things she wasn't ready to face. But if she did it fast, it might just save Elias's life, after all. Peace treaties required negotiation, and she knew what her first demand would be.

Safe—and fast—passage to Arborius.

CHAPTER 60

KALLIAS

Kallias was having a grand time sleeping off the wine binge that had left him slumped and drooling in the dungeons last night—he would have probably drowned down there if Seamus hadn't come and dragged him out— when his door slammed open so hard that the knob dented the wall. It *felt* like it had slammed into his *skull*, though, and he groaned, fumbling for the first thing his hand touched—a pillow—and throwing it with considerable force at the intruder. "Go *away*, Jericho. I learned my lesson, believe me."

"Good," said a voice that was *not* Jericho's. "Because I need your help."

His eyes flew open to Soleil leaning against his doorframe, her hair dripping wet. She was wearing a sunset-orange Atlas wrap dress, arms crossed over her chest, sand crusting her ankles and starfire in her eyes.

"You still drunk?" she asked.

Kallias grimaced. "Not even a little." Which wasn't fun, because it meant he was clear-headed enough to remember what he'd said to her . . . what awful things he'd let loose in that room. Guilt dislodged irritation in an instant, and he sat up, bowing his head to her. "Soleil, I am *so sorry*—"

"Fantastic. So you agree you owe me?"

"I—what?"

Soleil merely grinned, a thing of sunshine so bright and hopeful that he wondered if *she* was the one drunk. He'd never seen her smile like that before—at least, not the grown version of her. "Get dressed and pretend you still know how to be a prince. We're meeting in the dining room—ours, not the real one. You have twenty minutes." And then she swept out in a flicker of orange and gold.

He blinked after her, his mind sluggishly trying to process what she'd just said. "Ours?" he whispered.

Then he was *flying*, headache be damned, his fingers buttoning his shirt faster than he'd ever thought possible, barely remembering to throw on pants before sprinting out the door, his hair streaming unbound and unbrushed behind him. Jericho and Finn joined him moments later, both wearing similar looks of hope and confusion, keeping pace with him as they hurried to the dining room.

"Does anyone know what in the depths is going on?" Kallias asked.

"Maybe she's going to murder us all," Finn suggested, but his desperate eyes didn't match his voice. "Or maybe she . . ."

"Do you think she remembered?" Jericho asked, rubbing her arms, excitement gleaming in her exhaustion-dulled eyes for the first time in a while. Kallias had been too drunk to notice much in these past few days, but Jericho looked terrible; if not for the fact that she was just as healthy as ever, her cheeks still filled with color and her limbs strong, he would have worried she was ill. Something about her eyes just looked . . . wrong. Haunted, maybe.

Then again, they all wore that same look lately, thanks to walking dead. So maybe he wasn't being fair.

"Maybe," he croaked.

"No use hiding out here," Finn said. "We'll never know until she tells us."

He was right, for once. So they all pushed inside, completely unsure of what to expect.

Soleil sat at the head of the table, cross-legged on the seat, her skirt tucked around her ankles, her back straight and her chin tipped at a challenging angle. She gave them an uncharacteristically serious look, gesturing to the table. "Sit down, we need to talk. Just us four."

Kallias exchanged looks with Jericho and Finn, but slowly sat, his palms already gathering sweat in their creases. Whatever this was, they weren't prepared for it. He knew that much.

Soleil folded her hands on the table, taking in a deep breath. "Last night, I threatened Papa," she announced, as casually as one would announce it was cloudy that day, or that they had bought new shoes.

Finn's eyes widened, and Jericho jerked to her feet. "What did you—?"

"Relax." Soleil gestured for her to sit back down, and to his surprise, Jericho did. "I didn't follow through, obviously. You think I brought you here to announce I killed the king?"

"It does seem like the kind of thing you would do," Finn said.

"Fair. But I didn't, so be quiet for a minute." She took another deep breath and braced her hands against the table. She stared at her place setting so long that Kallias followed her gaze, wondering if she'd written notes on her napkin or something. He'd had to do that before. "You all know the sacredness of a vow. You swore one to each other when I died—us before all. But I . . . I was not part of that vow. And I shouldn't have expected you to act like I was."

Kallias's heart skipped a beat. Soleil's gaze snapped up, taking each of them in, settling on Finn—who looked away.

"But I swore my own vows," she said, "to the boy in your dungeon. Vows to stand with him, to protect him, to share his last breath as my own. And I cannot keep them without your help."

"We're not going to kill you when he dies," Finn mumbled, and Soleil put her head in her hands, with a sigh that suggested she was entirely fed up with him.

"Obviously not, and why would you even suggest that? That's horrible. I had another idea in mind. But Adriata isn't going to like it, and you three might not, either."

"Just spit it out, Soleil," Jericho said, her brow furrowed. "What's your plan?"

Soleil met each of their gazes. "This war started because I was killed. But I wasn't. I'm here now . . . different than you wanted, and still learning, and still Nyxian, but I'm here. There is no point in this war anymore. No fight left to be had, nothing to avenge. Nyx has paid enough, and Atlas has received everything they could have possibly wanted out of this. I'm not saying Nyx was without fault, and I'm not saying Atlas was justified in its motives. But it's time we stopped fighting over a murder that never happened. I'm going to tell Adriata that I'll be her liaison. I'll help negotiate a peace with Nyx."

"*No,*" Jericho blurted out, her eyes widening. "What? Soleil, they *stole* you, they took you away from us, they have to answer for that they will *never* have paid enough—"

"We don't *know* what happened," Soleil interrupted, surprisingly calm. Calmer than Kallias had ever seen. "And until we can sit down with Enna and *ask* her, I refuse to turn my back on the kingdom that raised me. Only one person is responsible for my being taken, and we should not punish *everyone* for her actions. Those are *my people* who are dying, my people being punished, and I won't let it happen a second longer. But I need your help to convince Mama. She won't listen to me on my own."

The three older Atlas siblings, bound by vow and blood and grief, exchanged looks across the table. Judging who was on what side. Picking allies and choosing opinions.

"I'm in," Finn said finally, shocking Kallias straight to his toes. He was never the one to make a decision first. He looked to Soleil, and his frown softened. "I promised you I'd get your friend his cure, and I meant it. Besides, I know it's not him making those skeletons waltz down the streets. He threw up for three hours after the first attack. It was kind of funny."

"I'm in too," said Kallias. "We've been at war long enough." And no war meant no need for Artem's weapons. He clenched his fist, refusing to look at his claiming ring.

Jericho was quiet the longest—too long. So long Soleil prompted, "Jer?"

"Fine," Jericho muttered. "Sure. I'll help organize a peace with the kingdom that stole you and tried to kill me. What could go wrong?"

Soleil beamed, the exact wrong reaction to that statement. "Great. We'll talk to Mama tonight. And . . . and thank you. All of you."

"Us before all," Finn said. "We didn't make that vow alone. We made it *for* you, and you'll always be part of it."

"No matter what you choose," Kallias said softly. "You're our sister."

Soleil smiled at him, a sure, steady thing that looked so much like his mother that he almost forgot the girl in front of him wasn't queen yet. "I know. I'm also your Heir—and don't you forget it. So move your asses. We have a peace to secure and a jackass to save."

CHAPTER 61

ELIAS

Deep in the pit of his gut, fire burned.

Flames licked his ribs, wrapping greedy fingers around them like the bars of a cage, climbing a ladder to his lungs, setting every breath ablaze. Searing pain stabbed him with every wheezing inhale, and the sweat pouring down his bare back and chest did nothing to cool him. Droplets rolled down his cheeks like tears, mixing with the blood from where he'd bitten his lip to keep from screaming in pain, iron and salt coating his tongue in a sticky film.

The poison was nearly to his heart. He could *feel* it, like tar thickening his blood, every heartbeat slower than it should be. It had stolen his breath first, then his strength . . . then his mind, heat swirling his thoughts into smoke clouds, gritty and toxic, looping in tilting circles like the wooden swing Soren once convinced him to climb on before she twisted up the strings and sent him spinning in whip-fast circles.

Delirium. Dizziness. He could hardly tell which way was up or down.

Atlas hadn't needed any magic to make him forget his name, his purpose, his peace. Their venom did that job for them.

He tried to raise his head, seeking something real to cling to, searching for steel bars and tide pools at his feet—gods, he would have taken just about anything over this. But dark spots bloomed in mosaic tiles across his vision, terrible patterns that promised something awful was waiting for him when he closed his eyes for the last time.

Infera or Arcaea? That was the only thought in his head today, hanging limply from his chains, chin touching his bare, blazing chest. *Have I done enough? Do you still hear my prayers, Lady of Silence, of Death and Mercy, of Flame and Vengeance and Righteous Fury? Or did you leave me when I left your temple?*

He didn't need an answer. The heat devouring the last of his strength told him enough: Mortem had given her fire-beasts free reign, and they'd decided his soul looked dark enough to play with.

He didn't know where he was going. And he was so, so very afraid.

The prison door slamming shut roused him from nightmares of Soren screaming his name from behind walls of fire, and he tried to stand straight, to no avail. His legs shook like wind chimes in a blizzard, and it was all he could do to lift his head once more, searching out his visitor with blurry, heat-stroked eyes. Before him, a freckled, annoying face swam into view—one he unfortunately recognized.

"What can I do for you, Prince Finnick?" The honorific fell from his mouth in a death-drunk slur, falling to the floor like a weighted training bag dropping from its rope.

The Trickster Prince of Atlas stood before him, face impassive, busy hands buried in his pockets while he watched Elias struggle to breathe. He tipped his head to the side, dark auburn hair feathering across his forehead with the movement, his eyes focused on the rotting hole in Elias's arm.

"I see why you were covering it up," he said. "Smells like death warmed over down here."

"If you're just here to gloat, I'm actually a little busy, so . . ."

"I wasn't aware dying was something that required effort on your part."

"Not the dying. The praying." Honesty—Elias didn't have the energy to lie to a man who would see straight through it anyway. "Why are you here?"

Finn cleared his throat, shuffling his feet, bending his knees, straightening his elbows, wearing just enough discomfort on the hinges of his joints that it caught Elias's drifting attention. "To gloat, firstly. And then to apologize."

Well, that settled it. He must have died already. The prince couldn't even pronounce *apologize* the right way, his nose wrinkling as he said it. "This is a joke, right?"

"Unfortunately not," Finn sighed. "I could use a laugh. I'm only going to say it once: I formally apologize for the way my parents have treated you. I know you're not the necromancer, and so does Soleil, and Kal would figure it out too if he'd get his head out of his—"

"Apologies aren't worth anything to me," Elias interrupted him, gritting his teeth against another wave of pain, his back bowing and straining against it. "I'm still dying in a dungeon."

"If you'd let me finish, you wouldn't be." Finn lifted his hand, a hint of gold flashing in his palm. "I convinced my mother to move you to a room. Still guarded, but I assigned Alia to it. You two are friends, right?"

Elias blinked, scanning the prince's face for any sign of a lie, any sign of a snake's tongue poking out between his teeth. The prince merely met his gaze, expressionless, dark-eyed.

"I promised Soleil," he said. "I promised I'd help her save you. And as long as you're praying, I'd throw up some thanks to whoever governs mercy, because Soleil happens to be the only person I keep my promises to."

Elias swallowed, trying not to flinch at the sandpaper rasp of his throat. If this was a trick, if he went with Finn, he might find himself gutted in the hall . . . but at least it would be a quick end.

"I can't walk," he said, in lieu of thanks.

"Seamus will come down to get you in a few minutes. I told him I wanted to talk to you first."

"And why is that?"

Finn's simple shrug belied the intensity of his gaze. "Because I want her to know I was telling the truth. And I want you to know it, too." He shuffled his feet again. "Better accommodations should buy you time. And Jericho might be able to ease the pain, even if she can't get rid of the actual poison."

Not a chance in Infera. "I don't want healing of her sort."

Finn shrugged, muttering under his breath about religious zealots. "Suit yourself. I'll ask Vaughn what he's got, then."

As the prince left, the echo of his departing footsteps blending seamlessly with Seamus's approaching ones, Elias swallowed down his pride, letting it boil in the fever and fear in his gut.

Between the nobility he'd seen in Kallias and the weakness he'd seen in Finn . . . he didn't know what to make of these Atlas princes any longer. And something told him that doubt was more dangerous than any poison.

CHAPTER 62

FINN

Finn dreamed of a girl surrounded by mirrors.

But today there was no throne, no smirk, no crown—only a faceless girl in a world of faceless girls, thousands of reflections scattered across an infinite space, purple jewels and blush-tinted mirrors flashing blinding gouts of light in Finn's eyes. Each flash stabbed like a white-hot knife into the center of Finn's forehead, over and over and over again, tines of dizziness threatening to fold him to the ground.

"You aren't a very good listener," said the mirror girl.

"You're not a very good speaker," he said, wishing his tongue didn't feel so numb. "What do you want with me?"

"Believe me, I want absolutely nothing to do with you," sighed the girl, her breath echoing in strange ways off the eternity of glass. "But if you don't pay attention, trickster, we're all going to end up playing a very dangerous game."

A threat or a warning?

"I think you'll find I'm very good at winning games," he rasped.

For a moment, the reflection before him changed—faceless no more. Eyes swirling with the color of candy floss, rich brown skin, a dimpled grin with a keyhole gap between her front teeth—

"Oh, trickster," she said. "You've never played a game like this before."

Light flashed. Glass shattered. Skeleton hands clutched Finn's ankles, his wrists, his throat—

"One more day, trickster," breathed that vertigo-inducing voice in his ear, laughter dancing on the edges of her words. "Make it count."

Finn woke up with something sweet on his breath, a circlet of bruises around his wrists, and a stone of dread compressing his chest.

Kicking himself free from his tangle of sheets, a shiver running through his shoulders as the sweat on the back of his neck cooled, Finn paced the length of his room, the lurid facets of his dream spinning in circles like a Lapis-made kaleidoscope.

He remembered every dream he'd ever had, and this one was no different. But no matter how he tried, no matter how sure he was that he'd seen it . . . he could not remember the mirror girl's face.

A knock on his door.

"It's open," he called, clearing the unease from his throat.

The door creaked open, and his father's head poked inside, hair rumpled from sleep and glasses slightly askew on his nose. He frowned, taking in Finn's heaving chest, his shaking hands . . . gods knew what his face looked like.

"Bad dreams?" Ramses asked lightly. "I heard you shout."

Finn's face burned. He folded his hands behind his back, forcing his next breath to go in and out in a steady whoosh. "It's nothing, Papa. Sorry if I woke you."

Control, control, control. He could panic over the lost memory later. What mask was his father expecting, which one would put him back where he was supposed to be—

Ramses merely gazed at him for a long moment, hands in his pockets, shoulder propped against the doorframe. Finally, with a slight jerk of his head, he said, "Walk with me, will you? It's been a while since we talked."

Damn. He hadn't found the right mask in time. "Sure."

He didn't bother changing out of his sleepclothes before padding into the hall—his father was wearing the same, anyway. King and Second Prince wandered down the hall, both stealing glances at Soleil's door, at the drawing no one had ever bothered to wash off.

"I have them, too," said Ramses suddenly, his eyes still focused on the door. "The nightmares. Your mother says I've scared a few years off her life waking up in fits."

Finn tugged his sleeves down to cover his shaking fingers. Most of the time, his heart shed guilt like a pair of ship-boots shed water. Lies came easier than truth these days, especially when it came to his family. Even with Soleil, truth was harder to tug free from his tongue.

He hated lying to his father.

When Adriata had pulled away from them all, shutting herself in her grief over Soleil, Ramses had pushed in instead—especially with Finn. Even when Finn had shouted and cursed and begged to be left alone. Even when he'd done nothing but sit in sullen silence while his father sat at the foot of his bed, waiting patiently to see if today was the day he would finally break, the day he would finally talk about the loss everyone else seemed content to let rot in their hearts.

He never broke. Never gave in. But every day, every single day, his father sat with him. Whether it was twenty minutes or from dawn to dusk, whatever time the King could give to his grieving son, he'd given it. Like he somehow knew that every time he left, Finn curled into his pillow and cried until his eyes were dry and burning. Like he somehow knew about the forbidden prayers and the locked-up letters and the dreams he had every night of Soleil walking into the palace like she'd never left, demanding to know why they hadn't looked harder for her.

"Do your dreams ever come true, Papa?"

He hadn't meant to ask it so plainly. He hadn't meant to ask it at all.

Ramses was quiet for a time, chewing on the inside of his cheek as they walked. "Sometimes. I think, anyway. There are some days when I find myself living in a moment I could have sworn I already lived once . . . but that happens to everyone, doesn't it?"

"Déjà vu," Finn agreed, his heart sinking. Some part of him had hoped to find a rational explanation for this madness that had started leaking from his dreams to his life. "What about the bad dreams?"

"What about them?"

"Do they ever come true?"

"No," said Ramses, more decisively that time. He fussed with the watch on his wrist, his golden-red brows drawing together over troubled eyes. "No, the bad ones . . . those are always about things that have already happened. Things I cannot change no matter how many times I relive them."

"The fire?"

Ramses shrugged. "The fire, yes, mostly. But also . . . Kallias's incident. That time Jericho nearly drowned off the docks when she was a girl . . . you weren't even born then. There was one battle, early on, before your mother stopped fighting . . . she caught a bad blow in the ribs . . ."

His father's eyes were beginning to take on that misty look they got when he was diving too deeply into the past, so Finn quickly laughed—a sound too sharp and nervous to be real, nowhere near his best work—and said, "No nightmares about me, huh?"

Ramses snorted, rubbing at the bridge of his nose before reaching out to wrap his arm around Finn's shoulder, drawing him close to his side. He planted an absent kiss on the top of Finn's head. "I never worry about you, Finn. Not anymore. You know why?"

Heart pinching in strange ways at that small affection, at the words, Finn shrugged one shoulder.

Ramses smirked—the one thing that always let Finn know he truly was his father's son, that he'd learned that cleverness somewhere—and said, "Because you remind me of me at your age. All of you are smart enough, but you, you have street smarts. That's rare in royalty."

"Mama has it."

"Your mother was taught it. And she was a very quick learner." As if in demonstration, Ramses pulled his arm away from Finn, holding his hand up— dangling Finn's glasses in front of his face. The glasses that had previously been stowed in his shirt pocket.

Finn smiled sheepishly and held up his own hand—showing off Ramses's watch. "You're getting rusty in your old age."

Ramses mock-groaned, shoving Finn good-naturedly before tugging him back into his embrace, the two of them swapping belongings. "All right, all right. I'm getting old, I know. No need to remind me."

"Hey, I still haven't caught you. You're not entirely washed up. What else did you get this week?"

Ramses shook his head with a long sigh, securing his watch back on his wrist. "Jericho's hairpin. Vaughn's wedding ring. I had Soleil's bracelets, but after the whole debacle with that Elias character . . ."

"Guilt?"

"Unbearable."

Finn nodded, pocketing his hands. "I had her earrings. I've got her battlemate's prayer beads, those daggers she gave him, Kal's cologne . . ."

"You've had Kal's cologne for two months. It doesn't count any longer."

"I think it counts as long as he hasn't noticed it's missing."

"Well, in that case, I still have your mother's heart. She has yet to ask about it. How many points does thirty years buy me?"

Finn faked a gag as Ramses chortled at his own joke. "Papa, please. You're better than that."

"I'm really not." His hand squeezed Finn's shoulder, warm, strong, bracing. "You're not shaking anymore."

And he wasn't. "I guess pickpocketing is a good distraction."

"I don't suppose you want to talk about those bad dreams you're so worried about coming true?"

Skeleton hands. Gap-tooth grins. *You've never played a game like this before.*

"No," he said softly, rubbing the goosebumps from his skin. "Feels like bad luck, you know?"

Ramses nodded. "If you ever do . . . you know I'm here, don't you? I'm always here."

A lump formed in Finn's throat. He cleared it away, forcing himself to nod as casually as he could. "I know. Thanks, Papa. I . . ."

His voice died in his throat. He'd run out of truths he was willing to give—all that remained were lies, crowding at the tip of his tongue, waiting eagerly to be let out.

"Thanks," he said instead, lamely. "I should get back to bed. Busy day coming up."

Ramses's smile was knowing, sad. "Aren't they all?"

A soft, wicked chuckle echoed in Finn's mind. *Oh, you have no idea.*

CHAPTER 63

SOREN

Adriata agreed to Soren's terms.

It had taken an apology, and an attempt at honesty that left her flustered and hot in the face, but with Kallias and Finn backing her up—and Jericho, albeit more reluctantly—Adriata had agreed to invite Nyx to negotiations. Only negotiations, no promise of peace yet. But she could work with that much.

Still, anxiety danced a continuous jig up and down every muscle for the next few days, so much so that she kept finding herself lying awake and staring at the ceiling, counting the distant chimes of various hallway clocks to add up how many hours of sleep she was losing.

Gods, this was ridiculous. She wasn't a prisoner, she could go wherever she liked, and the only way she was getting a wink of sleep tonight was with Elias next to her.

Shivering, she thrust herself out of bed, every hair standing on end as the chilly near-dawn air caught her in a dew-heavy embrace. She snatched up the plush robe she'd slung over her bedframe the night before, biting back a swell of unease.

She was beginning to lose her tolerance to the cold . . . another piece of her, taken by Atlas. How much of Nyx would be left by the time she was able to go home?

Sloughing off those exhaustion-tinged thoughts, she wrapped herself in the robe, nuzzling her chin into its collar as she padded out into the hall, woolen socks rasping gently against the floor. Every wall hung in the eerie shades of in-between, not quite night, not quite morning—a muddling of grays that tricked her tired mind into thinking there were monsters lurking just out of sight.

She hated mornings. Elias tried his best to coax her into the rosy little world of an early bird, telling her there was nothing more beautiful than the sight of the sun rising over the mountains. She'd informed him that she preferred sunsets and left it at that. In fact, if she could have slept till noon every day, if she'd been the sort of princess to devote her life to laziness and sitting pretty on a throne, she would never have given the sunrise another thought.

Her battlemate wasn't free, but he had been moved to a room, at least . . . Finn's way of apologizing, she guessed. Elias was still under lock and key, still guarded day and night, but at least he had a bed.

Maybe it would slow down the fever that had started to take him in the past few days, maybe it wouldn't. But this was his best chance to make it until Nyx sent back word if they were accepting the invitation to negotiate.

New nerves skittered down her neck, but she rubbed fiercely at the tingling skin, cracking the kink out of her spine as she snatched up a blanket from a basket of fresh laundry placed in front of someone else's room, tossing it over her shoulder like a training towel. Somehow, since the fever had started to worsen, Elias had started getting cold at night . . . his one blanket wasn't enough.

She was nearly to the stairway to the floor where Elias was being kept, trailing her fingers along the wall as she went, when a voice reached her ears— louder than usual, pitched frantic and frustrated, yet soft-edged—like the mumbling Elias did in his sleep.

Frowning, she slowed her pace, cocking her head toward the sound—it was back the other way, and even though every instinct told her to leave it—that she didn't want to know what was making Jericho so upset—her feet turned back toward her sister's office.

The door was shut, but light glimmered beneath the crack at the bottom—a halo of gold, like Jericho had lit candles within. It certainly smelled like it—the air was choked with the spice of incense, and for a moment Soren wondered if she should even be breathing it.

Jericho's voice looped like snowflakes caught in a twirl of wind, anger blackening the edges, and Soren pressed her ear against the wood, the cold wood aching against the shell of her ear.

"I have asked you for so little and given so much," said Jericho, "I have given and given and given, and I don't . . . I don't know what else you want. I—" She broke off, then started again, louder, angrier: "We tried that already! You know it didn't . . . sure, okay, let's try again. I'm sure it'll go much better than the first time, that nosebleed didn't stop for five *hours*."

That didn't sound like any prayers Soren had ever heard—Elias was never anything less than reverent with his goddess, coming to her each time like he was apologizing for even daring to exist. Elias's humility was a virtue, one so many—including her—lacked, but it made her sad to see him bent so low before anyone. Even a goddess.

Jericho didn't sound humble in the least. She sounded ready to storm the gates of the gods to get whatever it was she was after, and though Soren was far from pious, it still lined her spine with cold dread.

If there was one thing Elias had drilled into her head, it was that people should not challenge the gods. Question them, rage at them, weep to them, yes—but never challenge. To challenge the gods was to lose and lose greatly.

She tried to press her ear closer, to hear more as Jericho's voice dropped, but her shoulder pushed into the door, and the tattletale wood creaked so loudly that even Soren jumped, a curse nearly flying off her tongue before she snatched it back.

Jericho went silent within, and Soren barely had time to stumble back to a clearly-not-eavesdropping distance before the door swung open, her sister standing in the doorway sporting a scowl and pollen-stained hands, her eyes bruised with sleeplessness and her hair tied up in a messy knot.

"How long have you been out here?" she demanded by way of greeting.

Soren scowled back, pressing her nail into her arm to stave off her nerves and bring her focus back. "Not long. You didn't hear me knock?"

Jericho blinked at her, pink lips softening from scowl to frown. "Oh. I . . . I guess not. Sorry. I was praying."

"Didn't sound like praying to me. Anima pissing you off?"

Jericho hesitated. "I don't only pray to Anima," she said. "I find when you have a great need, it's best to appeal to any god or goddess who will listen. Sometimes one will take pity on you where the others won't. Did you need something?"

A trace of red glimmered in one of Jericho's nostrils—she wiped it away, but not before Soren caught the streak of blood on the back of her sister's hand.

"Jericho," she began, but Jericho shook her head, the shadow of desperation dulling those pale green eyes.

"Don't," she whispered. "Please, Soleil. I don't want to talk about it. Not today."

"Is this really about your prayers? Jer, if you're in some kind of trouble . . ."

"It's not me. It's Vaughn," Jericho said, tears budding in her exhausted eyes. She rubbed them away with both her hands, pressing her palms flat against her eyes for a moment. "Nothing's helping anymore, he can't seem to stay well, I don't . . . gods, Soleil, I've given everything I have to give and it's not enough."

A lump hardened in her throat like she'd swallowed a rock. "I know how that feels."

"At least you had hope. At least you still do." Jericho's breath came out in the broken shards of a sigh, and her knee buckled—Soren had to catch her, her calloused palms rasping against Jericho's elbows, and Jericho simply . . . broke.

She crumpled forward into Soren's arms, her face buried in her shoulder, and though she made no sound, Soren's shoulder grew wet and warm—tears soaking into her sweater, tears of a grief so deep and hollow that it had stolen the voice from Jericho's throat.

Soren didn't care for Jericho's grief, but Soleil ached with her, and together they lowered themselves to the floor, holding Jericho the entire way, until sister and sister were kneeling together in the hallway, rendered gray and grieving in the pre-dawn light.

"I knew from the beginning he wasn't mine to keep," Jericho whispered into Soren's shoulder. "But I always thought . . . you know, when someone tells you they're dying, you get that it's happening, but it just never . . . it never feels real. It never feels like it's actually going to happen, you keep waiting for the miracle, you keep rewriting the story in your head, and by the time you realize there isn't one coming—"

"It's too late," Soren whispered. "And you're not ready. You're never ready."

Jericho shook her head, a hollow laugh cracking off her tongue like a salt-laced whip. "Never. I've been losing him for twelve years and it's still not long enough."

Twelve years. Gods, what Soren would give for twelve years to lose Elias. Maybe it wouldn't be enough, but at least it would be more.

"Hey," she said softly, and Jericho raised her head, eyes red-rimmed, sticky tears trailing paths down her pale cheeks. "It's not over yet. We'll find a way to save him—to save both of them. Because we promised, and we don't break promises."

Jericho swallowed so hard her throat bobbed. "What if I can't keep this one?"

Soren held her gaze. "You can. Whatever it takes, we save them. And if we can't . . . then you'll still have us. Me and Kal and Finn. We're still here."

Maybe it was true, maybe it wasn't. But it was what Jericho needed to hear, and just then, that seemed more important than the truth.

And maybe Soren needed to believe it a little bit too.

CHAPTER 64

KALLIAS

The night before the end, Kallias Atlas dreamed of snow.

Rarely seen in Atlas and rarer still in his mind, ice-cotton flakes danced and whirled, settling heavy on his lashes and shoulders as he wandered the empty streets of his city. Every breath billowed in pale whorls before dissipating into the piercingly cold air, his lungs crackling in pain with every breath.

He may as well have been wandering the streets naked for all he shivered, for how gods-damned *cold* he was. Ice tipped his fingers, blackening them, killing them, and it was spreading, clawing its way up his bare arms and across his chest, his neck, over his mouth like a muzzle—

And when he tried to lunge out of his bed, shaking and beaded all over with cold sweat, he woke to his hands frozen to his sheets, and a voice echoing in his head . . . a voice like thunder and skyfire and the last defiant shout of a captain sinking beneath the waves with his ship.

He could not remember what that name that voice gave him, but he knew it was not his own.

Fear sank cold-tipped claws into his heart. And as he wrapped himself in a thick cardigan and made his way into the hall to pace, that cold did not abate.

FINN

The night before the end, Finnick Atlas dreamed of unholy things. Bones that told secrets and jokes that made the moon blush pink and people who walked between worlds on the edge of a mirror.

"Do you see what's coming, Trickster Prince?"

He did. He did.

Soleil stood in her room before a gilded mirror, her back to him. Her hair was too long, her back too straight, her head tilted in a strange way. Two skeletons flanked her, each with one fleshless hand resting on her shoulders,

"Soleil," he said. She didn't turn. "Soleil!"

"That's not my name."

He watched the skeletons warily for any threatening move toward his sister, slowly inching his fingers toward the dagger tucked in his waistband. "Fine. Soren, then."

She laughed—a delicate, giggling thing that raised the hairs on the back of his neck.

That wasn't her laugh.

"Not that one, either," she said, starting to turn, to face him. He caught a glimpse of gold, unnatural, otherworldly—

And then the image flipped, and he was no longer staring at the mirror, he was *in* the mirror, and the girl before him was fractured into hundreds of girls, *thousands* of girls with candy-floss eyes and gap-tooth grins and a laugh like a prophecy of doom.

His vision was tinted with pink. Everywhere he looked, everything he saw was coated in magic. His eyes settled on one of the skeletons—or at least, what started as a skeleton. As he watched, pink glimmers swirled around it, creating muscle and skin, creating hair and eyes, reconstructing the body for him until he saw a young man, dressed in a wetsuit, blue-eyed and smiling.

When he blinked, it all crumbled away. That smile turning ghastly, the eyes melting away until the sockets were hollow again.

"Hello again, trickster," said thousands of girls with one voice, one girl with thousands of faces. "Let me help you."

When she raised her hands, there was a round mirror nestled in each of her palms, reflecting his own face back at him. And when she reached through the mirror and clapped her palms against his temples, those mirrors *stuck*.

The sound hit him first—a hissing, a noise like searing meat, like water dropped on a fire.

Then the pain.

Burning wasn't the word. Freezing wasn't right either. His skin felt like it was curling away from the mirrors—like the glass had been made from something godly, like mortality shied from its touch. Volcanic and glacial. Terrible and tempting.

He wanted her to stop. He never wanted her to stop. He might have been screaming.

The girl pressed in, and pressed deeper, until he was sure the glass was going through his skin, through his skull, all the way to the center of his brain—

And there, pain became power.

An altar covered in dying flowers. Soleil screaming. Breaking bone. Saltwater tears. Death in every place he looked.

The pain sharpened, became focused, became a branding iron. And when he opened his eyes, mouth open in a silent scream—

He found himself back in his room. Awake . . . but not in his bed.

When he opened his eyes, his own reflection blinked back at him from the mirror hung on his wall, his hands clinging to the frame like it was all that was keeping him standing.

Later that morning, when one of the palacefolk asked him about the shattered glass in his room, he told them he'd tripped. And he did not give the girl with a thousand faces even one more of his thoughts.

ELIAS

The night before the end, Elias Loch stopped breathing twice.

The first time was when Soren slipped into his room, sleep-rumpled and wrapped in a thick robe, exhaustion stamping her eyes and a worried tilt to her mouth. Curled up on his side with his one thin blanket stretched taut across his shoulders, chills waging a war with the ravaging heat searing away all sense, he barely managed to mumble a proper "Hello, smartass."

He might have asked her to stay with him. He might have begged her until she crawled onto the bed, wiping at the sweat and tears mingling on his cheeks with blessedly cold fingers, her voice gentler than he'd ever heard it as she whispered to him that she was here, that she wasn't leaving, that they were going to make it through this night together. He might have called her beautiful, or maybe that was part of the nightmare he fell into afterwards, where he told her how he felt and she laughed at him.

Not the way she usually laughed at him, but with mocking. With pity. With a shake of her head that cracked something open in his chest.

The second time was deeper into the night, after waking from yet another nightmare of fire and flickering black feathers and the mournful call of a wake-singer. The second time was when he woke to Soren's head nestled against his chest, his hand tangled in her curls, her arms wrapped tightly around his torso and her leg hooked around his hips . . . like she was trying to hold him there with her strength alone. Like she could weigh his soul down with only her body.

He swallowed hard, his parched throat aching as he delicately untangled his fingers from her curls, pausing every time her snoring stuttered. Once his fingers were free, he carefully traced them over Soren's scarred shoulder. Over her freckled cheek. Her hard-earned crooked nose. The short lashes she always complained about. The one curl that was always a perfect ringlet, no matter how messy the rest got. The weird little mole on the lobe of her ear.

Memorizing every inch of her, memorizing everything he could to take with him when he finally went into Mortem's care.

And when he closed his eyes again, he held his breath. Held it, and prayed silently to Mortem to take him then—to take him here, in this one moment of peace he'd had in days, this moment where Soren was holding him and he could remember his name and the fire-beasts had taken their leave from tormenting him, if only for a little while.

But when morning dawned, Elias Loch was still alive. And when Soren woke and immediately felt for his heartbeat, when she met his gaze and slumped in relief and said "Good morning, jackass" with a quick kiss to his cheek, he tried desperately not to let her see just how much he wished Mortem had granted him that last mercy.

And when she held out the vial Vaughn had left to help manage his symptoms, eyes full of hope, he relented and downed it in a single gulp.

SOREN

The night before the end, the Heir of Atlas did not dream.

Instead, she slept when she could, and listened to Elias's heartbeat when she couldn't—timing every beat, fretting that the pauses between each one were growing longer, counting every second just to reassure herself that he wasn't slipping away while she laid there useless and snoring.

And for the first time in perhaps her entire life, she prayed.

To Anima, whose realm was life, which Elias was losing with every passing moment. To Occassio, whose realm was time, which Elias desperately deserved more of. To Tempest, whose realm was nature, who . . . well, he probably couldn't do much of anything for her, but she prayed anyway, because it was Elias, and he deserved her best effort.

To Mortem, whose realm was death. Whom Elias loved and served and prayed to. Whom she'd always resented, just a little, for the place she held in Elias's heart. Whom she desperately hoped did not love Elias as much as she did, because if Mortem loved him even half as much, there would be no persuading the goddess to leave her battlemate in this realm for much longer.

And finally, lastly, she sent up a vague, half-formed prayer to the fifth god, the one she could never remember and Elias never talked about, the one whose realm she didn't know and didn't care to know. But as long as she was following Jericho's advice, she might as well follow it as far as she could go.

In the morning, she prayed to each of them for Nyx to finally send back word, for them to agree to the peace talks, for this war to finally be over.

So when the alarm bells of Atlas suddenly clanged through the world, shaking the very bones of the palace, it felt like the gods were throwing her five divine middle fingers.

She'd barely thrown herself out of Elias's bed when Kallias cast open the door to his room, wild-haired and grim-faced, and said: "Undead. Climbing the walls, breaking the gate. There's already some in the palace."

Soren's heart sank. Soleil's lit with fury.

She saw it in his face, what he thought, what he meant.

She'd asked for an answer from Nyx. She should have specified which one.

CHAPTER 65

FINN

"**K**al!"

Screaming. Bells. The floor shook beneath him with the force of hundreds of people running for shelter, their shrieks blending together into a cacophony that threatened to burst his eardrums as he sprinted barefoot in the opposite direction, fighting the current of fleeing palacefolk to get to Kal's room. Some folks were running to hide; some were grabbing vases and frames, breaking the heads off brooms, determined gleams in their eyes and intent clear in their white-knuckled grips on their makeshift weapons.

The message had spread fast after the first bell: undead climbing the palace gate. Killing the guards. Killing anyone who got in their way. And when those bodies fell, they soon rose again—an army that added to their numbers with every kill they made.

Port Atlas was under attack.

"Kallias!" Finn shouted, but his voice was lost in the din. "Kal—"

Someone slammed hard into his shoulder, and pain exploded in his knee as he went down hard, rippling through his leg, through his bones, through his head—

A temple filled with life soaked through with death. Blood spilled on holy stones, Soleil's face stained with tears and rage and a grief that would consume her, consume all of them, burn the world to ash—

Hands gripped his shoulders and tugged him to his feet, pushing him back against the wall, away from stampeding feet. He blinked at Soleil, whose face and fluffy pajamas were speckled with blackish gore. Her hair was frizzy and puffed out like a frightened cat.

"You look pissed," he said by way of greeting.

"Oh, I am well past *pissed.*" Her lips were pursed in a tight bud, eyes flashing in rage. She stuck one leg out toward him, showing off her gore-soaked socks. "This is the *second pair of socks* they've ruined."

"Priorities," Finn managed, but gods, his head was spinning. He leaned into the wall, squeezing his eyes shut, trying to force away the pink haze encroaching on his world. "How bad is it?"

"They're all over the fourth floor," said Soleil, glancing over her shoulder at Elias, who must have taken the tonic he'd offered. The Nyxian zealot was standing straight, eyes bright and jaw clenched. Stronger, clearly, though he was still favoring his injured arm. "Alia made it out, but I don't know about anyone else."

Finn shook his head, tossing Elias his black Artemisian daggers and his prayer beads. The Nyxian caught them with a nod of thanks, not even bothering to ask how Finn had acquired them. "You three were the only ones up there. My parents didn't want to risk more bodies with what they think Elias can do. Where's Kal?"

"He was right behind us, I don't—"

"Over here!" Kallias elbowed his way out of the throng, still in his own pajamas, a cut bleeding across his jaw, blood flowing freely down his neck. Another gash above his eyebrow wept blood into his left eye. "The guard that made it back said they're through the front gate. All around the city."

"Mama and Papa?" Finn asked, his stomach dropping.

Kallias's throat bobbed. "They went into the city early this morning for a walk. No one's seen them come back."

The four of them exchanged looks, stealing time they didn't have, listening to the world descending into chaos beyond and inside their walls.

Finn was the first to open his mouth, but Soleil beat him to it, looking at Elias with a look so bleak Finn's chest pinched. "Elias, is this us?"

Elias blinked at her incredulously. "You're not actually asking if I—"

"No, no, I know it's not you. But is this *us*? Nyx? We're the only Mortem-worshipping kingdom with a reason to attack, we're the only ones who might—"

"Wait, wait," Elias interrupted, that furrow between his brows easing, the hurt softening into confusion . . . relief. "You think it's us because we worship Mortem?"

Soren blinked. "Well . . . yeah?"

Elias shook his head, gripping her shoulder in one hand, his beads in the other. "Soren, necromancy isn't one of Mortem's magics. It's one of Anima's."

CHAPTER 66

ELIAS

"You didn't think that *maybe,* just *maybe* it might have been a good gods-damned idea to tell me that a little bit sooner, *jackass?*"

Okay, so his battlemate was pissed. Rightly so. But to be fair, he'd been busy with *other* things, like her forgetting his gods-damned name, and playing the part of Atlas guard, and dying of an incurable poison.

They ran down the hall toward the foyer together, Finn and Kallias clearing the path ahead, his arm around Soren's waist, pushing her along while the stumbling steps and raucous screams of the dead chased them. "When did I ever have time to tell you that?"

She ducked under his arm and pressed her back to his, cutting the head from a skeleton that lunged for him. "Oh, I don't know, *every gods-damned day?*"

"You never asked—duck!" He whipped around as she obeyed, snagging a vase from a nearby column and chucking it at a body still wearing sagging bits of skin. He tugged her back up and pushed her forward until she started running, and he forced himself to keep pace, even though his body felt ready to collapse in its own pile of bones and flesh. Even with the medicine Finn had offered, every fragment of him was weak, quivering like a broken bridge about to give out, close to plunging him into the abyss below. *Just a bit longer. Just a bit longer.* "You never asked, and you always get all spaced out when I talk about religion—"

"I think I could have stayed awake for this one, thanks!"

"Don't shout at me."

"I'm not shouting!" she shouted. "Gods, Elias, I—so it can't be Nyx then! It can't be us."

"I *know*," he said—then quickly *regretted* saying, because the glare she threw his way practically stabbed into his brain. "Soren, I didn't realize you didn't know. I couldn't defend Nyx to Kallias without looking suspicious, and I *tried* to tell him it wasn't Mortem's magic after the first attack, but you two were so busy with Finn . . ."

Soren dug the heels of her hands into her eyes, pausing for a moment, squeezing them so tightly shut her entire forehead contorted. The princes continued to ford their way forward, not realizing they'd stopped. Slowly, Soren took in a breath. "You're right. I remember. Fine. We'll call it even. You're *sure* it's not Mortem's?"

Elias shook his head. "It's a common assumption for people who don't worship her or study her magic, but death can't create life. Mortem can prevent death or cause it, but she can't reverse it. Only Anima can do that."

Soren's gaze darted briefly to her swiftly moving brothers before she jammed herself into a deep closet full of mops and brooms and other cleaning supplies, tugging him after her as shambling footsteps echoed down the hall, more undead approaching. Her eyes were wide, her chest heaving, but her expression was calm, determined. She kicked the door shut, her fist clenched in his shirt, sweat beading the crown of her forehead already. "So if it's not Nyx, then who is it?"

"Arborius worships Anima," Elias croaked, bracing one hand on the wall behind her and the other on the door to hold it shut. He cast his mind back through the years, trying to dredge up his studies as a boy, trying to remember anything he could. Teachings on necromancy had been rare even then, and he'd only been allowed to read them at all because he'd wormed his way into being

Priestess Kenna's favorite. "But I don't know what motive they'd have to attack Atlas, or specifically target *you*. Who stands to gain if you went back to Nyx?"

Soren shrugged helplessly. "The attacks didn't start until after the ball. Until then, I was still planning on going home. Still am," she added quickly, when Elias's heart lurched so hard he was certain his chest jerked with it. "But things changed then. It . . . it might have looked like I was planning to stay here. So whoever it is, they were probably there."

Elias rubbed his eyes. There was so little to go on, so few things he could remember. "Necromancy is an extremely rare presentation for Anima's magic. The most common is healing. Sometimes more powerful gods-blessed have biomancy *and* healing, like Jericho, but other magics can't exist where necromancy is . . ."

Text swam before his eyes, blurry remnants of the books he'd pored over as a boy. *Necromancers can conceal their magic well, but there are signs no one can hide. It is a greedy, hungry magic, feeding on the remnants of life in the bodies its wielder animates—or, if one goes too long without practicing, it sinks its teeth into the wielder's bones. It feeds on life by seeking out decay, and if the magic cannot find it, the magic will create it.*

The wielders of this magic are especially dangerous, because if they don't use their magic frequently, they become desperate with craving. Desperate enough to seek out death. Desperate enough to cause it.

Because of this constant hunger, necromancers are naturally attracted to the dead and the dying. They can be found in hospitals and infirmaries just as often as graveyards and battlefields, and many take up the profession of physician or healer to keep themselves hidden. In a place where death is bound to happen eventually, any extra bodies often go unnoticed.

Necromancy, it should be noted, is illegal to practice in most kingdoms. It is a magic nearly extinct.

"It's an addictive magic," Elias croaked. "And if a wielder fights it, the magic turns on them and begins stealing the life from them instead. It makes them ill . . . if they don't use it often enough to regain their strength, it can kill them."

Soren stopped breathing. Her fingers loosened, falling away from his shirt. "It makes them sick. How sick?"

"Very. Though using their magic can bring their strength back, if only temporarily."

Soren's eyes came up to his—aghast, horrified. Maybe even grieved. "We need to find—Elias!"

Her eyes darted behind him as the door shoved in, pushing them both forward, and skeleton fingers tickled the periphery of Elias's vision just before

Soren snatched his daggers from his belt and sliced clean through it. She kicked past him, shoving the door shut with her foot, snapping the skeleton's arm.

In near-complete darkness once again, Elias gaped at her.

"Artemisian steel," she said with a heart-eating grin. "I told you. Through bone, like butter."

"Give those back."

"Finders keepers."

"I didn't lose them, you took them!"

Before she could argue, another scream came down the hall, fury and terror pitching it higher than normal, like the clang of blade against blade.

"Kallias." Soren pressed one of the daggers into his hands, keeping the other. "Let's go. Stay with me."

"Like you'd give me any other choice," he said, and she rewarded him with a smile that made his heart thrill. Then, side by side, they burst back into chaos.

CHAPTER 67

FINN

The dead had overrun the halls of his palace, and the future had overrun the halls of his mind.

Even as he and Kallias forced their way through the absolutely wrecked courtyard, nothing seemed right or real. Plants had been torn up, trees scratched from skeletons crawling up them. The grass was utterly wrecked, bloody mud left behind in its place.

There was no room for masks here. He couldn't play useless or lazy or *anything*, because today, that game would get him killed.

So when an undead came for Kallias, jaw unhinged and a ragged shriek rattling in its throat, Finn ducked and rolled, slicing its legs clean off. The undead collapsed, but immediately began clawing through the mud toward Finn, its fingers breaking and re-knitting with every movement. He scrabbled away, running backwards until his back collided with his brother's, until they were surrounded by the undead.

This wasn't just an attack. This was an ambush.

Where this . . . this *army* had come from, he had no idea, but they were . . . everywhere. Everywhere.

He could hear them . . . see them. Not just with his eyes, but with his mind. In the courtyard, in the city, outside the city limits.

Finn gripped Kallias's sleeve. "We need to split up."

Kallias shook his head, panting and bleeding from several places. "I'm not leaving you."

"Kal, trust me, I will be fine," Finn snarled—throwing away every mask and trick, letting his brother see the cunning, the anger, everything. He put his hand on Kal's bearded cheek for a moment. "Get to Mama and Papa. I'll find Jericho and Vaughn."

Kallias stared at him, torn, his hand flexing uneasily on his blade. He swallowed hard, something softening in his eyes. "Finn, I'm . . . I just—"

"Yeah, I love you too, dumbass," he said. "Now go!"

Kallias snarled a curse, but did as he said, spinning his sword in a quick arc before dashing off toward their parents' usual route. "Don't die!" he called back over his shoulder.

"I'll do my best!"

Just as Kallias disappeared, Soleil practically barreled into him, her hair stinging his face as it whipped around from the force of her skid. Her eyes were wide with dread, her teeth gritted, blood dribbling down her temple. "Where's Vaughn?"

"What?"

"Where is *Vaughn*?"

"I don't know! He was too sick to move yesterday, I haven't seen him. We looked in his room and he wasn't there, so my guess is the temple? He usually goes to pray in the morning if he's feeling well enough."

Soleil shoved his head down, lunging one arm over him. Brackish wetness spilled over his back, cold and slimy, and a head landed at his feet, the eye sockets empty. "Sorry. It was going to eat your neck. Which way to the temple?"

A temple filled with life soaked through with death. Blood spilled on holy stones, Soleil's face stained with tears and rage and a grief that would consume her, consume all of them, burn the world to ash—

"You can't go there." He had no clue why he was so sure, but he knew. Something horrible was waiting within those walls. "Soleil—"

Her eyes widened half a second too late, and this time, Occassio didn't see fit to warn him what was coming. Something stiff and clammy clutched at his ankle, the cold ground jarring his joints as something tugged his leg out from beneath him, and when he twisted—

His stomach lurched in earnest as his eyes met empty sockets, sickening magic glowing within them, the grinning skull tightening its grip on his ankles. The stiff remains of what had once been fingers slid over his leg, clutching at his tunic, digging sharpened bones into his skin and tearing through.

Elias was the one who moved this time, kicking the dead thing off so hard that its spine snapped before he crouched to slice its neck from its body.

Finn dug his hands into the mud and pushed, but pulsing pain shot up the muscles of his leg—the same leg he'd landed on earlier. There was no way he'd be able to put his whole weight on it.

Soleil glanced at him. Glanced up at Elias, whose expression was already falling, his lips already poised to say *no*, but Soleil said it anyway. "Get him somewhere safe and meet me back here."

"Soren—"

"Elias, please."

He held her gaze for a long moment. Two. "Right back here?"

"Not one inch from this spot."

Finn would have argued. But his vision chose that moment to dip back into dark dreams, tinted with a soft, almost taunting tint of pink.

CHAPTER 68

KALLIAS

As the city descended into pandemonium, a whirlwind of bone and blood and *screaming*, Kallias stumbled over broken cobblestones that gleamed like chipped teeth in the weak morning sun, desperately searching for his parents' faces in the crowd. He caught sight of someone familiar out of the corner of his eye: Maleko, one of the Kilgrave twins, roaring with the fury of an Tallisian mountain cat while swinging a hammer at an undead with sagging skin. Behind him lay Makani, half-buried beneath the wreckage of their ironwork stand, his arm bent at an awkward angle and his face slack in unconsciousness.

Gods, Kallias hoped it was unconsciousness.

He crossed the distance so quickly the soles of his feet barely brushed the stones, his heart lurching so hard it struck a rod of nausea deep into his belly when a harsh smell grated against his nostrils.

Smoke. Somewhere, something was burning.

No. No, no, no, gods no, not again—

Even as his mind fell into blind panic, he found himself beside Makani's limp body, tossing debris aside and tugging him free as Maleko finished off his undead and wheeled, shouted in relief when he realized who held his brother. "Prince Kallias! Thank the gods, when we heard they were in the palace—"

"No time!" Kallias hauled Makani up and pushed him into his brother's arms, bracing him until Maleko had a proper hold. "Have you seen the King and Queen?"

"They passed by the stand just a bit ago. I think they were heading for Sandi's place, your mother was talking about looking at tiaras—"

Kallias clapped a hand to the man's shoulder briefly, his mind already plotting a course to the jewelry shop. "Thank you. Get Makani and yourself somewhere safe, will you?"

Maleko's eyes blazed. "I'm not huddling in a hole while Nyxian filth tear apart my city!"

He didn't have time to explain what Elias had revealed in the palace—hadn't even had time to comprehend it himself, really—so he let that comment lie. But he said, "The more of us that fall, the more bodies they have on their side. I'm ordering you to keep yourself out of *their* ranks, understood?"

Maleko held his gaze. Kallias didn't blink.

Then the ironworker bowed—far more deeply than paying deference to a prince required. "At your command, Highness."

At his nod, they went their separate ways—Maleko dragging his brother along with murmured reassurances, Kallias sprinting toward the route his parents had taken, adrenaline tearing furrows in his veins every time smoke billowed or flame flickered in the periphery of his vision.

Not again not again not again not again

There—a flicker of scarlet in a shop window. Not flame this time.

Boots skidding on the street, Kallias collided with the door, slamming his shoulder into it, once, twice, again. It didn't budge—barred shut, probably. Of course a jeweler's door would be better fortified than others.

"Mama!" he shouted above the din of battle, drawing his dagger and slamming the pommel against the wood in their practiced signal—two quick taps, four slower ones. "Mama, it's Kallias! Let me in!"

For three heartbeats he waited, ear pressed to the door, blood pounding in his head and dripping into his eye. He wiped it away, rubbing it off on his pants, wishing to the gods that he'd had time to throw on even a little armor. But no, this was what his people would get: a sleepclothes-clad prince with his hair tied in a messy knot, his sword belt tied haphazardly around his hips, only a thin layer of cloth between him and these undead's awful teeth and sharp-tipped hands.

That thought had barely come and gone when the door finally gave beneath him—just an inch, an emerald-green eye peering through the crack. "Kallias?"

All Kallias's breath blew out of him in a rush, and he did a quick spin to show his mother he wasn't a dead man walking. "It's me, Mama. Is Papa with you?"

Her eyes flickered past him, surveying the damage beyond the door with a practiced eye. She cursed quietly, opening the door just enough for him to slide through. "No. He heard screaming and *ran* out there, I told him not to go but that gods-damned man never listens—where are your sisters? Finn?"

Oh, thank the gods you're okay, Kallias! he thought to himself, taking a single moment to taste bitterness. Then he shook it off. "Soleil's with her battlemate— he's not the necromancer," he added when his mother's eyes flew open, her mouth poised to shout. "He was asleep when the attack started. I saw him myself. Finn's looking for Jericho and Vaughn right now."

His mother cursed again, softer, sinking back with her spine pressed against the wall of the abandoned jewelry shop. She folded her hands by her mouth, chewing anxiously at a chipped nail, her dirt-smudged cheeks so pale he almost worried she would faint. Her face was stoic, queenly, but her chest heaved in a staggered way that reminded him of Jericho's bouts of terror when Vaughn's illness was at its worst. A shudder shook her body. "They're all out there. All of them. Oh, gods, *all* of them . . ."

Kallias swallowed, lifting his arms toward her—then letting them drop. What could he say, what could he do to comfort her? Their family was scattered. Their city was burning. He was wearing sleepclothes and someone else's boots, for Anima's sake. He was hardly a pillar of confidence. "Tell me what you need me to do."

Adriata stared at the wall, shaking hands pressed to her lips, eyes foggy with panic. Her breath came in stuttering, shrill gasps. "I can't—I can't do it again, I won't *do this again*—"

"Mama!" He gripped her shoulders, then her face, forcing her to look at him. "Mama, we are all going to make it out of this, you understand me? All of us. But I need you to tell me what to do."

Her face crumpled. Her hands wrapped around his wrists for a moment, as if anchoring herself. She gazed at him for a long moment, teeth worrying her lip.

"Your father," she said finally, and he tried not to let his breath out in a rush. "Find your father, then the rest of them. He's closest, it shouldn't take long."

"And you?"

"The palace is overrun?" At his nod, she shook her head, releasing his wrists. "Then I'm safer here than anywhere else. They haven't come by this street yet."

It seemed a shaky reassurance at best, but he couldn't argue. "I'll bring Papa back here, then I'll get the others. I promise, Mama."

Her eyes glimmered as she looked at him—he couldn't tell if it was tears or doubt that glazed her eyes. But she said, "I know you will."

He wished he could believe her.

"I promise," he said again, more fiercely, pushing every bit of conviction he carried in his chest into those two words. He turned away and reached for the door.

"Kallias!" His mother's voice shook, and when he turned, he found her gazing at him with trembling lips and an outstretched hand.

"Be careful," she said. "Come home. No matter what, you *come home.*"

His fingers flexed around the hilt of his dagger, and he swallowed the lump that tried to form in his throat. All he could offer was a nod.

Then he burst back into the fray.

He found his father in the last place he would've expected: the lower city.

He rarely ventured here, mostly because he preferred not being pickpocketed. Every city had shady corners, and while Port Atlas had fewer than others, it wasn't entirely exempt. This was where those who dealt in darker things liked to linger, stealing from travelers who didn't know any better or overconfident nobles who thought they could venture into the gambling houses here and emerge even richer for it.

Despite his unfamiliarity with this part of the city, it wasn't difficult to find his father; Ramses was defending the entrance to a dead-end alley, teeth bared in a feral snarl that reminded Kallias *far* too much of Soleil's, a borrowed sword in his hand and wildfire in his eyes. Undead crowded around the alley mouth—every shambling body Ramses struck down, another was there to take its place, a many-headed creature of bone and fester moving as one entity. Behind Ramses were several children, some nearly Soleil's age, some younger than she was when she'd been taken, all staring at the King with awestruck faces and fearful eyes. Some cried. Others shouted encouragements. All looked as though they hadn't seen a hearty meal in days, let alone a bath.

Kallias unsheathed his sword and plowed in, swinging blow after blow, not stopping to strategize or ponder or even breathe. He jammed his sword through ribcages, crushing them with a quick lever of his blade; he severed necks and legs, removing heads and feet, sending bodies crumpling to the dirty street with every movement. There was no time to stop and watch to see if they reformed and stood back up, no time to see which blows truly downed them—he had to reach his father. That was the only thought in his head, all sound drowned out but the roaring of wind in his ears, the snap of cold on his tongue.

Somewhere in the middle, he and his father met, both wild-eyed and breathing hard. They whirled, placing their backs to each other, splitting the final enemies between them.

When he drove his blade into the last fleshy puppet, sinking it up to the hilt with a sickening *squelch,* it took a moment to tug the blade back out. And when he looked down at that last adversary, he found ice creeping over the edges of the necrotic hole, frost growing from nothing on the tattered vest the dead thing wore.

Not now. Not now.

He hastily kicked the body over to hide the ice just as Ramses turned toward him. "Good timing," he wheezed before turning to the children, straightening his back, assuming the bearing of a king once more. "Get back to your caregivers or places of sanctuary, and hurry. The streets aren't safe."

With nods and a chorus of murmured *thank yous,* the children obeyed, filtering past while tossing up looks of admiration and gratitude to both Ramses and Kallias. One little girl stopped to give them each a hug around their legs, and Ramses chuckled quietly, rumpling her hair as she scampered away. Only when they were out of sight did the King huddle over again, grimacing, cradling his ribs. "Where are the others?"

"Mama's right where you left her. She sent me to find you." Kallias quickly braced his father, cursing quietly. "You're hurt?"

"One of those damned things threw a brick. Broke a rib or two." Ramses groaned through his teeth as they started to limp back toward the main district of the city. "And the others?"

"Finn's finding Jer and Vaughn. Soleil . . . I don't know."

His father's face contorted in terror, his hand tightening on Kallias's shoulder. "You don't know where she is?"

"Last I saw, she was in the palace with her battlemate . . ." How long ago had that been? Minutes? Hours?

Ramses gripped his shirt so hard it nearly tore, dragging him to a stop, forcing him to face him. "Kallias, these things have been coming for *her*. Nobody knows where she *is*?"

Kallias's stomach dropped as he caught up to his father's line of thinking. "Her battlemate won't let them hurt her."

"Her dying battlemate that's spent the past week in a sickbed? I'm not sure he'll have much say in the matter!" Ramses pushed off of him, staggering with a hiss of pain, already trying to draw his sword again. "I'm going to find her."

Kallias swallowed down his panic, lurching forward to block his father's way. "You can't fight."

"My *daughter* is being hunted out there, I can do anything I damn well please!" Ramses tried to push past, but barked in agony, one knee giving out beneath him, the tip of his sword scraping the cobblestones as he used it to catch himself.

Kallias carefully helped him stand again, bracing a hand on the back of his father's neck, giving him a quick shake to get his attention. "Papa. You *can't fight*."

Ramses's chest heaved as he met Kallias's gaze, the bone-deep terror in his eyes stabbing Kallias through the heart. "Someone has to find her."

Yes. Someone did.

Just as someone had before . . . a boy of fifteen who'd realized his baby sister was trapped in a burning palace and had run in to save her without a second thought. That boy had thought he could do it. He'd thought he, out of all the people on that beach, was the one who could get in and out fast enough to save her life.

That boy had been wrong. What hope was there that the man would be any different?

He steeled himself against doubt, against memory, and held his father's gaze. "I'll find her. I will—after I get you back to Mama. She's worried sick, you know how she gets."

Something about that broke through the thoughtless panic in Ramses's eyes, his shoulders slumping. "But she's safe?"

"As safe as she can be. But she needs you. I'll find Soleil—*Papa*," he repeated when Ramses's gaze started to drift, to look past him to the suffering city. "I *will find her*. I swear on my life."

Ramses finally blew out a shaking breath, bumping brows with him. "I know you will," he rasped. "I trust you."

Kallias squeezed his eyes shut. *Gods, I hope you're right to.*

CHAPTER 69

SOREN

Darkness pulsed hot and strange against the back of Soren's eyes. Voices bounced off the inside of her skull like shouts off a mountainside, waking up bruises she hadn't known were there. Everything sounded tinny and wrong, like she'd jammed pieces of straw into her ears.

Swallowing a groan, she lifted her head, trying to blink the crooked world into focus. White nothingness shuddered into a pale stone room with soaring ceilings, columns covered in creeping vines framing what appeared to be steps leading to a raw wood altar covered in piles of bones. Indoor garden boxes were planted at the base of every first step, sporting colorful flowers and fragrant herbs. A statue of a woman stood in the center of the altar, spouts of water pouring from her hands and mouth, gathering in a small pool at her feet. More creeping vines curled around her neck, her wrists, her head—a noose, a pair of manacles, a crown.

Anima. This must be the temple Elias told her about.

The temple. That was it.

Just as Finn had guessed, she'd spotted Vaughn ducking into the temple as the dead tore apart the city.

"Hey, necromancer!" The shout burst from her lips without thought, and when he whipped around to face her, eyes wide, hands shaking . . .

Everything had gone very dark.

Soren had been dumped in a heap at the bottom of the stairs, her nose inches away from one of the garden boxes. And standing before the wooden altar, arguing with Vaughn, eyes wide with confusion and anger . . .

"Jericho, don't." The words came out like sludge, syrupy with the heavy slur of a concussion. "Get away from him."

Jericho had clearly been through Infera already, her dress torn and bloodied, her hair cut to her collarbone on one side like she'd barely avoided a blow to the neck. Green light haloed her head and her shaking hands, bits and pieces of greenery poking through the dirt-smeared patches on her dress. Vaughn didn't look much better, his clothes hanging loose on his once-muscled frame, his collarbone protruding painfully from his broad shoulders, his eyes glowing pure white-green, the pupil and iris gone, cracks of light webbing down his cheekbones as if the magic was straining against his skin. The air somehow smelled of new growth *and* pungent decay, and both threatened to flip Soren's stomach.

When she spoke, both of them turned to look at her—Vaughn's expression tortured, Jericho's stricken.

"Soleil," she croaked, hurrying down the steps, reaching to cradle her face. "Soleil, it's okay. Vaughn's—"

"He's the necromancer." Gods, this was going to break Jericho, but better broken than dead. She gripped Jericho's shoulders to hold her in place, glaring over them at Vaughn, who folded his hands beneath his arms, pinning them against his sides. "Jericho, it's him, I saw him."

Jericho swallowed, gently extricating herself from Soren's grip. "Soleil . . ."

"No, no," Soren choked, already hearing the denial coming and reaching out again as if she could shake sense into her sister with her hands alone. There wasn't time to indulge Jericho's blind belief in her husband. "Jericho, you have to believe me—"

"No, it's not that. Soleil, I know what he is. I've always known."

Silence. In the temple, in her head, in her chest where her heart had clean stopped.

"What." The word was not a word, but a dare to prove Soren was so right and so wrong about so many things.

"I've always known," Jericho said again. "Before you died, even."

Soren looked at her, looked at Vaughn. Tried to wrestle her tongue into saying the words, tried to untangle her thoughts from the knot Jericho had just tied, but there was no way to make it make *sense*. "You're *helping* him?"

"I'm *saving* him." A plea rounded Jericho's eyes—for forgiveness or understanding, Soren didn't know, and didn't particularly care. She would give neither. "Without the war, without all the death, his magic turns on him. The life that lingers in the long-dead isn't enough for it to feed on. It needs the newly dead, the dying . . ."

"Did you start the fire." The first question of *far* too many swarming at the tip of her tongue. "Jericho, did you start the war on *purpose?*"

"No! No, that really was Nyx. But it did help him. Just before the fire, he was . . ." Her eyes drifted to Vaughn, who kept his own on the floor. Some haunted memory shone in both of their gazes, a ghost of desperation and grief, the shadow of days filled with suffering. "He was dying. We didn't make it to the dance that night because he had such a bad fit he couldn't stand. But so many people died that night, and then the war . . . gods, it practically healed him. A gift from Anima. Like she heard our prayers."

There was a ringing in Soren's ears that she couldn't shake, horror mounting slowly in her chest. "So my death was a *gift* to you?"

"No," Jericho snapped, a heartbreak Soren couldn't trust gleaming in her eyes. "*Never.* But you were gone regardless, and everything was wrecked, and I wasn't about to resent something good coming from all that ruin. But then Nyx's king died, and the queen offered peace, and when Mama said she was going to take it . . . I panicked."

"You killed them," she breathed. "The escort Enna sent. You said they attacked you, but they didn't, did they? You killed all of them."

Jericho's stare hardened from rose petals to stone, no longer apologizing for anything. "If the war ends, Vaughn dies. I wouldn't let it happen then, and I won't let it happen now. I thought if you went back there it would all go back to the way it was, but then you started remembering, and when you started talking peace . . ."

Gods, this was worse than even she could have come up with, worse than any story she'd been told of Atlas's ruthlessness. These attacks, this war . . . not born of vengeance, after all. No, all this bloodshed, all the pyres burned and mourning braids plaited, all the empty seats at dinner tables and crowded barstools in taverns . . . those had been born of love.

Worst of all, she knew that look in Jericho's eyes because she'd worn it herself.

There was no changing the mind of someone fighting that hard for a life not their own. And if it was only an enemy that faced her now, Soren would have rallied her strength and ended this with a swift strike and a vicious grin. Soren would have seen the desperation beneath the unhealthy shine in Jericho's eyes. Soren would have seen there was no saving her now.

But Soleil saw her sister. Her protective, silly sister who used to brush her hair and build sandcastles all day long until the tide came and swept them away. The sister who took her down to the beach at dawn to hunt for the prettiest shells, telling stories of mermaids who would brave the beach at high tide just to touch the shore one time, who left those shells behind as presents. The sister who'd sworn up and down that if Soleil held those shells to her ears at just the right time, when the moon was full and the ocean was calm, she could hear those mermaids singing.

Jericho had always been a creature of love and magic and taking a story too far. And maybe it made her a sentimental fool, but Soleil owed her one chance. One chance to say "The End" and come back to herself.

"Jericho," Soren rasped, "our people are dying. More are going to die if you keep this up. None of this is worth the life of one man."

Vaughn let out a shaky breath, and she guessed from that sound alone that none of this was entirely his choice. That he wasn't fighting for his own sake.

She thought of Elias, on his knees behind prison bars, tired eyes begging her to listen. *Let me go.*

Her heart clenched. She shook it off. "You swore oaths to our people, too," she added—louder, sharper, putting as much emphasis on *our* as she could. "Are you really all right with breaking them?"

Jericho didn't even blink. "I can live without my people. But not without him."

Fury without equal crested like a tidal wave, but Soren tamed it, keeping her voice low and even. Like speaking to a wounded animal. "And what about Nyx? What about the harm you've done to them?"

"What are you talking about? Soleil, these people—they don't belong to you! They don't love you! They *stole you* from us! They ruined *everything.*" Jericho spat the word through clenched teeth, fervent hatred catching fire in her eyes like a spark thrown on dry tinder. She stood up and paced away, throwing the words over her shoulder like arrows, counting off grievances on her shaking fingers: "After they killed you, Mama fell apart. Papa fell apart. Kallias and Finn shut themselves away—do you know how long it took to get them to leave their rooms after the fire? Do you know how long it took for any of them to smile again? No matter how many times I reminded them that *I* was still here, that *we* survived, that we still had a *family*, it didn't matter! Without Vaughn, I would've been *alone*."

The crack in Jericho's voice resonated through the temple, the aftershocks wavering in Soren's ears. The flowers in the garden boxes leaped, twisting together in chaotic bursts, like even Jericho's magic was off-kilter.

Soren's skin felt numb. Her ears felt dull. Everything felt hollow, like a knock against a false wall, like if she tapped on her skin it would echo back empty.

The war wasn't her fault, or Enna's, or Adriata's. It was *Jericho's*.

"Help me," Jericho whispered, her torn, sullied skirt streaking blood and dirt across the beautiful altar as she knelt before Soren again, grabbing her hands, holding them tight against her chest. "They broke us, they broke you, they broke *everything*. We're your family . . . me, Vaughn, the boys. Choose us. Help me save him. Us before all, remember?"

Soren squeezed her eyes shut, her hands clasped in her sister's, the love she'd once felt for her siblings and Vaughn and Atlas beating an anthem in her chest, swelling to the point of pain, a memory that lived in her heart instead of her mind.

This fight between the two halves of her heart would never be simple, but this choice was.

"I didn't make that vow," she said. "And I won't keep it."

Jericho's face fell. She dropped Soren's hands like they burned. "Soleil—"

The sound of a door creaking open broke through the still air of the temple like a battering ram, freezing them all in place.

"Vaughn," Jericho commanded, tearful princess snapping into ruthless queen in a blink. Vaughn met her gaze with a pleading look, reluctance clear in every line of his form, every twitch of his muscles, but Jericho held firm. "Hold her. I'll be back."

Soren lunged to her feet as the princess melted into the shadows at the edges of the temple, but something snagged around her ankles, rooting her to the floor. She looked down to find skeleton hands gripping her ankles.

Before anything more than the barest shred of scream could make it out of her throat, Vaughn made an erratic gesture, green smoke swirling from his fingertips and twisting around his piles of *supplies*. Finger bones clattered free from their pile and tumbled through the air, clicking into place around her mouth—a muzzle.

She dug her fingertips beneath the edges of the bones and tugged. Nothing. Vaughn's terrible power held them like they were plated with steel. She couldn't move them, couldn't break them, couldn't warn whoever was coming that—

"Soren?"

Oh, gods, *no.*

Why, why, *why* did he pick now to be the foolish one of the two of them? Why did he have to take those vows so *seriously?* If there was ever a place he shouldn't have chased her . . .

Soren clamped down on the instinct to scream, and for the first time, she prayed in earnest to Mortem. She prayed that the goddess didn't love Elias enough to wish him an early death. Prayed that the goddess *did* love him enough to have him turn around and leave this temple without ever catching a glimpse of her.

She held her breath. Refused to call. Because if he heard her, if he saw her, he wouldn't leave without her.

Luck—that was what she prayed for.

But Mortem was not the goddess of luck. She was the goddess of inevitability, and when Elias crossed the threshold into the temple, limping and bloody and breathing too hard, Soren knew whichever god held luck in their hands was no friend of theirs.

Elias scanned the temple, eyes widening when he found her, and she knew that at first he didn't truly take in the bones holding her in place, or the magic glowing in Vaughn's eyes, or the terror in hers. She knew he didn't realize that Jericho was lurking in the shadows behind him, armed with the Artemisian dagger she'd plucked from Soren's belt, the void-dark blade eating all light as it cut past the veil of shadow.

She knew, because when he saw her, he smiled. A smile that made her remember the admission she'd whispered to Jira that first night Elias joined the barracks, after she'd dubbed him *Elias the Pious* and had earned herself a long talk from her barracks captain.

He's beautiful, she'd said, as casually as she could manage with her blood still thrilling through her veins from the loathing look he'd shot her way. *The kind of beautiful that hurts.*

That smile hurt worse than anything else he'd ever given her. And he was still smiling when Jericho wrapped her arms around him from behind, like one lover surprising another, and shoved that blade deep into his stomach.

A noise escaped his throat—a startled sound, heartbreakingly innocent, a clotted hiccup.

There was no word for the feeling that swept through Soren at that *sound*. No word for the raw, untamed scream that utterly wrecked the back of her throat, shoving uselessly at the barrier of bone and joint clasped around her mouth.

Elias did not scream, or cry, or roar. He looked down slowly, his fingertips feeling around the edge of the blade, his brows furrowing when he found the wound beneath. Like he was confused by it. Like he couldn't feel it.

No. No, no, no no no—

Not him. Not now. Not this, damn it, *not like this—*

His eyes came back up to hers, and shock softened to sweetness. Like a *sorry*. Like a *goodbye*.

No.

Her heart gave out at the same time Elias's knees did, at the same time Vaughn shouted, "Jericho, what are you *doing?*"

"Getting what we need," Jericho replied, colder than every Nyxian blizzard Soren had ever been lost in. She bent down and jerked the blade from Elias's stomach, wiping his blood carelessly on her dress as she walked back to Vaughn. "Let her go to him."

Vaughn was staring at her open-mouthed, the color fading from his eyes, the power fading from his fingers. As his hands fell, limp and splayed like a worshipper's, the bones clattered away from Soren's ankles and mouth.

She should have ended it there. She should have remembered *inevitability* and not *luck*, should have known that all she could do for Elias now was to keep their final vow: to kill Jericho as Vaughn killed her, or the other way around, and race Elias to Infera after saving their people. Together or not at all.

But Soren wasn't smart, she was scared, and before the bones even clattered against the altar, she was running for her battlemate.

She hit the floor so hard next to him that her knees tore open against the stone, gasps ripping from throat as she gathered him against her chest, wrapping her arms around him from behind and stanching his wound with her twined hands. Blood gushed between her fingers, *so much blood*, and the growl of frustration that sobbed out of her jostled them both. Elias's head lolled against her neck, and her heart lurched at the shallow gasps he was breathing, at the rattle deep in his throat that she still remembered from a few weeks ago, a few lifetimes ago, when an Atlas blade ripped her open and ruined everything.

She knew what it meant when people breathed like that.

"You just had to follow me, didn't you, jackass?" she ground out, pushing harder against his wound, gritting her teeth against the quiver that tried to break her voice. "*I'm* supposed to be the one who doesn't do as they're told!"

A tired, barely-there laugh huffed against her neck. "What can I say? You're a bad influence, smartass."

"Don't you dare die. If you die on me, I'm going to kill you."

"Soren," he murmured, reverently, like a prayer. And that was all.

"I mean it, jackass!" Fear broke past her guard, a crack wedging itself between *jack* and *ass*. She lowered his head into her lap so she could cradle his face, looking into his eyes, baring her teeth in her best snarl, the one she saved for when she *really* needed to win a fight. "You're *not* leaving me like this."

The wan, loving smile on his face threatened to break her, and he reached up, touching his fingertips to her brows—pushing them apart. Smoothing out the furrow between them. "Don't look so worried. You'll get wrinkles."

The laugh that dragged from her throat sounded less like a laugh and more like a sob, and she caught his hand, squeezing it tight. Her eyes found Jericho, who was simply staring, arms crossed, jaw set in determination.

"Heal him." Not a request.

"No," said Jericho. "Not unless you promise to let the war continue. It's an easy deal, Soleil: you keep yours if I keep mine."

Soren blinked at her. Blinked down at Elias, who was still struggling to breathe, still looking at her. Inches away from entering the realm of his goddess, and he only looked at her.

"Do not give her one gods-damned thing," he rasped.

Pain clutched her chest, and she gathered him closer, digging the heels of her hands against the blood that just wouldn't stop coming. "What have I said about telling me what to do—"

"I wouldn't change a minute," he interrupted—pain and peace dulling his eyes, peace that she hated *so gods-damned much*, peace that only the faithful dying ever wore. He clasped her hand in his, his palm sticky and hot with fever and blood. "Do you hear me? Not one gods-damned minute I had with you. Not even the annoying ones. I'm dying anyway, and if you give up one inch of ground to her for my sake, I will *never* forgive you for it."

Gods, why did he have to be so good? Worse, why did he have to be *right?*

I can live without my people. But not without him.

Elias before all.

She gagged on the next sob, nausea thinning her blood as she held him, as her mind raced for any way out of this. Any way to save him.

It would be so easy. Nyx, Atlas, both of them were so used to war by now. Who knew if she could even convince Atlas to come back to the negotiating table a second time, anyway. No one would ever know she'd made this choice, that she'd sold their lives and their chance at peace for one man's sake, that she'd spent hundreds of lives to extend the one most precious to her by a few more weeks.

One person is never worth the lives of hundreds. No matter how much you love them. No matter how much you need them.

Her own words, self-righteous and foolish, knocked at the door of her conscience. Reminded her of how much she'd believed them when she'd thrown them out, careless and ignorant, not knowing exactly what it was that she was saying.

It was a much harder thing to believe now, when the one person being given up was *her person.*

But that didn't change the fact that she'd been right. She couldn't choose him over her people—either of her peoples. Because that would make her the same as Jericho, and maybe she could have lived with that, but Elias couldn't. If she made this choice, him over all, he would be ashamed of her.

And that she could not endure.

"No," she said to Jericho, burying her face in Elias's hair, whispering into it like it would hide this choice from the world. Like it could cushion her heart and keep it from breaking. "I can't."

"Jericho," Vaughn said, and she heard his footsteps echo on the steps, like he'd come closer. "Stop. Heal him. This has gone far enough."

"She'll change her mind," Jericho argued. "Trust me. She'll do anything to save him."

"Jericho, he's *dying anyway*, this is just cruel—"

Their arguing faded to nothing as Elias stirred beneath her again. Tried to raise his head. "Soren." His breath brushed her curls, warming her face, and she lifted her head, blinking tears back as she found his eyes. "Thank you. Th-thank you for all of it."

"Don't," she choked. "Don't, jackass. You're going to be fine. Just . . . find your anchor."

He stared at her, so heartbreakingly gentle, the corner of his mouth lifting.

"Will you stop looking at me like that?" she snapped, fiercely wiping hot tears from her cheeks. "I mean it! Find your anchor."

He held her gaze. Never blinked, even when his breath wheezed painfully, even when coughs shook his broken body, poison and wound working in tandem. "I'm sixteen. It's Winter Fair, and I'm falling in love with you for the first time."

Her heart crashed down, breaking every rib, cracking every brave and strong thing inside her.

Oh, she'd been wrong. So gods-damned wrong. She could have endured his shame. Mortem damn him, she could have endured his *hate*, so long as he was there to do the hating.

This . . . she couldn't endure *this*.

"I'm seventeen," he continued, reaching up and brushing away her tears, "and we're playing truth or dare. Jakob decides to be a dick, and suddenly I'm kissing you in the barracks closet. You taste like whiskey and you're calling me names every time you get a breath. I'm falling in love with you for the second time."

"Elias." A sob, a plea, an answer to a question he wasn't asking.

"I'm eighteen." His back arched beneath her hands as he fought for his next breath, face crumpled in sheer determination—like he was clinging on just for this, just to get these words out. He groaned in pain, fumbling for her hand, squeezing so tightly her bones threatened to break. But he kept talking, and talking, like he'd been *saving* these things, like he'd had them holed up inside him for years.

"I'm eighteen, and Kaia is dead, and everything is horrible," he said, letting go of her only to shakily run his finger down the bridge of her crooked nose. "You bait me until I break your nose. We fight until we're both too tired to throw a punch, and you look at me and you say, 'If you're done being a jackass, I'll show you where the best snacks are hidden in the kitchen.' I say, 'If you're done being a smartass, I'm in.' I fall in love with you for the third time while you're tossing cookies in my mouth. You're making me laugh when I never thought I would do that again."

"Don't do this now," she sobbed, catching his hand again and holding it against her chest, using her other hand to thumb a tear from his cheek. "Don't you dare do this like you're saying goodbye, jackass—"

"I'm twenty, and I'm dancing with you in an Atlas ballroom. I have the ring you liked so much in my pocket." Another laugh, quiet and breathless and *dying*, and he shook his head in a helpless way that killed her. "I'm sweating like a sinner at Mortem's altar. And all I can think is *I am so embarrassingly in love with you, Soren*

Andromeda Nyx, and I have been for four years, and I don't know how to say it, but gods, I'm going to try."

A half-hysterical laugh jolted out of her throat. "And of course you picked *now* instead, you dramatic—"

"I was going to ask you to marry me."

Just another whisper, just another confession that echoed softly off the temple walls. A breath that stole hers right out of her chest, that broke every rib, that shattered every excuse and *he doesn't mean it that way* and *pull yourself together, Soren* she'd ever whispered to herself in the dead of night, listening to him snore against her neck with his arm wrapped around her waist and his face buried in her hair.

Every secret wish she'd tossed recklessly to the stars, every almost-confession that had played hopscotch on her tongue when she'd had too much whiskey warming her belly, every time she'd nearly grabbed him by the shoulders and asked if he would just *kiss me already, gods, Elias*—all things she'd buried in her cowardice. And now it was too *late*.

"I would have said yes," she whispered. "No matter how you asked."

Elias didn't answer. He could only breathe, gentle gasps that grew shallower with every second, the light in his eyes fading away so fast her heart lurched in panic.

"Heal him," she said again, looking to Jericho, interrupting her and Vaughn's argument. "Please. Jericho, *please*, I can't . . . I can't."

Jericho looked at her, eyes dark, mouth twisted in a regretful knot. But still she said, "Promise to let the war go on."

With every lurch of Elias's chest, with every step he took away from her and toward his goddess, her resolve dwindled. Morality had a funny way of disappearing when it came to love, when it came to death.

Elias closed his eyes briefly—not briefly enough, so long that a panicky noise broke free from her lips before she could stop it. "Fine!" she snarled, spitting out her sin like a cherry pit. "Fine. I-I'll do it. I'll do it, whatever you want, just—"

"No."

Elias opened his eyes again—only halfway. And he didn't look at her anymore . . . he looked to Vaughn instead.

"If it's too late to save yours, help me save mine. Help me let go."

Panic gripped her chest in a fist so tight that she almost stopped breathing. "Elias, don't look at him, look at me—"

Vaughn's face crumpled. "Elias . . ."

"Please." Elias never broke his gaze, his own filled with some secret meaning she couldn't read. "Help me save her."

Soren put her hands on his face, trying to turn his eyes back to her. "Elias, what are you—?"

Vaughn raised his hand toward Elias, curled it into a fist, and *yanked*.

Crack.

A noise that echoed through the temple, through the air, through Soren's hands on Elias's head. A noise she *felt*, something breaking inside Elias, something shearing just beneath his skin. A noise so loud and sharp and awful that she *knew*.

Even before the light in Elias's eyes sputtered out, even before he went limp in her arms, even before she felt the unnatural way his neck bent against her hands . . . she knew.

She blinked down at him. "Elias."

Nothing. His empty eyes stared listlessly to the side. A trickle of blood ran down his chin, staining that scar she'd given him.

Her breath started coming faster, harsher, and she tightened her hold on him, bracing the break in his neck—as if putting him back together would somehow fix this. Her chest caved in as she screamed his name once more, shattering into a strangled roar: "No, no *no no no* don't you *dare*, jackass!"

But there was no *smartass*, no laugh, no roll of his eyes. He did not wake, did not breathe, did not come back to her.

Jericho's scream drowned everything else, and Soren's eyes drifted upward just in time to see her whirl on Vaughn, eyes wild, chest heaving, half-cleaved hair swinging with her movement. "What are you *doing*? He was our leverage, she was about to—"

"Jericho, enough!" Vaughn roared—the loudest she'd ever heard him speak, a battle cry that clashed with his wife's. His face was twisted in a mask of grief, of *rage* . . . of exhaustion. "*Enough*."

In the silence that followed, all she could hear was her own heartbeat, thumping a loud and mocking rhythm. All she could feel was the horrifying stillness in the crook of Elias's neck.

It wasn't fair, how some bones were more important than others. It wasn't fair that some couldn't heal once broken.

She thought there might be a bone in her like that, too. One that had snapped in tandem with Elias's neck, promising a pain without end, a wound without cure.

Vaughn lunged forward and gripped Jericho's shoulders, desperation burning in his eyes. "Love, please, enough. Look at me. Where does this end, where do we draw the line? At killing our people? At torturing a dying boy? This wasn't worth it at the start, and it's not worth it now! *Let me go!*"

Jericho blinked at him like she was genuinely confused. Her brows came together in a knot. "There is no line. There is *nothing* I won't do to save you."

Husband and wife, necromancer and healer, gazed at each other over bone and altar and corpse.

"It's too late anyway," Vaughn rasped. "The boy is gone. At least let her leave. Or are you going to kill your sister too? Is *that* a line you feel ready to cross?"

Jericho curled her fists, starting to turn to Soren. Then she stopped, hard, jerking back like she'd run into a wall. She turned her head to look over her shoulder, her brows furrowing again, a distant look dulling her eyes, a curtain of fog falling over sparkling green.

"What?" she asked distractedly.

"I said, is that—?"

Jericho held one finger toward her husband. "Not you."

Soren blinked dully at them, tugging Elias closer, running her hand absently through his hair. He liked to be fussed over when he was hurt—he always pretended he didn't, but he did. One time she'd brought him soup when he was sick and he hadn't stopped grinning for *days* after.

She'd spent so much time fighting with him. So much time fighting to stay, to find that antidote, being so gods-damned selfish. She should have spent every spare second wrestling with him and baking cookies and letting him keep his own socks for once. She should have taken him home when he asked the first time.

He wanted to *marry* her.

"You can't be serious," Jericho said to the air, turning incredulous eyes on Soren. "*Her?*"

Soren met her gaze, lips curling back. "Who are you talking to?"

Jericho didn't answer, merely studied her with a tilt to her head that sent chills through her, even this numb. "She won't agree. And we don't have any . . . oh. Will she?" A beat. "There has to be someone else. Not her . . . my family, we can't lose her again—"

"*Who* are you talking to?" Soren shrieked, so loudly that it hurt her own head.

Jericho opened her mouth, then stiffened. Her eyes rolled. Her shoulders jerked once, twice, like she was having some kind of fit—

Then she went very, very still.

A quiet chuckle rumbled from her chest—deeper, not at all like her, something that chilled Soren right to her core. Something edged with madness and chaos and the manic energy of a mob. Jericho's head lowered, and when she met Soren's eyes, hers gleamed gold.

"Hello, princess," purred a voice that was not Jericho's, her delicate tones layered with something much darker. "Let's talk business."

She tightened her hold on Elias instinctively. "What gods-cursed thing are you?"

"Watch it," said the thing inside Jericho, smirking with her mouth, a teeth-baring that promised dreadful things to follow. "Don't use our names in vain."

Adrenaline stood every hair on end, and Soren swallowed down some base, animal terror that rose inside her. Those golden eyes watched her throat bob with amusement, ancient and cruel, nothing kind in them.

Nothing *human*.

"Which one are you?" Soren rasped.

Elias was dead. Atlas was overrun with unholy creatures. At this point, the idea of talking to a god seemed laughably believable . . . though, that could have been the shock talking.

"My name is Tenebrae," said the thing inside Jericho. "God of Chaos. You probably haven't heard of me, heathen. It's been a long time since I was worshipped."

He was right—she'd never heard of *Tenebrae*. But she knew there *was* a fifth god, and more than that, she knew Elias was terrified to even talk about him. Like speaking of him would invite him in.

"I'm not really the religious type," Soren croaked. "Get to the point."

Using Jericho's body, the thing—the *god*—knelt beside her and Elias, gently trailing his fingers down Elias's back. "Interesting tattoos," he said, even though Elias's shirt covered them. "One of my sister's, then. Mortem always did have a weakness for holy men."

"Don't *touch him*. Just tell me what you *want*."

Tenebrae stood back up, wrinkling his nose. "Impatience isn't a good trait in royalty, you know. All right, love, listen closely—you see this?" He extended Jericho's arms, moving in a slow circle as if in demonstration, cocking one of her eyebrows. "Now, Jericho's only let me in for the moment . . . she's not quite ready to make it a permanent arrangement, we have a deal of our own to finish out first. But here's the thing. I'm in the market for a host—not for myself, you're not my sort. But my little sister Anima . . . part of our deal with Jericho is that she provides a host for her. Jericho offered herself, of course, but she's not meant for Anima. Turns out she's better suited to me. The princes are the same story, they're built all wrong for her. You, however . . . from what we can see, you might just do."

Soren blinked. Shock or no shock, that was too much.

"Okay," she said, burying her face in her blood-soaked hands, taking in several breaths that felt too fast, too tainted with fear. "Wake up, Soren. Wake *up*."

"Cute," said Tenebrae. "But I'm afraid that's not going to help you now, love."

"You're asking me to be a host. For a *goddess*."

Tenebrae sighed, letting Jericho's head loll back. "I don't have the patience for this. You handle it, pretty."

With a jerk of her head and a strangled gasp, Jericho's eyes snapped back to green. She stumbled, and Vaughn caught her, the pain in his eyes utterly indescribable.

"Anima needs a host," Jericho rasped, as if her voice was hoarse with overuse. "And if you let her in, she'll bring Elias back."

The pain howling in Soren's chest went dull, briefly. "What?"

"You heard me." Jericho clutched Vaughn's arm, pale and trembling, grief and determination waging a war of their own in her eyes. "You let Anima have your body, and Elias gets to go home."

Soren raised burning eyes to the two traitors standing above the altar, scorching them in a pyre of her own making, wishing with all her heart that she could make it real.

"No. Bring him back." Not a plea anymore. A raw command that would accept nothing less than obedience, immediate and thorough. A general's voice— a queen's. "He doesn't deserve this, just bring him *back*."

Jericho had the gods-damned nerve to look sorrowful, wearing it as prettily as she did anything else, two delicate tears sparkling on her cheeks like diamonds. Soren wanted to claw them from her face. "I can't, not now. He's too far gone. My magic can't reach that far."

Damn it. Damn it, damn it, damn it.

Knees aching against the tile floor, chest numb, hands shaking, Soren cradled Elias's head in her lap. No matter how she shook him, no matter how many times she smoothed out his brow and told him to get back here before she kicked his ass in a way he'd never recover from, no matter how many times she whispered *I love you, I love you, come back, come back, jackass* . . . he did not wake up.

No matter what it meant for her, she'd promised him that she would get him home.

She bent her head, pressing her lips to his cold forehead, willing warmth back into him—willing him to blink awake, to smile at her, to call her gullible for thinking he was really dead. One last try. One last prayer.

But his skin only made her lips cold.

"You kept your vows," she whispered to him—gods, could her voice even reach him anymore? "Now let me keep mine."

She didn't care if he never forgave her. She would never forgive *herself* if she left him here, if she let this awful place be his deathbed when she could still save him.

She'd thought she could endure it—for her peoples, her kingdoms, she'd thought she could. But the moment Elias's neck had snapped beneath her hands, that had all changed.

Jericho was still waiting when Soren looked up, gritting her teeth so hard they hurt, grief steeling her bones with strength.

Breathe in. Hold it. Breathe out.

Control what you can.

She couldn't change her failures. But she could change this—she could control this.

Elias over herself.

"Will it hurt?" she asked.

Jericho's face crumpled, like she actually cared, and she shook her head—opened her mouth to say more, than closed it again.

"And she can really bring him back? Not as a necromanced body, but him?"

Jericho nodded again. "My magic's not strong enoug, but hers will be. We'll get him home safely. You have my word—and Tenebrae's."

Jericho's word was worth nothing to her now, and the god's even less, but anything was better than this. "Then do it. And hurry. I don't want to look at your face another second, you Mortem-cursed traitor."

Jericho descended the altar, her head lowered, her chin quivering. "Soleil, I swear, I didn't want this—"

"You don't get to call me that," Soren said flatly. "Get this over with."

Jericho's hands circled the crown of her head, palms covering her eyes. Sudden terror jolted through her, and she instinctively grabbed for Elias's hand.

Wait, she wanted to say. *Wait, I'm not ready, I'm not ready.*

She wanted to say goodbye to the others. To Kallias and Finn and her parents and her sisters and Enna.

But for her battlemate, her jackass, her Elias . . .

"You have to say it out loud," said Jericho. "You have to willingly allow her in."

"I give my consent," Soren whispered, clinging to Elias like he could somehow shield her. Like even in death, he could give her strength, give her courage. "Let her in."

Emerald light exploded in Soren's eyes, and it wasn't pain that flooded her body, wasn't agony that swept all that she had been, all that she was, all she would ever be away into oblivion.

Not pain at all, but power.

Not a shot of flavored liquor, but a bottle. Not a storm, but a hurricane. Not magic, but divinity.

Soren and Soleil and Atlas and Nyx and war and peace . . . they all wilted away, curling up into nothing, dormant seeds that would never come to life again, replaced by the weight of deific passion. By wildness and growing things and new life where there had once been none.

She smelled lavender and herbs. Gardens and leaf piles. Seasonings and medicines.

An exultant, ecstatic laugh warbled through her head like birdsong, and something stretched inside her mind—a long, leisurely sensation, like a cat arching its back, like a snake uncurling, like a bird spreading its wings.

It started in her head. Then went lower, and further, spreading through every vein, every muscle, every hair and nail and bone . . .

Real and not real. Here and not here. Alive and dead.

She couldn't remember her name.

But the boy beneath her hands, the wolf, the worshipper, the pious, the jackass . . .

He was her home and her heart. There was no part of her that did not know him. No power in this world that could render him a stranger.

So the girl who'd once been Soren wrapped her hands around that divinity, that power, and tugged—ignoring the startled cry that burst from her own mouth, in a voice that was barely hers, with a fear that did not belong to her. She took that power and held it, clutched it until it burned, until every inch of her sang with intoxication, with godhood, with glory.

She wrapped her arms around the boy, burying her face against his empty chest, pouring all that power into him, giving him the last of her, giving him all that she could—

And the last thing she felt, before the thing that was *not* Soren stole all breath and thought and being, was his neck knitting back together.

His heart lurching back to life.

CHAPTER 70

ELIAS

Death smelled like home. Like cinnamon pastries and rose-and-peach shampoo and new yarn.

Soren.

As darkness flooded in, claiming him with gentle hands and stealing away all pain . . . Soren was there with him. Holding him close. Walking him home.

He was not afraid, not with her at his back. And when golden light teased the edges of his consciousness, when he began to remember how it felt to be warm . . . he knew where he was going.

Mortem had not forgotten him, after all.

But just as he began to reach out, to grasp for that bud of light and warmth, the promise of peace singing over his soul . . . something caught his other hand.

Tugged him back, back toward dark and pain and cold, back toward blades and blood and Soren's tears soaking into his hair.

No. He wrenched himself away from it, soul-deep yearning twisting him forward, hands stretched out toward his goddess's welcome. *Let me go.*

Not now, Elias Loch. You aren't finished yet.

The voice that answered him was not his battlemate's, but it was familiar. Grave as a funeral and soft as velvet, uncompromising but always gentle. A voice he had sought after all his life . . . a voice he had always known he would hear in death.

But he hadn't guessed that she would be turning him away.

The smell of home turned rank in his nose, rose and peach rotting, yarn soaked in iron-scented blood. For a moment, he smelled herbs, wildflowers, fresh grass . . .

Sunfire burst into supernova inside Elias's chest, something *snapped* back into place in his neck, a pulse of pain radiating across soul and body—

Cold slammed back into his bones. And he knew nothing else after that.

Elias woke up with a headache from Infera and a crick in his neck he couldn't rub out.

His mouth tasted horrific, like he'd taken a bite out of a half-eaten carcass a wolf left behind, and every single inch of him *throbbed*—not with pain, not really, but a sensation not unlike wearing a coat that was too small . . . like his soul fit uncomfortably to his body, like every inch of his insides had been stripped raw. His eyelids were shut so tightly it took him a moment to wander close enough to wakefulness to open them, and even then he had to pry them apart.

Sand-colored walls and Atlas-blue blankets greeted him, the sharp smell of herbs and clean sheets tickling the scent of death from his nose—the infirmary. He'd come here briefly when Kallias gave him the tour of the palace, but he'd never planned on visiting it again. And while it was a welcome change from the dungeon, every movement brought a fresh wave of aches without end, a body bruise that reached from skin to soul.

Gods, what had happened to him?

"Welcome back," greeted Kallias, who was sitting on a stool nearby, looking surprisingly put-together. His hair was wet, like he'd just bathed, and he was wearing training pants and a sleeveless cotton shirt that billowed a bit. He was bruised, sporting a black eye, and stitched in several places on his chest and arms, but he was alive. And sober, which was unexpected.

"Is it over?" Elias asked. Gods, even his voice sounded wrong.

Kallias nodded, but the unhappy tilt to his mouth told Elias he wasn't convinced. "Ended just like the last time—we didn't do anything special, they just stopped attacking. Fell apart and didn't get back up. Jer and Vaughn and I dragged you and Sol . . . Soren back here. You four looked like you got dragged out of Mortem's pit."

That . . . didn't sound right.

He swallowed. "Soren?" He'd never been injured in battle without waking up to her fussing and pretending the whole time that she wasn't. She should have been here insisting he eat something and adjusting his sheets and telling him how useless he was for getting himself hurt.

Unless she was hurt, too.

Kallias's eyes sharpened. "You don't remember?"

Temples and bones and his own knife in his stomach and Vaughn gripping him with magic, tugging, snapping—

Golden light and fire.

"I don't know," he choked. Gods, what little he *thought* he could remember felt like a fever dream, like a nightmare. "Is she okay?"

"She's fine," Kallias said with a shrug, but something was off in it. Something that seemed uncertain, or outright false.

Cold terror bloomed in Elias's gut, but he smothered it. *Stay calm. Breathe. Whatever it is, we will fix it. She's alive, that's all that matters.* "You don't sound sure."

"No, I am, I just . . ." Kallias hesitated. "She's not hurt, not anymore. Jer healed her up. But she's seemed off since you all got back. I thought maybe she was worried about you, but she's just been . . . distant. Dazed, maybe."

There was something coiled up deep inside him, a knot of dread, something that felt like memory, a dark tangle with nothing helpful to offer beyond *something is wrong, wrong, wrong.*

He had to think. Had to remember. Something had happened when he'd run to find Soren, something . . .

A temple. Soren kneeling at the altar, alive but afraid, something pale and strange clamped over her mouth.

Pain—explosive and scalding, burning like fire, even though the steel was cold against his skin, his guts, deeper—

Saying goodbye. Giving his last confession at an altar that did not belong to his goddess.

Something reaching into him, under his flesh, wrapping cold claws around his spine. A crack that echoed through his skull, through the temple, through the world.

Forcing himself up, he groggily pushed off the blanket covering his legs, rubbing the bridge of his nose. The sweat that gathered on his chest and arms cooled as the morning air rushed to greet him, and as he pressed his feet to the floor, tiny pinpricks of pain danced beneath them. Gods, even the soles of his feet hurt.

"Let me see her." If he knew Soren, she was probably just fretting in her own way. Whatever had happened in that temple, it was . . . bad. Worse than bad. But he was here now. "Or am I still a prisoner?"

"No, I handled that," Kallias said, rubbing his black eye with a grimace. "Since you saved Finn's life—thanks for that, by the way—you're free to go home whenever you like. One-way immunity. We won't stop you from crossing the border this time, but if you try it again, your life is forfeit."

Home. He would be allowed to choose his deathbed, after all.

"Pity. There go my plans for a beach sabbatical," he deadpanned, and Kallias actually snorted, a sound that bordered on a laugh. "Thanks."

"Least I could do." Kallias circled his hand over his chest, shuddering. "Really, the very least I can do."

He wasn't wrong, and Elias considered demanding jewels or something just for the fun of it, but dismissed it. Now wasn't the time, and it wouldn't be funny unless Soren was there to witness it, anyway. "What happened to Jericho and Vaughn?" he asked, fingers tightening on the edge of his cot, remembering Vaughn's cracked skin and terrified eyes, Jericho's reckless demands and the merciless edge in her eyes as she wiped his lifeblood on her skirts.

Kallias frowned at him, that black eye squinting nearly closed, leaning back to study Elias at a distance. "They're recovering," he said slowly, as if suspicious of Elias's intentions. "Why do you care?"

Elias blinked at him. Kallias blinked back.

"Kallias," he said, "didn't Soren tell you?"

Kallias's brows knit, and he stood and stepped back like he was dodging a blow. "Tell me what?"

Unease tingled in Elias's fingertips, and he squeezed his hands into fists. Soren should have told them. If she was okay, if she wasn't hurt, she should have *told them* Vaughn and Jericho were behind this.

Out of habit, Elias reached up to rub his injured shoulder—then paused.

Before the temple, his shoulder had burned with Infera-touched fire, crawling sensations shivering up and down his skin, poison gnawing the flesh from his bones and the strength from his limbs. He'd been dying. Truly dying.

Now . . . now there was nothing.

Slowly, half-afraid it was an illusion that would break the moment he pushed it too far, he pressed his fingers over his skin—his *completely intact* skin. Where there had once been nothing but rot in his arm, a hole festering with death and decay . . . his shoulder was whole again. The only reminder it had ever existed was a knot of scarring, a star of dark veins reaching jaggedly outward . . . scars that almost resembled thorny brambles.

No fever. No infection. And when he curled his fingers into a fist, when he lifted that arm up . . .

No pain. No weakness.

Healed.

He was *healed.*

Breath whooshed from his lungs faster than a kick to the gut, and he fell back against the wall behind the cot, running a probing finger over the raised tissue knotted at his shoulder. The skin didn't even tingle when he touched it.

It should have made him joyous—it should have been a miracle. He should have been throwing himself to his knees and worshipping until he lost his voice.

Instead, a horrible feeling wrapped around his gut like a pronged net. Every instinct stood at attention, knowing deep in his core that something was *wrong, wrong, wrong.*

Miracles didn't come for free, not in this day and age. And for one of this magnitude . . . the price that must have been paid . . .

"Take me to Soren," he croaked. "Now."

The palace was wrecked.

Bits of bone were buried in the carpets, blood painted the walls, and there was a hollowness in the eyes of every palace worker that echoed his. But he didn't have time to slow down and take it all in—not with doom riding on his heels, dread clinging to his back like the shadow of a guillotine hanging over his head.

Something horrible had happened, but gods, he didn't know *what.*

So when he and Kallias entered the sibling's dining room and found Soren laughing with Jericho and Vaughn . . . his heels caught on the floor.

He held the frame tight in one hand, supporting himself while he studied her, searching for any sign of injury or magic, trying to understand why she was sitting with *them* after all that had been revealed in the temple.

"Soren?"

Jericho and Vaughn looked to him first—Vaughn with a look of guilt that quickly shuffled itself into a smile, placid and normal. But Elias had only seen eyes that broken on tortured men.

Jericho, however, met him with a grin that seemed too perfect to be real. "We were wondering when you'd be up," she said, but happiness wasn't supposed to sound that tense.

"Go to Infera and rot," he rasped back, and her smile dropped. "What did you do to her?"

"I don't know what you're talking about," Jericho said, enunciating prettily, but her eyes went viper-cold.

He'd thought Finn was the snake that would bite through his boot. He should've paid closer attention to the one with prettier scales.

Soren didn't look up at all, and the expression on her face sent a wave of tension through his whole body. He'd seen that lost look before; that unbelonging had shadowed her after her fit at the ball, when she'd forgotten his name and her own.

"Soren," he repeated, louder.

"Soleil," Jericho prompted after him, and finally his battlemate's eyelids cracked open—not enough for him to see more than the faintest slit of white. She smiled, sort of, barely turning her head in his direction. Like she was *hiding*.

She certainly *looked* fine. There wasn't a scratch on her, not a bruise to be seen, and her cheeks were flushed the same soft pink as her dress. The chiffon skirts stirred gently in the breeze from the open window—not something Soren would normally choose, but not *entirely* out of the realm of possibility. Her hair was clean and tied back in a ponytail—normally she didn't wear it like that, unless she had a head injury that made braids too painful, but there wasn't a mark on her head at all.

Just off enough to make every notch in his spine go stiff.

Worse, there was a strangeness to her smile, an uncertainty to it he'd never seen . . . almost a shyness. And the way she held herself was all soft edges, too, her shoulders curved in, her arms positioned defensively in front of her middle.

"Not going to say hello, smartass?" he asked, with a smile that didn't seem to fit on his face, either. Terror writhed and riled in the pits of him, waiting desperately for that *jackass*, for the taunting grin, for the echo that would tell him she was okay.

Her brow wrinkled, and she flinched slightly—like he'd hurt her feelings, if that was even possible. "That's not very kind," she said, with a light, melodic laugh that sounded *absolutely nothing* like Soren.

When she finally blinked her eyes open, still smiling, green flickered gold.

Elias's stomach dropped to his feet. Through them. All the way into the bedrock beneath the palace.

Priestess Kenna's voice came back to him, a whispered rhyme in the shadows of a stormy night: *If you meet a man with gilded eyes, drop your knee and bow. That's not a man before you, son—a god speaks to you now.*

No.

"If you let Anima have your body, Elias gets to go home," he heard, in a place out of his reach, in a place he'd left behind.

"You kept your vows," Soren whispered in his ear. *"Now let me keep mine."*

"Soren," he breathed. "Soren, tell me you didn't . . . come on, smartass, tell me you didn't."

Soren—*not Soren*—smiled at him again, that small, soft thing that held nothing of her at all. And this time, when she blinked, the gold stayed. Unnatural, terrifying . . . *deific.*

"Okay, really, enough," she laughed, rising with impeccable grace, no slouch to her back, no swagger to her gait. She crossed the room like a ballet dancer, patting his once-wounded shoulder with gentleness that betrayed her. "What did I do to deserve the name-calling?"

Illness swept all feeling from his legs, and it was all he could do to hold himself up. All he could do to stay standing as he stared at this woman, this stranger, this *thing* in his battlemate's body.

There were stories—older than him, older than the priestesses, older than the kingdoms—that told of times when the gods walked the earth.

Tempest, Anima, and Occassio had all been known to take hosts. Even Tenebrae had taken one once or twice, though legends on that careless god were few and far between. Even the bravest of the priestesses were afraid to whisper his name, and no amount of pleading on Elias's part had convinced them to say much more than what he'd already managed to read.

"Tenebrae is an ambitious, ruthless god," they'd said. *"Even his brother and sisters have turned their backs on him. Do not speak of him in your prayers, Elias. It will only anger Mortem."*

Yes, there were legends of people gifted with something just beyond mortality. Of humans born with the strength to bear the weight of godhood on their bones. Some were discovered early and raised as sacrifices, and there were some who sought the gods out and sold themselves in exchange for miracles. But the gods had not stirred that way in *centuries*. Some had even begun to whisper that they were dead.

The Atlas family was rumored to be blessed by Anima. Not just with beauty, but with long lives, with strength . . . and maybe something more.

Elias gazed into those golden eyes and saw nothing of Soren in them.

There was no defeating deity. Not even for his stubborn, smartass battlemate.

But gods, he had to try. He had to *hope*.

He swallowed. Hard. Steeled himself against all grief, all hesitance, all pain. *Mortem, give me strength. Give me discernment.*

"Soren," he whispered. "Give me something. Just one thing to tell me you're there."

"Elias?" Kallias asked from behind him, caution deepening his voice to a growl. Elias ignored him, searching the face in front of him, desperately seeking out *anything* of the woman he knew and loved.

She had to be there. She had to be. If anyone could hold up under a goddess's soul . . . if anyone could fight . . .

She tilted her head, studying him like he was a particularly interesting bug. She laughed a little more sharply, but irritation tinged her eyes. "You're not making sense. Is everything okay?"

"Say my name," he said.

"Elias."

"No, not that one." He got so close that he could smell flowers on her breath, could see the shades of gold layered in her eyes. He hoped she could smell the death on his. "Try again."

She looked to Jericho like she was searching for an answer, and that was all Elias had to see.

Grief would come later. Anger would come later. All of the dark and horrible things tangling themselves permanently between his ribs would come later.

He'd once told Soren a story of souls without rest. How they wandered the world beyond with backs bent by the burdens they carried, clothes torn by winds like talons as they begged Mortem for sanctuary.

But they would find none. No peace, no rest—not until their deaths were avenged.

He owed Soren that much . . . peace for her soul. If that was all he could give her now, he would not fail her.

He held the goddess's gaze. Reached out and framed her face with his hands. Took one last look at his battlemate, memorized her—the clusters of freckles, the crooked bend in her nose, the scars that dappled her in all her reckless glory.

I was going to ask you to marry me, he'd said to her. The last secret he held that she didn't know, the last thing he could give to her.

I would have said yes, she'd sobbed against him, her tears washing the blood from his face.

"I'm sorry," he said softly. "Soren, I'm sorry. Forgive me."

Then he wrapped his hands around her throat.

CHAPTER 71

FINN

Forty-two minutes.

That was how long Kallias could rant without pausing.

Finn stayed quiet while his older brother paced before Elias's cell, where they'd unceremoniously thrown him after he attempted to choke the life from Soleil. Kallias was shouting himself hoarse with dry rage, things like *just how mad are you exactly* and *what in the depths were you thinking* and *you could have killed her, you backstabbing bastard!*

He probably should've been yelling too—after all, Elias had gone mad and tried to murder his sister. Instead, he was slouching against the wall, picking at the grime beneath his fingernails with one of the black daggers he found discarded on the floor of Anima's temple while Kallias roared, and Elias stared at the floor.

By the time he'd gotten to the temple after the battle was over, limping on his barely-healed leg and trying not to panic over the way his visions had suddenly stopped, Elias had been unconscious, and Soleil had seemed disoriented, her eyes rolling like she couldn't get control of them. Kallias and Vaughn had hefted Elias between them, and Jericho had tugged Soleil's arm over her shoulders to support her as they walked out.

One of the daggers had been coated in blood. Elias's shirt had been torn and soaked crimson at the midriff with no wound beneath. And when Finn had grabbed Soleil's face and turned her toward him, her eyes had winked gold in the torchlight.

Just like in his visions.

He didn't know what that meant, but he would bet every coin in his coffers that Elias did. So he stood. And he listened. And he waited.

And when Kallias paused in his threats to hang Elias and feed his body to the sharks, his chest heaving, his lip gnawed red and raw, Finn looked up and met Elias's gaze.

Fear was not an emotion Finn indulged in. A scared man was easily manipulated, and he preferred to be the one doing the intimidating. But the look in Elias's eyes struck terror so deep inside him that he wanted to turn and run.

"You saw through it, didn't you?" Elias rasped. "You can see her eyes."

Finn held his gaze, flexing his jaw, tasting the words before he spat them out. "Soleil's dead, isn't she?"

He'd seen it already, and not in visions. When he'd tried to talk to her after her return, when he'd tried to get the truth of what had happened out of her, she'd lied—and not the way Soleil lied, with bluster worthy of an accomplished card player. She'd avoided his eyes, and laughed too much, too nervously, and changed the subject until he stopped asking.

He didn't know who was behind those wishing-coin eyes, but it *wasn't* his sister.

He'd gotten there too late.

"What? What do you mean, she's dead?" Kallias snapped, his boots squealing as he came to a sudden stop, his head whipping around to pin Finn down with such a severe look that he almost took a step back. "She's fine. I mean, she almost wasn't, since *Eli* over here decided to try and *strangle* her—"

"That's not her." Elias's voice was dull as a river rock, his eyes unfocused, fixed on something only he could see. His fingernail tapped erratically against one of the bars of his cell, the corner of his mouth still dripping blood from Kallias knocking him out. His gaze held no grief, no anger, only a deep, unending emptiness that sent a shiver down Finn's neck. A man with nothing to lose was not a man he messed with. "Jericho tricked her. Promised her my life if she gave up hers to Anima. Now they both have what they want—Jericho gets to have her war, and Anima gets to have a body."

"Anima? The *goddess*? Elias, I don't know what you've been taking for that shoulder, but that's absurd," Kallias scoffed. "And Jericho had nothing to do with this, why would she—?"

"Vaughn's the necromancer," Finn and Elias said together—earning Finn an appalled look from Kallias and a shocked one from Elias.

"You *knew*?" Elias asked.

Finn shrugged, looking away. "Not until after the battle. Wasn't hard to piece together what happened when I saw the bones, the blood . . . how much stronger Vaughn looked." Too bad he'd been too gods-damned late.

Kallias's eyes flickered between him and Elias, pain and disbelief warring over his expression, his hand curling and uncurling around his sword's hilt. "Explain. All of it. Now."

So Elias did, weaving a tale so disturbing that even Finn thought he might be sick. Grief began to pull at his strings, reminding him how easily he had unraveled before, reminding him how easily it could be done again.

He shook it off. He was a boy back then, a boy with nothing sharp to wield. Things were different now. He was dangerous now.

"Anima isn't as good at illusions as Occassio, but any god can manage to hide their eye color. I can see through them because of my tattoos," Elias said. "I don't know why you can, Finn."

"I'm talented," he said.

They didn't laugh. It wasn't funny anyway.

"With Anima in Soren's head, she'll encourage them to end the peace effort," said Elias. "And as long as the war goes on, Vaughn will live."

"And Soleil?" Kallias choked. "How do we get her back?"

Elias didn't look at Kallias. He looked to Finn, the pain on his face immeasurable. Unbearable. Conveying through silence what he could not say in words.

"There is no bringing her back," Finn murmured. "There's only Anima in there now . . . that's why you tried to kill her."

Elias nodded, letting his forehead fall against the cell bars, closing his eyes. "There are a million reasons gods could take hosts, but if Jericho is consorting with Tenebrae, it's not anything benign. I don't know enough about him to have any idea why he and Anima would be in league, or what they're after. All I know is this: if gods are choosing to walk among us again, something big is coming. Something terrible. And we don't want to be fighting a war on top of it."

Kallias rasped his hands down his beard, studying his feet like the answers to everything were written on the laces of his boots. Then, without so much as a goodbye, he turned and walked out the door.

"Where are you going?" Finn called.

"To talk to Mama. To tell her who she really needs to arrest."

"Wait," said Elias, and Kallias turned back to look at him. "There's something you should do first."

CHAPTER 72

KALLIAS

Everything had gone utterly mad, and Kallias was far too sober to handle it. But he couldn't drink this away—wouldn't. Not now that he knew.

He drifted through the halls in a daze, the back of his neck burning, emotions rising and falling like a storm-tossed tide, anger and disbelief and grief and terror converging in a whirlpool that threatened to drown him.

Jericho and Vaughn. Gods, there was no way to make sense of it, no angle that made it seem right, nothing that eased the sting of his sister and brother-in-law having betrayed them all.

Worst of all, though, was the tiny part of him that was *smug.* The tiny part of him that was so gods-damned pleased with itself for being *right* about Jericho that it almost took the edge off the knife in his back.

His mother was seated in her office, which hadn't been touched by the shambling army of corpses. She wore simple pants and a dark gray top, her eyes skimming reports without reading them, the frown lines by her mouth looking deeper than they had the day before. But the shaking, scared mother he'd found in the jewelry shop was gone—all that remained was the stoic queen.

He swallowed. Braced himself. Rubbed the bandage on the back of his neck, where he'd been mad enough to let Elias cut a symbol into his skin—something he claimed would help Kallias see through Anima's illusions, though he had yet to test it. He knocked lightly on the doorframe, and though his mother didn't look up, the tension in her shoulders let him know that she'd heard him.

"May I sit?" he asked.

Adriata merely gestured to the seat in front of her, which Kallias took to mean yes. He sat down, trying not to wince at the pains that the movement woke.

Adriata looked up from her papers, anxiety lighting her eyes brighter than he'd seen in some time. "Are you all right?"

"As all right as I can be," he mumbled, resisting the urge to shield his black eye from her. "Are you?"

Adriata shook her head, lowering her gaze to the papers in front of her once more. "I should have known better. I should never have tried again. But at least Soleil sees them for what they are now. We can move on."

Kallias swallowed down the lump in his throat. Tried to steel the shakes in his hands.

The part with the goddess . . . that was for later, if ever. He still didn't quite believe that himself. But Jericho and Vaughn . . . "Mama, it's not them. It wasn't Nyx who attacked us."

She waved a dismissive hand, mumbling something under her breath before saying, "I know it wasn't Soleil's boy. You don't have to keep pushing that."

"No, not just him. Mama, it's Vaughn."

She snorted, not even bothering to look up, flipping the paper she was studying over. "Love, I'm not in the mood for jokes."

"It's not a joke. Elias saw him, Mama, and Finn too, and . . . I believe them. I believe him." Somehow, over these weeks . . . even though so much had been a lie, he'd come to rely on Elias. Had almost begun to see him as a friend. And even though he no longer trusted the man, he trusted his love for Soleil.

He wasn't lying about this. No matter how insane it seemed, Elias had seen Vaughn perform necromancy . . . and seen Jericho involve herself in it as well.

Kallias pushed on, telling her the story Elias had told him, leaving no detail out but the ones that involved Anima. when he was finished, his mother had finally given him her full attention for once—her eyes hovering on his face, studying him carefully.

Then: "I'll get a healer."

"What?" He stood, taking a step back when she reached for his hand.

"Obviously someone didn't treat you well enough," Adriata said, getting up and following him backward, concern darkening her eyes—but not for her kingdom. For him; for his sanity.

He gritted his teeth. "Mama, I am not *hurt*. Aren't you listening to me? The man has my trust, and he—"

"Kallias, sit," his mother commanded—talking over him. Once again ignoring his opinion, his knowledge, in favor of her own.

His knees ached to obey. To bend. To bow beneath the authority in her voice. But instead, he stood taller. Gripped the back of his chair. Raised his chin and met her gaze head-on. Not like a prince. Not like a son.

Like a king.

"You are not listening to me," he snapped. "We have agents in the palace who have manipulated you into waging a war we did not need to wage for *ten years*. Ten years of our people suffering, of *their* people suffering, and for what? We could have had peace eight years ago, and Jericho killed twenty men to ruin it. We could have had peace *now*, and Jericho ruined it again. We need to take Vaughn into custody, question Jericho, and make peace with Nyx *now*, before this gets any worse!"

Adriata's hands lowered. "You actually believe this nonsense the Nyxian boy is feeding you."

"It is not nonsense. I have worked closely with him for these past few weeks, and while he lied to protect himself, he's never lied about anything else. I believe he's a good man, an honest one, and I believe what he says he saw. And even if I didn't, we have to follow up on it, we need to—"

"I will not have a Nyxian telling me what I have to do," Adriata snapped. "Not even if his words come through my son. You really think your sister had anything to do with this? Kallias, she can barely heft a sword. Go lie down and stop wasting my time—and while you're at it, start studying those books I dropped in your room. You only have two weeks left before Artem arrives, and this doesn't change that."

Her words stole all the breath from his lungs, aching in his stomach like a kick to the ribs.

She didn't believe him. Worse, even after all this . . . she was still going to sell him off.

He stared down at his hands—hands that would never hold a crown, but had held the hands of his people. Had held a sword in defense of them. Had held hammers to rebuild their homes, had held children eager to tell him their newest games, had held a surfboard and the edge of a sailboat and the paddle to a canoe.

As a prince, he could not save them.

But maybe he could as something new.

"I need to abdicate," he whispered.

"Speak up, Kal," Adriata sighed, rubbing her temple as she lowered herself back into her seat. "My hearing isn't what it used to be."

"I said," he snapped, so loudly that he nearly startled himself, "I abdicate my title as First Prince."

His mother's eyes snapped up to his. "What?"

Fine. So he would have to make it official, then.

"I, Kallias Alexandros Atlas, hereby abdicate my title as First Prince," announced Kallias, and the moment he did, the weight of all his twenty-five years lifted off his shoulders.

"Kallias," choked his mother, but he wasn't done.

"I pass the title to my brother, Prince Finnick Aurelius Atlas, and—"

"Kallias, *stop*—"

"—And release all responsibilities and privileges of the position to him with no ill will. May he serve his kingdom with dignity and pride." Unlikely, seeing as it was Finn. He'd serve the station with sarcasm and inappropriately-timed jokes.

And he would hate Kallias for forcing him into it. But Kallias was done serving the whims of other people.

Adriata gaped at him, fury and horror taking turns darkening her eyes—and behind them, heartbreak. "Kallias, this is . . . you're tired, love, you don't have to do this, just . . . just rest, and we'll talk—"

"I don't know why you don't love me like the others," he interrupted, a crack creeping into his voice. "I don't know where I failed you to make you so eager to get rid of me. But I've stayed quiet for far too long. I've been the perfect son for *far too long*, and I'm done with that. You're not a great queen. You're a great *warmonger*. Did you think the war would bring her back? Did you think it would somehow heal you? It hasn't. It's only turned your people into widows and widowers, orphans and child soldiers. And Soleil wasn't even dead! She's been out there all along, and if not for Jericho, we might have known that in time to save her. Even now you won't listen. Something *is* wrong in Atlas, Mama, but it's not me. It's *you*."

Every time Kallias Atlas opened his mouth to offer his truth, he broke things. Sometimes irrevocably. And he knew, staring into his mother's tear-filled eyes, that this was one of those times. But maybe this was something that needed to be broken.

"Kallias . . . I don't want . . . I didn't mean to make you feel like I wanted you gone, that's never been . . ." Adriata took a deep, shaky breath. "I'm sorry. But—"

"I know," Kallias interrupted softly. "But that doesn't fix it."

And nothing would. Not until his mother came to terms with the things she'd sacrificed in her quest for revenge. Not until she found it in her heart to forgive him for not being the right son, the son that could have saved her daughter from the flames that devoured their home.

Adriata didn't seem to have an answer for that, and Kallias didn't have anything left to say.

Well. One more thing.

"If you won't set your pride down to protect Atlas," said Kallias, "if you won't save our people . . . then I will."

He left feeling lighter than he had in years, even as his mother's shock-dulled eyes followed him out the door.

All his life, he'd been looking toward a throne, waiting for a ring to be forced onto his finger. All his life, he'd been striving, never resting, always having to be better. Always having to be perfect. The First Prince of Atlas.

But he was no longer a prince. No longer anything at all.

So he took all the responsibility, all the fear, all the anger and bitterness and grief . . .

And he let it go.

"Kallias!"

Finn's voice followed him as he stalked down the hall, his shoulders thrown back, no weight left to curve them into a perpetual bow. He'd always thought a crown would be his salvation. He'd never realized it was actually his cage.

"Kal!" Finn cursed under his breath as he caught up to him, heaving for breath, gripping his shoulder and jerking him around. The Second Prince—no, the First Prince now—looked at him with something like betrayal, something like pain. "What do you think you're doing?"

"I'm saving my kingdom," Kallias replied, pushing past him, heading back toward Elias's cell. "Whatever that takes."

"And what part of that means you giving up your gods-damned crown, huh?" Something wavered in Finn's voice as he chased after him—Kallias thought it might have been fear. "Kallias, you have no idea what you just did, you have *no idea* what's going to happen to me—"

"Well, you won't be able to gamble anymore, for starters."

That tugged Finn to a halt—for a moment, at least. Then he picked up his pace again. "You knew?"

"Elias told on you. It's a bad habit, you know."

"So's alcoholism."

"Fair point."

"Why didn't you tell me they'd approved an arrangement?" Finn moaned, raking his hands through his hair, picking up his pace so he could cut in front of Kallias, blocking him from going any further. He stared at him, the pain in his eyes like nothing Kallias could remember seeing in him . . . at least, not for a long time. Not since they were ten and fifteen, grieving in their own separate ways, unable to look at each other for too long without being reminded of their loss. "No wonder you've been so miserable this past week, gods, I—Kal, you should have told me—"

"There was nothing you could have done," Kallias said gently, but Finn scoffed.

"I could have *helped you*," he said desperately. "Gods, Kal, you could have at least *talked to me!* Don't you think I deserved to know that my brother was leaving me? Did you even *think* about what that was going to do to me? You're my only gods-damned *friend*, you idiot!"

Kallias's heart cracked straight down the middle. "Finn, you *hate* me."

"Who told you that?"

"No one had to! I promised you I'd get her out, and I didn't, I . . . I failed you. I failed as a prince . . . and as your brother. These last few years especially." *I failed all of you.*

Finn blinked at him, his mouth opening and closing like a fish dying on a dock. "Kal, there are a lot of things you've failed. Being my big brother isn't one of them."

Tears pricked at Kallias's eyes. "Finn . . ."

"No, listen to me, you ass." Finn gripped his shoulders, looking him in the eyes—tears of his own shining there, a sight that astonished and frightened Kallias in equal measure. "Listen to me. You're not the smartest of us, and you're not the strongest of us, and gods know you're not the best-looking of us—"

"Is this going somewhere?"

"But you are the best of us. Far and away the best of us. And you've not always done everything right, but you've always done right by *me*. And maybe I hate you sometimes, but I always love you. Us before all."

Kallias's tears fell in earnest then, and he gripped Finn's shoulders briefly before tugging him into a tight embrace. "Us before all."

It felt tainted now, knowing what Jericho had used it to justify. But he still meant it—and always would.

"So," Finn cleared his throat, "what now?"

"Now, I need you to do something for me," Kallias said. "I need you to stay here, to keep an eye on Jericho and So . . . and Anima. I need you to make sure they don't do any more damage while I'm gone."

Finn pulled back, eyes sharpening. "While you're gone."

Kallias held his gaze. "I'm going to Nyx. To tell them Atlas has been deceived into escalating the war. Maybe I can keep Infera from falling on our people's heads. And I'm taking Elias with me. If anyone will be able to find out what the . . . the *gods* are scheming and what we have to do to stop it, it'll be him."

Finn swallowed so hard Kallias saw his throat bob. "So you're leaving."

"And I need you to lie about it," Kallias said. "Do you think you can manage that?"

Finn laughed—a wry, wretched thing Kallias didn't really understand. "Oh yeah," he said. "I think I can handle that."

CHAPTER 73

ELIAS

"All right," Jakob said, settling back with his arms folded behind his head, Varran lying across his lap. Both of them sported half-drunk grins, Varran's shirt half-unbuttoned. "My turn. Elias, truth or dare?"

Raquel and Jira leaned against each other's backs, still woozy from completing their dare—eating an entire chocolate cake in five minutes flat—and Kaia was nudged Elias with her shoulder, grinning at his sour look, at the discomfort in his eyes as he clutched his beads. Soren sat alone, cross-legged and smirking, swirling her glass of Nyxian whiskey in one hand, her head tipped to one side. She studied Elias with hungry eyes, picking out his every weakness, her tongue swiping over her lips with predatory intent.

He wished someone would kick her ass, if only to teach her a little humility. Maybe then she'd take a break from torturing him day in and day out.

"He picks dare," Kaia said over Elias, who had definitely said "Truth." She met his horrified look with an innocent grin, and he softened; it was hard to be mad at her. It was why sweet, giggly Kaia was a good match for him—she didn't have a grumpy bone in her body. Meanwhile, just about all his bones had at least a little grouchiness buried in them.

"Perfect." Jakob's eyes gleamed. "I dare you to kiss Soren."

Soren spat out her sip of whiskey. "Excuse me?" she choked, at the same time Elias said, "Oh, pits, no."

They met each other's eyes across the campfire, scowls mirrored in each other's faces.

"What's so wrong with kissing me?" Soren demanded.

"Well, to start, I'm sure the forked tongue would make things unpleasant."

Soren started to stand, Jira supporting her by putting a hand on the back of one of her wobbly legs. But Jakob held up one finger. "Ah ah ah. I dared you to lock lips, not fists. Elias, do remember that anyone who refuses a dare takes a dip in the pond."

The extremely frozen pond.

At least if he did this, the torture would be over in five minutes, tops. If he even touched a toe in that water, he would be training through a cold for weeks.

"Fine," he muttered, setting aside his own barely-touched glass of whiskey, giving Kaia a playful shove as she giggled at his expense. Soren bowed mockingly as he passed her, twirling her arm in a flourish, directing him to the barracks which housed the nearest closet.

"A bit of privacy for you, sir," she said, in a voice thrown to sound unbearably stuffy. "I assume you don't want an audience for your deflowering."

Elias flushed. There was no way she knew that this would be his first kiss—not even Kaia knew that. But the way she was looking at him . . . he wouldn't put it past her to have somehow tracked down one of his siblings—or gods forbid, his mother—and sweetly plucked that knowledge from their overeager mouths. She didn't seem to know when to stop when it came to making life miserable for him.

"After you," he said, holding the closet door open for her. He was a lot of things, but he was always a gentleman, even to girls who could have given Occassio a run for her money in terms of wickedness.

Her eyes gleamed as she slipped into the closet, trailing her fingers across the front of his shirt, fussing with one of the buttons, sending a horrified thrill straight from his navel to his spine.

Horror was definitely the right name for it. He refused to call it anything else.

"Come on, then, jackass," she said. "Let's have a little fun."

Elias sat on the foot of his cot, fingers fussing absently with the string in his hands, eyes focused on the charm at the end of it.

Kallias would be there any minute to break him out, promising him quick and safe passage back to Nyx in exchange for his assistance in sorting out the godly half of this horrific scheme. The ex-prince seemed convinced that there was still a chance they could find something to bring Soren back to them, and Elias didn't have the heart to tell him he was wrong.

He held the charm up to the light—not his prayer beads. He'd shoved those in some corner of his pack yesterday and hadn't pulled them out since.

He didn't feel like praying. Not after all this. Not after he'd lost everything, piousness be damned. He'd lived his life according to Mortem's teachings, had worshipped her as best he could, had prayed to her until he was hoarse most nights . . . and still, she'd taken the one thing he couldn't bear to lose.

So he no longer wore his beads. Instead, he wore Soren's ring, pressing it into his palm whenever the ache got too close to real, chest-crushing grief.

I was going to ask you to marry me.

I would have said yes.

He couldn't give in to it, this thing he could feel just behind the wall of his chest, a heaviness, a pain he could not endure. He had nothing to say for it, no title or name that seemed to encompass all the ways he was being eaten alive. No way to describe how it felt like his heart had been lifted clean out of his chest, with nothing given to replace it, a hollow cavern that was inches away from collapse.

Besides, it wasn't time for that yet.

Here, numbness was his friend, his companion, and his weapon. Indifference was his new battlemate, the thing that would see him through this fight. He would cling to that nothingness until it was safe to let go. Until he could crumble without taking anyone else with him.

But first, he would help Kallias save his people. And he would save his own, as well—because Soren would have been ashamed of him had he done anything less.

He pressed that ring to his lips and squeezed his eyes shut. Remembered a whiskey-sweet mouth and curses passed between lips and how he'd been a little bit surprised to discover that her tongue was not actually forked.

Pain struck, hard and fast, worse than the blade Jericho had driven into his gut—one of the two Finn had returned to him once again late last night.

"She'd want you to have them back," he'd said, scratching his neck, avoiding Elias's eyes. "And for what it's worth . . . I loved her too. I'm sorry."

"Will you do me one favor?" Elias had asked.

"Depends on the favor."

Elias had looked him dead in the eye. "Make them pay."

Finn had merely smiled—the wolfish smile he'd learned from Soren. And that was enough.

Footsteps approached from the steps. Keys jingled in the door. He slid the ring's chain over his neck—let it dangle over his heart, where he could always find it, where it would remind him why he could not fall apart. Not yet. Not until it was over.

He took the other thing Finn had handed him out of his pocket—a tiny scrap of the tunic Soren had been wearing in the temple, an Atlas-blue one.

Good that he hadn't let her cut his hair.

Pain, again—but he crushed it, shoving it back into that hollow in his chest. Later. Later. Later.

He threaded the new cloth into his hair until he had two braids—one laced with bright blue, one dull, time-worn brown. He bound the new braid tightly, his hands tying the cord at the end with an unfeeling, vicious tug.

Kallias came inside, a leather bag strapped across his back, his hair hidden beneath the hood of his thick coat. He was already wearing the grief worse than Elias, his face a bit blotchy, but his jaw was set; and though his eyes were red-rimmed, there was no gleam of alcohol in them.

"Are you ready?" he asked.

"Let's go," Elias replied, and those two words held a promise of death for those who had dared come between Elias Loch and his battlemate. For those who had dared to come between two souls so closely intertwined that even Death had hesitated to cleave them apart. "We have a war to end."

EPILOGUE

Anima loved her new body.

She loved it, even though it was barely strong enough to contain her; after all, human bodies weren't built for divinity. Only luck of birth and strength of blood had made this one capable at all. If it had been any other body, her power would have broken every bone, torn every muscle. She would have burned through it in moments.

As it was, her form groaned and strained against the restraints of tendon and skin, heart and lungs, skull and soul. *Not enough room. Not enough for me.*

A visceral longing cut through her, a homesickness for her *old* body. Her first body. But that one was dead. This one would do.

She stood before the mirror in the body's chambers—her chambers, now. She gazed at herself in the polished glass, soft fascination blooming as she ran her fingers over the dips and curves, the freckles, the disorderly waves of red-gold hair.

The well-toned arms, the thick thighs, the soft stomach with muscle corded beneath. The harsh, knotted scars. This body knew battle.

She'd never worn a warrior before.

Princess Soren Andromeda Nyx. Princess Soleil Marina Atlas. Soren. Soleil. Officer. Your Highness. Milady. Killer. Kid. Smartass.

She mouthed the names to herself as she memorized her body. Too many names for one person, but she would learn to answer to them. She would smirk and snark and sink her thorns in, playing her part to these people as long as she had to.

Just as her brother had ordered her.

Anima looked at her palms, calloused and dry, bending her fingers inward to test them. They obeyed without hesitation.

A giddy smile curled at one corner of her mouth. *Mine.*

Somewhere deep inside her mind, a quiet echo sounded—*mine.*

Her fingers twitched of their own accord, straightening themselves out.

That smile faded. Twisted into a frown.

She bent them again, forming a fist, repeating to herself, "Mine."

One finger leaped out of formation—the middle one.

And in that place within her mind, some dark, cold corner she hadn't yet explored, that echo came again—not an echo at all. Another voice.

Mine, it said—*she* said. *Mine. Get out of my head.*

Anima shook her hand violently, and the fingers went limp, once again at her command.

"Who's there?" she asked out loud—then chided herself for being silly. The room was empty, and this head held no one but her. She hadn't finished clearing out the lingering traces of memory, that was all. Old patterns of thinking could linger in the mind even after the soul fled.

No one answered. As expected.

Anima squeezed her eyes shut, casting her consciousness toward that last bit of her new mind, ready to sweep the last of the old owner out—

She collided with a wall. A solid, dark wall.

She pushed. It didn't budge.

"What in the pits?" she muttered, the slang word for her sister's realm tumbling off her tongue far too easily. The old owner's vocabulary should have been gone by now.

Uneasiness pinched her brows together, and she leaned closer to the mirror, studying her new green eyes as if the answer lay somewhere within.

She'd never had trouble extending herself through a new mind before. Was she doing something wrong? Was the mind damaged? Brae had promised that Jericho wouldn't harm her host. He'd *promised* they would be kind.

She gritted her teeth, squeezing her eyes shut, using all her strength to shove at the block.

"Mine," she muttered. "You are mine now. I'm—"

The wall pushed back.

Anima staggered forward as if she'd been shoved from behind, her head colliding with the mirror, the *crunch* of breaking glass followed immediately by a sharp, hot pain across her forehead.

Shock bubbled through her as she lifted a hand to her forehead, bringing it away bloody. And as she met her own gaze in the mirror, the cracks distorting her image into something unfamiliar once again, the dark corner of her mind hissed, *Just* try *it. I dare you.*

"Who are you?" Anima choked. "You aren't supposed to be here."

She didn't understand. She didn't—

You said my names. Do you remember them?

She was dreaming. Surely she was dreaming. Did this body sleepwalk?

My body, snarled the voice within. *Mine. It's still mine.*

A chill ran down Anima's spine, and she stepped away from the mirror, her hands beginning to shake. "This isn't possible."

Princess Soren Andromeda Nyx. Princess Soleil Marina Atlas. Soren. Soleil. Officer. Your Highness. Milady. Killer. Kid. Smartass.

Anima's breathing came fast and hard. Panic built in her chest.

The stranger in Anima's head whispered, *Still here, Goddess Great.*

With a scream of frustration, Anima shoved back against the voice, the stranger, the *intruder* until her head was quiet once more.

"Not for long," she panted, leaning with her palms splayed against the wall, closing her eyes as blood seeped from the cut on her head. "You'll fade away soon. They always do. Y-You're just a nightmare."

There wasn't an answer. But the darkness still lurked.

Watching. Waiting.

Alive.

Alive.

A knock on her door. "Are you all right, Your Highness?"

Your Highness. That was one of her names now.

"I'm fine," she called, in the best imitation of Soren's voice that she could muster. It wasn't the way she was used to speaking—her voice liked to pitch higher, softer. "Sorry. Something startled me is all."

At least this tongue knew how to lie better than her first. She could work with that.

Tenebrae had promised that this would be temporary. There were only a few things left to do, a few more steps to take before Jericho became desperate enough to agree to their terms.

She clenched and unclenched her fingers one more time—just to be sure. They obeyed her.

Some of the tension eased from her shoulders. *Better.*

Opening her palm, she blew a soft breath against her skin. Green dust shimmered on her breath, a gentler form of her magic that gained weight and form as it swirled into a vibrant pink hibiscus. She set it aside for the moment, slipping her fingers into her hair, testing the weight and thickness of it. She'd washed the dirt and sweat and oil from it this morning, removing a dirty old piece of cloth that had been braided into it—likely a memento for the old owner, but nothing that concerned her. She'd used her magic to grow it out longer, nearly past her waist, the way she liked it. Hopefully no one would pay too close attention.

The strands were like silk against the roughness of her skin, catching the light in a way that delighted her, flickers of fire roaming from her head to her waist. Red hair was new—neither of her other bodies had been redheaded.

"Mine," she murmured, carefully twisting that hair into a thick braid, tucking the flower behind her ear.

"Mine," she repeated, dressing herself in a green gown that matched her eyes, a gown that emphasized the muscles in her arms and the curves of her body.

"Mine, mine, mine." A chant she repeated with every step, every change, until the person she saw in the broken mirror was no longer Soren—or Soleil, or smartass, or whatever she liked to be called.

Yes, she still had Soren's eyes, her hair, her nose, her chin. Her body and her scars. But the smile she offered herself was entirely her own: a broad, brilliant smile that shone with all the warmth and fire of the sun. The poise with which she held herself, the gold limning her irises, the flower in her hair and the perfect dress—that was all Anima.

And it always would be.

She refused to think of the darkness. Refused to listen for it as she slipped on a pair of sandals and made her way out of that room, refused to worry about it as she offered the guards a sheepish smile and a smooth lie about the state of her mirror. The cut had already healed, thankfully—her magic was beginning to settle.

This was her body now. Nothing and nobody could take it from her. She was Goddess. She was Divine.

But she kept her fingers clenched tightly at her sides, just in case.

THE END

ACKNOWLEDGMENTS

First and foremost, to God, who gave me the spark to be a storyteller, who gave me the mentors and friends I needed to foster that spark, who continues to give me more than I deserve every single day. You gave me the courage to choose the path I needed to follow. This journey would have ended long ago if not for Your grace. This journey is dedicated to You, always.

To my own siblings (and sibling-in-law!), Caleb, Joshua, Katie, and Alita: you four fill my life with ridiculous joy. Thanks for the Markiplier Try Not To Laugh challenges, the antique store adventures, the Mario Party tournaments, the Netflix binges, the GMM marathons, the Psych movie nights, and for being my alpha readers. Thank you for loving me through my moods and my crises and my writing rants you didn't totally understand, but listened to anyway. Thank you for driving me to an author event early so I could get a good seat, and for hanging out in the bookstore with me all day. Most of all, thank you for being my very best friends.

To my parents, who have never once discouraged me from pursuing what I love, who let me take out twice as many books at the library as my siblings because they knew I would finish them before they were due back. To my dad, who let me steal his Eragon books and read them until the covers fell apart, who sat through every single Twilight movie with me without complaining even once because he knew how much I loved them. To my mom, who sat on the porch swing and read us Peter Pan and rubbed glittery lotion on our hands so we could have our own pixie dust, who taught me how to read, who taught me how to write. You two gave me the gift of unconditional love, and this book wouldn't exist without you.

To Miranda, who has read every story I've written since we were fifteen, who grew from the cousin I was most excited to see on Thanksgiving to someone I haven't gone a day without talking to in nearly ten years, who lets me sleep on her couch and gets McDonald's with me at midnight and scream-sings Les Miserables and Taylor Swift with me. Da, there are no words to encompass all that you mean to me. My life is infinitely brighter with you in it. Thank you for loving all my characters, from Raven to Seymour to Soren. Thank you for journeying with me from the Yankee candle shop to the Birdhouse and all the way to Atlas. Thank you for Textland and reality shows and Trolls. Thank you for being my friend for every single one of my twenty-five years. I love you. <3

To Kristin: Thank you for always opening your home to me, for giving me a safe place to talk in your salon chair, for the movie nights and the Target runs and the Red Robin girls nights. Thank you for the pictures and the laughter and always making my hair look fabulous. Thank you for ranting about Grey's with me and feeding me wheat toast. Thank you for the sunshine box that made me feel loved after my first big heartbreak. Thank you for kitten cuddles and trying so hard to get my dad to let me take one home. I love and admire you so much!

To Renee: my editor, my CP, my publishing mom, my *malatanda*. I thank God every day you reached out and asked if I wanted your copies of the Grisha books, and that I said yes, even though you were a Scary Internet Stranger™. Your books reminded me of why I love reading (do you know how long it'd been since I'd stayed up all night to finish reading a book before Darkwind crashed into my life?), and you remind me why I love writing. I am endlessly thankful that your job cancelled whatever event they were supposed to have and you were able to meet me and Da at that writing conference. I mean, after getting food poisoning together, there wasn't anywhere for our friendship to go but up! Thank you for putting picky-eater groceries in your fridge, for putting up with my rotating obsessions with your various Starchaser ships (one in particular), and for tough-loving the heck out of me. You are the reason I believed I could actually pursue self-publishing, and your love of these characters reminds me of why I write. Thank you for your unshaking faith in me, for reminding me that my worth is not measured by my productivity, and for gently nudging me back on the right path when I start to go down the wrong one.

To Sam, Wes, and Danny: Thank you for letting me borrow your wives/fiancées, sleep on your couches, and eat the food out of your fridges. You guys rock.

To Levi, Kenzie, Autumn, and Charlie: You guys make my life so much brighter! Thank you for the hugs, the Minecraft lessons, the cookie-baking, and the dancing. I love you all SO MUCH and can't wait to come over again soon!

To Joey: HI JOSIAH-BIAH AUNT CASSIDY LOVES YOU AND SHE'LL SEE YOU SOON! I tried to get your mom to name you after Finn, but she wouldn't budge. You've only just made your grand entrance into the world, but you're already a joy-bringer and a heart-stealer. Tell your mama to bring you to Michigan soon, okay?

To Lina: I am not exaggerating when I say this book would not even be finished yet if not for you. Trading SOTS and TSH pushed me to stay accountable to my own deadlines, and gave me the confidence to actually let other people read this monster. I go back to read your comments when I'm in need of a reminder that I can do this writing thing, and they always make my day brighter. Thank you for the gorgeous chapter headers, the Porthladd/Atlas AUs, the very first fanart I ever received, your love of Finn the problem child, and for always being ready with an encouraging or reassuring word when I have doubts. And, last but not least, thank you for the gift to the world that is Griffin Branw—ahem, I mean, DOTD and SOTS. Your stories matter, and I'm so grateful that you're telling them.

To Emily: thank you for the Olive Garden and Applebee's dinner dates, for the mall days and road trips, for camping and sleepovers, for One Tree Hill and Grey's, for getting me through high school and college with your constant support and friendship. You're my best friend forever, no code words needed. (Unless Sad Alarm or the Meatloaves are around, anyway.)

To Kayla, my first ever beta reader and first ever writing friend who wasn't related to me, who gave me the privilege of meeting her witchy girl and soldier boy first, then her gorgeous cast in her fish book: LET ZAVENIK AND NESH BE HAPPY YOU MONSTER. Ahem. But really, thank you for being the first to love Seymour and Hughes, for all the Disney tips and the check-ins and helping me stay sane when I was applying for mentorship programs and struggling with revision plans. You're infinitely cooler than me and I'm privileged to know you.

To my beta team, Alli, Gee, Stephanie, China, and Brianne: you guys are the BEST. The beta process was the most terrifying part of this whole thing, and you all made it absolutely painless. Thank you for being some of the first to love this book and for all your suggestions that made it better. Thank you for the memes and the gifs and the flowers and all the yelling that let me know I was doing something right, LOL! I'm eternally grateful for each and every one of you!

To Katie Marie and Sapphire Ink Press: YOU ARE A GODSEND. Thank you for all the work you did to help me get this book out into the world. Having you on my team made this launch infinitely easier, and I have no idea how I would've managed it without you. You're amazing!

To Fran (@coverdungeonrabbit): I can't thank you enough for the incredible work you did on the cover! You took my vision and made it something I could never have even imagined. You're so talented and so wonderful to work with!

To my coworkers in custard hell: Y'all are the real MVPs. Thanks for laughing with me and complaining with me and getting me through the difficult shifts. I'd give you all raises if I could.

To Aunt Shawna and Uncle Jesse, who let me come down to Florida to finish writing this book, who take me to the ocean whenever I need some saltwater of my own: thanks for believing in me, and for giving me the inspiration I needed to write an ocean book.

To the rest of my family, who has waited very patiently for me to finally get a book published: TA DA! I finally made it happen!

And last but not least, thank you to YOU, the readers that made it this far. I hope you loved taking Soren's journey with her, and I hope this adventure brought you joy and laughter along the way. I am immeasurably thankful that you took the time to pick up my weird, flower-y, necromancy lost princess book. Just by reading, you've made a lifelong dream of mine come true. Thank you.

Sorry about the ending…but not really <3

See you in the next one!

ABOUT THE AUTHOR

Cassidy Clarke is a proud Michigander, barista, and Hallmark movie expert who loves all things fantasy, from Disney movies to Dungeons & Dragons. Her debut series THE BLOOD AND WATER SAGA is a high fantasy love letter to the lost princess daydreams of her childhood and an attempt to put her experience growing up with three younger siblings (all of whom are cooler than her) to good use. She spends her days writing like she's running out of time, binging Critical Role campaigns, hoarding pretty dice like a dragon, and baking the world's best chocolate chip cookies.